A Soft Place To Fall

Amber Wynn

Dedication

To All My Beautiful Black Brothers,
Your Sisters love you and need you to be that Soft Place to Fall.

XO,

Black Love

COPYRIGHT

CHRISTOPHER RASHAD GLOBAL ENTERPRISES, INC.
Fist Edition: August 2014; Second Edition: August 2015
ISBN-10: 0990519724
ISBN-13: 9780990519720
Cover photo by John Knight http://reelpangea.blogspot.com
Model: Sydney Hamilton

Acknowledgements

Writing a novel is hard work. Publishing it is scary.

When I published the first version of *A Soft Place to Fall* I was scared for a different reason. July 2014, I found a lump in my left breast and was waiting for the results. My mom had passed away in 2011 from breast cancer, so I was facing a high probability that my life as I knew it was about to change. In that week as I waited, I reflected on my life and the only regret I had was that I hadn't published my novel. So I pulled it out, purchased an ISBN number, got it copyrighted, designed a cover, and literally uploaded it to Amazon.

Bam! Published. Okay. Now, I could die with no regrets.

News came back that it wasn't cancer, but I had accomplished one of my biggest goals in life. The reviews started coming in, and I was hooked! *OMG*, There were so many mistakes in that version because my only goal was to get it out. As I edited this version I became so grateful to all the readers who pushed through the grammatical errors, typos, and layout issues and just embraced the story, *yikes*! Thank you, and I hope this version is easier on the eyes.

I would like to thank Christopher Williams for this new look and feel. It was his idea to shoot a new cover that captures the essence of McKenzie, the main character. The model, Sydney Hamilton, is a

beautiful young sister who was so amazing and supportive. Thank you Sydney. Besides the cover, I got a couple of cute pics from the photographer John Knight for my website redesign, another really cool idea of Christopher's!

So here I am, a year later. And here is the updated version of *A Soft Place to Fall*. Is it perfect? Hell no. ASP2F is still too damned long! It's a fast read, but now that I've written a second novel, and had it professionally edited, I know that it's just too long. AND, I will edit it down next go around. I promise. But for now, she's my first baby, my labor of love and please, just embrace her as such!

For me, this is novel is purely about stepping powerfully into my dream! I didn't have a manual. I did so many things wrong. And, I didn't ever really '*get it right*,' but I did it! That, to me is the most empowering thing about this novel. I did it.

ASP2F moved me from, 'one day I want to publish a book, for anyone to read', to 'I'm a published author.' I'd tell any author out there wondering if they can do it: Yes, you can! I thought I had one week to live and got mine out there. Just do it. And if it sucks, guess what, go back and do it again . . . like I did. :D

Life is so Amazing!

Table of Contents

PART ONE

"What's Done in the Dark"

The room was almost pitch black. But the light in the corner illuminated the space her bed occupied. He stood there, motionless for a moment, afraid to move. She lay still in the bed, a mass of blackness as the light cast a shadow on her lifeless body, a silhouette, empty, cold, and motionless. An oxygen mask covered her nose and mouth.

"Hey, Mac," Christian whispered. Slowly, she struggled to face the voice. Her strained movement caused Christian to move quickly by her side.

"Don't try to move. Here, I'm here." He moved to the side of the bed facing her, but, as soon as she saw his face, tears began to flow. Before he knew it, he was crying too.

"McKenzie, I am so sorry! I'm so sorry—will you forgive me, please?" he said in between sobs. He laid his head next to her face on the pillow, afraid to touch her swollen and bruised skin. McKenzie reached over and rubbed the back of Christian's head. He looked up into her eyes.

She was unrecognizable. Her left eye was completely closed, swollen and purple. Her right eye was open, but there were stitches over it. There were traces of half-wiped blood around her nose and mouth. Underneath the oxygen mask, her nose was bandaged. And her mouth was bruised and swollen. There were scrapes and cuts covering her face and hands. Her shoulder was in a splint.

She didn't look anything like the McKenzie Batiste h had come to know, meticulously color coordinated, with smooth peanut butter complexioned skin. Even her curly hair was flat and lifeless. Christian forced a smile. She motioned toward the facemask. Christian lifted it slightly away from her face.

"For… give you for what?" she forced out the words with a half-smile.

"For sending you into that bitch's house, so he could do this to you." Christian placed his head back on the pillow and cried softly. McKenzie tried to say something, but inside the oxygen mask, it was muffled. Christian sat up and lifted the mask.

"You . . . fucked . . . him . . . up . . . right?" Her eyes locked onto Christian's.

"I fucked him up real bad, McKenzie." He dropped his head for a moment. "I think I may have killed that spineless piece of shit. I don't know. I told the detective—I think she's sending someone over to check on him," he said, returning his gaze to her. She didn't speak. But something in her eyes communicated relief.

Christian replaced the mask. McKenzie closed her eyes and drifted off to sleep.

♋   ♋   ♋

"Pete died today." Christian informed McKenzie. It was late afternoon.

"Oh no," McKenzie said into her cell phone. She was sad for Melvin remembering how devastated she was when the woman she considered her mom passed.

"Yeah, April just called." Christian said. "She was going to go by and pick up their summary because Melvin won't be able to make the meeting tomorrow, obviously. But her sister got hung up at work and she had to go pick up her niece on the Westside."

"I can go by and pick it up."

"Really?" Christian said. "Are you sure? I was going to see if I could get in contact with Fern. I can do it if I pass on the gym tonight—"

"Go get your fake work out on Christian. I'm not far from his house; about a half hour or so. I'll stop by," McKenzie said. Christian laughed.

"Alright, cool." Christian said.

♋   ♋   ♋

"Hey, Melvin," McKenzie said as she entered his house, "Sorry to hear about your dad."

Melvin was a mess. He was beet red. His eyes were swollen. He stumbled toward the table, grabbing the summary.

"No, you're not!" he slurred. "You always looked at him with disgust," he said, glaring at McKenzie. "Just take this and get out," he held out the summary.

The truth was, McKenzie *didn't* give a fuck. She wasn't happy to see Melvin sad. She wasn't happy that his dad had died. But the truth was the man had no idea Melvin was alive in the world. The few times she had seen the old man, he was oblivious to what was going on around him. She thought at least now he was in a better place.

McKenzie took the summary and walked out of the house without saying a word. As she jumped into her jeep, she called Christian to tell him what had happened.

"Mac, the man is mourning; that was grief speaking. He was looking for some sympathy. My goodness, are you that cold and unfeeling?" Christian said. "It's one thing to dislike a person; it's another thing to treat a grieving person unkindly."

McKenzie felt like shit. "OK Christian. I get it. I mean, OK—I fucked up! What do you want me to do, I already left!" she said.

"Go back."

"What? I'm almost on the freeway," she said. *How inconvenient.*

"Go back, McKenzie, and take him something to eat. He's probably been drinking all day and hasn't eaten a thing," Christian said. "He may want to talk, but then again, given your strained relationship, he may not. Regardless, you will have shown concern and kindness by bringing him some food, right?"

McKenzie thought about it for a minute. Melvin probably wouldn't want to be bothered. If she took him something to eat, Christian would get off her back. And he did look like he hadn't eaten in a while.

"Oh kaaay!" McKenzie screamed into the telephone. "I'll talk to you later," she hung up and busted a "U" into El Pollo Loco. She got him a three-piece meal with beans and rice and lemonade.

As she pulled into Melvin's driveway, she felt pretty good about herself. Christian had begun to have a major influence in her life. Before, she could have cared less about what anybody thought about her. But she cared what *he* thought about her. So much so that she was back at this asshole's house with food and drink! McKenzie knocked on the door. She heard him fumbling around. She knocked again.

"Melvin! It's McKenzie. Open up!" she yelled into the door. Melvin opened the door. He must have thrown back a couple more drinks since she left because he was looking even worse.

"Uh, maybe you should slow down on the liquor, Melvin," McKenzie walked past him into the house.

"Maybe you should mind your own business Muh Kenzie Bah-fucking-Teest!" She rolled her eyes and ignored his statement. He was obviously drunk.

"Look, I brought you something to eat--" She started to unwrap the chicken and lay it on the dining room table. But Melvin charged her, knocking her down to the floor—catapulting the food across the room. McKenzie's right shoulder took the brunt of the fall as she landed

"I don't want anything to eat! Do you hear me?" he said, moving toward her. McKenzie lay for a minute blinking; trying to process what was going on. She tried to get to her feet, but Melvin grabbed her arms.

"You always think you know everything don't you, bitch?" he screamed, the hot stench of alcohol filled her nostrils.

"Melvin, let me the fuck go before I--" McKenzie tried to rip herself free. But his grip was too tight. Between clenched teeth, he replied,

"Or you'll do what? What the fuck are you going to do to me?" He threw her down on the couch. She hit her head on the wooden arm, ripping a deep gash above her right eye. The blood oozed down the side of her face.

"Ouch! You mutha fucka! You're drunk, Melvin!"

"Yes, I'm drunk, McKenzie. My fucking father just died this morning, and I'm drinking. But you don't care, do you?" He grabbed her shirt, yanked her up into his face. She turned her head.

"Do I repulse you? Why are you turning your head Muh Kenzie?" he said. McKenzie didn't reply. He grabbed her cheeks tightly in between his fingers, forcing her to face him.

"I know I do. I can see it every time you look at me. I fucking repulse you—don't I?" He slapped her across her face. McKenzie screamed.

"Melvin, let me go." McKenzie's heart was racing. Her head was throbbing. And she was petrified. He was a little scrawny man, but with the alcohol, he was incredibly strong.

"Or what?" he said, slamming her up against the wall.

"Ouch!" McKenzie tried to swing at his face, but he grabbed her hand. He grabbed the other one and slammed her down on the floor.

"What are you going to do to me bitch? You can't do shit to me, do you hear?" He leered down over her. He looked her up and down. Rage covered his face like burning lava. "But we both know that, don't we, Muh Kenzie? You wouldn't ever do anything to me—or with me." He ripped her blouse open. McKenzie kicked and screamed. She fought to get free.

"Because the Queen Bitch Nigger is too good for old Melvin the white boy—right?" He pinned her arms over her head. She turned her face away from him. The act infuriated him. He switched hands, pinning her arms with his left and with his right, he reached back and socked her in the face.

McKenzie let out a gutturally shrill scream. Blood oozed down her face. A sinister smile formed across his face. His eyes darted with excitement.

"Isn't that right, Miss 'I'm above you'? Are you above me now, you whore?" he said, slapping her across the face. She bit the inside of her bottom lip and clenched her fists tight. She screamed. But she refused to cry.

McKenzie was defenseless. He straddled her, pinned her arms over her head, and sat on her pelvis.

Melvin was delirious. He ripped off her jeans. She tried to kick him, but he used his body to dominate her.

Fear gripped her. She quickly looked around for something to grab, or push him into--something to get her out of this situation.

"I'll show you. Black men ain't all that!" He tried to sound hip. "I'll show you, once you go white, everything will be outta sight. Ain't that right Miss 'I only like Black men?' He tried to kiss her. She spat in his face and stared into his cold green eyes.

He socked her closed-fist. McKenzie could feel the bone crushing in her nose. The pain seared through her head. Everything became cloudy for a moment. She was jarred back into the moment by the burn of flesh tearing inside her. She screamed as she tried to free herself from him.

"Be still, bitch. I'm going to give this dick to you and you're going to love it. Do you hear me? You move—you move and I will kill you!" He looked down into her eyes with hatred that made her believe he would.

McKenzie turned her head and didn't move. She felt him ram himself inside her over and over. It felt like sandpaper ripping her apart inside. She lay there motionless while he kissed her on her neck. He gently nibbled her earlobe and slid his mouth across her cheek to cup her mouth. He sloppily and eagerly forced his tongue in her mouth. He left a slimy, sticky, smelly trail of spit across her face. His rank breath engulfed her bloody nostrils. The pain in her face was excruciating. Her right eye had started to swell and close.

But she lay still as he went through the motions of a sex-starved lover. Running his fingers through her curls and smelling her fragrant skin, Melvin slid off of McKenzie. He nestled himself behind her, slowly grinding her butt. He reached over and massaged her breast as he kissed the nape of her neck. McKenzie shut down completely. She could feel Melvin's dick getting hard again, poking her in her back. She closed her eyes. He slowly kissed her down her back. Each kiss felt like nails being pounded in her flesh.

Melvin pulled her hips back toward him, and slid his fingers inside her. He was disappointed to find her vagina dry. He was so hard, and wanted her so much. She lay there allowing him to touch her. He thought she'd be dripping wet by now.

"What's wrong, McKenzie?" he whispered into her butt cheek. He rubbed his face on each one over and over. She didn't reply.

Melvin pulled her up on her knees. He inserted his finger inside her from behind, moving slowly and deliberately until he felt her walls moisten. He smiled. He gently massaged her clitoris until her body submitted by gently shaking. Melvin quickly positioned himself behind her, and entered her.

"Yeah baby," he slurred into her back "Let's cum together." He lifted himself upright, grabbed McKenzie's hips and pulled her back and forth, pounding her butt against his midsection. McKenzie clenched her teeth and closed her eyes, never moving—never uttering a sound. He pumped back and forth until he came. "Uh. Uh. Um."

He fell on top of McKenzie. She lay there, listening to him breathing deeply until he drifted off to sleep.

McKenzie flipped him off of her. Startled, Melvin tried to grab her. She moved quickly, grabbing a nearby plant pot and smashed it on his head.

McKenzie didn't stop to see if he was alive or giving chase. She grabbed her keys and ran for the door. She missed six of the eight steps outside his house, and fumbled to get her car door open. She almost ran over an old lady walking her poodle as she screeched out the driveway.

It was almost dark now. She glanced at the clock on her dashboard; it read 5:37 p.m. She dialed Christian's number.

"Hello?" a female voice answered. McKenzie paused for half a second; surprised a woman answered his cell.

"May I speak to Christian?"

"May I tell him who's speaking?"

"No thank you," McKenzie said. There was a thud and a muffled *whoever she is; she didn't see fit to tell your wife her name.*

"Hello?" Christian answered. Before she knew it, McKenzie was sobbing. The hot salty tears stung the gashes and cuts in her face. She winced as she told him the horrible details.

"Where are you?" he said, grabbing his keys. Jada was fast on his heels.

"Who is that Christian? Where are you going?" she said. He motioned for her to be quiet.

"Turning into Emergency. Kaiser Cadillac." McKenzie mumbled, rubbing her temples. She was exhausted.

"I'm on my way." Christian said. Before McKenzie could object, he'd hung up the telephone.

"Who the hell was that?" Jada said, grabbing Christian.

"Why, Jada?"

He was not in the mood for a bitch session right now. His stomach felt sour from what McKenzie had recounted. She was vague, only saying he had socked her in her face and ripped her clothes. That she couldn't see, and could barely breathe. He wanted her to pull over and call the paramedics, but she refused. He was too embarrassed and angry to ask her if Melvin had violated her.

"Maybe because I'm your wife? And some bitch just called my husband who refused to identify herself, and now my husband is rushing out of the house." Jada crossed her arms across her chest. Christian didn't have time for this. But he knew she wasn't going to just let this go.

"It's one of my classmates. She's in trouble and needs my help," he said, grabbing a jacket from the closet. Jada followed close behind.

17

"And why is she calling you? She doesn't have a husband, boyfriend, father—hell, a brother—she can call?" She said as she grabbed her jacket.

"No she doesn't, otherwise don't you think she would have? Where do you think you're going?" He demanded, pausing at the door.

"With you--or you ain't going nowhere."

Christian was outraged. But he didn't have time for a fight. He walked out the door and Jada jumped in the passenger seat.

For the twenty minutes it took him to get to his destination, Jada bombarded him with nonstop questions. *Which classmate was it? Why did she feel so comfortable calling him? Why didn't she think it was disrespectful calling another woman's man to help her?* Then she went on a tirade about how quickly Christian had moved for this mystery woman, but when *she* asked him to do anything, it was like pulling teeth.

Christian didn't respond the entire time. All he could hear was McKenzie crying in the phone. He'd never heard her cry before. It was his fault. He had sent her back there. She only went back because he made her feel bad about how she had treated him earlier. He felt like shit.

Christian made a right, and a quick left, and before Jada knew what happened, he had jumped out of the car.

Stay here was all he said to her. And he said it in a way that Jada knew he meant business.

They were in front of a peach colored house. Jada watched from the passenger seat as Christian took the stairs like Michael Jordan flying across the court. *Bam! Bam! Bam!* He hit the door so hard the windows shook. *Bam! Bam! Bam!*

"Hey—hold up! I'm coming." Melvin stumbled toward the loud noise. He unlocked the door, and tried to peek out the crack he made, but Christian had other ideas. He shoved the door open, sending Melvin reeling to the floor. Christian walked in the house, stepping over him. He flicked off the lights in the foyer near the door, and walked purposefully to the dining area, dragging Melvin behind him by his collar.

Confused, Melvin tried to get up. But Christian yanked him with so much force Melvin fell back down.

When Christian reached the back of the house, he pulled Melvin up by his shirt until they were staring each other in the eye. Melvin's eyes were bloodshot. His face was swollen, and it looked as if dried blood covered the top of his head. He scanned Melvin—his pants were still unzipped. This sent Christian into a rage. He punched Melvin in the gut.

"Ugh! Christian!" Melvin saw the anger in Christian's eyes and panicked. "Let me explain what happened."

Christian balled up his fist and punched Melvin three times in the face. Melvin let out a blood-curdling scream.

"Shut up bitch!" Christian screamed at Melvin as he threw him against the wall. Melvin's lanky body slid down the wall. Christian saw El Pollo Loco chicken spewed across the dining room floor. He walked over and kicked Melvin in the ribs.

"*Uhhh*" was all Melvin could grunt. The kick knocked the air out of his lungs.

"You can't explain. There is no explanation for what you did to her."

Just looking at him created a rage inside of Christian he had never felt. He imagined McKenzie in this house, and Melvin violating her. The fear she must have felt. She said he pinned her down. Christian grabbed him by the neck and socked him over and over in the face. He didn't stop until blood covered Melvin's face. He wanted to kill him. He wanted to watch him take his last breath.

"She . . . she…" Melvin raised his hand in submission. He gasped in between strained breaths. "She . . . it wasn't like . . . that." He winced.

"It wasn't like what—you piece of shit?" Christian said, shaking him. His head bobbed around.

"She . . . wanted it. I swear!"

"What the fuck are you saying?" Christian said, tightening his grip around Melvin's neck.

"No, seriously. She . . . lay there. She didn't fight. She let me kiss her . . . and caress her. If she didn't want me, wouldn't she have fought me?"

Christian slapped him.

"Ouch!" He said. "I'm . . . telling you the truth! She gave herself to me."

Christian socked him in the stomach. Melvin fell to the floor. Christian stomped him until he didn't move any more. Christian stood over him, shaking. All he felt was shame—knowing in his heart that none of this would take away McKenzie's pain.

A yellow puddle slowly formed around Melvin's midsection.

Jada heard the thumping and bumping in the house, and she could've sworn she heard screaming.

Christian walked out the house with a scowl on his face. He climbed into the car, turned on the ignition, and pulled off. Jada did a quick inventory. His shirt was covered in blood—his knuckles were bleeding!

"Christian! What the hell is going on?"

"Not now, Jada."

"What? You get a call from a woman who refuses to leave her name, you jump in a car—race over to a house, obviously beat someone to a pulp—and all you can say is 'Not now Jada?'"

"I didn't tell you to get in the car. That was your call, remember?"

"Because you weren't offering me any explanation."

"Why the fuck do I have to explain everything to you?" Christian said, staring Jada in the face.

"Maybe it's because I'm your wife."

"That's right, Jada. You are my wife, not my mutha fuckin' momma. I am a man, dammit—not your child. I don't have to answer to you!"

"Well, that's what you're supposed to do with your wife— you know, *share* things like this?"

Christian quickly turned the corner. "So, because we're married, you're supposed to know my every move . . . and my every thought?"

"Yes!"

"It ain't gone happen."

"Then why are we married—if you're just going to keep secrets from me?" Christian pulled the car in front of their house.

"I don't know why we're married." He looked at Jada. She opened the door and got out of the car.

"Fuck you Christian!" She said and slammed the door. Christian pulled off without a second thought. Jada was safe. McKenzie was another story.

♋   ♋   ♋

Christian rushed into the emergency room.

"Excuse me . . ." Christian said to the nurse behind the desk.

"Yes?" she looked up and smiled.

"I'm looking for McKenzie—McKenzie Batiste," he said, wiping sweat from his forehead, eyebrows furrowed. He placed his swollen hands on his hips and breathed in and out deeply while the nurse shuffled through her papers.

"One moment please." She picked up the phone and dialed. "Hello? Yes. Can you come to the front? There's a gentlemen here for Ms. Batiste. Yes. No problem." She returned the phone to the base. "Someone will be out in a moment to take you back to her." She said.

"Thank you." Christian paced back and forth then turned to the nurse. "But do you know how she is?" The nurse dropped her head for a moment.

"She's pretty bad," she said. She tried to prepare him for what he would see when he saw her, but she could see the anxiety rising in his face. Christian rubbed his head. "This is all my fault!"

The nurse looked surprised. "No, whoever did that to her is a monster. You're no monster," she said in a gentle voice.

"Hello, Mr. Batiste?" came a female voice from behind Christian. He turned to face a tall sister in a grey blazer, blue blouse, and grey slacks. Long skinny braids fell down her back.

"Christian." He said, not admitting to being her husband, in the event that only family would be allowed in to see McKenzie.

"Detective Anderson, I'm the investigating officer on this case." She extended her hand to Christian and gave him a firm hand shake.

"If you follow me, I'll take you back to Mrs. Batiste." They started the long walk down the corridor. "I'm sorry about what happened. But McKenzie came right in after the assault and we were able to get good samples for the rape kit." Christian stopped mid-stride. Hearing the word rape nearly brought him to his knees. The detective stopped to find Christian leaning against the wall.

"I'm sorry, I thought you knew? McKenzie said she'd called you and—"

"No—She did . . . I'm sorry." He paused. Detective Anderson waited patiently. She had covered special victims cases for 15 years and seen all kinds of husbands' reactions—from stoic anger, to complete breakdowns. She gave Christian time to have his moment.

"It's just . . . ." Christian wiped sweat from his forehead. "It's just that this is my fault," he said, banging his hand against the white hospital wall.

"It's no one's fault but the rapist's," she said. But after Christian explained what led up to McKenzie's brutal attack, she understood why he felt so guilty. Detective Anderson walked up to Christian and placed a gentle hand on his shoulder.

"I know you feel responsible. I know you feel horrible. But you've got to understand that for as badly as you feel—the woman that you love feels 100 times worse. And you have to realize—this is about *her*, not *you*. She's riddled with guilt, shame, helplessness—and on top of all of that she'll be worried about how you feel about her." Christian looked bewildered.

"She's been raped," Detective Anderson said, "She doesn't know how you're going to view her. Will you think she's dirty? Damaged goods—"

"Of course not! She's the victim—she was violated!" He said. Detective Anderson smiled warmly.

"She was violated. But Mrs. Batiste is no victim. Do you know that less than 20% of rape victims report the crime? And of those, less than 10% preserve any of the evidence? And of those, less than 3% go to trial to testify?" Detective Anderson motioned toward the room.

"She was violated. And from what I can tell, she's angry and hurting, and trying to be stronger than she is. But she's no victim. C'mon, she needs you right now." But before she could enter McKenzie's room, Christian told her about what he did to Melvin.

"Is he dead?" she said, pulling out her cell phone.

"I hope so." Christian said as he walked into McKenzie's room.

♋   ♋   ♋

CHAPTER ONE

McKenzie

"The deeper she hurt inside, the better she looks outside"

A manufactured rooster cock-a-doodle-dooed at 5:30 a.m.

McKenzie lay quietly till the rooster crowed the third time. She opened her eyes, reached over and whacked the "off" button, killing the rooster.

Sigh.

She rolled out of bed, slid her feet into fluffy white house slippers as she grabbed the matching white robe and tied the belt snuggly around her waist.

"Ahmad! Time to wake up!" McKenzie yelled toward the hallway.

She walked over to her closet, slid open the door and stood, hand on hip as she did every day, deciding what outfit she would wear.

McKenzie decided on her two-piece navy blue Jones New York suit. She grabbed the suit with her right hand as she scanned the row of button down shirts. She pulled out a white shirt with blue pin-stripes. She stood up on her tippy toes and grabbed the leather navy blue Nine West sling backs.

OK, she whispered under her breath.

McKenzie pulled open the second dresser drawer, grabbed matching navy blue Victoria Secret bra and panties, and headed for the bathroom.

"Ahmad! You up?"

24

"Yes, I'm up ma," Ahmad shouted from his room.

"Ok, thank you." McKenzie walked over to the TV stand and searched for the remote control.

"Where are you?" she said, scanning the area. "Ah! There you are." She grabbed it and pressed the "On" button. "TiVo. Man's greatest creation," she said as she walked back to the bathroom.

"On today's show, we have Dr. Robin Smith, licensed psychiatrist, talking to us about women's power and how to access it." Oprah said.

"Dr. Robin, you said in your book, Me, Myself, & I – *The Three People You Need to Know to Create the Life and Relationship of Your Dreams,* that women need to kick to the curb 'waiting on the sidelines for someone to care about them, love them, or help them', and get excited as they uncover the secret key to their own success." Oprah flipped through the pages of the hardcover, stopping at the dog-eared pages.

McKenzie stood in front of the sink and turned on the cold water. She watched the bubbling effervescence rush down the drain. She grabbed her purple toothbrush and mechanically applied the Sensodyne toothpaste onto the bristles.

Up and down. Up and down. She brushed the front. *Spit!* Front to back. Front to back. She brushed the left side. *Spit!* Front to back. Front to back. She brushed the right side. *Spit!* This was her morning routine--always three times.

McKenzie grabbed the buff puff and applied the Murad exfoliate. She scrubbed her left cheek, her nose, her right cheek, then her forehead. Next she scrubbed her chin. Then her right cheek again, back to her nose . . .

"Ma! I'm ready" Ahmad shouted.

McKenzie jumped. "OK. I'll be ready in about 10 minutes Ahmad."

"What really spoke to me was this partnership you talked about. Can you share with our audience more about that?" Oprah said.

"Yes of course, Oprah. YOU! Me, Myself, and I are an unbeatable team—it's a partnership required for true success," Dr. Robin said. "I shared my own personal journey that actually lead me to this revelation. I found myself struggling to identify where I

25

belonged in the world, and what truly inspired me. By the world's standards, I was doing great. I was educated in great schools, had traveled around the world, was building a successful private practice, and started pursuing a career in television. Yet, something was missing. What was missing was a secure personal sense of my worth, value
and purpose."

"I think we can all relate to that-- right, audience?" The TV audience clapped.

"What are some basic things you say we can do to tap into this source?

"Great question, Oprah. There are a few exercises, if done every day, can help alter our relationship with ourselves."

McKenzie, in panties and a bra, walked back into the room, brushing her teeth. She stood in front of the television and watched Dr. Robin give her instructions.

"So, every morning, what I want every woman in your audience to do is stand in front of the mirror and repeat these statements to themselves:

I am a beautiful and powerful woman.
I am deserving of all things great and grand.
I accept all the wonderful things the universe is placing in my path today.
I love you!

"So, just by saying these affirmations, women can expect to alter their relationships to themselves. Is it really just that simple?"

"Oprah, you'd be amazed at how many women feel uncomfortable with these four simple statements. And it's because they don't acknowledge who they are for themselves. Or, they're waiting for someone else to say these things to them so they can feel good. And most times, Oprah, like myself, we look the part and play the role, but the honest to goodness truth of the matter is—they don't believe it. They don't believe they deserve greatness, love . . . and they can't say 'I love you!' because they secretly don't believe they're worthy of love—not even from themselves.' Dr. Robin leaned into the camera.

"Here's the thing, Oprah, self-knowledge is a fundamental key to the success of any fulfilling relationship. There is no more important relationship than the one we have with ourselves.

Unfortunately, most women spend so much time either running from their past, or taking care of others, that they never get to know who they are and what they're really capable of being. But you can never fully be happy until you get to truly know you."

"Thank you, Dr. Robin. When we come back, we'll talk more about manifesting a future you love. More, when we return."

McKenzie walked back to the bathroom with a mouth full of toothpaste. She spat in the sink, stepped into the shower, and turned on the hot water. She loved the feel of the pulsating jet streams of water on her neck and shoulders. It was like a wake up massage that got her going in the morning. She stepped into the shower, closed her eyes and dropped her head as she thought about what Dr. Robin said earlier.

That's some white people shit, McKenzie said out loud. If only life could be instantly and miraculously changed through daily affirmations. Some shit just cuts too deep, and is etched in your soul to the point where it doesn't matter what you say . . . it's just who and what you are. McKenzie soaped up and rinsed off three times. Then she applied a thick glob of body wash to her loofah and moisturized her body.

McKenzie stepped out of the shower, towel pat dry, and oiled her body with baby oil. She put on her suit and pumps, then walked back into the bathroom and applied her make-up: foundation, chestnut brown eye shadow, and a neutral shade of lipstick.

As she finished the last touches of her make-up, McKenzie paused. She stared at herself in the mirror. She looked at her face . . . the two blemishes on her cheek from this month's cycle had been expertly covered, as well as the scar near her right temple that she had gotten in a "Yo Mama" childhood fight.

"Perfect!" She said, scanning herself one last time in the mirror. McKenzie hesitated for half a moment. She looked into her eyes in the mirror.

"I am . . . a . . . a beautiful . . . and . . . and . . . powerful. Woman." She cleared her throat, and looked away. McKenzie took a deep breath, and looked into her eyes.

27

"I . . . *am* . . . deserving . . . of all things . . . I . . . *am* . . de-" McKenzie turned and flipped off the light.

"That's some white people shit." She said as she grabbed her backpack and walked out the door.

Swish, Swish. Swish, Swish.

McKenzie heard her boss before she saw him. She envisioned the beige khakis— now a dark taupe from the heat and sweat oozing down the insides of his thighs. The dark wetness spreading with each step, the rubbing of the folds of flesh gathered between his legs as he waddled his way over to her cubicle.

"McKenzie, can you get this over to Sandra Nelson in legal before you go?" James said.

He placed the manila envelope on her desk. She rolled her eyes. She had asked him at two thirty if he had anything that needed to go to legal. What did he say? *No not today.* And now here it was four thirty, and as she was walking out the door—

"Oh yes." He snapped his fingers. "That reminds me!" He stood there for what felt like twenty minutes, tapping his toes and staring into space.

"Yes. What did you remember?" McKenzie took three slow breaths in and out. He did this to her every day. It was like he had to make sure he had gotten every minute of work out of her—but at four thirty—when she was walking out the door.

"I volunteered us to do the Kreeger account mock-ups."

He smiled as if he genuinely believed the "we" constituted a "him" and a "her," when she knew good and well that the proverbial 'we' meant her. She turned to face him. The stupid grin was still plastered across his round shinny face.

"Really?" McKenzie said. She paused and carefully chose her words. Instead of saying *And when the fuck am I supposed to have time to do that?* She said "And when are *we* doing that?"

Mr. Johnson looked at her, paused, and said, "It's due tomorrow by close of business."

He shuffled some papers around on her desk. He didn't dare look her in her dagger-filled eyes. She still had the mail merge for the 2012 upgrades to collate, whole punch, and assemble, to run the stats for the quarterly report for upper management, to talk to the caterer for the luncheon for the support and technical team—not to mention order the awards—

"Kathleen was swamped, so I told Bill we'd do it."

"Mr. Johnson have you forgotten? I still have the quarterly reports, and the support lunch—"

"Ms. Batiste!" He tossed the papers across her desk.

"I don't have time for the minutia," he spoke with his back to her. "We all have a heavy load. It's called time management and prioritization. I'm sure you'll figure it out. Just make sure you get those mock-ups done by close of business tomorrow. My word is my bond. I can't look bad in front of Bill." He started to shuffle off down the hallway.

Fat fuck, she thought. She wanted to say it out loud. Actually, she wanted to get up in his face and scream it. She really couldn't stand him.

She thought of thirteen ways she could inflict pain on him. He never once looked at her. Never bothered to ask if she had something do—like leave—it was way past four thirty. *Quittin' time for the Mac.*

Just because his ass didn't have a life, didn't mean she didn't. She packed up her stuff, grabbed the envelope, and headed for the FedEx machine.

"Oh, and McKenzie?" James slithered back around the corner of her cubicle. "Are you leaving already?"

"It's four thirty. I have class tonight, remember?"

James Jordell Johnson—what a bitch-ass name! His momma didn't like him either. She fucked him up before he even got started in this world. James Jordell? Seriously? And then he had the nerve to try and go by Jim. Jim! Punk-ass sell out! She could not stand this man for so many reasons.

He looked at her as if this was the first time he heard about her being in school. In reality this was probably the fifteenth time she had to remind him. Just like she had to constantly remind him she had a son.

After two years, four months, and six days working for a person, you'd think they'd remember something about you.

"Class?" James said. He scratched his George Jefferson head *bald at the top, hair on the back and sides*. "Uh no, I don't recall approving that."

She sighed, placed her things down, and turned to look at him. "I've been in school two semesters, Mr. Johnson." He looked at her through those 1980 glasses that were so big they sucked up his face. *In her torture chamber, she had fat boy tied up. He'd been there for eight days. She was starving his ass. He was sweating and dehydrated.*

"What else do you need me to do?" McKenzie smiled.

"Uh, yes. I need you to get this letter out to Compliance before close of business. I promised Bob I'd have it to him today."

He ripped off a handwritten letter from a notepad, tossed it in her general direction, and turned and walked away . . . like she hadn't just told him—for the sixteenth time—that she had class tonight. Not to mention, she still had to go pick up Ahmad. *Shit!*

He was so lucky she needed this job! She placed her things down and quickly whipped out the letter. He would sign it 'Jim'. *Jim!* Black men just didn't go by Jim! James. You called a Black man James.

But James Jordell Johnson didn't know a thing about being Black. He didn't know a thing about being a boss. He didn't know a thing about nothing—except how to run the shit out of his department. Recognized the past four quarters as "Outstanding Employee of the Month" for sales and revenue, James knew software. Last year, he had earned the company over three million dollars in revenue. He was one of the top sales accountants, second only to Chip. *Chip! What the fuck?* His name was—oh hell, she forgot what the hell that white boy's name really was. She wanted to say Chad . . . no, that was Chandler. Hell, she didn't know.

Anyway, James was determined to out-do Chip. Try as he may, Chip always topped him in over-all sales. James won the rinky-dink award, but Chip got the prime office space. Not to mention, everybody but Jimbo knew Chip was being waxed, molded and shaped for BJ's position. BJ was the CEO of Braxton Jiles' Industries.

Dumb ass James couldn't see he was Uncle Tom, House Nigga, Affirmative Action Boy. He'd walk around laughing and joking with the higher ups, and all the while they were stiffing his dumb ass. Chip got promoted— Jim got an award. Chip got the corner office—Jim got an award. Chip got stock options—Jim got an award. Fat boy was getting fucked all the while holding out for something bigger—something his dumb ass was never going to get. Dumb Fuck.

But none of this would bother her—seriously—if James Jordell Johnson kept it real. Everyone had to play the game—it's the white man's world. But you don't have to sell out. But more importantly, don't take it out on *her*!

"Here's your letter, Mr. Johnson. I really have to go. I'm going to be late for class and I still have to pick up Ahmad."

He didn't look up. "Who is Ahmad?"

McKenzie turned around and walked out. *Day nine, roll in a cart of pipin' hot fried chicken and let it just sit there in front of him*

♋   ♋   ♋

"Hurry up, Ahmad!" *Honk, honk, honk!*

"Dammit, I'm late!"

McKenzie's head was half way out the window. Ahmad was standing on the corner, talking to his homeboys. He towered over all of them, even though he was the youngest of the bunch.

Ahmad looked out of place standing with those thug-looking boys. He was neat and clean. His hair was cut in a low fade with waves—theirs were unkempt corn rolls and big lopsided naturals. He had on a crisp white polo, and fitted grey khaki's—her compromise. Khaki's were gang-banger clothes, but she couldn't argue that Dickies had thicker, sturdier material. At the end of the day, McKenzie was going to always go with quality. The thug boys all wore some variation of blue shirts (*Crips*) and big sagging baggy

31

jeans, held up by belts right up under their asses. All of them (Ahmad included) wore spotless white Air Force Ones. The thugs had blue shoelaces in theirs.

Ahmad was 6'2", a deep rich dark chocolate—like the Hershey's Special Dark chocolate. That's what she called him when she was feeling tender, *Her Special Dark.* When he was four he asked her why she called him that. "Because you're not just a beautiful Black man, son, you're special," McKenzie answered.

"What makes me so special?"

"God blessed you to be extra dark."

"Why is that a blessing? Kids at school call me blue-black!" He lowered his head. She smiled. *Kids can be so mean.* She lifted his eyes to hers.

"It's because they are jealous, son. You know what my grandmother used to say—and it applies to you," she said. He shook his head *no*.

"The darker the berry . . ." She smiled.

"The sweeter the juice!" He said. His little eyes lit up. She kissed his forehead.

"Hi Miss. Batiste!" Tony said. Ahmad jogged over to her shinny black jeep.

"Hey baby! How are you?" She reached down and clicked the button to unlock the door.

"Why you all frowned up Black woman?" Ahmad said as he slid into the passenger seat. He leaned in and kissed his mother gently on her cheek. She smiled.

"You know why!" she said. She gassed the jeep and bust a 'u' in the driveway. "I ain't raising no thugs, no gang bangers, and no pimps, Ahmad."

"Ma!" He threw his hands up in the air as if to say *hold up!*

"I was standing outside waiting for you, like you said I better be. At what time?" He leaned in and pointed to the clock. "At five o'clock. Not five o' five, not five o' three, not five o'one! No, Ahmad Malik had his rusty crusty behind outside, curbside at fo' fiddy nine to be exact! Just so I wouldn't hear *yo* mouth. And look—" He furrowed his brows, and squinched up his nose.

"I got the look *and* the mouth anyway! I tell you, a brotha can't win!" He turned to face the window, shook his head in mock disbelief. "I tell you, there are times like these that I understand why brothers turn to white women."

She socked him in his shoulder as hard as she could without losing control of her truck. "Boy I will slap the taste out of your mouth for saying some stupid shit like that to me." Ahmad fell out laughing.

"Hot buttons, hot buttons. Push them hot buttons!" He laughed and pushed imaginary buttons in front of him. She rolled her eyes. He was so playful sometimes it made her sick. But most times it just eased away her stress. She laughed.

"You know what I'm referring to smart ass." She jumped onto the 110 freeway going north.

"I don't want you hanging out on the corner, son. You're just asking to get shot up. And quite frankly, I didn't support our local farmers all these years, feeding your ass just for you to get killed." She merged into the carpool lane. Ahmad laughed out loud.

"Is that all I am to you, an investment that you're waiting to collect on?"

"Shit, I'm still waiting for you to mature." She laughed.

"Aw, that's cold, momma. That's real cold." He turned the radio up and bobbed his head to the music.

"Naw, on the real tho' ma . . . I was waiting for you when T-bone—"

McKenzie shot him a look.

"*Tony*, Cedric, and Damante 'nem rolled up." Ahmad said.

"Who the fuck is 'nem?"

"I'm not paying $14,000 a year on an education for you to be walking around here talking Ebonics like some uneducated thug." She merged right two lanes. "Boy, you better talk right before I bust you in your mouth."

"Mother! Pleeeease!" Ahmad said. "I'm code switching."

He faced her, eyes stretched open wide so you could see the whites of his eye balls, and started flaying his arms around.

"I need a good 20 minutes to get my baring! Projects . . . Affluent Black community . . . Projects . . . Affluent Black community—It's hard, OK? Give a brotha a break!" He looked at her with a pained expression. They fell out laughing for about five minutes.

"Stay away from them trifling ass Negroes Ahmad," she said as she pulled off the freeway.

"Yes mother. I will stay away from the trifling, uneducated, gang banging thugs," Ahmad answered. She socked him in his arm.

♋   ♋   ♋

McKenzie exited the freeway and made a right going East onto Century Blvd. She remembered taking the bus down Century with her grandmother Dia. They used to go down Century to go grocery shopping. That was before they built the shopping center on 103rd: before the Food-4-Less and Popeye's, before the Sav-On's and the Koreans' $1.00 store, beauty supply, and nail shops.

They used to walk to Century because the buses only ran once an hour, and by the time it came they had already passed the bus stop. That was when Dia was full of life. That was when the Projects were full of life. They'd walk down the rows, and everybody would speak.

"Hey Muh Dia! Is that McKenzie? Lawd that chil' sho nuf is growin'—you must be feedin' her some of Mrs. Petey collard greens?" Ms. Hazel would say.

Mrs. Petey used to grow the prettiest, thickest, greenest, collard greens on both sides of the Jordan Downs. She had some special concoction she'd make to keep the bugs out and make them grow tall and dark green. They said it was voodoo. Mrs. Petey's people were from Louisiana. She was high yellow and spoke Creole. More importantly, that woman would kick some ass over her greens!

Many people tried to steal her greens, and many asses were whooped as a result. She said she used to wrestle alligators back in Louisiana. No one knew whether or not that was true, but she had a reputation: you were better off a pair of gators on somebody's feet than to get your ass kicked by Mrs. Petey. The kids called her crazy, the grown ups thought it was all that voodoo she practiced. But Mrs. Hazel loved Dia. She gave her a bunch of greens every time she picked them.

The Jordan Downs had two sides: the *103rd and Grape Street side* and the *92nd and Juniper Street side*. They were separated by a big empty field. And there wasn't any difference between the sides in terms of the buildings. They were all that ugly, pasty, opaque lime green. They all had upstairs down stairs. They all had a clothesline in the back. They all looked alike. They all had poor people living in them. The only difference was one side bordered Grape Street, and the other bordered 92nd St.

But people knew which side you were from. Back in the day, everybody knew who everybody was. When Dia and McKenzie walked to the store the old women would be out sitting on their porches.

"There go Muh Dia and McKenzie." Mrs. Hazel would say. "You know the momma left that child after Don Don got killed."

"Lawd, it probably was fo' the best. Diane ain't never been right since her momma up and left her," Ms. Simms would say. "That's why she ain't right in the head. Every girl needs her momma. Before she left her, Precious spoiled Diane shitless. Then she left that child to fin fo' herself, best way she could." They would all sit there and watch them walk by. They'd nod and look at McKenzie like she was the spawn of something pathetic.

Precious was Diane's mother, and lived off her looks. She slept with men for money to buy clothes, get her hair done, and pay her bills. She got pregnant with Diane when she was fourteen. She went out with several men to get enough money for what she needed. When Diane was six, Precious left her with her grandmother to go live with a sugar daddy—a man old enough to be her father.

McKenzie was unaware of Diane's past and what haunted her. She held Muh Dia's hand and walked, oblivious to the stories that surrounded her.

McKenzie remembered those days. Those were the happiest days of her life.

♋   ♋   ♋

She made a left onto Grape, and a quick right onto Juniper. Ahmad was blasting the radio. McKenzie was annoyed because Mr. Johnson kept her after work. Then she rolled up and saw Ahmad posted up with Tony and his crew. *Trouble.* And tonight was her first night of class. She was running late. She was dropping Ahmad off at Mrs. Petey's.

She turned left onto 97th Street, Muh Dia's row. There were police cars and ambulance everywhere.

"Ma!" Ahmad said. "They're at Mrs. Petey's!" He was out the car before she could find a spot to park. He ran up the walkway and into Mrs. Petey's unit. McKenzie threw the jeep in park and quickly ran behind her son.

She pushed through the crowd. She spotted Mrs. Hazel who had tears running down her face. "What happened, Mrs. Hazel?" McKenzie said. Mrs. Hazel grabbed her hand so tight McKenzie flinched.

"Mrs. Petey had a heart attack," Mrs. Hazel said. McKenzie pulled loose and ran inside and up the stairs. Ahmad was at Mrs. Petey's side. He turned to look at McKenzie. Tears streamed down his face.

"Momma."

The paramedics were packing away their stuff.

"Is she OK?" McKenzie looked at Mrs. Petey and knew she wasn't. She was dead. There was no air filling her lungs. She looked small and fragile. It reminded her of her last days with her grandmother, Annie Mae. Everyone called her Muh Dia. But to McKenzie she was simply *My Dia.*

All her childhood Dia was larger than life. Not in stature, she was only 5'5", about 140 lbs. But she was big in presence. Dia would walk in a room and command it. She was always impeccably dressed—matching from head to toe.

She'd always say, *Just cause you live in the ghetto don't mean you have to dress like you're from the ghetto.* Dia had been an administrator for LAUSD. She was retired but when she first moved to L.A. from Arkansas back in 1952, she could only afford to live in the Projects. Her husband, Donald Senior, died in August 1952. By September, she had packed up her few possessions and her son, McKenzie's daddy, Don Don, and moved to Los Angeles. Over the years, she obtained her bachelor's degree and master's degree in education, but she never moved out of the Projects.

This is my home, she'd say *I don't need a fancy house in Ladera to be happy. I have my son, my McKenzie and God—everything else is gravy.*

For years, it was just Dia and Don Don, her only child. He attended 103rd Elementary, Markham Junior High and then Jordan High, where he met McKenzie's biological mother, Diane. They dated the 11th and 12th grade of high school. Don Don 'won' an academic scholarship to Howard University thanks to Dia's connections with the school board. He attended Howard, obtained his degree in Finance. Her mother attended Spelman and received her degree in Liberal Arts.

At twenty-four, Don Don was stable. He was working for one of the top law firms in the city as an accounting consultant, making a substantial amount of money. Diane became pregnant with McKenzie and became a stay at home mom. Dia told McKenzie that Diane was content staying at home while Don Don supported her even though she had a degree. Diane lived the cush life of a stay at home mother and wife for four years until the day Don Don was shot and killed.

He had been visiting Dia when he stopped at Mr. Lee's corner store. Two boys from Nickerson Garden projects were inside. The Nickerson and Jordan Downs gangs had been feuding for years. It was like the Hatfield's and the McCoy's Feud —20 years of fighting and they don't even know what they were fighting about anymore. It's just what they did because it's all they knew. Some Grape Street OG's (*original gangstas)* rolled up and saw them walking out the store and emptied two clips from an AK47. McKenzie's dad lay dead at the base of the cash register; a casualty of the Nickerson Garden/Jordan Down gang war.

Dia was never the same after that. And Diane fell apart. Watching her mother walk out on her, then having her husband shot and killed—she couldn't take it. She dropped McKenzie off at Dia's one night and kept it moving. McKenzie didn't see her for three years after that.

Dia said McKenzie saved her life. She told everyone that God sent McKenzie to her. That without her, she probably would have shriveled up and died—But McKenzie gave her a reason to live.

But Dia didn't have the same passion for life after McKenzie's daddy was killed. She had the mouth, but the spark in her eyes was gone. They were dull, lifeless. Her spirit had been broken. Dia's health started to deteriorate. It started off with high blood pressure and hypertension. The doctor told her she needed to cut down on salt and fried foods.

"Then I might as well just roll over and die!" she'd say, "bland, baked food? Why the hell bother?" And she kept eating the way she always ate, deep-fried food, chicken, pork chops, fish. If it was meat, she'd find a way to fry it. She even prepared her vegetables with too much seasoning. She flavored them with seasoned salt, lemon pepper, garlic salt, and salt pork or ham hocks. Tasted damned good, just did damage on the arteries.

Dia slowed down tremendously. They stopped walking to the grocery store. She stopped walking McKenzie to school. After a while, she stopped walking altogether. She barely left her apartment. They'd watch the Soaps together. Her favorites were on channel seven: *All My Children*, *One Life to Live*, and *General Hospital*.

"I hate that evil cow!" She'd say about Carly "She's a triflin' ho, sleeping with Tony—that's her momma's husband for heaven's sakes!"

"Her momma left her. She just wanted to hurt her mother the way she hurt her." McKenzie said in a whisper. Dia turned to look at her.

"You look here, McKenzie, that's some crazy white folk shit. Black people don't sleep with they momma's husbands. That's some nasty shit." She said. "When you hurt, you deal with it head on. You hear me?" McKenzie didn't reply.

"McKenzie Batiste, look at me!" McKenzie turned to look at her.

"Yes, Muh Dia."

"Your mother is not well." She said, looking off. "Death has a way of turning your insides into mush. Making you stop believe . . ."

"She loves you," she said, "the best way she knows how."

"I don't need her love." McKenzie said. And she meant it. All she needed was her grandmother's love. It filled her heart and made her happy. Just to have Dia smile at her set her world right.

Dia grabbed McKenzie's hand and kissed it. "I feel sorry for Diane. God don't like ugly child." She said. She shook her head.

"Your grandmother ran off with some man who had a lot of money. And your momma stood and watched her pack up, walk out the door, and never come back for her. She's broken. But you are whole, McKenzie. You're whole and full of love. Don't let hate ruin you. You have to be bigger and stronger than hurt. Don't let them cheat you out of life like it has me and your mother."

♋   ♋   ♋

Over the next year, Dia would deteriorate before McKenzie's eyes. Her diabetes robbed her of her eyesight, her left leg, and eventually her will to live. She died early May in King Hospital. As she thought back, McKenzie believed anything closely resembling pure love died inside her that day too.

Diane picked McKenzie up two months after the funeral. McKenzie stayed with Mrs. Petey until they found her. Diane had gotten married to a preacher and was living somewhere in Ladera.

♋   ♋   ♋

CHAPTER TWO

Christian

The cell vibrated on Christian's hip. It was Jada calling—*for the eighth time that day.* He flipped the phone open.

"Hello?" he said. He stepped out of his car and closed the door.

"Some bitch named Lisa just called my house!"

Christian rolled his eyes and took a deep breath.

"Lisa who?"

"The bitch didn't want to leave her last name! As a matter of fact, she didn't want to leave a name, a number, or the reason why she was calling you. Why is that, Christian?"

"How do I know Jada?" He said. *Sigh. Here we go.*

"Well, she called and left a message, so I called her back. When I asked her who she was and what was the nature of her call, she said you knew who she was and if you could just return her call, she'd appreciate it. What kind of bull shit is that?"

"Jada! Why did you call her? The message was for me." The woman walking in front of him turned to look at him. He stopped and let her get far ahead of him.

"I'm your wife, Christian. It shouldn't be a problem—unless there's something going on. Is there something going on?"

"No, of course not." *Not that it mattered at all what he said. It never mattered. If he argued with her she'd say he was arguing too hard, so he must be guilty. And if he didn't, in her mind that meant she was right.* Christian's goal was always to get her to shut up as soon as possible. The best way to accomplish that was to let her rant and rave until she got tired of hearing herself.

"Then why the fuck couldn't she just tell me why she was calling you? Why the secrets, Christian?"

41

He searched his mind for who Lisa was, and it hit him—she was the secretary from the Masters' program department. He never gave his home number out to women. She must have taken the number off of the application. He thought he left his cell as the contact number. But he wouldn't waste his breath trying to explain that to Jada.

"I don't know. I'm not in her mind. I can only speak for me." Christian shifted the phone to his other ear, and placed his hand on his hip.

"And I can only speak for me. I don't want women calling my house, Christian. It's disrespectful."

He scratched his forehead and sighed again. "OK, fine Jada." He just wanted to get her off the phone. "Whatever."

"Whatever? What the fuck does that mean? Are you going to check that bitch or what?"

"Yes," he said, teeth clenched. "I will make sure she doesn't call the house again."

Jada's voice softened. "Good. You can call her while I'm here, so I can hear you tell her."

He paced in between two cars. "I said I would tell her, Jada."

"Yeah, just like you said you would tell Trish, right?"

Christian sighed. *Here we go*. He had to hear about Trish—again. Trish Davenport was a cool sistah Christian kicked it with for a couple of months while he was in North Carolina—the *first* time he attended Grad School.

Early one summer, he and Jada were driving home from a dinner party in Northern Cal.

"Christian where is our relationship going?" She said, "We've been together for five years and need to make some decisions."

"What kind of decisions Jada?"

"I think we should get married."

Marriage was the furthest thing from Christian's mind. It was the only thing on Jada's.

They argued for weeks. "Jada, I need to be able to support you before we get married, so I need to finish Grad school."

"I don't know why we can't get married first? I can move to North Carolina with you."

However many ways there were to be bound, gagged, and have the life sucked out of you—she suggested them. Three months later Christian was enrolled at North Carolina A&M.

Christian had a ball. New friends, new experiences, and the first in his family to obtain a Master's degree—he was on his way. More importantly, NC A&M offered him the escape he needed from Jada and the looming idea of being married.

Jada called questioning him every night. And it just got worse as the weeks passed. Christian made excuses like he was in the library studying with a study group, or in the computer lab writing a term paper. The truth was, he loved Jada. But things had changed. He was dating other women; nothing serious, but it was nice to be around women who didn't question his every move—let alone, his every thought. The women he dated talked politics—about the state of African Americans. They talked and *listened*—to what he thought, to what he felt. They didn't spend the entire evening questioning him about who he *was* with and who *wanted to be* with him.

Jada was so vexed by Christian's waning availability she came out to visit. Jada was in North Carolina three days before she "found" the telephone bill. And Trish's number on the bill—every night for the past three months. Jada called Trish and confronted her—only to learn that she and Christian had been dating. Jada was devastated. She cried hysterically and Christian felt like shit.

Christian went home for Thanksgiving, and never returned to NC A&M.

"You can transfer your units to Cal State Long Beach; they have an excellent Educational Development Master's program." Jada handed him swatches of material in a variety of colors. "Which one do you like baby?"

Christian's mouth was dry. *How did I let myself get into this mess?* They were getting married—the only way of proving to Jada that Trish didn't mean anything.

"We're starting off new, fresh. We don't need to be separated ever again." Jada whispered in his ear. "We need to be close so we can rebuild the trust you destroyed. We're going to be so happy together." She wrapped her arms around Christian's neck and pulled his face into hers. It would be the first kiss of many in the years to come that would turn his stomach sour.

"I have to go to class, Jada."

"You know I love you, right Christian? I'm sorry I'm being a bitch, but I'm trying to make sure we have a solid marriage. I'm still trying to help rebuild trust. I mean, it's hard when the one you love has been unfaithful to you."

Christian took a deep breath. He was so tired of hearing how badly he fucked up. And he was tired of being punished for it.

"Yeah. OK Jada. Look, I gotta go. Talk to you later." He hung up the phone.

♋   ♋   ♋

Christian walked toward class, deep in thought. He passed by the gold and brown maple trees, and the beautifully manicured lawns, made plush and green by the reclaimed wastewater doused on them twice a day by the high-powered oscillating sprinklers.

Some people smoked spliffs to escape their problems . . . some drank . . . others shopped. Christian went to school. *Damn, that shit sounded corny.* But it was the God honest truth. It was the only safe haven he had . . . the only place he could go without his wife that was not perceived as an impropriety.

Christian looked back and wondered how he got here—to this place where he was so miserable. It was a place where he fought so hard to maintain some sense of himself. He felt like every day he was pulled into this vortex where his manhood was questioned, his individualism was challenged, and peace did not exist.

It was amazing because Christian clearly remembered hating that feeling. That uneasiness he felt so often these days. As a child, hearing the arguments, the screaming and shouting—and eventually the slaps, punches, and thumping and bumping from his mother and her husband—left him feeling helpless.

Not being able to save his mother made his stomach curdle like sour milk in the refrigerator. It was cold and lumpy, and stank some terrible. Stank so bad it made you turn away in disgust and have the worst scowl on your face. That's how Christian felt as a child.

But here he was, a grown man—feeling the same way. Wishing he could become invisible just like he wished when he was six years old. Doing whatever it took to keep the peace because he honestly believed he could change the outcome. As a child, he sat quietly. He cleaned up even though he didn't mess up. He did everything he was told. Hoping it would make a difference. He even lied. He hated lying, but his mom didn't play.

"What happens in this house ain't nobody's business!" she'd say after her husband beat her burgundy, purple and black. She was fair-skinned and bruised easily.

"If anybody asks, you don't know nothin' you hear me?" she'd say to him and his siblings. Christian was the youngest, and the most obedient.

"Yes, momma," they'd all say.

His stomach would be in knots watching her expertly apply make-up to cover the bruises. He wanted to kill her husband for hurting his mother, but she kept distance between them. She was a human shield—or punching bag—however you chose to look at it. Christian was young and scrawny. Her husband would have kicked his ass for sure, but Christian would have enjoyed trying to beat the shit out of him, even if he did lose.

So they'd go to school, church, to his dad's —nobody knew. They were on lock down like Vegas—*what happened in that house, stayed in that house*. On the outside, everyone thought they were just the happy little family. But on the inside, everyone walked around on edge trying to dodge another one of the husband's bouts of rage.

Christian's escape was to leave for school. He won a partial academic scholarship to Cal State San Francisco. But even if he hadn't received financial assistance, he would have found a way to get away from there. The partial scholarship just covered tuition. He lived off of the meager work-study check, paying for books,

46

microwave popcorn, and the top ramen noodles he would live off of. He didn't care; he was free.

That was, until he received a call from his sister telling him his mom had an aneurysm. She was in the hospital, on life support. He never felt so much guilt and shame for leaving his mother with that monster than he did at that moment. He watched her lifeless body being force to rise up and down by the ventilator, and nearly choked on the hot bile that filled his throat.

Christian tried to remember their life before *him*. How his mom used to play hide and go seek with them in the house. That stopped when the husband moved in. He said they were making too much noise. *How they used to laugh and dance.* That stopped too. He said they were wild and out of control. Slowly, the happy home they had turned into an intolerable hellhole where everyone walked around on egg-shells trying to miss the landmines laid inconspicuously about, waiting to go off.

Christian silently promised his mom as they unplugged the machine and removed the ventilator, that he would never disrespect a woman. He would always hold her in the highest esteem and treat her like the queen she deserved to be treated like. He would redeem himself. He would show his mother that he loved her more than anything, even though he didn't save her. He would honor her memory by being the honorable man she raised him to be.

It was a promise that proved to be a challenge every time he laid eyes on Jada. She would say and do some of the most outrageous things—hurtful, mean, and stupid things. Sometimes he just wanted to shake her. But he would never put his hands on a woman. If he were the kind of man who did hit a woman, he would have slapped the shit out of her by now over some of the things she'd done.

But he wasn't. He would think of his mom and overlook it. He would take a deep breath and bear it. Besides, everyone thought they were so happy. And he liked feeling that his happiness brought others joy.

♋   ♋   ♋

CHAPTER THREE

Grad School

Christian felt McKenzie as he walked through the door. There were at least forty other people in the room, but Christian was drawn to her energy. Although she sat in an empty row of desks, her presence filled the room.

He stood in the doorway for a moment, inconspicuously watching her. Her peanut butter brown complexion, tucked under a white, orange and blue bronco baseball cap, was smooth and creamy. She stared off into space, deep in thought. She sported a short hairstyle, barely any showed outside the cap.

No make-up, just a faint touch of orange lipstick to make the ensemble complete. Her only adornment was a tiny diamond nose-ring in her right nostril. He noticed only because the light caught it just so—creating a slight sparkle that made him take a closer look. She wore navy blue sweat pants, with an orange stripe down the side, an orange t-shirt, and white, orange and blue Nike's. *Cute*, he thought, as he made his way toward her. She hadn't said a word and already he was intrigued.

♋   ♋   ♋

49

"Excuse me, Sistah," he said, as he approached. Every strand of hair on the nape of her neck stood on edge.

McKenzie looked up. *Oh my freakin' God!* Was what she wanted to say. Her eyes locked on one of the most beautiful, creamy, dark chocolate Black men she had seen in a long, long time.

He wore a ribbed cream turtleneck sweater, some black nut-huggin' jeans, a tight pair of black leather Kenneth Cole boots, and a black baseball cap that dressed the outfit down just right. His face was smooth; his beard was thin, faded, and neatly shaped. The diamond stud in his right ear wasn't too big, but it sparkled enough to let you know it was real. *Sexy.* He had small, almond shaped, chestnut-brown eyes that pierced into her as he spoke.

"Yes?" McKenzie said.

He smiled. *Good Lord, what a dazzling smile.* He looked around the room.

"Do you mind if I sit next to you?" The corners of his mouth inched up as he asked. McKenzie looked around the room. There were plenty of empty seats.

"Of course not, King, have a seat."

She motioned for him to sit next to her. He raised his eyebrows, showing intrigue at her response. A white girl, sitting two rows behind her, grunted. McKenzie turned around to face her.

"You got a problem back there?" McKenzie stated, more than asked.

The white girl's eyes widened. She sat motionless and shook her head 'No.' McKenzie turned to face the beautiful Black man with the dazzling smile. He was shaking his head, laughing. He slid into the chair next to hers.

"You're bad," he whispered. McKenzie smiled.

"Yeah, I am." She half-turned to face the white girl again. "But if people would mind their own business we wouldn't have any problems. None at all." The white girl fixed her eyes on the paper on her desk and didn't respond.

"Leave her alone. She's scared to death. Look at her face," the guy with the dazzling smile said.

She looked the white girl up and down, and turned up her nose.

"Whatever. I ain't the one." She said. She rolled her eyes.

He smiled at her as he unzipped his bag. He pulled out a notepad and a pen, placed them on the desk and turned to her.

"My name's Christian, by the way" he said, extending his hand. McKenzie took it, shaking it firmly.

"McKenzie. Pleased to meet you, of course." McKenzie said. Christian looked at her oddly.

"Of course?" Christian said.

"Of course. I'm always pleased to be in the presence of royalty." McKenzie said as she looked back at the white girl. Nothing—no looks no responses. They both laughed out loud.

"Why, thank you—Queen?" Christian said.

"That's right. But you need to say it with a bit more authority. Don't question. Know," McKenzie said, leaning in toward him.

"I bet you know?" Christian said leaning in toward her.

"Put all your money on *that* bet baby." McKenzie grinned.

"OK, ladies and gentlemen. It's time to get started," said a tall, dark-haired Latina woman. "This is Psychology 502, Psychology of Education, a prerequisite for Psych 504 and 507—required core courses for the Masters of Educational Leadership degree. If you are trying to add, see me at the end of class.

"Right now, I'm going to take roll—not that it's going to be at all accurate—so humor me, will you?" She smiled warmly, then walked toward the dirty chalkboard and began erasing the notes from the previous class.

"I am professor Telfair," she said as she scribbled her name on the board, followed by a Ph.D. She turned to face the class. "We're all adults, and I'm not stuck on titles—so, whatever you're comfortable with."

"Now, for the roll—please, let's just get that out of the way," She began reading off the names.

"Henry Heins-rucken-ger, Did I completely butcher that?" She looked around the room for the victim. A linebacker looking blonde guy with piercing blue eyes sat up and responded.

"Yes ma'am, you did. But you did it better than most," Henry replied with a light-hearted chuckle.

"I'll get it straight. Give me a couple of classes, please"

"Don't bother. Hank is fine."

The instructor scribbled notes on the side of the roster.

"Christian Malveaux?" The instructor looked around the room. Christian raised his hand.

"Right here."

She smiled and checked off his name. She read off the rest of the names on the roster.

"Is there anyone I missed?" She glanced across the crowded room. There were half a dozen hands raised. She jotted each name down at the bottom of her roster. "Yes?"

"McKenzie. McKenzie Batiste," she said. The professor paused. "Did I speak with you earlier in the week, Ms. Batiste?"

"Yes ma'am, you did." The instructor nodded and jotted down a few notes. "Can you stop by after class, please?" McKenzie nodded. There had been an issue with her enrollment, so McKenzie needed her to sign off on her Add Form to secure her place in the class.

The professor reviewed the syllabus for the course, took questions, and handed out a group assignment.

"OK folks. You've all completed your prerequisites satisfactorily. Not to say that any of those classes weren't challenging." She stopped at each row, handing the person on the end a stack of papers to pass down.

"But these are 500-level courses you're taking now. They're going to require much more effort . . . more thought . . . and more teamwork," The professor said. She moved to the front of the class. "This is your cohort. You will see these faces for the next year or two, for some of you—three." The class laughed. "You will get to know each other, probably better than you'd like—but it will be a worthwhile experience, trust me. Many of you will leave the University with friendships that will last a lifetime."

They all looked around the room at each other, wondering who would fit that category for them. Christian looked at McKenzie and smiled. She smiled back.

"The purpose of this course is to provide each of you with the skill sets needed to be effective in your teaching role. The

University is committed to creating a pathway for disenfranchised
youth to complete post-secondary education. Your role begins in the
classroom, ladies and gentlemen. With you being able to adapt to
less than perfect situations. And equipped to teach *students* with a
myriad of barriers in their day-to-day environments.

"Your first assignment," announced the professor, "will be a
group project." The class moaned. "Yes, yes—I know. Not so much
enthusiasm, please," she said, placing her hands on her hips. "This
project calls for you to observe organic situations, identify the
potential barriers, and make recommendations on how to best
support youth so that they, along with their families and, or, support
systems, can remove these barriers—perceived and real—and create
positive environments that help encourage post-secondary
matriculation."

"OK! Let's do this the old-fashioned way and count off. I'll
go up and down the rows."

The professor divided the class up into groups of five.
Everyone moved to their designated area of the room and into their
groups. They turned their seats to face each other and began their
introductions.

"If everyone is OK with it, let's start by telling everyone
your name, and what you're going to do with your degree once you
get it. Who wants to go first?" Christian said.

"I'll go," an older woman said. "Hi. My name is Camille
Miller." She was in her mid-fifties with blond hair that was fading
into grey. "Well, currently, I sit on the L.A. Commission for youth
education and social services, and, while it's a volunteer position, I
thought the degree would help me with the legislation and initiatives
that I vote on regularly."

Camille shared that she had two grown children, Justin and
Chase, who were both now in college. When Chase, the younger of
the two, left for UConn she packed up her things and moved out.

"It was a loveless marriage," she said. "I married Stanley
because he was safe, and it was expected. We had been together
since high school, and before you know it we were getting married,
buying a house and having children. It was all so boring."

She said they stayed together for the children. Once the boys
were gone, so was their reason for being together. Camille said the
divorce was easy and they're cordial because of the boys.

"But when I look back, I realize I wasted twenty good years of my life. I was miserable. And so was Stanley."

She seemed sweet. Like one of those people you could pour your heart out to and never have to worry about it getting out.

"What about you Miss McKenzie?" Camille said, smiling at McKenzie.

"My goal is to teach in middle school."

"That's a difficult age!" Furnell said.

"Yes, I suppose. I just remember being in middle school and how challenging it was—and wishing I had someone I could turn to to tell me the truth about life. I want to offer our youth as many resources as possible. And I want to do it within the context of truth and hopefulness—I don't think our kids have much hope these days."

McKenzie sat for a moment in deep thought.

Christian was next. McKenzie couldn't wait to hear his story. He kept it sweet and simple. He was in the program because he wanted to become a Principal of a high school. He transferred from NC A&M, and hoped the degree would position him to make an impact in the K-12 educational system.

"Specifically, my goal is to make systemic changes as it relates to equity and access for urbanized youth with limited resources." Christian said.

McKenzie tried hard not to smile. *A Black man after her own heart.* She thought it was just those tight ass jeans that drew her to him—but the beautiful Black man had a brain and some ambition—her mouth started to water.

"Hi, I'm April," said a Sistah around 24 years old, with exceptionally large boobs and ass, and long, wavy dark brown hair.

April was short, with curves that could stop a Mack truck. She was light complexioned with full lips. And she wore tight-fitting clothes that made you notice her curves. She wasn't subtle at all. McKenzie used all of her restraint not to turn her nose up at the young woman. It was very distasteful. And the truth was, she was pretty. She didn't think the girl needed to do all of that to get attention.

"My desire is to open a group home." April looked around the group for what McKenzie thought was dramatic effect.

"I want to help young emancipated girls believe in themselves and set professional and personal goals of achievement."

McKenzie did roll her eyes on that one.

"Too many of our young girls have low self-esteem these days. I believe through proper education, life skills, and role modeling, our young girls will have a fighting chance for success. This degree will move me closer to my goal and demonstrate the importance of post-secondary education to the young girls as I will, of course, be the role model that they will first try and emulate."

April ran her long acrylic nails through her wavy hair. McKenzie stared at her in disbelief. She caught April batting her eyes at Christian. She shook her head and turned to face Furnell. *How pathetic.* McKenzie thought. Was that a show for Christian?

Furnell wanted to start off as a history teacher in high school and eventually transition into administration. "I am a History buff!" He got all hyped up in his chair, shifting from side to side, moving around his syllabus—he was grinning from ear to ear.

"Any particular country or era?" Christian said. "American, England, Post WWII?"

"Aw man," Furnell sat and thought for a second. "I think it's more about the impact on humanity for me." He scratched his head and nodded vigorously. "Yeah. You know that saying, 'You don't know where you're going until you know where you've been?'"

Everyone in the group nodded.

"My focus is more about creating systemic change—sort of like Chris there—by understanding how we fucked up our past, so that we don't repeat history, and so we can make a better future for our children."

McKenzie watched Melvin roll his eyes. She was instantly annoyed.

"And—"McKenzie said, dragging out the word, looking at Melvin, "how would this degree help you accomplish that?

"Well," Furnell said, "there's a saying in Africa 'How are the children?' And basically what that means is, children in Africa are the most fragile, easiest displaced, and unprotected in the village—in the continent. So, if the children are OK, then it's safe to believe that as a people, as a society, things are on the right track."

The group smiled and nodded at the rationalization. Again, Melvin rolled his eyes and started doodling on his note pad.

"Sorry this is such a long explanation guys—but I'm totally amp'd about this" Furnell said. "So, if I can focus on education," he looked pointedly at Christian, "and make systemic changes, changes that we know did not work in our past—and if it's with our most fragile beings, our children, then I believe I can positively impact our future."

"So you will be working with disadvantaged communities as well, then?" McKenzie said.

"Oh, hell yes!" Furnell said. Camille chuckled. April smiled. Christian nodded his head in approval. Melvin smirked and continued to doodle on his note pad.

"And you—Melvin?" McKenzie asked. Her voice was flat, and even though she looked him in the eyes, it was more of a mad-dog stare than a sincere look of interest. Melvin looked up from his doodling.

"This degree qualifies for loan forgiveness," Melvin said, picking lint off his white and blue striped Benetton sweater.

"What's that?" Furnell said.

"Oh, you work in a poor community for two years and they wipe out your loan," Melvin said. "I'll show up, dodge a couple of gang fights, fly low under the radar for two years and have the government pay off my loan. Voila!" he said with a smirk.

"But if you had to choose?" McKenzie said between clenched teeth.

"Who would *choose* to drive to the ghetto to teach a bunch of prison-bound kids who don't know the difference between a comma splice and all spice?" Melvin chuckled to himself. McKenzie glared.

"Actually, I would," Furnell said.

"And what the hell is wrong with you?" Melvin said, running his fingers through his wavy red hair.

"What the fuck is wrong with you?" McKenzie shouted.

Melvin turned to look at McKenzie and met a scowl so ferocious he had to turn away. Furnell gently touched McKenzie's hand.

"What I would choose to do, Melvin," Furnell said, "is to give those same bunch of kids you're referring to the same quality education those Westlake kids get. Maybe me being in front of the class will inspire them to make other choices besides going to prison. You ever think about that?"

"What *I* think about," Melvin replied, "is serving my two year sentence and getting my loan forgiven, then transferring to a school that has text books, and a computer lab—not a meth lab on campus."

"Now," the Professor interrupted before anyone in the group could reply to Melvin's statement. She walked around the class and distributed an assignment sheet.

"If you have any problems with a group member, feel free to come see me. It's important that each of you carry your weight on this project, it's 40% of your final grade in the class." The students moaned, groaned, and complained. "Let's review so we can make sure everyone is on the same page. Be sure to jot down some preliminary ideas for the next time your group meets."

Professor Telfair scanned the room. The groups looked evenly distributed. The majority of the class was white, about 65%. This was typical, not many minorities in this Master's program, even less minority males. She sighed. "OK, we have a lot of material to cover, let's get started." She walked the room reviewing the syllabus. Next, she provided an overview of the course group project.

"The purpose of the study is to observe youth in their natural habitat. You'll introduce different variables and observe how they affect the control group and gain insight on how external factors impact the learning process."

"During your project, you will be asked to rely on the use of observations to create the data that mimic the types of information you might collect in social service research situations," she explained. "Essentially, all you need to complete these exercises are several subject matters to observe independent and dependent variables, and an experimental and control group.

"You should begin these exercises by generating data. You cannot do the subsequent exercises without doing this one first because you will use the data generated in the first exercise as the basis for all the others. After completing each exercise, you can compare results to get a clearer picture of whether your data patterns are typical or more unusual. You'll be able to determine the validity by using the information I have provided you, and the information in your text." Professor Telfair said.

"Tonight, I just want you guys to meet each other, exchange numbers and email addresses. You have the assignment there on the third page of the syllabus. Be sure to reference it during your observations. I can't tell you how many disappointed students I've had—going off on tangents 'thinking' they're doing a research project, only having failed—yes, I do fail people—because they didn't use the resources provided to them."

♋   ♋   ♋

On the way out, Camille and Christian walked together.

"Twenty years wasted, huh?" Christian said. He had a half-smile plastered across his face.

"Yep. Wasted."

"You really believe that? I mean, you raised two healthy kids to go on to college, right?"

"Are they healthy?" Camille said, shuffling her backpack to her right shoulder. "Yes, we raised them. And yes, they've gone on to college—but I don't know if they're healthy—mentally, I mean." Camille stopped and faced Christian.

"What they learned, Christian, was how to stay in a bad relationship. You know what I mean?"

"No. What do you mean?"

"We were their role models. I taught them what a wife and a mom are supposed to be: essentially, unhappy, because that's what I was. That's what they saw every day. Stanley taught them what a husband and father are supposed to be—again, unhappy. And that you're *supposed* to stay with a woman who doesn't get your juices going—even if you're miserable."

"Yes, but you taught them commitment and how to stick things out, even when it was tough. Not many people can commit to something for 20 years." Christian said.

"No, no. That's what society tells us, kiddo. But the truth is, they learn by example." Camille patted him on the shoulder. "And we didn't get a damned thing out of sticking it out, but wasted years. Those are years we could have spent loving someone who loved us back."

Christian stood for a minute, contemplating.

"But it's hard to get out Camille. It's not that easy. You make it sound so easy. Just leave . . ."

"Nom kiddo, it ain't easy. It's probably the hardest thing you'll do." They stood in silence as she watched Christian fight back tears.

Christian had never confided in anyone before, and couldn't really explain why he felt comfortable or even compelled to pour his heart out to this stranger, except that her story sounded just like his life.

For the next hour, Camille listened to Christian tell his story. Her heart ached, knowing all that he was enduring. Her rage grew, realizing as he spoke that he was where she was at year ten—miserable enough to know it wouldn't get better, but too bound by fear and obligation to do anything to change the situation.

♋   ♋   ♋

Lecture in Professor Telfair's Psychology of Education course had been very interesting. She covered many of the controversial topics that were being discussed on the daily news and highlighted in the Dateline, 20/20, and 48 Hours evening shows: academic inequity, access to quality education, and biased aptitude testing, to name a few. She covered a broad range of psychological theories, cultural and societal dogmas, as well as the standards of education and their evolution over the years.

McKenzie really enjoyed this course. She enjoyed being forced to consider issues outside her normal realm of thinking. She enjoyed the challenge of learning something new, and understanding how things came to be. She was an active participant when it came to class discussions, and on more than one occasion, a worthy adversary in one-on-one debates.

It was the fourth class meeting, and the groups would start meeting more frequently to prepare for their group projects.

"Can you guys meet on the weekend?" April said.

"Weekends are bad for me," Melvin said. "Evening meetings during the week work better for me, preferably on Tuesdays or Thursdays. But nothing after 8:00 p.m.--"

"And maybe we should come to your house, so you won't have to walk?" McKenzie said as she rolled her eyes.

"Excuse you?" Melvin replied.

"Excuse you!" McKenzie said. "Last I checked this was a *group* project. We're all going to have to make sacrifices—meaning meeting times and places. What's with this shit—"?

"I'm sure Melvin was not implying that he was not prepared to make sacrifices, McKenzie," Christian said.

"He was probably just trying to narrow down some dates and times to see if it would work with the rest of the group." Christian looked at Melvin for confirmation. Melvin didn't respond.

"Well, I'm open," Camille said.

"Thank you Camille," Christian said, smiling. "Now, how about we start over, following Camille's lead?"

The group finally decided to meet at least once a week, on Wednesday evenings at 7:00 p.m. for now. As the presentation grew nearer, they would meet more frequently to make sure they had enough time to complete their project successfully. The group agreed and adjourned for the night.

McKenzie was the first to leave the table. She headed toward the back of the room. Christian watched her as she purposefully made a B-line through the room to a young man sitting in the corner. He had on a red and gold 49er's sweat suit, with a matching baseball cap, and matching red, white, and gold Adidas tennis shoes.

McKenzie said something to the young man and he stood up. They walked toward the door. Christian quickly grabbed his things and headed toward the door. As he approached the exit, he met up with McKenzie and the young man.

"You outtie?" Christian said to McKenzie as he stepped to the side to let her pass.

"Yeah." She said as she walked through the door.

As the young man followed close behind, Christian realized that he was just a teenager. He stood about 6'2"—a couple inches shorter than Christian, but he looked about 14 years old in the face.

"What's up, young blood?" Christian said to the young man, extending his hand. The young man took it, shook it once, cupped his fingers, slid them across Christian's into a snap *the Black man hand shake* and pointed his index finger at Christian as he walked passed.

"You got it."

"Aw, I can't call it," Christian said, walking behind them as they left the building.

"If you can't, then who can?" said the young man.

"I'm gonna have to leave that up to the young blood, like yourself." Christian watched the back of McKenzie's head as they walked. She never responded, and never missed a beat in her step.

"Then you can stop worrying. You're in good hands." The young man cupped his hands together, like the 80's All State Insurance commercial. "With Ahmad." The teenager smiled and trotted off to catch up with McKenzie. Christian laughed.

"All right Ahmad, you stay up Black." Christian stopped in the quad. "Good night McKenzie Batiste!"

"Good night Christian Malveaux!" she yelled back. He could hear her smiling. He smiled and walked off toward the "C" parking lot.

♋   ♋   ♋

The next class, Christian approached McKenzie. "Was that your little brother with you last class?" McKenzie smiled.

"Ahmad is my son," she said, staring him directly in his eyes.

"Your son? You're kidding, right? What, did you have him at ten?"

He looked her up and down. She couldn't be a day over twenty-two or three. Ahmad had to be all of 14. Doing the math, that wasn't possible.

"Close. I had him at 15," she admitted, "and he's 16."

"Fifteen, my goodness, how old are you now?"

"Getting a Masters and you still can't do math?" McKenzie smiled. "I'm 31 years fine." She laughed.

"That's right."

Christian couldn't argue with that. McKenzie was beautiful. And after learning about Ahmad, she somehow looked even finer. McKenzie smiled a gracious smile.

"We didn't talk much, but he seems like a fine young man. You've done a wonderful job raising him."

"Why thank you, Mr. Malveaux." She hesitated. "If he turns out half as good as you have, I'll be more than pleased."

Christian was touched. She didn't know him very well. That was a very sweet thing to say. It especially took him off guard because McKenzie wasn't big on compliments. She was generally spinning heads with her quick wit and smart-ass remarks. "Well, thank you," was all he could say.

The group was meeting regularly on Wednesday nights. Sometimes, they met at restaurants, sometimes, at each other's houses. Tonight they were at Melvin's house. McKenzie couldn't stand Melvin. She told Christian that on their second group meeting.

"He irritates the lining of my ass," McKenzie admitted to Christian as they walked toward Melvin's house that night. They pulled up at the same time.

"He's all right."

In all fairness, McKenzie was just as clueless in her Blackness as Melvin was in his whiteness—fair exchange, no robbery. But Christian did side with McKenzie because he was a Black male who had felt the harshness of the struggle all his life.

McKenzie rolled her eyes at Christian. He knew it irritated her that he always tried to see the best in people. McKenzie said she got that, but this time she felt he was way off.

"He ain't all right. It puts the fear of God in me that one day he's going to teach our children." McKenzie walked next to Christian with a look of consternation on her face.

"He doesn't like us, Christian. White folks who don't like Black folks definitely shouldn't be standing in front of the classroom teaching them jack."

She looked at him with such pain and worry he felt compelled to reach out, hug her, and tell her everything was going to be OK. But he refrained. They had become close over the weeks, talking about the lectures, their project and the state of the educational system. But none of their conversations were on a personal level. Even a hug would cross the line. And even though Christian was very attracted to McKenzie, he didn't know if she felt the same. Not to mention, he was a married man.

Melvin had snacks on the table in the den where they sat.

"Help yourself" Melvin said as he placed the blue bowl full of bugles on the oak wood colored table. Christian, McKenzie, and Furnell sat on a black leather couch across from a 36" T.V.

Furnell was the coolest white boy McKenzie had ever met. He was so real and unpretentious, unlike most white people she had encountered. Furnell had a way about him that made you feel at ease. *If all white folks were like Furnell, this world would be all right*, McKenzie thought as she sat between Christian and Furnell watching Melvin piddle around.

Just then, a little old wrinkled white man walked in the room, stark naked.

"Oh shit!" Furnell said, sitting straight up.

"What the—" Christian said. McKenzie covered her eyes. "Hey Mel!" Christian shouted. The old man just stood there. Melvin came running in the room.

"Dad! Got dammit! Get your ass outta here. Now dad!"

Melvin ushered his dad out the room because he wasn't going anywhere on his own. Over his shoulder Melvin apologized.

"Sorry guys, I thought he was asleep by now." The doorbell rang. "Can one of you guys get that?"

Furnell looked at Christian and mouthed, *What the Fuck?*

Christian threw his hands up in the air, and McKenzie sat shaking her head in disbelief.

"I'll get it," Furnell said. He jumped out of his seat and opened the door. It was April. "Hey you!" Furnell said.

"Hey, what's going on Fern?" April replied with a big smile. Everyone loved Furnell; it was just his personality.

"Good evening everyone!" April said as she entered the back room where everyone sat.

"Good evening," Christian said with a smile.

"Hi," McKenzie replied. Not rude, but not overly enthusiastic either. She just didn't appreciate the way April carried herself. As a Black woman, McKenzie felt that Black women should be more unified, supportive, and appreciative of other Black women. But more often than not, she found herself in this intangible tug-of-war over Black men—*I'm going to get him first* and *no holds barred*—to get him. *Sistahs!* McKenzie had learned early in life that it wasn't worth it. Both sistahs ended up wounded, dejected, and the brotha, more than likely, had played them against each other—only not be with either of them. What a waste. What a terrible cycle of deception and sisterly betrayal.

No, she wasn't going to play this game with April. McKenzie had a notion to just pull her to the side and tell her about herself. But she feared losing control, and taking out all her anger from this, and all the other fucked up situations in her life, out on her—so instead she just didn't participate.

"How are things coming along?" April said, bending over a little too much as she placed her things down. All the men stared.

"Actually, we haven't gotten started yet," Christian replied quickly.

"Yeah, we had a little side show, right before you came in," Furnell chimed in.

"What happened?" April said.

"It's not important," goody-two shoes Christian replied. "We can get started now that you're here. Camille should be pulling up any minute now." Everyone followed suit and pulled out their notes. Melvin returned to the room.

"Did I miss much?" he said, sitting down.

"Nope, just in time," Furnell said. There was a knock at the door.

"Camille!" Everyone shouted. It's what they did every time the last person of the group arrived. You could hear her cackling through the door. Melvin jumped up and opened the door.

"Hey everybody!" Camille said as she rushed into the room. "I'm sorry I'm late, traffic was horrible."

"No problem, Camille, we were actually just getting started." Christian made room for her to sit next to him. April rolled her eyes. McKenzie smirked. *Dumb, dumb girl*, she thought to herself.

"So here's the situation," McKenzie said. She'd been sitting silently for the past few minutes, "we need three observations. Look at practicum three, four and five."

They flipped through their syllabus.

"One focuses on observing male and female youth in a controlled setting, another in an uncontrolled setting, and the last with adults present—either controlled or not."

"Ok, there are six of us, so we can break up into groups of two," Camille said. Everyone nodded in agreement. "It asks for male and female interpretation." She looked around the group. "We have that—three males and three females." April sat up in her seat.

"Well, how will we decide who goes with who?" April said in feigned innocence. McKenzie rolled her eyes.

"I think we should decide based on geographical location. That way it'll be easier on both parties, not having to drive all across town," Melvin said.

Everyone, except April, agreed. Camille lived in Torrance, so she was paired with Furnell, who lived in Manhattan Beach. April lived in Cypress, so she was paired with Melvin, who lived in Cerritos. McKenzie and Christian lived in L.A.—so there you had it. April sat pouting the rest of the night.

"Don't you think we should decide based on the topic or something?" April said, in a last ditch effort. But the group discussion went along the lines of *it didn't matter because it was a group paper with male-female observations, as long as the data was collected, who cared who gathered it?*

"Are we going to decide as a group where the observations will be made, or should we just let the partners decide?" McKenzie said, as if to say to April, *It's a done deal darling about the whole partner topic. Let's move on already.*

"Um, I think it's fine to let the partners decide," Christian said. He looked around the group. "It'll probably be easier for them to choose a location that's logistically feasible for them, rather than having all of our input. What do you guys think?"

The group agreed. April was still pouting.

"Then, let's review the research questions to make sure every element of our research project is consistent," Christian said. "We don't want to compromise the validity in any way. Then we'll let the partners take it from there,"

Christian didn't even pick up on April's foul mood. They were there for about 45 minutes. After the partner assignments were finalized, they set their next meeting date and shook the spot.

♋　　　♋　　　♋

Christian was walking across parking lot "F" when he heard a thumping system approaching. He turned to look for the car. It was blaring "Keep Yo' Head Up" by Tupac. He looked to the left, then to the right, but couldn't spot the car with the slammin' system anywhere. As he approached the Administration building, one of his fraternity brothers walked up and greeted him.

"What's up C?" his Frat said, as they acknowledged each other with a Black man half-hug, half-shake.

"Aw, not much bruh, what's crackin'?" Christian asked. He couldn't concentrate on what the brother was saying because he heard Pac's song again, blaring, and saw a black Jeep Wrangler making its way up the road. *Bose system,* he thought to himself. *It's got to be a Bose system. It's too crystal clear not to be.* He watched the Jeep coming up the aisle.

It was shiny and impeccably detailed as the sun showed off a high-end professional wax job that was obviously recently done. The tires were oversized, but not too big; just enough to have the driver sit higher up than in most trucks. Armoralled tires—*That jeep was bangin'!* He thought as he admired the truck.

"Are you coming to the benefit Saturday?" his line-brother (*fraternity brother he pledged with*) Tony said, interrupting his thought.

"Yeah. Yeah, I'll be there for sure." He turned his attention back to Tony. He looked around for the Jeep, but it had escaped into the multitude of cars lining the parking lot.

"Cool. I'll see you there!"

They gave each other dap and walked way in opposite directions. *Thump thump, thump thump*. The Jeep. Christian turned to watch the sparkling black jeep turn into a parking space about 100 yards away. And to his surprise, out stepped McKenzie.

She was wearing a turquoise, orange and white sweat suit—Miami dolphins—with an orange baseball cap. She had on all white K-Swiss tennis shoes. Her stride was purposeful and she looked focused as she strutted across the parking lot.

Christian decided to follow. He found himself breaking a sweat trying to keep pace with McKenzie. He looked down at his watch, 4:30 p.m. *Maybe she's going to class*, he thought. Christian glanced around, suddenly embarrassed as he realized that he was following McKenzie. But he wasn't too embarrassed because he continued to creep slowly behind.

McKenzie made a left into the University gym. Christian lingered outside for about ten minutes, then crept inside. As he walked through the gymnasium he spotted some athletes working out in the weight room, others were playing basketball on the court, and still others doing their own workout routine either in a corner, or near the bleachers. He didn't see McKenzie.

Christian waited ten more minutes before he walked over to the aerobics room, adjacent to the gym. No McKenzie. *Where is this woman?* He thought. He had been watching the door and knew she hadn't slipped by him. Christian walked around until he came to the aquatics center. He stuck his head inside and looked around. In lane three, making the most even strokes he had ever seen in his life, was McKenzie Batiste. He stood watching her from a distance for about 15 minutes. The stadium was filled with the mellow sound of classical music. She swam free-style, then the backstroke, next, the butterfly, and then free-style.

The water polo team filed in and began warming up. A curly haired blonde boy waved at McKenzie as she gracefully flipped and started a lap of backstrokes. None of the team members seemed bothered by the classical music as they stretched and dived into the pool in the lane next to McKenzie's.

McKenzie free-styled her last twenty minutes. She was in a world of her own as she swam back and forth like a fish in a lake.

Christian ducked out the Center as McKenzie exited the pool. He felt foolish for watching her—knowing he wouldn't have a legitimate excuse if she had busted him and asked him why he did it. He made his way back to the Student Union and lounged, looking out the big glass window, and waited for McKenzie to pass.

Christian looked at his watch, 5:45 p.m. She should be making her way to their 6:00 p.m. class soon.

No sooner had he calculated the time with her schedule, than she came strutting around the corner. As always, McKenzie was walking like she was on a mission—fast, purposeful strides— moving around any and everything in her way. Christian jumped up out of his seat in pursuit of the woman in the Miami Dolphins' sweat suit.

"Hey! Wait up!" McKenzie turned around and waited for Christian to catch up. She smiled. He liked the reception.

"Hey you," McKenzie said.

She shifted her books to the left side so Christian could fall in step on her right. He moved in close. Her perfume was intoxicating--light and sweet. He inhaled deeply for a few seconds before he spoke.

"Slow your roll sistah. That classroom ain't going nowhere." She smiled. *She should do that more often,* he thought, engulfed in all her womanness--voluptuous lips, captivating eyes, scintillating smile, and a soft sensuous fragrance.

Christian looked McKenzie up and down. Of course he had noticed her before, but for some reason today, she looked different. She had on sweats—she always wore the tightest sweat hook ups— always color-coordinated, always a matching baseball cap, all that was the same. He couldn't put his finger on it, but today, McKenzie just exuded something different.

"You gotta keep up, Black man. I'm a Black woman in demand. I got places to go" Christian chimed in, "*people to see, things to do.*" They laughed.

"You not going to class tonight?" he inquired. It was almost six.

"Yeah, I just need to drop this book off at the library first. I'll catch you in class though," she said, dismissing him.

"I'll walk with you."

"Oh, OK—I just didn't want to make you late—"

"A couple of minutes won't hurt."

As they walked to the library, Christian struck up idle conversation. He wanted to get to know her outside of the academic environment. So he started with something light and easy.

"What would you do if you won the lottery?" Christian said, "I'd pay off all my debt, buy a Harley, and travel."

"Hmm . . ." McKenzie pondered for a moment. "I'd buy a four-bedroom house with vaulted ceilings, huge bay windows everywhere, a whirlpool tub, and a built in barbeque in the back yard."

They weaved in and out of the quad area, walking around passing students.

"Oh! I know what else!"

"What else?" Christian said.

He watched her animated expressions and dreamy eyes as she described her purchases.

"I'd buy a lakeside cabin, deep in somebody's woods, where the leaves turned colors with the changing seasons, and I'd travel—all over the world."

Christian wanted to ask her about swimming, but never found a segue, and thought it would be too weird to ask without giving away that he'd been watching her. So he left it for another day.

In class, professor Telfair lectured for about an hour on gender stereotyping and then the class broke up into their groups. Their group had completed most of their assignment so they met in their partner-pairs to select the locations for their observations.

"Where do you want to go?" Christian said.

"Well, how about this. I'll choose the first location, and you choose the second?" McKenzie suggested. Christian didn't have any objections.

"But I get to lay the ground rules at my location—no psychoanalysis, or comments on my observation style, OK?" she said.

She pointed her finger in Christian's face. He took her finger in his mouth and gently bit it.

"Ouch!" she said, pulling her hand back quickly. "Boy! Are you smoking crack? What are you doing?" she said.

Christian laughed, knowing he hadn't hurt her. She was stunned, it threw her off-guard and he knew it. He grabbed his bag as he stood to leave the room. He watched McKenzie's eyes follow him as he moved.

Christian had on a crisp white V-neck t-shirt, some baggy blue jeans, a dark brown belt, with matching dark brown Sketcher boots. He wore a shiny silver chain around his 18" neck and a small silver hoop in his ear.

McKenzie smiled. He watched her eye him up and down, and when she smiled, he knew for sure she wasn't hurt.

"You've got one more time to call me boy— "

"Or else what?"

She tried to fake an attitude. He leaned in and whispered in her ear.

"Or else I'm going to have to *show* you what the difference is between a boy and a man." He stood up straight and walked out without waiting for a response. McKenzie laughed out loud. She shook her head from side to side in disbelief, as everyone around her watched. She smiled. Christian's back was to her, but she knew he was smiling too.

♋   ♋   ♋

CHAPTER FOUR

Getting to Know You

They met at the Administration building in the "F" parking lot. McKenzie arrived first. Christian drove up in a cream colored STS sitting on 20's. It was clean. His system was clear as he drove up thumping DJ Quick's "Tonight". *Old man car,* McKenzie thought as she watched Christian gather his things. She told him last class to wear shorts, a tank top, and some sandals—her observation, her rules.

"Just because you picked the location, doesn't mean you get to dictate what I wear." Christian had replied when McKenzie gave him his instructions.

She just smiled and didn't say anything. He showed up wearing a pair of beige shorts that touched the top of his knees, a taupe colored tank top, and a cream and taupe colored baseball hat with a pair of brown sandals. The cream-colored pooka shells and gold hoop set the outfit off just right. McKenzie smiled as he walked up to her truck.

"What are you smiling at?" He threw his things in the back seat of her jeep. It was impeccably clean. The roof was off, but you could distinctly smell the jasmine air freshener.

"Yo fine ass. Now what?" She stared him down as he slid into the front passenger seat. He laughed and quickly turned away.

"Now, let's go."

McKenzie had on blue jean shorts with an orange halter-top, and orange leather sandals. Her curly wild hair barely showed over the top of a matching jean visor. Outside of the swimming pool, Christian had never seen McKenzie's hair. It was always tucked underneath a baseball cap.

She saw him through her peripheral vision looking her up and down.

"What are you looking at?" She said.

She turned the black jeep out of the parking lot. Christian laughed.

"I'm looking at your fine ass, how about that?"

"That's right!" she laughed, unfazed. She shifted into third gear and sped off to their destination.

♋   ♋   ♋

"What type of music do you have?" Christian said. He thought he'd change the subject. All that flirting had him spending the last few minutes beating himself up for not even thinking about Jada, *his wife*.

McKenzie adjusted her rear view mirror.

"Is there anything in particular you'd like to listen to?" She weaved her way in and out of traffic. She nodded in the direction of the CD case.

It was a perfect southern California day. The sun was shining brightly; the wind blew her little curls all over the top of her head. She looked sporty with her small, square framed sunglasses on. Outside of the pool, Christian was used to seeing McKenzie in sweats. Her peanut butter skin was smooth and shiny under the beaming sun. She looked good without so many layers of clothes on. She looked light, happy. And she was smiling. He couldn't remember her happy or smiling in class or during their meetings.

Christian grabbed the CD case and sifted through her CD's. Rap. She had a nice mix of artists. Hip Hop, Gangsta, R&B, Reggae, and a few crossover artists—but it was all rap. Oh, wait a minute . . . she had one full sleeve of—classical music.

"I take it you like rap?" He shook his head as he smirked.

"Yeah. Why? You one of those intellectuals who don't like rap?" She said. She eyed him up and down, ready for a debate. Christian laughed.

"Calm down. I just asked a question. Why you gotta go bite a brotha's head off?" He continued to leaf through the CD's. "Aw! Here's the cut!" He pulled out a CD. "Do you mind?" he asked politely.

"It's a Bose. You can't break it."

"And if I did—"

"I bought the warranty. It would get replaced."

Christian paused. He slid the CD in. The changer shuffled the disks. Tribe Called Quest's *Benita Apple Baum* started to play.

"Is it me?" He turned to face McKenzie.

"Is what you, Christian?" She seemed puzzled by the question.

"Do you just not like me—or are you this hard, and keep your guard up like this with everyone?" He pulled at his shorts at the knee, adjusted in his seat, and shook his head.

McKenzie looked hurt. She paused before responding.

"It's just you."

"Well what the hell did I do?"

Christian threw his hands up in the air "I started off a King, now I feel like a homeless bum under the freeway."

McKenzie sat, mouthing the words to the song, ignoring Christian for a minute. She slowly turned to face him, not paying any attention to the road.

"You're still a King sweetheart. That's your inherent birthright." She returned her attention to the road. She pressed the button, changing the song.

"I thought I was choosing the music?"

"I'm tired of that song."

"Are you tired of me?" Christian said. McKenzie paused.

"No. Not yet. But I'll let you know when I get there." She made a right turn and jumped onto the 405 freeway. McKenzie reached down for her purse. She grabbed her lip balm and applied a fresh new shiny coat.

"I won't hold my breath," Christian said as he flipped through the CD's.

McKenzie's insides turned flip-flops. As they made their way through the surprisingly light Saturday morning traffic, McKenzie tried to recount her interactions with Christian. To her, they had been fine. She tried to engage with him intellectually during their conversations, and to joke with him about other, less serious topics. McKenzie was stumped at why Christian felt she didn't like him, especially because she found herself extremely attracted to this man.

"You wanna hear my anthem?"

"Sure," Christian said, without looking her way.

She pressed CD number 4 in the changer, and song number 10. She turned up the volume. *Dunt, dunt dunt dunt dunt* the music began . . . then Lauryn belted,

Everything is everything,
What is meant to be, will be,
After winter, must come spring,
Change, it comes eventually.

Christian turned to look at McKenzie. She smiled.

"This is my war song. The song I play before I walk onto campus. This will be the song I play for my kids before we start class every day, you know what I mean?"

Christian shook his head and laughed out loud.

"Are you serious?"

"Hell yeah, I'm serious!" she screamed over the music. "This is the shit Melvin wouldn't know a thing about—" She nodded toward the music, referring to the lyrics of the song. "He'd probably deny that it's even true, you know what I mean?"

She bobbed her head to the beat and mouthed the words. Christian watched her. She was probably right about the Melvin's of the world, he thought, believing that everyone has an equal footing in the game. Or, just not believing kids of color have a chance at all.

"If it's your anthem—then sing the damned song!" He said. McKenzie laughed, and then happily obliged. She sang the song as if Christian wasn't in the car, loudly, freely without any reserve.

She had the mannerisms of a female rapper, moving her head and hands to the beat, hitting every word on cue. She was in a world of her own.

Let's love ourselves then we can't fail
To make a better situation
Tomorrow, our seeds will grow
All we need is dedication

She turned to Christian and smiled.

"Now sing it with me Black man!" She shoved her right hand in his face as if she held a mic. Her energy was infectious.

Christian shook his head. But leaned into the mic, and they sang the chorus together.

McKenzie merged onto the 10 freeway West. Christian lay back and bobbed his head to the menagerie of rap, hip-hop and old school songs randomly selected by the changer. She watched him from her peripheral vision. His long legs, stretched out comfortably in front of him. His thighs, wide and muscular, were a contrast to his medium sized legs, and even smaller-sized ankles. McKenzie smiled at his ankles. They looked almost feminine. *Sexy*, she thought. *I could kiss those ankles for hours—Hold up! What am I doing?* McKenzie interrupted her twisted sexual exploits with this man's ankles. She laughed out loud.

Christian looked surprised.

"What's so funny?"

He smiled at her vibrant laugh. McKenzie looked at Christian and wondered if she should tell him about her crazy thought. *What the hell!* She thought *At least he'll know I do like him.*

"Oh, I was just laughing at myself," she said as she turned off PCH to a road that led underneath an overpass.

"Oh-kay, and?" He said.

McKenzie wanted to just say what she was thinking, but something stopped her. Her heart actually started pounding fast and her mouth became dry.

"And, I do that from time to time." McKenzie said.

She looked straight ahead, now completely tensed.

Christian turned away from McKenzie shaking his head as they crept along the deserted road, blasting Ice Cube.

They arrived at Zuma Beach. McKenzie turned in the parking lot, found a parking space in the shade, and turned off the truck.

"You ready?" McKenzie said. She beamed. Christian shook his head in disbelief.

"So, did you hear anything I asked you on the way over here?"

"Every word." She jumped out of the jeep.

"And?" he said, still seated. She walked around, opened the door and extended her hand to him.

"I'm sorry, Christian . . . I've got problems."

He looked at her. She stared him in his eyes. He took her hand and jumped out of the jeep.

"What kind of problems, McKenzie?" Christian spoke softly, not trying to press, but not allowing her to change the subject. She walked beside him.

"It's hard for me to open up to people." McKenzie said. She paused. Christian listened. "You're right about me being hard. I've heard it from other people before." She looked a little embarrassed. "And believe it or not, I've gotten better." She turned to him, and they both laughed.

"I'd hate to see the 'before' if this is the 'after'." Christian said. McKenzie socked him in the shoulder.

"Fuck you, Christian."

"What's with the rap?" Not that women weren't into rap. But McKenzie only had rap and classical music. That was odd.

"I don't know" she said and then paused. Christian walked beside her, silent. "I just don't like that mushy shit." She looked off at the ocean.

"I love you, I need you, let's make love this way—" She threw her hands up in the air "Who needs to hear that shit 24-7? Not me." They walked along the bike trail toward the shore. The sun's rays were beaming off the water. "I like rap. I like the beats, the stories, the mixes. I like the hooks, the sampling. I'm not into the mushy shit. That's it," she said as if the topic was closed. They walked a couple of feet in silence.

"What about the classic mushy shit?" Christian said. "The Stylistics, the Chylites, Frankie Beverly and Maze?"

"Oh, those are the worst!" McKenzie said. "Their lyrics are so filled with fairy tale bull shit. No real relationship could ever live up to what they sing about." She waved her hand, as if she had brushed the whole lot of them off.

"So you've never thought that they might be singing about real situations Ms. McKenzie?" Christian said with a broad smile across his face.

"Yeah, well maybe. They're just not any I've ever, or will ever experience," she said, and then quickly changed the subject. "Do you want to hear my thoughts on how we should approach this observation today?"

"Yes," he conceded. He realized she had no intentions of speaking further on the mushy song topic.

"What are your thoughts my Queen?" Christian said turning to look at her. McKenzie smiled.

"That's right! Well—"

They approached a public restroom. McKenzie scanned the area. It was still early morning. The beach was practically empty. There was an occasional biker or jogger on the bike trail. Up ahead, she noticed three teenage girls taking off their skates, getting ready to go into the restroom. Three teenage boys milled around outside on the nearby basketball court, obviously waiting for the girls.

"Follow my lead," McKenzie said, and took his hand in hers.

Christian's hands quickly started to perspire. But McKenzie held on tight, not fazed by the moisture between his palms and hers.

They walked up on the group. When McKenzie saw that they had noticed them, she leaned in, and on her tippy-toes, kissed Christian on his cheek.

"I'll be right back babe." She smiled up at him.

Following her lead, he smiled back. Christian casually scanned the area for on-lookers, or someone who might know him. There was no one else around.

"OK. I'll wait out here."

He took a seat outside the restroom a couple of feet from the teenage boys. They checked Christian out.

"You ball?" one of the teenage boys said as he took a seat next to Christian.

"Yeah," Christian said to the boy. "You?"

"Hell no!" one of the other guys said before the boy could respond. "He ain't got no handles whatsoever!" the boy said and gave the last boy dap.

"Shut up Daniel!" the boy sitting next to Christian shouted. He looked over at Christian, embarrassed. "I love basketball," he said, almost inaudibly.

"Too bad it don't love you!" the last boy said.

The two friends laughed. The boy rolled his eyes and dropped his head. Christian assessed from the boy's response that he wasn't much good.

"Won't ya'll chill man." Christian said to the boys who immediately cut out the put-downs.

Christian looked at the boy. He was small, scrawny—not baller material at all. But Christian could tell he had heart, just by the way he approached him.

"What's wrong with your game?" Christian said.

One of the boys started to say something, but Christian shot him a warning glance so he kept his mouth shut.

"They're right." the boy said, "I suck." He drew circles in the sand as he spoke.

"And why is that?"

"Look at me . . . I'm short—" He practically cried, "I have no coordination . . . and I get pushed around on the court by the bigger guys." Christian looked at the boy.

"But do you got game?" The boy shrugged his shoulders.

"Now, either you have skills, or you don't. Do you have skills? You know whether you do or not." Christian stood up, extending his hand out to the little curly-haired boy who stood.

"When I'm playing by myself, I do." The boys laughed, but quickly went silent when Christian shot them a look of death.

"What do you mean?" Christian said.

"I mean, I make the baskets down the middle, I got the moves in the inside—and my outside shots always go in."

"But?"

"But, when I'm on the court with other guys I can't connect."

He kicked the sand and walked off.

∽   ∽   ∽

Inside the restroom, the three girls were reapplying make up—*a little on the heavy side,* in McKenzie's opinion. The older girl was outlining her lips with black eyeliner. McKenzie reached in front of her to get some soap to wash her hands.

"Excuse me sweetie," McKenzie said. She smiled at this girl who couldn't be more than fifteen or sixteen.

"No problem."

She tried to appear much older and confident than she was. She pulled out a tube of clear lip-gloss and filled it inside the dark black lines. McKenzie stopped drying her hands and looked at the girl.

"What?" The girl said. McKenzie grabbed some tissue and started to wipe off the lip liner from around her thin lips.

"This is not summer make-up sweetie, this is . . . well—" McKenzie didn't want to embarrass the girl. She noticed the other two girls were younger and followed her lead.

"It doesn't accentuate your beautiful face."

The girl eased up with that remark. The other two moved in closer.

"What do you all have in your purses?" McKenzie said.

She waited for each of the girls to dump their array of glosses, powders, tubes, and sticks onto the sink counter. She shuffled through them all until she found the right colors for each outfit. She meticulously applied each girl's make up in a matter of minutes.

"There you go darlin'" McKenzie said to the last girl. She had lightened up their faces by thinning out the liner around their eyes, blending the shadows on their lids, and using color to line their lips instead of the loud and bold black eyeliner.

"This way, we draw attention to your face, and not the make-up," McKenzie explained as she put away the last of the make-up.

"Make-up is supposed to bring out your natural beauty—not hide it." McKenzie smiled. The girls looked fresh and youthful.

"Thank you . . . Hey, what's your name?" The fifteen year old asked. She stood and admired her new look in the mirror.

"McKenzie. No problem." McKenzie replied, and walked toward the door.

"That's a cool name. Kind of tomboyish—" the middle girl said.

"Yeah, I guess so" McKenzie said. "I like it. It seems to fit me. Most people would probably describe me as a tomboy." The girls all disagreed.

"Tomboys don't know nothing about applying make up the way you do," the oldest girl said.

"And tomboys wouldn't put together a fly ass outfit like that—matter-of-fact, they wouldn't be caught dead in something that feminine," the middle girl said.

The other two agreed. McKenzie smiled. She knew if they saw her Monday thru Friday they'd know that she fit the bill of a tomboy.

"And a tomboy most definitely wouldn't have such a fine ass boyfriend like the one you got outside!" the youngest girl said.

All four of them screamed in delight. Even McKenzie had to agree with her. They all gave high fives on that one.

"He *is* hellah fine, huh?" McKenzie laughed with the girls.

"Hell yea!" The middle girl said. "How you get him?"

McKenzie leaned in. The girls leaned in too. She looked them in their eyes.

"The secret, ladies . . ." They waited on edge. "Is to just be you." She stood up and walked out the restroom. The girls followed behind her.

"It's hard keeping up the fantasy, the make-up, being helpless, not having opinions." She turned to look at them with a knowing look.

"Listen, if a guy can't handle your thoughts, your opinions, and the fact that you're not some prissy little damsel in distress waiting to be saved by some knight in shining armor—then kick his twisted ass to the curb." McKenzie made a sweeping motion with her right leg like she was on a soccer field kicking a goal. The girls giggled.

"Trust me, you don't need him." They made their way around the building. "He'll end up being more trouble than good--all that handholding, all that biting of the tongue."

83

She stopped. Christian was crouched in front of a young boy, his hands out to the side as if they were playing basketball and he was sticking him. His ass was sticking out, and all the girls paused to get a good look.

"Nope. He's got to know you're real—and love you for being that way." McKenzie finished.

She stepped down off the steps and into the sand and headed toward the guys.

Christian stopped to face her as she approached.

"Don't stop on my account." McKenzie said. She signaled for him to continue. He nodded and returned to his stance.

"What's your name?" Christian said.

"Jonathan."

"Christian."

The young boy nodded as he resumed his position.

"OK J," he said. He focused his attention back on Jonathan. "When I step out with my left foot, what are you going to do?"

Jonathan was concentrating.

"Step in with my right foot?"

"Are you sure?"

He pivoted on his left foot into a right turn.

"You have to think about where I need to go. I'm going for the rim J. So, if I pivot on my right foot I'm coming right into you— why would I do that?" Christian said as he demonstrated the move.

"So, thinking defensively, I'm going to anticipate that the person with the ball, standing in front of me, will step out on his left foot, pivot and go right, so that he can post up and make that shot right up under the basket—right? Can you see that?"

Jonathan smiled. "Yeah. I see it."

Christian extended his hand out to the curly haired boy. He pulled him into him, tousled his hair, and gave him a hearty hug.

"This is what I mean by mind over matter J. If you don't have a mental game—you don't have game at all. Size means nothing if you have no strategy." Christian lead Jonathan off to the side, still coaching him.

"You can be the smallest man on the team, but if you can make the plays—even if it's in assists—you're the most valuable player on the team, and everyone's always going to want you to run with them. Remember that." He patted him on his back.

"What was that, make believe I have a basketball 101?" McKenzie said as she walked over. Christian placed his hands on his hips; he was sweating cats and dogs.

"Hee hee hee."

"I have a basketball in the jeep if you want one?" Jonathan's eyes lit up.

"You do?" Jonathan turned to Christian. "Can we try it with the ball, Christian?" Christian turned to McKenzie.

"Do you mind, babe?"

The girls cooed at that. Christian instantly felt a twinge of guilt. He couldn't remember the last time he had called Jada babe, or anything warm and endearing for that matter. Yet, here he was with a woman he'd known for only a couple of months and it was rolling off his tongue with ease.

"No, not at all. I'll go get it," she said as she walked off toward the jeep. Christian trotted to catch up with her.

"Are you sure?" he said as he placed his hand on the small of her back. "What about the observation?" McKenzie stopped.

"Man, what do you think we've been doing the past 30 minutes—socializing?" She placed her hands on her hips, attitude in full blast. "When I told you to follow my lead, what did you think I meant?" She frowned.

"I mean, I don't know?"

"Well why did you think I was kissing on you, and referring to you as my boyfriend?" McKenzie said. Her mouth slowly inched into a smirk as she folded her arms across her chest.

"Well, it all happened so fast. I didn't really process it. I mean—it felt so natural and—" *Oh shit*, Christian thought to himself. He didn't mean to say that.

"What I meant to say was, we didn't have a discussion about what it was we were going to do, so I wasn't really clear—"

McKenzie turned and walked away.

"Well, I hope you can recall your interactions during all of this natural feeling Mr. Malveaux. I told you my approach was unorthodox. But I have no intentions of trying to find another group to observe in the name of authenticity." She reached in the back seat of the jeep and grabbed Ahmad's basketball.

"Don't worry. I remember everything vividly," Christian said, with his eyes fixed on her shiny orange lips.

Christian turned to face McKenzie. "You up for a bite to eat?" They were on their way back to campus. "If you're not in a hurry, I was thinking we could jot down our observations over an early dinner at Red Robin?" He was trying to find a plausible reason to stay in this woman's company.

"Mmm. That sounds like a great idea!"

They ordered, Christian a BBQ burger, McKenzie a grilled chicken sandwich with bacon and guacamole. As they waited for the order, they discussed the environment, in which the study was conducted, the independent, dependent and extenuating variables that contributed to the findings.

"What made you choose Zuma beach?" Christian asked. "Did you know those kids were going to be there or something?"

McKenzie looked up as she finished writing a sentence.

"No, I'd never seen those kids before today."

Christian looked into her eyes. They were beautifully shaped, but so unrevealing.

"I just really like that beach." She moved her papers onto the seat across from her as the waiter approached with their food. "It has the most spectacular sunsets."

Christian laughed a loud robust laugh. "That's the reason why you chose that location, McKenzie?"

She shoved a French fry in her mouth.

"Yes. Why?"

"Well, let's see." Christian said. "Oh, maybe because we were trying to do a study that required *observing youth*? Hello?" He laughed. "Beautiful sunsets have nothing to do with observing youth."

She laughed with him. "I guess you have a point there, Mr. Malveaux. I never thought about that. I just knew I wanted to go to Zuma beach. It never occurred to me that we wouldn't be able to complete our assignment. Good thing it all worked out, now isn't it?" She said as she bit into her sandwich.

"Yeah, good thing, huh, Ms. Batiste?" Christian shook his head.

"You like strawberries?" McKenzie said. She sipped her strawberry lemonade.

"Yes I do--"

Before he could finish his sentence, she slid a huge slice of strawberry gently into his mouth. Surprised, he accepted her fingers between his lips. Her mouth slightly parted, she slowly and sensuously pulled her fingers out of his mouth.

"Good, huh?" McKenzie said in a soft sensuous whisper. She licked the remaining juices off her fingers. She raised her eyebrows in feigned shock. "Delicious." She smiled.

Christian knew she was talking about *his* juices. He looked away.

"What? It's not like I haven't been kissing you all day Christian. Geesh," she said, laughing.

"True. But it wasn't in the mouth," he replied. McKenzie slid next to him, gently pulled his face into hers, and slid her tongue into his mouth.

The kiss was five seconds long, but it felt more like five minutes to Christian. As they broke away, their eyes locked on each other.

"Sweet," McKenzie said. The corners of her mouth turned up.

Christian smiled back. "Listen, Mac." He shifted uneasily in his seat. "There's something I need to tell you." His smile disappeared.

"Hey look—I'm sorry. I was out of line just then. I shouldn't have done that." She started to slide away from him.

Christian grabbed her hands to stop her from moving too far away. "No, it's OK. I mean—I don't mind." He paused, took a deep breath. "You weren't out of line. It's just. Well, I'm married Mac." He looked her in her eyes.

McKenzie paused. "Did I just make you commit adultery or something here?" She looked pained, and somewhat confused. "Are you one of those fanatical Christians or Jehovah's Witnesses or something?" She wiped her mouth and threw the napkin in her plate.

"No! I just didn't want to give you the wrong impression is all," he said as he wiped his mouth.

"How? By allowing me to kiss you all day? Shit--" McKenzie frowned. "If we had been fucking all day, that'd be different. What we did amounted to about the same as a cordial handshake, OK?"

Christian nodded and reached for the bill. McKenzie threw a $10 bill on the table.

"I'm going to the restroom, be right back." She left before Christian could say anything.

♋   ♋   ♋

Melvin was in the University bookstore when he saw McKenzie walk in. As hard as he tried not to, he couldn't help but smile. He watched her walking—always with a purposeful stride—even for mundane acts as grabbing a Hostess Ding Dong, Funions, and a bottle of coke. She had on her standard warm up suit, red, white, and gold—with a matching pair of red and white sneakers.

McKenzie didn't notice him, which was not surprising. Melvin knew she didn't care for him. McKenzie had been exceptionally cold toward him since the loan forgiveness comment. AND . . . she had made it a point to let everyone know *she didn't do pink meat*. She wouldn't have been interested even if she could tolerate him.

Well now, that's just her loss isn't it? Melvin thought to himself as he watched her. She looked as if she was gliding up and down the aisle. He kept a safe distance, but racked his brain to try and come up with a clever greeting. Something cool and hip that might make her see him differently.

Two athletically built African American men entered the bookstore laughing and joking with each other. They grabbed a couple of bottles of Gatorade and headed toward the cash register about the same time as McKenzie. The "brothers" motioned for McKenzie to go ahead of them. She smiled brightly, and thanked them. Melvin inched up to the line behind the two young men.

"That'll be $5.75," the cashier said. McKenzie opened her purse and fumbled around for a couple of seconds.

"Shit!" McKenzie looked distraught as she tossed things around in her purse.

"What's the problem Sis?" one of the young men said to McKenzie. "Did you change purses and forget to put your wallet in there?" He gave her a wide knowing smile.
They all laughed. "My girl does it all the time. She calls it 'The casualty of matching accessories.'"

"Yes!" McKenzie said. "I hate when I do that!" She grabbed the stuff off the counter.

89

Melvin stepped in front of the grinning young man in the purple jacket with gold lettering. "Hi McKenzie! Here, let me pay for that for you." Melvin said, handing her a twenty-dollar bill. His heart was racing, and his face was flushed. But he was thrilled that this opportunity had presented itself. He looked into her flawless caramel complexioned face and waited for her look of relief.

But what she gave him was a look of disgust. "No, that's OK. I'm cool."

Melvin was crushed. "No really, take it. I *want* to pay for it."

"No really, I *don't want you* to pay for it. I'll just put it back." She continued to pick up her items off the counter.

"Oh no," the brother in the purple jacket said as he picked up McKenzie's key chain acknowledging the emblem with a nod. "Can't have our Soror go without her Funions and Ding Dongs. That's brain food for the gods!" He handed the cashier a card of some sort. He looked at McKenzie for approval. McKenzie smiled and nodded.

"Thank you, Frat!" she said and walked over and gave him a long, long hug.

"Oh, you know it's all about the Coleman Love. I should have known you were a Soror in all that crimson and cream."

They laughed and continued their conversation as they walked out the bookstore. Melvin stood idle at the register and watched the trio leave the store. McKenzie had no idea the colossal strength he had just mustered up to offer to pay for her snacks.

The cashier coughed. Melvin placed his yogurt and granola bar on the counter and tried desperately not to make eye contact.

The group gathered at Jake's, an old fashioned pub up the street from campus. They ordered pizza and beer while they discussed each pair's observations. Christian was at the counter getting the beer when the last person arrived.

"Furnell!" everyone yelled and clapped as the stocky blonde slid into the booth next to April.

"What's up my peeps?" Furnell threw his backpack to the side and reached for a slice. Christian walked up with the beer. Everyone held out a glass as he started to pour. Folks were engaged in side conversation while they ate and chugged the beer. McKenzie got up and walked over to the jukebox. As she perused the selections, Christian crept up behind her. Tonight's sport ensemble was a snug fitting terry jumpsuit featuring the blue and gold of the St. Louis Rams.

"Yeah, I doubt very seriously that ol' Jake has some Rhakim or Chuck D. in that there selection." Christian stood with his index fingers through the two front loops of his jeans, legs bowed, as if he was getting ready to line dance. McKenzie laughed, but continued to look through the songs.

This was the first time they had seen each other since Christian's confession at Red Robin. The ride back to campus had been uneasy. McKenzie only talked about the assignment, what type of cross tabulations and studies they could reference to support their position. Christian didn't push the issue.

McKenzie typed up her report and emailed it to Christian the next morning— never mentioning anything else. Christian combined their reports and sent them back to McKenzie. She made minor changes—and via email, they solidified their submission for tonight.

"Well, that may be true, but he does have some "Funky Cold Medina" and some "Bust a Move" if you're really into the latest top 40." They laughed, and McKenzie walked back over to the table.

"Hey sweetheart," Camille said as McKenzie slid next to her at the table. McKenzie opened her messenger bag and pulled out the summary report she and Christian had written up about their observation.

"How are things going between you and Christian?" Camille said, and elbowed her in the ribs.

"What?" McKenzie replied more to the nudge than the question.

"You two make the cutest couple—"

"Girl that is a married man. The Mac don't do sloppy seconds."
McKenzie noticed April leaning in trying to ear-hustle.

"He's not happy in his marriage. He's just a good man, trying to do the right thing. But he needs some happiness in life. I think you'd be good for him, Mac," Camille said softly. McKenzie paused. She sat there a half second looking as if she was deep in thought. Before she could reply, she was interrupted by loud clapping from the group. She turned to see Christian approaching the table with his arms held high in the air, fingers snapping, and his hips moving slowly from side-to-side.

"Hey!" he shouted over the noise. McKenzie couldn't hear any music. He leaned down and whispered in her ear, "What you know about this Miss Rap star?"

"I can't hear the song." She strained to hear what was playing. Christian lifted her up by the elbow.

"C'mon. Get closer to the music."

She got up and followed him to the middle of the makeshift dance floor. The Isely Brothers were playing. McKenzie turned to face Christian with a grimace across her face.

"Here you go with that mushy shit, huh Black man?" She stood in the middle of the dance floor with her hands on her hips. Christian smiled as he grabbed her hands and stepped into her space.

"Let a brotha show you a thing or two about this kind of music--" He began to cha-cha. "It's called--"

"The mutha fuckin' cha-cha!" She moved in step with Christian.

"What hole you think I was raised in not to know what the cha-cha is?" She looked up into his eyes and laughed. They were in step—with each other, and the Isely Brothers as they sang,

Driftin' on a memory
Ain't no place I'd rather be
Than with you . . . yeah, loving you . . . well-well-well

McKenzie and Christian moved fluidly. She looked up into his eyes and they both sang the chorus. McKenzie felt the words to her core. She couldn't explain it, but she wanted to be living for this man's love. Her heart skipped a beat at the thought. The corners of her mouth slowly inched up as she moved across the floor to the song, knowing in her heart that there truly was no place she'd rather be than where she was at that very moment.

"What?" Christian threw his head back in laughter. "The rap star can cha-cha?"

"Uh. Yeah! Better than yo' stiff ass—any day!"

She threw a dip in her turn for emphasis. The group clapped wildly. She laughed, looking back over her shoulder at Christian's response.

"Oh! It's like that, is it? You think you got some skills Mommie?" Christian walked up behind her. They moved in step as if they were one person instead of two. He gently placed his hands on her hips and let them rest.

"More than you—Papi." McKenzie indiscreetly pressed her bubble back into his now erect dick. McKenzie smiled. She placed her hands on top of his as they effortlessly moved across the dance floor.

The people in the room had disappeared. It was just McKenzie and Christian filling the tiny space. The words engulfed them as they moved.

"You all right?" McKenzie asked over her right shoulder.

"Yeah. I'm cool. Why?" Christian said into her right ear. Her ass was small, but seemed to fit perfectly into his pelvic area, causing his dick to jump into a rage of excitement.

"That rod back there is doing some gymnastics. I don't want you pointing at anyone when this record stops. That's all. A sistah's trying to look out for a brotha," she said with a slight giggle.

93

"Oh, ha ha." He pulled away from McKenzie's booty. Luckily, he had on a loose pair of tan khaki slacks. He waved at the mesmerized crowd, and they waved back. He reached for McKenzie's hand and walked off the dance floor as the song faded into the next selection.

As they approached the table, their classmates stood, clapped, and cheered like the two had just won a talent contest. McKenzie shook her head. Christian gave Furnell a bunch of high-fives.

"Dayum man, that was tight! When did you two choreograph that?" Furnell said.

Christian and McKenzie looked at each other and burst into laughter.

"That's the first time we've ever danced together, Furnell." McKenzie said.

"Really?" Camille said. "You two moved like you'd been dancing together for ages. Smooth and natural." She smiled. April rolled her eyes.

"People, please. Black folks learn how to cha-cha before they learn how to read. Especially the older generations," April said, trying to diffuse the crowd. Christian laughed. McKenzie ignored her as she always did.

"I thought it was a bit too provocative," Melvin said. He looked appalled. McKenzie leaned over the table in Melvin's face.

"When a Black man and woman are that close together, you can't get anything *but* provocative. Good observation," McKenzie said, and then rolled her eyes. Melvin glared at her.

"Can we get started on our assignment, please?" April said. "I have no intentions of being here all night." Everyone started pulling out their papers.

Christian reached for his mug of beer. McKenzie watched him as he moved. He was glistening from the heat of the room and all the grinding they did on the dance floor. He seemed to be moving in slow motion has he lifted the mug to his lusciously full lips.

McKenzie sat entranced. She felt her panties getting wet from the thoughts swimming around in her head like that golden liquid swishing back and forth in Christian's mug. She crossed her legs, intensifying the pulsating between her thighs. Christian slid his lips around the rim of the mug and slowly gulped the amber-colored liquid. As his bottom lip moved slightly back and forth across the bottom of the glass, McKenzie couldn't help but imagine his tongue caressing her clit in that rhythmic motion. She closed her eyes . . . and bit her bottom lip. When she opened them, she saw Christian fighting back a smile.

Melvin watched the chemistry between Christian and McKenzie. They weren't verbally saying anything, but he could feel the energy transmitting between the two. McKenzie was such a bitch. Always had a quick, flip, fucking "Black Woman with an Attitude" response! Melvin watched McKenzie watch Christian lick the foam from around his lips. McKenzie looked as if she was going to explode. Melvin looked at Christian, who winked at McKenzie. McKenzie turned her head toward the group as if she was paying attention to the conversation about one of the observations.

Melvin watched the corners of McKenzie's mouth turn slowly upward. He knew why she was smiling.

♋   ♋   ♋

Week six, and Christian was picking the location of the next observation. He had given her no clue as to where they were going and what they were doing. He had gotten directions to her house and said he would arrive there around 3:00 p.m. When he showed, Ahmad opened the door.

"What's up, young blood?" Christian said, extending his hand out to Ahmad. Ahmad stepped into Christian, grabbing his hand for a quick shake, reaching around to give him a half-hug.

"Aw, I can't call it!" Ahmad said, teasing Christian. They laughed.

"Well if you can't bruh, who can?" Christian replied, throwing his hands up in animated question.

"I got it covered. Don't worry about nothing," Ahmad said. Christian stepped into the townhouse following the 6'2" lanky boy. Ahmad had on some baggy blue jeans with an oversized navy blue Fat Albert t-shirt, matching white and navy blue Adidas tennis shoes and navy baseball cap. *He got it honest,* Christian thought as he followed him into the living room.

Christian wore khaki green nylon cargo shorts, a brown t-shirt, a khaki green baseball cap, and a pair of khaki Nike running shoes.

"Have a seat," Ahmad said as he ushered Christian into the spacious room. It was nicely decorated—African theme. *Of course, what else?* Statues, framed papyrus pictures, and masks, all adorned the walls and corners of the earth-toned room.

"Would you like something to drink, are you hungry—I can whip you up something real quick before moms comes down?" Ahmad offered.

"No thanks. I'm good. But I saw the hoop you got hanging from the garage when I pulled up. Wanna catch a quick game of 21?"

"You mean do you want to lose at a quick game of 21? Man, I got mad skills, you didn't know?" Ahmad said as he opened the screen door that led to the back.

"You talkin' more head," Christian said as he snatched the ball out of Ahmad's hands. "What you got planned for today?" he inquired as they made some warm up shots.

"Aw, my girl is coming by in a couple of minutes, and we're gonna just chill I guess," he said, lobbing up a three pointer from the corner of the driveway.

"Yeah?" Christian said smiling. "She a hottie?"

"Yeah, she the bomb. And she's smart too. She has a 3.8 GPA".

"Is that right? What do you have Ahmad?" Christian said, tossing the ball to him. Ahmad tossed it back to start the game.

"Well, last report card I had like a 2.9 or 3.0—it wasn't bad. It just didn't have nothing on my girl, you know what I mean?"

"I feel you."

"You guys have a lot in common?" Christian said.

"Oh yeah. She likes basketball—you know that's my first love next to my mom's, right?" Christian smiled. "Oh, you a momma's boy?"

"Hell, yeah. Through and through," Ahmad said with no shame. "I'd take a niggah out for my mom's, on the real tho'. My mom's has been through so much, and made so many sacrifices for me, how can I not be, you know what I'm saying?" Ahmad said as the ball glided gently into the hoop, touching nothing but net. He stood with his hands arched for the follow through.

"No, not really man. Like what?" Intrigued, Christian prodded.

Ahmad paused. "Well, she's a single mom. It takes a lot to raise a boy into a man." Ahmad moved to the other side of the key. He concentrated on the rim as he spoke. The doorbell rang. Ahmad threw him the ball and headed for the door.

"Hold up G."

Shit, Christian thought, *just when we were getting to the good part.*

Ahmad came back outside with two Pepsi's in his hand, followed by a tall, dark chocolate girl, about 16 years old. It was his girlfriend, Crystal. She was a cutie. She had pimples on her fourhead, shiny black eyes, black hair pulled back into a shoulder-length ponytail. She was tall, about 5' 9". Her pink and white polka dot tennis skort accentuated her long muscular legs. She commanded full attention as she entered the backyard with long, graceful, yet intentional strides—back straight, and an intense look on her face.

"Christian, this is Crystal." Christian walked over and shook Crystal's hand. Firm shake. "Crystal, this is my mom's classmate, Christian—what's your last name?"

"Uh, Malveaux. But Christian's fine," he said, as Crystal made her way around the patio table to sit.

"Pleased to meet you, Mr. Malveaux," she said. *Good home training*, Christian thought. Kids don't address their elders by their last names anymore, manners is such an outdated thing with today's youth.

"Ahmad, did you get that?" McKenzie called from the upstairs window.

"Yes mom, it's Crystal," he yelled back.

"Oh, OK. Hi Crystal!"

"Hello Ms. Batiste!"

"How you doing down there, Christian?"

"Oh, I'm straight. Ahmad's keeping me entertained."

"I'll be down in a sec, OK?"

"Take your time, I'm enjoying the company," Christian said, smiling at Ahmad. He was a smart, observant kid. For him to

97

understand his mother's situation like that, required quite a bit of maturity. Much more than Christian felt most 16 year olds had these days. Ahmad handed Crystal a Pepsi. "Christian, you want one?"

"How about some water?"

"With ice?" Ahmad said, walking toward the kitchen.

"No thanks. You got any room temperature?" Christian said, following Ahmad. He reached under the sink cabinet, and grabbed a bottle of water.

"Think fast!" Ahmad said, tossing the bottle in Christian's direction. Christian caught the bottle easily.

"I told you son, I got skills," Christian said, twisting off the cap of the water, laughing.

McKenzie jogged down the stairs. She was wearing short black corduroy shorts, a white tank top, and a pair of white K-Swiss tennis shoes, with black stripes on the sides. Christian couldn't help but wonder how many pairs of shoes she owned. She clearly had a pair for every outfit! They moved toward the living room.

"Sorry about that, Christian. Hey Crystal, what's going on honey?" McKenzie said, walking into the living room.

"Hello Ms. Batiste. Not much."

"Mom, you want something to drink?" Ahmad yelled from the kitchen.

"Sure. A Coke please." Ahmad brought McKenzie a can of Coke. He walked over to the sofa and sat next to Crystal.

"So, what type of homework are you two working on today?"

"Oh, just some follow up to an assignment," Christian answered. "You said you and Crystal were just hangin' out today?"

Ahmad looked around from Christian to McKenzie. "Uh, yeah. Why? Do you guys need some privacy? We can shake the spot."

"Naw, young blood. We're cool. Besides, I still have some ass to tap outside . . . or did you forget about our game?" Christian said, moving toward the backyard.

"You didn't get enough?" Ahmad said, jumping up off the couch.

"Enough of what?" Christian said, looking back at Ahmad. "That was just me letting you warm up. You're about to get embarrassed, son." He laughed as he grabbed the basketball from the kitchen. Before he stepped outside, he turned to McKenzie. "You two want to play?"

Crystal smiled at the invitation, but turned to McKenzie before she moved.

Aware of Crystal's hesitation, McKenzie stood. "Well, sure, if you really want your ass tapped." Crystal laughed.

"I see where your son gets his trash talking. I hope Crystal has skills because the only thing you two have been able to show me is that you got mouths and a gang of tennis shoes." Everyone laughed.

"Boys against girls?" Christian said.

"Beauty vs. Brains?" McKenzie countered.

"How about couple teams?" Ahmad said, snatching the ball out of Christian's hands. He threw it up. *Swoosh!* All net. "Unless of course, you're afraid of our youthfulness—you know, think that gives us an unfair advantage?" he said, with a wide grin plastered across his face.

Christian retrieved the ball, bounced it twice, and shot it up. *Swoosh!* All net. "Youth is no substitute for experience, son. Remember that," he said, eyeing Ahmad.

"Enough of this macho-testosterone crap already," Crystal said, going after the ball. "Are you two going to spend the day talking, or are we going to play some ball?" She stood at the top of the key, McKenzie moved to the free-throw line.

"Check," McKenzie said, throwing the ball in. Crystal caught the ball, stepped back one step, and put the ball up. *Swoosh!* The ball fell through the net and into Christian's waiting hands. "If that is what all of you are going to do all day—I'm going inside!" McKenzie said, hands on her hips.

Ahmad came from behind Christian and ripped the ball out of his hands. He moved around him and laid the ball up. "Don't worry mom, they won't all go in that way—but Cris and I will get more in before you and the old man there." Ahmad said laughing as he ran toward Crystal.

McKenzie stood with her hands on her hips, watching Ahmad as he and Crystal gave high-fives. She walked over to Christian.

"We have got to whip their asses." Christian looked in

the young couple's direction. "Let's do it." He picked up the ball. "Celebration time is over youngins, let's set the stakes and play this game." Ahmad and Crystal walked toward the adults.

"Well, Ahmad ain't got a dime," McKenzie said. "So the bet can't be monetary." Ahmad frowned.

"That's alright. The bet is dinner and a movie," Christian said, throwing the ball to Ahmad.

"And what part of 'Ahmad ain't got a dime' didn't you hear?" Ahmad said, catching the ball.

"No, I heard it. When we win, you and Miss Crystal will cook the dinner. Whatever we decide we want to eat. And, you can break your piggy bank to find $3.99 for a rental," Christian said. "If you win, we pay for dinner and a movie at a restaurant and the theater." Christian looked at McKenzie for approval. A grin coaxed the corners of her mouth. "Deal?" Ahmad looked at Crystal. She smiled and nodded in agreement.

McKenzie snatched the ball out of Ahmad's hands and passed it to Christian who easily lifted it into the basket. Ahmad was stunned.

"Oh, now it's on!"

♋   ♋   ♋

Christian slid Ahmad a sweaty fifty-dollar bill as they clasped hands, and gave each other a half hug.

"Yeah, you know we let you guys win, right?" Christian whispered into his ear.

"I know no such thing," Ahmad said as he pulled away. They smiled at each other. The game had been close, 20-21. It was fun because both teams had been competitive—giving up no easy shots. Crystal out-scored them all. She was a natural.

Sticky and sweaty, they moved inside for something to drink. McKenzie passed out cold water. Crystal and Ahmad moved toward the front door.

"You guys outtie?" Christian said.

"Yes Mr. C, I'm going home to shower. I stink!" Crystal said. She scrunched up her face, and fanned her hand underneath her armpit. They all laughed.

"Ahmad—" McKenzie said.

"I'm going—I'm going! I'll see you in a half hour Cris." Ahmad kissed Crystal as she walked out the door. Then he dashed up the stairs to the shower.

Christian reached for his backpack in the corner of the living room. "Are you ready to write up this observation, Ms. Batiste?" He said as he pulled out a notebook.

"What?" McKenzie said. She looked confused. Christian loved it.

"Observation? You know the second one we were supposed to do today?" McKenzie stood and walked into the kitchen, pulled open the drawer and said, "When did you decide that, Mr. Malveaux?" She grabbed a pen and tablet.

"What's the problem, Mac, you think you have the patent on winging things?" Christian looked directly at her. McKenzie turned to face him.

"Absolutely not." She stared at him intently. "I'm thrilled you're picking up a thing or two from a sistah." Christian chuckled.

"But before we begin," he said as he lifted a CD case out from his bag, "I've got *my* collection of music today." He watched McKenzie roll her eyes.

"Is it that mushy-smushy shit?" She said in a sing-songy tone. Christian laughed.

"No it is not mushy-smushy shit—funny lady."

He walked into the living room and opened the glass door of her entertainment center. He put 6 CDs in the changer.

"They are the classics," he corrected, "and today is your first Survey Course in the Classics." Christian walked back into the kitchen.

"My what?" McKenzie said. She sat at the table and watched him closely.

"Survey Course. You know, like in English undergrad— they'd have you read several authors from a specific time period so you could get a good sampling from the era?" McKenzie nodded.

"Yes, well consider this your survey course of The Classics."

McKenzie ignored Christian, and started writing up the day's observations. The CD started to play the first song. The crowd whistled and clapped in the background. The piano banged out the first chord. A raspy voice bellowed.

Oh, you give your hand to me. And then you say hello.
And I can hardly speak, my heart is beating so.
And anyone can tell, you think you know me well,
But you don't know me . . .

"Oooh!" Christian said clapping. "Starting you off with the Genius! You are being made right, girl!" He said with a huge grin. McKenzie stopped writing to listen.

"He sounds like he's got the blues. You got me listening to some country music singing Black Man?"

"Listen to the words, *woman!"*

Christian grabbed her hand across the table, and looked her squarely in her eyes as he sang the words along with Ray Charles.

Oh you don't know the one who dreams of you at night,
and longs to kiss your lips, and longs to hold you tight,
to you I'm just a friend (naw), that's all I've ever been—
and you don't know me . . .

Christian's facial expressions illustrated the pain and frustrations of the words in the song. Christian had a beautiful voice, deep and smooth. But what captivated McKenzie most was the sincerity this man put behind the words of this song.

McKenzie was mesmerized listening to Christian tell this story. He sang about a man not knowing the art of making love, though his heart ached with love for this woman. The man was afraid and shy – so shy that he let his chance that she might love him pass him by.

Christian looked pained as he described this man's world. The man watched the woman walk away with some other guy, all the while he was silently dying inside because she'll never know the one who loves her so, because she didn't know him.

Christian let her hand go as the song faded out. He smiled and paused the CD player with the remote.

"Well, what did you think?"

"About the country song—or, about your animated Karaoke moment?" Christian sucked his teeth.

"C'mon Mac," he said, "I'm trying to show you something here. If you're not interested--" He started to push away from the table. She reached over and grabbed his hand.

"No wait! I was just fucking around. I do want to hear you out. Go ahead. I'm listening." Christian studied her face for a minute.

"That was Ray Charles. The Genius. And you're right—it does kind of have a bluesy, country feel to it. That's because this man crossed so many genres with his songwriting!" Christian was so excited as he talked about Ray Charles, McKenzie couldn't help but become engrossed in his explanation.

"But check out the words. He's telling this woman that he loves that she doesn't really know him. Apparently, they're good friends. She doesn't know it, but he's in love with her. So much so, that he dreams about kissing her and holding her at night. He says his heart aches with love for her."

"I don't know," McKenzie squirmed in her seat.

"You don't know what?"

"I'm hearing you . . . but that sounds—mushy to me."

Christian smiled. "This is a man who is confessing that he's not 'the Mack.' He's admitting that he's not smooth or fly. He's saying that he never knew the art of making love—but his heart aches with love for her. What red-blooded woman wouldn't want a man to say some shit like that to her?"

McKenzie sat and thought for a minute. *I guess that's some good shit.* She tried to imagine a man confessing something like that to her.

"OK, I guess so."

"You guess so? Do you understand the magnitude of vulnerability in that statement? Shit, McKenzie, ain't no brother gone let a woman know that kind of shit—that's giving up way too much power." He laughed at her. She thought about it a minute.

"I guess so." Honestly, she didn't think men were ever vulnerable—or *really* loved women, for that matter. She thought they did just what they had to in order to get what they wanted. That's not love. That's bullshit wrapped up to look like love. Mushy shit they said to get women to believe they love them.

Christian was exasperated. "You didn't get any of that from the words?"

"Um. Not really, but I haven't had time to really digest it either. But honestly Christian?"

"Yeah, honestly." He really wanted to hear what she thought.

"He sounds like he's blaming her for not being able to read his mind. I mean, how the fuck is she supposed to know he's in love with her? If he doesn't *do* something to let her know . . . If he stands there like an ass and watches her walk off with another guy? C'mon! He's a wimp!" Christian shook his head in disbelief.

"You are brutal."

"Here this brother is—probably friends with some nut-crackin' sistah like *you,* assertive, self-assured—and he's just intimidated by your beauty. He probably figures you wouldn't be attracted to him. So, he's just happy to be in your company. Just happy to engage in conversation with this whirlwind of a woman."

McKenzie was floored. First of all, to find out this is how Christian saw her. Then—because she didn't see how in the hell he could get this scenario from those lyrics.

"I suppose that scenario could be possible. Sure," she said quietly.

Christian pressed the play button. And for the next forty minutes they argued back and forth about the lyrics of Stevie Wonder's *My Cherie Amour*, Earth Wind and Fire's *Reasons*, and Teddy Pendergrass' *You're My Latest, Greatest Inspiration*.

"OK Ms. Batiste. Class is over." McKenzie couldn't tell if he was disappointed or not.

"Will there be more?" she asked, testing the waters.

"Absolutely, I don't scare that easily," he said smiling, "and I'm going to leave these here with you to listen to. Just play them over and over—and listen to the words."

They returned their focus to completing their write-up. The music continued to play in the background. And McKenzie found herself unconsciously humming the chorus.

Christian smiled.

Ahmad showered, dressed, and left for dinner and a movie with Crystal. Christian and McKenzie wrapped up the write-up on the observation of the afternoon with Ahmad and Crystal.

"Ew," McKenzie said. She lifted her arms and smelled under each armpit. "I stink."

Christian looked up. "What's with these hygiene confessions?" He smiled.

"The truth is painfully evident." She said, fanning in front of her nose. "Look, I'm going to jump in the shower. It'll be quick; if you want to wait maybe we can go grab something to eat? Are you hungry?"

Christian watched her as she stood before him. He was sticky, but he didn't stink. The day had been wonderful—more than he had anticipated, actually. He was curious about McKenzie. He was happy he had come up with the idea to observe McKenzie's son and his girlfriend. It gave him more time in this remarkable woman's world. What bothered Christian was why he wanted so badly to be in it.

"Yeah, I'm starving. But go ahead. I'll wait for you to get the stink off so we can go eat. What do you have a taste for?" He asked.

McKenzie moved toward the stairs. "You decide. I'm easy." She said taking the stairs two at-a-time.

The shower came on. The walls in McKenzie's townhouse were so thin he could hear the powerful flow of the water in his classmate's upstairs shower. Christian sat in the kitchen looking over his notes about the day's observation. He looked up to find his attention fixed on McKenzie's K-Swiss.

Christian tapped his fingers on the table. *I wonder how many shoes McKenzie has?* He looked at the shoes, then up at the ceiling where the noise of the shower rumbled.

It was a crazy thought, but Christian was overwhelmed with the desire to creep up those stairs and find out. With the shower going strong, Christian inched up the stairs. Mid-way, the shower turned off. Christian froze. The water switched from shower to tub. Christian listened closely, ready to dash back down the stairs. But the water from the tub continued to run. *A shower and a bath?* Christian sat across from McKenzie at the table, but didn't think she stunk—certainly not enough to warrant a shower *and* a bath.

At the top of the stairway, Christian waited and listened. He moved quietly toward the open door to the right. His mind raced, and remembered how he followed McKenzie to the pool on campus. *If Mac ever found out about that, and me, now, she'd think I was some sicko stalker.* Christian thought to himself. *And justifiably so.* What he was doing was insane. Yet, he moved toward McKenzie's walk-in closet.

Slowly, he slid the door open. "Oh my—" Christian whispered in disbelief.

The closet was filled with easily over 100 pairs of shoes: mostly tennis, but quite a few other styles. He was just about to take a closer look when he heard a deep, throaty moan from the bathroom. He paused to listen harder.

"Mm . . . uh, oh . . . mm"

Christian instinctively moved toward the sensual sounds. The bath water was still running.

"Ah. Ah. Oooh. Yeah."

Christian peeked his head around the corner, trying not to be seen—but trying to see why McKenzie was making these erotic sounds. The door was opened only a crack. But what he saw held him captive in his place. From his vantage point, he saw McKenzie, lying back in the tub. He was standing behind her, so she couldn't see him watching. He slowly and gently pushed the door open a little.

Her legs were spread wide open, feet propped up in the corners of the tub—and a steady stream of hot water was running down to her vagina! Christian's mouth dropped open. He inched closer. She lay back in the tub, her head halfway submerged into the water. She was cupping her butt in her hands. She slid further up under the running stream of water, lifting her pelvic area up as if she was moving in closer to a man's body . . . as if she was pushing so as to take his penis deeper inside of her. The motion created a deep reaction in Christian's shorts. But he kept his eyes fixed on McKenzie.

She lay there, submerged in the water. As he watched, he noticed her abdomen rising and falling in a quick, repetitive rhythm. McKenzie was whimpering.

"Uh. Uh. Uh. . .Umm . . . Oh. Uh." her breath was short. To Christian, it sounded as if she was about to . . .

McKenzie sat up! Propped up on her elbows, she spread her legs even wider. She leaned in forward, and froze. She reached up to the nozzle and turned the water to make it hotter. Christian watched intently. He reached down and stroked his enormously hard dick. He was so turned on.

"Ohhhhhhh!" McKenzie's outcry jolted Christian forward.

"Oh!" He said as he stumbled partway into the bathroom.

He stepped back out quickly, and hurried down the stairs, flustered, embarrassed, and with his erect dick leading the way.

McKenzie slowly stepped out of the tub. She dried off, reached to open the mirrored medicine cabinet door. As she pulled out the baby oil, she closed the door and smiled. Her eyes locked on the place where Christian stood watching her masturbate in the tub.

♋   ♋   ♋

Christian was downstairs, pacing. *Did she hear me?* He wondered. It was quiet upstairs. He didn't hear McKenzie walking around. He was anxious. But more than that—he was still hard.

Christian quickly walked into the kitchen, opened the refrigerator, and grabbed a Coke. Taking the stairs two at-a-time, he yelled:

"Hey Mac!" At the top of the stairs, Christian paused. "Mac?"

"Yeah, what's up?" McKenzie replied from her room. "I'm over here Christian."

Christian walked toward her room. "Hey, I brought you a Coke--" Christian came to a complete stop. McKenzie was in a champagne-colored robe, oiling herself down. She looked up at Christian and smiled.

"Thank you."

She walked over to Christian and handed him the bottle of oil. As he took the bottle, she turned around and dropped her robe. His dick had gone down—but quickly returned to attention when she dropped the robe. His brain was a mass of confusion. He stood behind her, looking at her back—her beautiful ass, and her long silky legs. Christian felt as if he'd been standing there for hours . . . looking like a clumsy boy, instead of a thirty year old man. McKenzie waited patiently.

"Have you ever tried Neutrogena body oil?" Christian said.

He applied the baby oil on McKenzie's shoulders. Her skin was so soft. He gently massaged her shoulders and neck. She tilted her head to the side, closed her eyes, and leaned back into the massage.

"Uh uh." McKenzie said.

"It's not as oily as regular baby oil, but it moisturizes the skin really well."

Christian couldn't focus. He was scared McKenzie would lean back into his extremely hard dick. He tried to move backwards, but she just moved with him.

Christian became extremely uncomfortable. He had oiled her back and shoulders three or four times. He didn't move down to her supple ass like he wanted to. Everything in him wanted to caress her butt.

McKenzie pulled away. She walked over to her bed, climbed up and slid back in the bed, facing Christian. He stood there, motionless. She was beautiful. Sexy. He was speechless. McKenzie watched him. She looked as if she could sense his uneasiness.

"I figured since you liked watching me, Mr. Malveaux, I'd let you get an up close and personal look." She stared at Christian intently.

Christian froze. *Oh shit!* He thought to himself. Anxiety filled him from head to toe.

"Do you always sneak around watching folks masturbate?" She slid her right leg up under her, exposing her full bush. She leaned back into the headboard, causing her breasts to protrude. Immediately, Christian's bulge began to grow.

"Do you like it when people watch you masturbate?"

McKenzie smiled. "I like it when *you* watch me." She ran her fingers through her hair. She extended her hand to him.

For a split second he thought of Jada. He knew what he was doing was wrong— even though, technically, he hadn't done anything. But it wouldn't matter to Jada, if he *thought* about another woman that was cheating.

Christian didn't know which was throbbing more, his heart or his dick.

Christian walked over to McKenzie and took her hand in his. He watched her the whole time.

"What else would you like for me to do?" he said in a soft whisper. She pulled him down to her.

"Kiss me. I like it when you kiss me."

She looked so innocent as she looked up into his eyes. Everything about McKenzie oozed sensuality. Christian leaned down and kissed her. First, a soft peck. McKenzie closed her eyes. He kissed her again, this time a long passionate kiss. McKenzie opened her mouth and took him all in. She slid her arms around his neck and gently pulled him in. He moved his hands inside her thigh. McKenzie opened her legs to him. He slid his fingers slowly inside her. McKenzie moaned inside his mouth. Something about that stirred up more desire in Christian.

McKenzie moved down to get more of Christian's finger inside of her. The motion reminded Christian of her motions in the tub. Christian pulled his hand out. McKenzie opened her eyes.

"What's wrong? Why did you stop?"

Christian stood, licked the juices off his fingers, and began to move away from the bed.

"I'd better stop now before this gets to a place where I'm unable to." He said. He looked into her eyes. She watched him attentively.

"Make me cum." McKenzie said.

McKenzie lay back flat on her bed, in a most erotic pose. She commanded Christian without speaking a word. Christian smiled and walked back over to the bed.

"With what? My fingers? My tongue?" Christian said in a whisper.

He slid his finger slowly inside her. McKenzie closed her eyes. Christian gently massaged her clit. She twitched with pleasure. Slowly, he explored her engorged walls. They were warm and slippery. He imagined her underneath him as he gently slid inside those magnificent walls. Her eyes were closed. His were open. He watched her as she moved in concert with each gentle stroke.

Christian leaned in and kissed her neck. McKenzie sighed. He kissed her clavicle bone. McKenzie moaned. He kissed the area in between her breasts. McKenzie bit her bottom lip. He slowly slid his tongue down the center of her body until he reached her navel. McKenzie wiggled under his touch. He patiently and gently caressed her navel with his tongue, exploring every angle—leaving no area untouched. McKenzie grabbed the back of his head.

Christian moved himself in front of McKenzie. He took both hands and gently ran them up the inside of her thighs. McKenzie lay back, eyes closed, and fell limp under the touch of Christian's hands. She was dripping wet. He saw the juices oozing down her vagina and became enormously hard.

He slid his finger inside the slippery walls. McKenzie moaned. He gently massaged her erect clit causing her to moan and groan out loud. She propped up on her elbows, tossed her head back, and spread her legs open wider.

Christian loved the thought of McKenzie giving herself to him. It was so sexy, so sensual, and so erotic. He wanted to take his hard dick and— He pulled her lips apart.

"Ohhh!" She moaned. "Oh. Mm."

Christian watched her body become anxious to his touch. He barely brushed the tip of her labia, and she instantly moved down to try and coax him into touching her more. He smiled.

"You want it?" Christian whispered.

"Y-yes," she replied, guttural—barely audible.

"You want me?"

"On top of me . . . behind me . . . underneath me—I don't care, just as long as you're inside me. I want you inside me, Christian, please baby. . . "

Christian slid up to her wet, hot, bush and slowly . . . gently . . . stuck his tongue inside her.

"Oh shit," McKenzie moaned.

She thrust her pelvic area forward, causing Christian's tongue to inch deeper inside her.

"Yes, baby, yes," she whispered.

Christian pushed her lips further back and lunged his tongue deeper inside her, with quick forceful thrusts. McKenzie tossed her head from side to side. Her eyes were shut tight.

Christian watched her. She looked so fucking sexy.

He slid his finger inside her as he transitioned his tongue to her clit.

"Oh fuck, yes, yes!"

Christian loved it! He sucked her clit, stretching it until McKenzie whimpered. Then he adjusted himself between her legs. He grabbed her hips, pulled her vagina up to his face and quickly brushed the very tip of his tongue across her clit over and over and over—until the feather light wisps sent McKenzie into a frenzy of a climax.

She tried to clamp her legs shut, but Christian kept them parted as he intensified his strokes. McKenzie called out as she reached her orgasm.

"Ohhh! Yesss! Oh Yesss! Uh, Uh, Uh . . ." McKenzie fell back onto her back. She shook with an intensity Christian had never seen before. She lay there, shaking, as Christian watched. She lay there, breathing deeply while he slowly rubbed her stomach.

McKenzie rocked back and forth as Christian rubbed her stomach. She turned on her side, smiling. Christian smiled at her mischief."

"What?"

McKenzie reached over to her nightstand. Christian watched her reach for a long white—*what was that?* She sat up and flicked on a switch. She held the buzzing penis out to Christian with a smirk on her face.

"I need penetration. I'm wet . . . and hot."

Christian took the vibrator and played around with the switches. One controlled the pearls inside the vibrator that supposedly simulated the throbbing motion of the shaft. The other controlled the butterfly contraption that hung under the bottom and replaced the nuts.

McKenzie laughed, watching Christian try and figure out her toy. She took his hand and turned the vibrator upside down. He was perplexed by the move until she took his hand and guided the butterfly antennas toward her clitoris.

She slid down and spread her legs. She rubbed her thighs while Christian adjusted the speed on the butterfly. McKenzie's body instantly responded the moment he anchored her clit between the vibrating antennas. She turned her head, grabbed the sheets, and slid into a burst of convulsions. Christian was amazed at how quickly she came. He watched her deep breathing, her flat stomach rising and falling.

"I need penetration," she said, eyes half opened.

Christian adjusted the vibrator to slide the shaft inside McKenzie. She was so wet her walls sucked in the rubber penis, and smacked from engaging the thick juices inside. Christian's dick instantly went hard. His mouth literally started to water.

She took his hand and helped him find the rhythm for the simulated thrusts. She gasped, moaned and groaned and rocked back and forth in time with Christian. He watched the pleasure sweep across her face, and wanted so badly to experience it with her.

Christian slid on top of her, kissing her breasts gently. She moaned and grabbed the back of his head, stroking it softly. He positioned himself over her as if he were inside her, and slowly pulled the vibrator out—to the very tip. McKenzie gasped. He paused, then slid it back inside just as slowly. McKenzie lifted her butt to try and take in more, but Christian pulled it out to the very tip again.

"C'mon baby. Stop. I want to feel it inside me."

Christian paused. He wanted her to feel *him* inside her. He kissed her, sliding his tongue gently inside her mouth. She eagerly took him inside her, returning the kiss with passion and urgency.

Propping himself up over her, he quickened his motion—being careful not to plunge too deep.

"Oh yes!" She said. He slid it in and out, over and over, sending McKenzie into frenzy. She grabbed his shoulder and dug in deep with her fingers. McKenzie closed her eyes and bit down on her bottom lip. Her body jolted once again into convulsions. Christian watched her body shake, and her face relax into a placid look of contentment.

"Mm . . ." She said. Christian slid next to her on the bed, and affectionately rubbed her stomach.

"How was that mama?" He whispered.

McKenzie smiled. "Two down, one more to go." McKenzie took Christian's hand and showed him how she needed to be touched.

"It takes me three orgasms to set me straight." Christian smiled at the confession, and allowed her to take his fingers and move them slowly across her clitoris, then slide them deep inside her. She moaned. She took his index finger and, with short, deliberate strokes, rubbed a flat, ribbed area in her vagina.

McKenzie's body began to quietly convulse. The shaking began slowly. Then erupted into a full body shake. McKenzie held on to Christian's hand as she began to climax. Sounding much like she did earlier in the tub, McKenzie let out a loud scream. Christian watched as she reached an orgasm. She held her hand over his, inside her as she shook. It was the sexiest thing he had ever experienced in his life.

♋   ♋   ♋

"Wait, wait, wait!" Denise said. "What did you just say?"

Denise was McKenzie's best friend since elementary school. The only female she was able to have any type of relationship with, ever. They became close the first day McKenzie transferred into her class after going to live with her mother.

Denise went out of her way to show McKenzie around the school, which was three times the size of her school in Watts. The other kids whispered and pointed, but Denise smiled and took McKenzie's hand. From that day forward, they were inseparable.

"Denny, I *said* I just dry-humped thee most beautiful Black man like a high-schooler in the back of a car." McKenzie squealed.

"Oh my God! Are you kidding me?" Denise laughed.

"No. It was the dumbest shit ever." McKenzie laughed with her friend.

"Then why did you do it? How old is he? Oh my God, McKenzie—is he legal?"

"Whaaat? Yes, of course, he's legal!" McKenzie said. "I can't believe you even went there. He's our age, just so you know."

"Really? Shit, with you there's a high possibility."

"What? What the fuck does that mean?"

"Let's see, there was Douglas, and Hector, and John . . ."

"Yeah, yeah —they were all legal. And pretty. But this is different."

"They were fuck buddies, according to you. How is this one different? Is there a possibility of a relationship?" Denise said.

"Nah. He's married."

"Married?! What are you doing?"

"Just having fun. Stop worrying. The Mac don't do sloppy seconds."

"Then what do you mean this is different?" McKenzie heard Jermaine saying something in the background. Denise placed her hand over the telephone. Jermaine was Denise's husband whom McKenzie could not stand. He was an asshole. They had two beautiful boys, Jared and Daniel, who were three years apart. Jermaine moved the family out to Texas under the pretense of a better life for his family.

The truth was, he didn't give a damn about his family. Jermaine only cared about himself, and flossing. They purchased a mansion-sized house compared to what they could afford in L.A. and Jermaine loved to be able to brag about it.

He didn't spend any time with Denise and the boys. She was pretty much a married single mom. Denise was a good woman. She supported Jermaine. McKenzie believed that she loved him. She was the dutiful wife. But Jermaine didn't give the same to his wife.

Their entire marriage, all McKenzie saw was Jermaine slowly and methodically tear down her best friend's self-esteem. Put downs and public ridicule that Denise would stomach and blow off. She'd make excuses and take the blame—your typical abusive wife syndrome. Denise said he'd never physically touched her, and McKenzie believed her. But the verbal abuse had done so much damage that he didn't need touch her.

"Listen McKenzie, I gotta go." Denise said in a whisper. "I'm going to call you back so we can talk about this more. But this doesn't sound like something you should really pursue, if you know what I mean? You had your fun, done and done. Right?"

"Maybe, maybe not. We'll see. But, I hear cave man in the background. Go make his dinner. I'm not going anywhere. Call me later."

"Stop," Denise said, laughing. "Love you. Good night." McKenzie heard Jermaine call them dykes in the background.

"Love you more." McKenzie said. "And tell Neanderthal his little dick made you turn to women." They laughed.

115

The next morning, and every morning following, McKenzie received an email from Christian with a song attached as an MP3 file. It was one of his 'Classics'. He'd send her a series of thought-provoking questions to answer.

What is she saying to her lover?
How do the instruments in this song intensify the mood?
If you could compare this song to a season, which would it
be?
What emotion does this song make you feel?

And every morning, she'd eagerly open her email, looking for the next song and series of questions. Each song had its own set of specific questions. McKenzie began to anticipate the emails. She would answer the questions and, in turn, ask questions of her own. This dialogue around these songs gave her insight to Christian's thought process and personality.

Christian: What does Al Green mean when he says
'It can't be measured by no sign. In your heart
or even in your mind'?
McKenzie: I think he means that love is
intangible and is defined differently - even
from how you feel in your heart or in your mind.
Christian: Yes. I think we get caught up in

```
stuff like Valentine's day, where there's this
expectation to buy the biggest bouquet of roses, or
the biggest karat ring as if that measures a person's
love. And it's not about that - and it's so deep,
sometimes it can't even be measured by what you feel
in your heart or what you think it is in your mind.
```

McKenzie found herself seeing the songs through his eyes. And, as time passed, she had to admit that she began to gain an appreciation for the slow, mushy stuff.

She'd also begun to have favorites: Teena Marie, Al Green, Frankie Beverly and Maze, Etta James, Anita Baker, and Luther Vandross. She hadn't figured out if it was the songs themselves, or how she'd come to view them because of the way Christian formulated his questions about them.

McKenzie didn't know it, but Christian put a lot of thought into the songs he sent her. Secretly, he was sending her messages through the lyrics. He said things through their words that he hadn't gotten the courage to say to her himself, like the lyrics from "When We're Dancing Close and Slow" by Prince.

When we're dancing close and slow
I never want to let you go, no, no
I feel your warm embrace
The softness of your face
Tell me, baby, are we here alone?

These lyrics were the closest description of how Christian felt cha-cha-ing with McKenzie. Prince described kissing his love interest long and hard and almost being able to taste the thoughts within her mind: sex-related fantasies – which were exactly the thoughts Christian was having about McKenzie. He loved those moments cha-cha'ing with McKenzie - the closeness, the intimacy, being in sync – everything he loved most about sharing his space with McKenzie.

But the line that resonated the most, and that Christian would repeat over and over, said *when they're dancing close and slow he's not afraid to let his feelings show*. That's exactly how Christian felt. It was as if that time on the dance floor removed all of his inhibitions. It freed him to touch McKenzie in a way he would never have the courage to do otherwise. It put him closer to doing what he was becoming consumed with doing.

I want to come inside of you
I want to hold you when we're through
Can't you feel my love touching you?

As the weeks passed, McKenzie's responses seemed to become more thoughtful. At first, she ripped the songs apart, citing silly fantasies of the crooner, bad word rhyme choices, or unrealistic and completely unattainable expectations of the person whose affection was being sought. But, as the days passed, she seemed to begin to really listen to the words, and put thought into answering his questions. Her answers changed from short, 2-3 sentence answers, to three and four paragraph commentaries. Christian loved it.

Pretty soon, these lyrical analyses became their morning ritual, like a cup of coffee. And like a caffeine addiction, they had to get their fix—every day.

♋   ♋   ♋

In class, the groups were allowed the last portion of the hour to work on their presentations. April and Melvin were sharing their team observations about six elementary aged kids, being supervised by a 23 year old at a Chuck E. Cheese.

Melvin wasn't listening. He was watching the dynamics between Christian and McKenzie. Since she walked in the door, Christian hadn't taken his eyes off her. McKenzie flirted coyly with him. It was subtle, unless you were watching, like Melvin had been, you wouldn't have noticed.

Melvin watched McKenzie. She moved around the room with ease, talking to the group members and other classmates on a variety of topics. She smiled her genuine smile at the African Americans—but was short or insincere with the white people. Melvin glared at her. There was no denying she was gorgeous. The perfect smile, full, supple lips, pretty straight teeth. The perfect figure--well proportioned. And that mind—McKenzie was brilliant. She was just the biggest bitch on the face of the earth.

CHAPTER FIVE

The Major

Christian found himself thinking about McKenzie all the time now. They had fallen into a routine where they'd meet up at the Student Union after McKenzie's afternoon swim and walk up to class together.

He was running late today. Jada had gotten into an accident the day before and informed him as he was leaving the house for campus that she needed a ride to the rental car facility. This unscheduled request had him running thirty-five minutes behind.

His frustration level rose higher as he spent ten minutes circling Lot 'F,' driving up and down rows looking for a parking space.

McKenzie left the aquatic center at her usual time, she anticipated meeting Christian at the Student Union. They had been meeting up there for a couple of weeks now, and she had come to look forward to that personal time together.

They didn't discuss their intimate encounter at McKenzie's townhouse. When Christian tried to bring it up, she quickly changed the subject. But she thought about it every day. How he touched her . . . the fullness of his lips . . . his hard dick. She wondered what it would be like to have him inside her.

Instead of talking about her curiosity with Christian, McKenzie continued to function around him as if it never took place.

McKenzie waited at the Student Union for 15 minutes before she decided that Christian wasn't showing. Disappointed, she headed toward class. *This is why you don't set your heart on men, they're so flaky*, she reminded herself. As she rounded the corner to cross the quad, she was snatched back so hard her books flew out of her arms and across the grassy area.

121

"What the fuck—" But she was slammed so hard against the brick wall, that it knocked the rest of the sentence out of her mouth.

"Listen to your foul vulgar mouth!" The deep baritone voice hissed.

When McKenzie regained her senses, her heart froze with fear. Huge hands gripped her arms, swung her around, and pinned her up against the wall. McKenzie tried to focus on her assailant. As her vision cleared, she found herself staring up into a pair of crazed black eyes. Her body went limp.

"How did you find me?" McKenzie said, barely able to stand, let alone speak.

"I told you. You can never leave me. I'll always find you." He seethed. He towered over McKenzie. And under his grip, she was defenseless.

Christian finally found a parking space. He ran to the Student Union, hoping McKenzie was still there. But when he got there, she was nowhere to be found. He looked at his watch, *McKenzie hates to be late; she's probably already headed to class*. He started a soft trot to class, more because he was anxious to see McKenzie than because he was late.

He took a short cut through the IT building. As he crossed the quad, he glanced to the right—and had to do a double take. In the corner, a woman was pinned to the wall by a huge older guy.

Christian couldn't be sure from that angle, but, as he moved closer to the scene, it became increasingly clear that it was McKenzie being pinned up against the wall. Christian tried to assess the situation to make sure he wasn't seeing things wrong. But when he moved in closer, he could see fear all over McKenzie's face. Rage gripped him, and he switched into protective mode.

Christian grabbed the man by his shoulder, and spun him around. Shocked, the man released McKenzie. She quickly moved behind Christian, and grabbed the back part of his jacket tightly in her hands. He moved in front of her and used his muscular torso as a shield.

"Is everything OK here?" Christian said slowly. A scowl covered his face.

"Nothing you need to worry yourself about, son." The man replied, tight-lipped, as he straightened out his heavily starched, crisp white button down shirt.

Christian tried to turn to McKenzie, but she grabbed his jacket in such a way that let him know she didn't want him to move. She was pressed up against him, and he could feel her heart racing.

"Oh, I'm not worried at all" Christian said.

"This is family business. You can excuse yourself now so that I can finish my conversation with McKenzie."

McKenzie pulled Christian's jacket tighter.

"I don't care what kind of business it is—you can excuse yourself because whatever 'conversation' you thought you were having is over." Christian straightened his stance and eyeballed the older man. He looked him up and down. *Family business?* There was something familiar about the man's face. Christian couldn't quite put his finger on it. *Was this McKenzie's father?*

The man stood there, quietly glaring at Christian. Then, he slowly turned and walked away. When he was about 50 yards away, McKenzie rushed to pick up her books and, without a word, headed off to class. Christian gave chase.

"Mac? Mac! Will you wait a minute?" McKenzie was walking, but at a pace that felt like she was jogging.

"Christian—we're already late for class. Can we do this another time?" She managed to get out between silent sobs. Her chest burned. She could barely breathe. And she was shaking like a leaf. All she wanted was to get away from Christian.

Before he could catch up with her, she made it to class. She hurried into the room and sat in an empty seat between two of her classmates. Christian entered the class and scanned the room. When he saw where she sat, he got the picture. He found a seat in the back of the class. He watched McKenzie the entire time. She was a mess. She tried to inconspicuously wipe the tears that kept trickling down her face.

Christian was furious at the old man who had her pinned to the wall, at himself for being late today, and at McKenzie for shutting him out like this.

♋ ♋ ♋

After lecture, McKenzie practically ran out of class. April tried to start a conversation with Christian, but he pushed right passed her to go after McKenzie. She was running toward her car when Christian finally caught up with her. He grabbed her, and turned her around to face him. When he saw her frightened face, he immediately released his grip.

"I'm sorry, Mac. I didn't mean to grab you so forcefully."

"That's what they always say," McKenzie said as she riffled through her purse for her keys.

"What? What are you talking about?" Christian replied. "What the hell have I done to you? Except try to protect you from that asshole today?" He stood, brows furrowed, hands flailing about.

McKenzie was flustered. She knew her feelings had nothing to do with Christian. He was right. He had saved her today. But she wasn't ready to deal with this right now. Right now, all she wanted was to get away *so she could breathe.*

"I'm sorry, Christian. You're right." She turned to face him. Tears were still streaming down her face. "Thank you for today. You haven't done anything to me at all. I'm sorry." She held her head down. Christian moved in to hug her. McKenzie pulled away.

"What? I don't know what to do here. Can you help a brotha out?" He paced back and forth.

"Just let me go, Christian." McKenzie didn't look up.

"I can't, babe. You have to talk to me. I won't be able to sleep tonight until I know that you're safe." Christian paused. "Who was he, and why did he have you pinned up against that wall?"

McKenzie walked over to a planter stand and sat. She dropped her face in her hands and sobbed. Christian sat next to her, and wrapped his arms around her. She cried in his chest for about twenty minutes. He waited patiently, rubbing her back, kissing the top of her head as she cried.

"He's my stepfather. His name is Charles Winslow. But everyone calls him 'The Major.'" McKenzie's voice was dry, crackily—almost inaudible. Christian leaned in close to hear.

"Why do they call him the Major? And why did he have you pinned up against the wall?"

"He was a major in the Air Force. He's a Bishop in the church now. But he was a decorated officer with all these medals and shit. And because he was a distinguished Black man in the military, folks were more than happy to acknowledge his accomplishments by calling him by military rank. Major." She paused. "He had me pinned up against the wall because he is an asshole."

"OK. And?"

"And. He's pissed because I moved out of his house."

"You're a grown woman. Why would your moving out cause him to pin you up against a wall? I don't understand."

"You'll never understand, Christian. Hell, I still don't understand. He's been my stepfather since I was seven—and I still don't understand. He is an asshole." Christian waited patiently. McKenzie fiddled with her fingers trying to figure out how to formulate the words.

"When I was nine, I decided I wanted to be an R&B singer. As I grew older, I wanted to be the equivalent to a Lauryn Hill, Sade, Mariah Carey. In my teens and early twenties, I had their pictures on my wall. I had their albums—knew the lyrics to all the songs." She wiped tears with the back of her hands as she told her story.

"Major came into my room one day and ripped all the posters off the wall, took all my albums, broke them into pieces, and made me throw them away."

"It's OK . . ." Christian rubbed her back. She looked so pained recounting her experience, he wondered if he should have her continue? But the way she responded today was so uncharacteristic—he'd never seen McKenzie so emotional--he wanted to know as much as possible.

"He had just been ordained a minister and said he wasn't going to have his stepdaughter singing secular music. He said it was Satan's music. So he banned it from his house, and made me start taking Opera classes."

"What? At nine? Did you want to sing Opera?"

"No. Not at all."

"Why didn't he have you singing gospel music? And where was your mother? What did she say?" McKenzie stood up and walked off. Her back was to him.

"She was there. But she never said anything. She always went along with everything the Major did."

Christian couldn't imagine McKenzie's mother being docile and submissive—what happened to the fruit not falling far from the tree?

McKenzie turned to face Christian. She smiled. It was so fake and pathetic. Christian reached out and grabbed McKenzie's hands. Slowly, he pulled her in between his legs. She was standing. He was sitting. He looked into her eyes, and for the first time since meeting her, she did not look confident. If he had to describe it, she looked hollow—empty. Christian was touched in a place, deep inside. He wanted to find this Major asshole and rip his head off his neck.

Christian could see that McKenzie was struggling with what to say. He could feel her heavy heart. He could see that her talking about the Major caused all kinds of emotions inside her. She hesitated, then stepped further into Christian's space. She slid her arms around his neck, and rested her head on his shoulder. He gently held her close. It was something about the way he rubbed her back that made her relax, he could feel her body loosen under his touch.

"Where were you?" Jada said as Christian entered his house.

"I had to meet with my professor after class," he said, placing his backpack on the floor. He rubbed his eyes, yawned, and headed for the bathroom. Jada watched him. He didn't offer her another word.

"Are you hungry? I made some Enchiladas—"

"No thanks. I grabbed something on campus. I'm just going to turn in. I'm tired." Christian exited the bathroom. He took off his clothes and put on his pajamas. He quickly slid into bed and closed his eyes.

Jada turned off the television, washed her face, put on her nightgown, and slid into bed next to Christian. She moved in close to him, rubbing his back. Christian didn't respond. She moved her body in to cup his butt, and slowly started grinding it. She kissed the back of his neck. Lying there, motionless, he hoped she would assume he was asleep. But Jada didn't give in that easily. She reached over and took his limp penis into her hand. She patiently stroked it, trying to bring it to life.

Christian dreaded these moments. They always caused him so much anxiety. Jada would try to entice him into having sex. When he wouldn't respond, she would beg, and then demand.

"C'mon baby," she whispered into his back as she kissed him.

"I'm tired Jay." Christian said as if she had woken him out of a deep sleep.

"You're always tired. Or sick. Or busy. It's always some excuse." Jada said. Christian didn't reply. It was useless. He knew how the argument would end. It was one they had every month. "Who are you fucking, Christian? It's certainly not your wife."

127

"I'm not fucking anyone, Jada," Christian replied without emotion. It was true. Sex was the last thing on his mind. He simply didn't have the desire. 'A thirty year old man—not wanting to have sex?' But it was true.

"Why do I always have to beg you to have sex with me? Don't you find me attractive?" He could hear her crying next to him.

"Of course, you're attractive. You're a beautiful woman," he assured her. And she was. She had an ass that would stop traffic. Back in the day, Christian could just look at her ass and would get an instant erection. These days, Jada could be lying next to him in bed and push her butt into his dick, and he wouldn't rise at all.

"Do you think you have Penile Erectile Dysfunction?"

"I don't know. Maybe."

"Maybe you should consult your doctor, Christian. This is not normal," Jada said. "We used to have sex two and three times a week. Now, it's a fucking act of God to get it once a month." Christian remained silent. He knew what she said was true, and a part of him felt bad. They used to have a very exciting love life— back in the day.

"Yeah. Maybe," he said, hoping it would salvage his night.

Jada pulled at his shoulder. "Christian. Look at me." Christian turned to face his accuser. "I'm young. I have needs. Most people would just go outside their relationship to get their needs met if they were in my situation." Christian wasn't fazed by her underhanded threat. He couldn't honestly say that it would bother him if she did.

"C'mon baby. Touch me." Jada took his hand and place it between her legs. Christian instinctively rubbed the area he knew would get Jada off. She closed her eyes and spread her legs. Christian closed his eyes and pictured McKenzie in her room, lying naked on her bed . . . legs spread open . . .

"Ahmad!" McKenzie shouted as she bolted through the door. "Ahmad!"

"Yes, mom? What's wrong?" Ahmad answered, rushing into the living room. He heard the anxiety in McKenzie's voice.

"Did anyone come by tonight?"

"Anyone like who?"

"Ahmad, answer the question, dammit!"

"No, ma. No one came over," he replied.

"Any hang up calls? Any packages delivered today?" she said pacing back and forth. Ahmad watched his mom move aimlessly around the room.

"No, ma. Will you tell me what's going on, please? Why are you buggin' like this?" McKenzie removed her baseball cap and ran her fingers through her curly hair. She plopped down on the couch and placed her face in her hands. Ahmad stood, watching her.

"The Major found me." She looked up. "He showed up at campus, today."

"What?" Ahmad shouted. "How did he find you? Mom, did he hurt you—I swear, I'll—"

"He didn't hurt me. Christian showed up and ran interference. I just wanted to make sure he didn't show up here." She looked up at Ahmad. She recognized that scowl on his face: he was worried. McKenzie smiled at her little man. "We're fine, Ahmad. Come here, baby." He walked over and sat next to his mom. She hugged him and kissed him on the forehead. *She had to believe they would be fine. She went through an enormous amount of work to make sure of it.*

♋   ♋   ♋

The telephone rang. "Hello?" McKenzie answered.

"Hey Mac, it's Christian. I'm around the corner. Is it OK if I come by?" McKenzie knew she would have to have this conversation sooner or later.

"Sure. Come on."

Ahmad had left for school already. And McKenzie was doing the laundry.

There was a rap on the door. McKenzie opened the door and let Christian in. As Christian walked past McKenzie, she grabbed his hand. He stopped and turned to face her. But, before he could say anything, McKenzie wrapped her arms around his neck and began to kiss him.

Surprised, Christian slowly relaxed and received the gentle motion of McKenzie's tongue in his mouth. He pulled back to look at her. McKenzie smiled nervously and waited. Christian leaned down, and kissed her on her forehead.

"What's up?" He took her hand and led her to the couch to sit.

"What's up with you?"

"Well. I didn't sleep all night. I was worried about you. Did your stepfather come by last night?"

"No. I don't think he'll come by here. He's much too arrogant."

"What do you mean?"

"Well, on campus, it was open. He'd have to be let in here—and he wouldn't risk the humiliation of having to stand outside and not be invited in. We're fine."

"Are you fine, really? I've never seen you look so frightened—"

"Yes, I am fine. Look Christian. The Major is a controlling, conniving, hypocritical asshole." McKenzie paced.

"OK, and that made you afraid of him?" Her explanation didn't make sense. McKenzie stopped pacing and turned to face Christian.

"And he was physically abusive." *There! She said it.*
Christian stood up.

"He physically abused you?" He shouted.

"He called it discipline. It was some military bullshit. And, as soon as I could get out of his house, I bailed." McKenzie grabbed Christian's hand. "He's such a control freak, he never got over it." She moved in closer, took his palm and slowly started to kiss it.

Christian watched her. She was so sweet. He couldn't imagine that huge man laying hands on her—especially as a small, innocent child. Christian had heard that there were a high percentage of men in the military and on the police force who abused their families--something about displaced anger and aggression.

McKenzie paused. "Christian?"

"Yes, baby?" McKenzie smiled at the term of endearment.

"Thank you . . . for yesterday, I mean." She hugged him, wrapping her arms around his waist. He placed his arms around her neck.

"You were . . . awesome," she said as she smiled into his chest, thinking of the shock across the Major's face when Christian dismissed him.

"And I really appreciate what you did," she said. And she meant it. Besides Ahmad, she never had anyone to defend her. It felt odd—which was why she didn't know how to respond at the time. But it felt good.

"I should have socked him in the back of his head—" he said, thinking about how "the Major" hit McKenzie. Thinking about how he could still instill fear in her as an adult. McKenzie laughed at the visual.

"You should have. I would have loved that."

"You would have?" he said, lifting her chin up so he could see her face.

"Yes, I would have loved to see somebody hurt him." McKenzie's eyes went cold for a few seconds. Then she squeezed him.

"But he's a cruel man. I would have gone crazy if he hurt you, Christian." McKenzie said.

"He wouldn't have hurt me. He's an old man."

McKenzie knew the Major was older than Christian. But she also knew he fought dirty.

"Thank you for being there for me," McKenzie said, lifting Christian's shirt up over his head. She unbuckled his belt and unbuttoned his pants. Christian watched her undress him. His dick stood at attention under his briefs. She slid her hand inside his waistband and caressed him. His dick began to throb. Christian's thinking became hazy.

McKenzie pushed Christian down on the couch. She stood in front of him and removed her t-shirt, revealing small perky breasts. She pulled down her sweats. Stepping out of them, she exposed a full bush of shiny black hair covering her vagina.

Christian was nervous, *turned on, hard as hell,* but nervous. As McKenzie slid on top of him, she grabbed the tip of his dick between her lips and gently brushed it—with slow, short, strokes—against her clit.

McKenzie's nipples were in Christian's face. He grabbed the right one, sucking it into his mouth. She let out a sexy moan and moved in closer so he could take more inside his mouth. He used the tip of his tongue to outline her areola then he kissed her hard nipple. He sucked it with force and gently bit it.

"Oh," she murmured. She slid down on Christian's dick, moving him halfway inside her. Her walls were silky from the gush of juices flowing. McKenzie was hot.

"Mac . . .?" Christian said, struggling for words. "Mac, baby—wait." He pulled her off of him. She was so light, he lifted her higher than he'd meant to.

Surprised, McKenzie looked at him. "What's wrong? What's the matter, baby?" Christian was blown away by the "baby".

"Nothing. I'm feeling good. I'm hard—you are so sexy," he said, kissing her. She took his tongue inside her mouth. She began kissing him, eagerly. Christian had to concentrate to complete his thought.

"I . . . I just don't want you to think you have to do this," he said, seriously.

McKenzie stopped kissing him and looked down into his eyes. "This isn't 'thank you' sex, Christian. I want you. I've wanted you ever since you watched me cum in my bathroom. You remember that day?" She grabbed his dick and slid him back inside her. Christian closed his eyes and lay back.

"The question is . . ." She slid all the way down, covering Christian's dick with her wet juicy walls. Christian grabbed her waist and gently moved her hips up and down.

"Oh yeah. Mmm. Ma—ooh. McKenzie, gurl. You feel sooo good!"

"The question is . . ." McKenzie increased her speed. She gyrated her hips, moving them in a figure eight motion.

"Do you want me?" She stopped moving. Christian opened his eyes to find McKenzie smiling mischievously at him.

Christian smiled. In one swoop, he pushed them off the couch—grabbing her around the waist—he pulled her into him. He carried her up the stairs and into her bedroom. She kissed his neck as he laid her across her bed.

He kissed her slow and hard, shoving his hard dick deep inside her. She pumped eagerly under him, taking all of him inside her. They moved together. Christian was sweating, the droplets showering McKenzie's face. She laughed, licking the salty sweat from around her mouth.

"I'm sorry baby," he said, smiling. McKenzie laughed.

"Here, I've got a remedy for that." she said sliding back.

As he slid out of her, McKenzie turned over on her stomach. She grabbed a pillow and, scooting up on her knees; spread her legs open, welcoming Christian.

"Now, you can sweat as much as you like on my back."

Christian took a good look. It was so sexy. That bush, her lips, hanging. Her full fat vagina, juices oozing down her legs. His dick throbbed. He moved up on the bed, and sat back on his knees. McKenzie pushed back, searching for his dick. He guided himself inside her.

"Umm." she said.

"Oooh." he said.

And their bodies, eagerly, began to move back and forth. Sweat covered McKenzie. Christian kissed her neck and back. He held her hips and pulled her into him. He became harder watching her ass move up under him. She was enjoying herself as much as he was. Her thrusts, the way she was moaning, the way she was grabbing the pillow and scratching at the sheets.

"You like that, McKenzie?" Christian cooed in her ear.

"No baby, I LOVE it. I love your dick inside me," she called back to him, moving faster and harder back into him.

She got him hot. He couldn't remember ever being this excited. Christian could hear his heart beating in his ears. It was loud and speeding up with every stroke.

"Mac! . . . Baby! . . . Oh shit! . . . Baby, I'm . . . I'm . . ." He leaned back, grabbed her hips and watched as he moved in and out of her from behind. McKenzie tightened her walls around him, sending him into a frenzy.

"Let go, baby. Let go!" She called back to him.

"Ahhh. Mmm," Christian grunted.

He could feel the sensation shooting through his body. The heart beat in his head turned into a steady single stream of noise. As the heat rose in the room, and the sweat gushed from his body, Christian felt his chest tighten. The air became thin. And his thighs became taut. His toes curled . . . and . . .

"Ohhh! Mac!" He pulled out, his juices splattered across her butt and back. Then he fell on top of her, exhausted. Satisfied, but exhausted.

♋   ♋   ♋

"You did what?" Denny screamed into the telephone. "Sex. I said, we 'did it'. You know, *We Had Sex*" McKenzie said. "And it was good!" she laughed.

"Okaaay, what happened to 'The Mac don't do sloppy seconds?'"

"Good dick trumps sloppy seconds."

"McKenzie Batiste! He's a married man, for heaven's sake."

"That's their problem, not mine, dear heart."

"Are you kidding me, right now? You're not taking *any* ownership in this adulterous affair?"

"Adulterous affair?" McKenzie laughed. "Really, Denny? That's so mellow dramatic. Are you a writer for The Young and the

Restless? Look, It's not like I'm asking him to leave his wife. I just fucked him— or should I say, he fucked me. And girl, it was good. Did I say he has some good dick?"

"OK. TMI. And really, McKenzie: You're smarter than this. You know how this is going to turn out. They never leave their wives, whether you ask them to or not. You're just going to end up hurt—"

"You can only end up hurt if you don't get what you want. I don't want him to leave his wife. I don't want to be his wife. I just wanted to see what he felt like."

"I hear you, McKenzie. But I know you, hon."

"Oh yeah? And what is it that you know, hon'?"

"I know you play this hard bitch role. But you're a softie underneath that hard shell." Denise paused. "Just promise me you'll be careful, OK? I worry about my friend."

McKenzie smiled. Besides Ahmad, Denise was the only person left in this world who really loved her. This she knew for a fact. She'd give Denny her left kidney, no questions asked. That's how deep they rolled.

"I promise, Kiddo. But you got your friend twisted. I'm not an actor playing a Bitch on TV. I *am* a bitch," she laughed. "Softie died a long time ago."

CHAPTER SIX

Christian

Christian sat in his car, windows up, music off, hands firmly gripping steering wheel, replaying over and over what he just did.

"What the fuck did you just do?" He said into the mirror as if his reflection would answer him back. "Shit! Shit! Shit!"

Christian rubbed his forehead. He looked down at his dick.

"What the fuck did you just do?"

Who was he kidding? His dick wasn't the only one participating in that phenomenal act of passion with that amazing woman upstairs. He wanted her.

"So what, Christian? Every man wants her. *You* are a married man . . . *who doesn't have sex with his own wife!*" He thought about Jada. She wasn't an unattractive woman. If she was walking down the street, any normal brother would try and get at her. Physically, she was quite beautiful. She still took care of herself, worked out, got her hair and nails done, dressed well.

And the bottom line, regardless—was that she was his wife. *His wife.* He couldn't rationalize that away. He had become the asshole of a man he promised himself he would never become: so much for cherishing his wife, so much for being a different kind of man.

Christian sighed, deeply. He felt guilty about having sex with another woman. But he didn't feel bad about making love to McKenzie. His heart was so happy. Christian shook his head.

How the hell did I get here? He said to himself as he scratched his head.

He sat and reflected on their relationship. How it started, how it got to where it is, what he was going to do now.

It was hard for Christian to believe that he had ever experienced happiness in his relationship with Jada. It had been so

137

long since he felt it. But there was evidence: pictures of them cuddling and grinning from ear-to-ear, college friends who recounted how much in love they were *You guys were inseparable!*

Yes, they were the perfect couple. But, somewhere in that perfection, Christian had lost himself and he just didn't know how to get back to that place where he recognized himself. Christian—independent Black man. Not Christian—Jada's boo, Jada's boyfriend, Jada's fiancé, Jada's husband.

Christian was a late bloomer. At seventeen, he hadn't had a real girlfriend. There were girls he talked to, dated—if you wanted to call it that—they went on a couple of dates, but nothing 'official' and definitely nothing long term. He was a tall and lanky looking fellow. Deep chocolate with beautiful straight teeth, and a jheri curl like most other teenagers—but he just didn't have the charisma or the confidence.

To make matters worse, his older brother, Matthew, was *Smoove* and *Fly*. This smooveness only added stress to Christian's already stressful unsocial life. The expectations were unreal. Christian spent the majority of his middle and high school years staying out of Matthew's way and perfecting the craft of *beatin' his meat*.

By the time he reached college, he was completely ready to leave his house of horrors and delve into the richness and freedom campus life had to offer. What he was not prepared for were the women: so many women, so much stress.

Christian was awkward. His height had always made him stand above the rest, causing him to intentionally slouch to try and fit in. Then, he was clumsy. It could have been the size twelve shoes, or just his synapses not connecting properly. He didn't know. What he did know was that his hands got wet and his mouth got dry whenever a fine woman was in his space.

His homeboys would jokingly tease him, but most times try and offer him 'brotherly advice' on how to mack down the women. Desperate to fit in, Christian would try the lines and the techniques, but not many were successful.

It was by chance, one summer, home after his freshman year that he hooked up with an older neighbor for his first sexual experience. He used to do odd jobs for Ms. Williams, growing up— take out her trash, empty her mousetraps, and help her unload groceries from her car. This summer, Ms. Williams was interested in more than help with her household chores.

"Christian," Ms. Williams said, walking into her bedroom. "Come here and help me."

"Yes Ms.—"

Christian's mouth dropped open. Lying in the middle of the bed, stark naked, was the most beautiful pair of titties Christian had ever seen. And he had seen every Hustler issue his stepfather owned, so he'd seen quite a few.

"Come here. There's something I need you to do."

Nervous, Christian inched over, slid on the bed and followed the older woman's lead. He instantly broke into a sweat. He watched Ms. Williams' lips moving, but couldn't hear a word she was saying because his heart was beating so loudly. Frustrated, she took his hand and showed him what to do.

Amazed at the production of warm liquid between her legs, Christian lay quietly next to Ms. Williams, obediently moving his fingers to the rhythm she set. She reached over and slid Christian's pants down, releasing his rock hard penis.

"Come on baby. Come do me. That's what I need you to do."

Christian, nervously, slid on top. Clueless about what to do next, he kind of lingered there. Ms. Williams took him in her hands and guided him in. Five triumphant pumps later, Christian felt a hot rush come from his toes, travel up the inside of his thighs, and forcefully burst through his pulsating dick.

Before he knew what was happening, Christian was lying dizzily next to Ms. Williams breathing deeply, and smiling broadly.

"Wow," was all he could mumble.

Ms. Williams stood up and wrapped her robe around her voluptuous body. She turned and smiled.

"You did well, Christian."

Proud of his accomplishment, he was promptly dismissed and sent back into the world a de-virginized man, ready to experience more of that explosive feeling.

Christian returned to SFSU, a new man. By the end of the summer, he had grown two inches, filled out, and developed a broad chest, some ass, and definitely a confidence he didn't have freshman year. And did the women pick up on it.

It wasn't like there was an onslaught of women jocking. But he had to hustle on his work-study job to get extra hours so he could afford to date—which he was doing regularly. Nothing serious, but he did have an opportunity to pop off more than two pumps during his infrequent romp sessions, *he could still count the number on one hand.*

It was in Dr. Rhasheed's African American class that Christian caught Jada staring at him. He was passing a stack of papers with a class assignment on it to the right, when he caught those big Walt Disney doe eyes locked on him. When their eyes met, she smiled coyly and turned away.

A couple of weeks of this and Christian felt confident that Jada was interested. After the last class, right before Spring break, Christian decided to approach her.

She was walking down the hall with two of her sorority sisters, when he jogged and caught up with her. Christian's mouth watered at the sight of all that ass stuffed snuggly in a pair of dark blue jeans. He strained to focus on her face, but with all that junk in the trunk he was finding it extremely difficult.

Gold shirt, he said to himself, *she has on a gold shirt and white tennis shoes. And gold bamboo hoop earrings. Focus, focus, focus, Christian.*

But man, I'd like to grind up against all that ass stuffed in them blue jeans! His dick replied.

"Uh, hey—excuse me," Christian said as he touched Jada's shoulder.

Jada slowed down, while her sisters snickered and walked off. Smiling, Jada turned to face Christian.

"Yes?"

"How you doin', I'm Christian," he said, extending his hand nervously. Jada shook his hand and shifted her books to her right side.

"Jada."

"Jada. I'm sorry I pulled you away from your girls."

"Oh, it's OK. I'll catch up with them later." Christian smiled. They turned and walked down the hall.

Christian discreetly slid his warm, wet palms down the sides of his pants.

"What are you doing for Spring break?" Christian said.

"I was trying to get out to Freak 'Nic, but couldn't pull together enough money for the plane ticket."

"Oh yeah? You been before?"

"Mm Hm. I went last year with my girls. You?"

"Naw. Never been. I hear it's over the top, though."

"Yeah, it's that all right. But its fun, I mean, I had fun hanging out with my girls."

"So, what's your Plan B, then?"

"I'm going to stay here over the break, actually. If I can't get to hotlanta I won't be going home to mom's curfews and restrictions. You know what I mean?"

"Yeah, I do. I'll be here too." Christian cleared his throat. "Maybe . . . I don't know. Maybe we can go catch a movie or something?"

"Sure, I'd like that."

Christian spent every night of Spring break at Jada's apartment.

♋   ♋   ♋

"What up, son?" Ronnie said to Christian, shoving his feet off the coffee table as he plopped down on the couch, next to Christian.

"What up, dog?"

"Where the hell you been? We swooped up some AKA honeys at the Student Union the other night, after that whack ass Sigma party."

"Uh huh," Christian replied, "what's that got to do with me?"

"A bruh was gone hook you up, son—I mean, I can handle two or three or more, but being the brotha that I am, I was gone give you one. You know what I mean, son? Just trying to be a generous brotha and all."

"Nigga, you couldn't give away air if you wanted to, let alone give away a broad. Shut the fuck up!" Brandon said, throwing a koosh ball at Ronnie.

"Man, cut that shit out. Call me a nigga one mo' time, and you, son, will part with several of those monstrously large horse teeth in yo' grill, yo."

"Man, cut that shit out. It don't matter. I was busy, anyway." Christian said.

"Christian was *busy* getting pussy whipped with baby dip with the bodacious ass!" James said. "What's honey's name? She's a Delta, right?"

"SG Rho, son!" Christian said, throwing a pillow at James. "And get out of mine, OK?"

"Yo, son, is that Ant'ny's girl? Short, 'bout yay high? A-symmetrical bob, with the sexy swoop in front of her eye?" Ronnie said, in animated form.

"Yep. That's the one. Short— wit' ass for days!" James chimed in.

Christian threw another pillow at James.

"Shut up, dude. Damn. Is that all you see?" Christian said.

"When she's in my path, hell, yeah!" James said.

"Yo, son, on a serious tip. You better watch out for that one." Ronnie said, shaking his head.

"Man, why are you trippin'? Jada is cool," Christian said. He got up from the couch and walked to the kitchen. He'd been kicking it with Jada since Spring break, and he was really feeling her.

"Chris, yo—why would I lie to you? I am a staunch supporter of *Get the ass, Get the snatch movement*. Seriously. I'm just saying—she was with Ant'ny a long time. And yo, that mutha fucka is craay-ay-zee!" Ronnie said.

"What's that got to do with Jada?" Christian said, pouring himself some water out the fridge.

"Son, word has it he used to beat that ass—regularly."

Christian swirled around. "What? He hit her?" Anger rose in Christian's throat.

"Yep. Regularly." Silence held the room.

"Well, obviously she wasn't with that. They ain't together anymore," Christian said.

"Dude, they ain't together because star cornerback left her for that AKA honey, what's her name, Jay?"

"Janine. Now that's one fiiiiiiiine honey right there!" James howled to the ceiling.

"Yo, son, you stupid," Ronnie said. They all laughed.

Christian stood behind the counter contemplating the news that Jada was once in an abusive relationship with Anthony Carter. He was solid. Buff. Christian couldn't imagine him putting his big ass hands on Jada. He'd break her. She was so small and fragile.

"Anyway yo. If he hadn't left Jada for the new shorty, she'd still be with him. That says old girl ain't wrapped too tight to me."

"Yeah, well, we all make mistakes. I'm sure she sees the error of her ways," Christian said.

"She's high maintenance dude. Trust me. Ant'ny may have been kickin' her ass, but the booster club keeps his wallet lined and he kept her tight," Ronnie said. He and James gave each other dap.

"Jada's not like that. She's down to earth," Christian said.

Christian didn't have a lot of money. The partial scholarship paid for tuition, but Christian had to work for book money and his other expenses—rent, food, and extra-curricular activities. As a matter of fact, things had gotten so tight; he'd gone downtown and gotten on public assistance. He qualified for, and received, monthly food stamps. It was those food stamps that paid for the steak dinners he had been preparing for Jada the times she came over to his place.

"No, she ain't. She's high maintenance son, and bougie." Ronnie said.

"No, she's not. Ronnie, man—you know my finances ain't all that. And we've been kickin' it strong. I'm telling you, she's real."

"You been taking her out, buying her gifts and shit?" James said.

"No. I ain't got it like that."

"Well, what are you doing?" Ronnie said.

"The most I do is cook dinner. And we rent movies. But that's pretty much it," Christian replied.

And it was true. He didn't tell the fellas they were candlelight dinners—grilled filet mignon steaks, with sautéed vegetables, handmade cheese potatoes, French bread, and a dessert.

"What do you cook, Betty Crocker – what the fuck? Ain't the bitch supposed to do the cooking," James said. "She got yo ass pussy whipped for real nigga." James looked, quickly, at Ronnie.

"I heard you, son. And don't refer to our women as no bitches either. One more slip up and I'ma have to split your lip yo."

"Aw'ight. Aw'ight. Chill. It's habit. I don't mean nothin' by it. Damn," James said. He slumped down in the couch.

"Check this. I'm not going to have that conversation with you again. And in response to Romeo over there, *what do you cook*, Mr. Renaissance Man?"

"Oh, hee hee hee." Christian said sarcastically. "You guys are making way too much of this. I cook normal, regular, meals. You know? Steaks."

"Steaks!" Ronnie and James said, at the same time.

"Dude. High maintenance. Say it with me," Ronnie said. "Trust, son, you stop grillin' up the steaks, ol' girl's gone stop giving up the goodies. Trust. A bruh wouldn't lie to you."

"Yo, Steak Ums! Yo boys wouldn't lie to you," James said, walking over to Christian and slapping him on his back.

144

Christian didn't reply. Cooking steaks was the last thing on his mind. The information about Anthony had him twisted.

♋   ♋   ♋

A couple of months had gone by and Christian was struggling financially.
He had been spending a lot of time at Jada's. One night she confronted him.

"How come we don't go out anymore?" Jada sat on her chair in her bedroom, arms folded across her chest.

"Because I just don't have it right now, Jada." Christian had noticed Jada was getting snippy and irritable when he came through lately.

"Well, *why* don't you have it anymore?"

"Because I have bills, Jada, and I've been trying to help you out here and there." Jada sat quietly.

"So that means we can't go out at all anymore?"

"Do you have money for us to go out, Jada? Because I just don't have it." Jada sat, looking at her nails.

"Christian, you spend a lot of time over here. I think you should go half on
my rent and groceries."

Christian looked at her like she was crazy. He had already paid hertelephone bill. She said it was going to get cut off because she had been calling him so much. And then there was the money for her Poli Sci textbook because she was short and 'needed a little help'.

He was trying to help Jada, but the truth was, he was barely scraping by himself.

"I spend a lot of time over here because you don't like coming over to my place, Jay." Christian said.

"You have roommates. We have more privacy here."

"Yeah, but I have groceries at my place. I just happen to eat here because I'm over here."

"Exactly. You are here. You eat here, so you should contribute Christian." Christian didn't reply, but he made a mental note to spend less time at her place.

It didn't use to be a problem. Christian remembered back to a time when they could barely stay away from each other . . .

Christian was hard as a rock, dry humping Jada like he was in high school—*for most boys; it was early college for him.* They had been spending every day together for the past two months, kissing, grinding, touching. He was trying to take it slow, be respectful, and move at her pace. But, honestly, he thought he was going to burst.

They were completely naked and sweaty. Christian slowly slid his fingers inside Jada until she arched her back and wiggled around her bed. He watched her face squint into pleasure, and listened as she whimpered in response to his touch. Jada was wet.

Christian gently slid between Jada's legs. Usually she protested, but this time she spread her legs open. Excited by the invitation, Christian swirled the tip of his penis around Jada's ready opening. She grabbed his butt, and pulled him down toward her.

Ready to slide in, Christian heard the familiar strobe of his heartbeat fill his head. *Swoosh, swoosh, swoosh.* Just before he slid inside, Jada froze.

"Christian?"

Incoherent, Christian continued to try and gain entry into the wet pleasure dome he had dreamed about for weeks, imagined vividly the feel as he choked his chicken.

"Yeah?"

"Christian, look at me. Christian."

"Yes, Jada? Yes, what's wrong?" Christian said, focusing.

"You love me, right?"

Christian watched Jada's lips move, but wasn't quite sure he was hearing straight. Did she just ask him if he loved her? Loved her? *Um, no.* He didn't love Jada. He was diggin' her, and he definitely wanted her, but he was sure he wasn't ready for love.

"Jada, I—"

"Because I can't give myself to you unless you love me."

146

Christian paused for an entire second. He was a sociology major, but it didn't take a rocket scientist to figure out this equation and how his next word could move him closer to getting his hard dick inside her luscious pussy.

This was the moment. Like Adam and Even in the Garden.

The "PG" version is the version told in the bible. *Eve handed Adam the apple, and told him to bite of it.* The true version is probably rated "R" and closer to the truth.

Adam, after weeks of creating animals and mates for each of them, and watching them get their swerve on, decided to get his hump on with his mate, Eve. They kissed, and touched, and discovered what that serpent under Adam's fig leaf was really created for.

The bible says, "This 'serpent' began to coax Eve into eating an apple . . ." And then she, in turn, convinced Adam to take a bite from the forbidden Tree of Knowledge. The likely way it went down is one of two ways: 1. Eve ate the apple. Women do what the hell they want to do—end of story. Or, 2. Adam and Eve were told not to do the nasty because doing so would take you to a place of forbidden knowledge. So, they were dry humping. Eve *decided*— because everybody knows, sex only happens when the woman decides it's going to happen— that she was going to let the serpent swim in her ocean. So, Adam is kissing Eve, grinding her naked body—just lovin' her up. He slides two fingers in the coo coo. Eve spreads them creamy thighs open, evah so gently. GREEN LIGHT! GREEN LIGHT! GO ADAM! GO! Excited, Adam starts to guide the serpent in, when BAM! Eve pumps the brakes. Errrrr!

"Adam?" Eve coos. Adam is still trying to guide Mr. Serpent in that elusive hole. "ADAM!" Adam is jarred out of his sexual fog. "Look at me, Adam."

"Yes baby, what is it?" Adam says.

"You love me, right?"

"Eve, baby I . . ." What he started to foolishly tell Miss Eve is that Love wasn't necessary. None of the other primates needed it. They just found their partner, got hot and bothered, and did the do. What is this love shit she was talking about?

"Because I can't give myself to you if you don't love me,"

Eve said, dripping
wet. Adam's dick, steel hard . . . tip in, shaft throbbing and ready for
slippery friction, is looking at him like, *You betta not fuck this up for
me.*

Adam paused for an entire second. He was a Neanderthal,
the first Man on earth, but it didn't take a rocket scientist to figure
out this equation and how his next word could move him closer to
getting his hard dick inside her luscious pussy.

"Yes." <Insert any man's name here> *Adam, Christian,*
ANY man's name will do, said.
<Insert any woman's name here> *Eve, Jada* smiled and
opened her legs.

Did he bite the apple? It probably was a cherry, lodged
deeply in the silky fleshy folds of the woman who started it all. But
the story is still the same, thousands of years later. Men saying yes,
when they really don't mean it. But are too smart *or maybe dumb,*
depending on how the relationship ends up, to say No, knowing
where that *won't* get them at the end of that conversation.

So much is lost over the years in translation. But Christian
was pretty sure his version was as close to truth as you were going
to get about the serpent, the apple, and the power of the pussy.

The next day in the quad, Christian was sitting with his
homeboys, when Jada and her girls walked up. Jada slid her arms
around Christian's neck.

"Hi baby," Jada said. Christian smiled

"Hey you," he said, returning her kiss. Jada smiled and
linked her arms inside his. She laid her head on his chest. Christian
felt warm inside.

"What's this all about?" Ricky said. "I thought we was boys?
When were you going to tell me J-J here is your new shorty?"

Christian was about to tell Ricky that they were cool but it
wasn't nothing official like that.

"Christian, you haven't told your boys you're my
boyfriend?" Christian sat, looking dumbfounded. "Sorry fellas, I'm
off the market. I'm Christian's and only Christian's. She wrapped
her arms around his waist. "And he's mine all mine, right, baby?"

Christian looked over at Ronnie, who was doing circle
motions around his right ear. He mouthed, "Crazy". Christian rolled

his eyes. Jada wasn't crazy. She was moving a bit too fast for him, but it was cool. He was feeling her, and what he felt surely felt good.

It made him nervous actually; he couldn't remember the last time he felt this way. It had been so long since he trusted anyone. Since he felt safe. For the first time in a long time Christian felt a part of something that made him happy.

♋　·　♋　　♋

Christian was seven when his dad left his mom. Those were the exact words his dad used when he told him.

"I'm leaving your mother. I'm not leaving you or your brother and sister. I want you to understand that."

Christian stared at his father. Of course, he didn't understand that. How was he supposed to know the difference between him leaving his mom and leaving him and his brother and sister, when his dad wasn't living in his house anymore? He wasn't seeing him every day, and he was no longer a part of his, and his brother and sister's normal routine. In his mind, his dad was leaving them all.

"We got married too young, and for the wrong reasons."

"Well, how old are you supposed to be when you get married, and what are the right reasons?" Christian asked. His father rubbed his beard, pulled out his cigarettes, lit one up and took a long deep drag.

"There is no set age, son. It's more about knowing yourself, first. You need to know who you are before you take on the responsibility of trying to keep someone else happy. If that person ain't happy, there ain't nothing you can do to make them happy." He knelt down on his knee and stared Christian in the face.

"Love is not enough. Don't ever believe love is enough, son. You have to want the same things—share the same values. Otherwise, you grow apart. Once that happens, you become angry, and frustrated, and unfulfilled. We weren't put on this earth to live like that. If you're not happy, son, it's a waste of a life." He looked down at Christian, who looked completely lost.

"I know you're too young to understand right now. But remember what I'm saying to you. A relationship can work, but you have to want the same things in life, and believe in the same things. When you get old, sex and good looks ain't the glue no more, all you got is each other—if you don't like that person, you are fucked."

He took another long drag on his cigarette, flicked it in the street, and walked over to his brick red Lincoln Continental. The

150

red Continental his family would load into, and go to the beach in, on Saturdays. They'd spend the entire day there. His mom would pack fried chicken and potato salad, his dad would help them build sand castles with amazingly deep moats, and he, Angela, and Matthew would spend hours splashing in the water. They'd get the big waffle cones with three scoops of ice cream. Christian would always get three scoops of vanilla, but Matthew would get three different flavors. Angela would have chocolate chip.

The red Continental was Christian's limo. He'd sit in the backseat and his driver would take him to destinations all around the city. Along the way, he and his siblings would lay claim on their cars.

"I got the red one!" Christian would scream.

"I already called that one," Matthew would say.

"No, you didn't!"

"Yes I did. That one is mine. And so is that green one, right there!" Matthew would say, laughing. Christian would sock his brother. Matthew would shove him into his sister, who would scream bloody murder.

"Cut it out, back there!" his dad would say, and the boys would quickly quiet down. No more family days in the long red limo.

"Chris. Son?" his father said. "Look at me." But Christian couldn't look at his father. His head was swimming. The words his dad said were swooshing in his head like the waves at the beach—*you're fucked*. His dad felt fucked. He was leaving them because he and his mom didn't share the same values. What did that mean?

"I love you, son. That won't ever change. I will always be there for my kids."

The tension in Christian's throat was so tight he thought he would pass out from a lack of oxygen. He took a slow, strained breath. His chest shook as the air filled his lungs. It felt like hot splinters were floating down his nasal passage and lodging inside the lining of his chest cavity, searing into his soul, like a hot brand on an unsuspecting animal. Like how that moment, and that conversation that day, were forever branded into his mind.

At seven, all Christian could understand was that his mother was in pain. Seeing her cry more than he had ever seen her cry his entire life left him feeling helpless and angry. How could his dad do this to her? She almost lost her job for calling in sick so many times. Her wardrobe consisted of a turquoise terry cloth robe and a pair of raggedy, worn pink slippers. Her accessories, his dad's purple and gold Laker's commuter cup of whatever alcoholic beverage she could get her hands on (or, make Matthew get Jasper, the neighborhood wino, to buy at the liquor store on the corner), breath mints and Visine.

His dad left her. And true to his word, he was there for his kids. He had them every other week, bought them clothes and was active in school and extra-curricular activities. He was no longer in the home, but he was still a part of their lives.

But, he had left his mom. And in her despair--her drunken stupor—she turned to Derren, the neighbor across the street. At first it was just a hook up, every now and then. But the vulture slowly sunk his claws into her and, before you knew it, he had moved in. Desperate to have a man, *obviously any man,* in her life, Christian's mother tolerated the abuse.

Christian felt she was afraid of another man leaving her because there was no reason for him to be there. He didn't add to the household. He didn't like her kids. He was short, unattractive, and not the sharpest tool in the shed. But he wasn't too stupid, he got his mom to put his name on the deed to the house. He took out loans against the equity to pay for toys and live the lifestyle his meatpacking job couldn't pay for alone.

Christian blamed his dad. If he hadn't left her, she wouldn't have turned into an alcoholic who needed a man – any man. And him, his brother, and sister wouldn't have had to live in that hell hole all their childhood, miserable, in fear, feeling unloved and unwanted, keeping secrets, and watching his mother's husband beat his mom to a pulp.

It would take years before Christian would learn the truth about his mom. He would learn that his mom had been a functional alcoholic the majority of his parents' marriage. That was one of the reasons why his dad left her. The other was that he felt smothered. *Drowned*, his dad would say, *by her neediness.* It was too much responsibility for one person to bear.

"I couldn't be responsible for another person's happiness," his dad would say.

It was ironic and scary that Christian found himself repeating the same words about Jada. The difference between him and his dad, though, was that he didn't have the courage it took to leave his marriage, although everything in him told him to.

It would take Christian going through his own living hell before he understood what his dead meant that day. Years of trying to fix the unfixable, arguing for three days straight over something so mundane, that by day three he'd just apologize because he had forgotten what the hell they were arguing about and just wanted to have peace.

Christian saw the red flags early, but he ignored them. He loved Jada and didn't want to believe that she wasn't the woman for him. She was his first true love, college sweetheart. Christian tried hard to keep her happy, believing that in the end she would see the value in that and work just as hard to make their relationship work. But she didn't. Instead, she moped and pouted until she got her way.

Years of watching his words and where his eyes wandered in Jada's presence for fear that she'd mistake a statement or read into a look, wore on him. He did it to try and prevent setting her off on another one of her tirades, where she'd need convincing that he loved her only, needed her only, and wanted her only – an exercise that became more draining every time. And the more he did it, the more he resented her.

At first, there was a part of him that thought it was cute. He'd come in and save the day, being what he wished his mom had, a man to save her, treasure, and protect her. He wanted to be that man who rode in to save the day. Being there for her like he was in college, providing for his woman. But years later, they were in the same situation and he was still giving, and she was still taking. The expectation set, Jada wasn't prepared to give up her hold of the reins. It was her way or no way.

At the time, he really believed that their issues were things they could work on as a couple; or that they were things that compromise would remedy. But as time went on, he became resigned to the fact that Jada worked inside a vacuum, and somewhere within that space, compromise didn't exist outside of her belief that Christian should be the one doing the compromising.

♋   ♋   ♋

CHAPTER SEVEN
Jada

By the end of sophomore year, Christian and Jada were an established couple. Christian was happy and Jada was thrilled. Christian was very attentive and supportive, not at all like Anthony. Anthony was – well, a jock. While Jada enjoyed the prestige of being Anthony's girl, there was something to be said for being the center of someone's world.

She knew she was the center of Christian's world because he had a mini-shrine of her in his room. There were fourteen pictures of her and of them on his dresser, along with little mementoes: a teddy bear she had given him for Valentines; candles from a few of their dinners; and tickets from a play, a concert, and some other fundraisers they had attended at the University— memorabilia of the things they had done together.

She knew Christian was sprung. Anthony wasn't ever sprung. As a matter of fact, most times, she couldn't keep Anthony's attention long enough to know he cared. The only time she knew he did was when he saw her talking to another guy. Anthony got hot. And that's when he'd show he was jealous. That's also when he'd lose his temper and lay hands on her. It was crazy, but he would get so enraged she knew he loved her.

"I don't want to see you talking to another man!" Anthony would say.

He'd slap her, or squeeze her arm real tight, but then he'd become so loving and attentive. And their sex was phenomenal afterward. But it never lasted long. Nothing lasted long with Anthony. Even though Jada endured the abuse and tried her best to make him a better man, he hurt her and eventually left her for someone new.

Jada didn't have to worry about any of those things with Christian. He wasn't an aggressive man. He never raised his voice, never once forcefully touched her, and he never made her feel invisible. And she didn't have to worry about him leaving her. He wasn't the type to leave a woman.

He was the type of man her mother called *A Keeper*. Not that her mom ever had one herself. Her mom went through men like she went through underwear, always looking for *Mr. Right*. A generational habit Jada was determined not to repeat. All of the women in her family managed not to find a good man. She was so proud to have landed Christian. He was college educated, handsome, smart, and a provider. The day they got married was the happiest day of her life. No one in her family had been ever been married. It was a badge of honor that she wore with a great sense of pride. Christian was a keeper, and Jada would do everything in her power to keep him.

"A Keeper," according to Janet Smith, "was a good man who loved his woman, had a good upbringing, a good job, and would do everything in his power to take care of his woman." It was a bit soon to know about Christian's earning potential, but based off what Jada had experienced this past summer he would do everything in his power to take care of her—even if he couldn't afford it.

She loved that about him. How he wanted to make her happy, even if it meant he had to make personal sacrifices to do it. It proved to her how much he truly cared. Over the years as he demonstrated less and less how he felt for her physically and emotionally, she found herself making him demonstrate it in other ways: purchases they couldn't afford a lavish wedding at twice their budget, a new car, jewelry. Christian would always make it happen. He'd take out a loan, or take on the extra debt. Jada didn't want for anything--except the emotional demonstration of his love.

Back in college Christian could look at her and she knew without a doubt that he adored her. They used to lie on her couch and watch TV while he ran his fingers through her hair and stroked her back. Now days, sex was horrible. In college they fucked like jack rabbits; now she practically had to beg him to have sex with her twice a month. This emotional distance made her feel insecure. He did everything else that demonstrated his love and commitment, but the lack of physical and emotional commitment drove her crazy. No matter how much she tried to make him, he wouldn't turn back into the amazing romantic he used to be when they first fell in love.

Christian was a smart man. But he needed a push every now and then to get on the right track. Jada would do things to *help* make sure things went her way, like getting his dad to make her case for her. Christian hated arguing with his dad. And even worse, he hated anyone thinking he didn't have his shit together or that they were having problems in their marriage. So she'd *drop in* on dad and casually *share* information with him so he could convince Christian to go along with her plans. She quickly became friends with his sister and did the same. Jada would work all angles to get what she wanted.

There was a small part of her that understood what Christian meant when he said her manipulation and jealousy pushed him away. But she knew better. She knew that everything she'd done and continued to do was in the best interest of their relationship. Christian just couldn't see it right now. Like the wedding: waiting on Christian to pop the question, they probably would have never gotten married. But her strategically using his infidelity to lock in a wedding date helped him to secure a wife who would be by his side through thick and thin. As Christian's dad said at their reception; he'd gained a strong, beautiful, smart helpmate. She was all those things, and more.

They would have everything she had imagined for her life: wealth, prestige, and a family. Christian was just so slow to move. He needed to weigh out everything to make sure it was the right choice. She knew what she was doing. He just needed to trust her. These days she was working overtime in getting him to do that. Which annoyed the shit out of her. All he had to do was review all the decisions she'd made thus far; he'd see that they had moved them closer to where they needed to be as a couple.

Instead he seemed more and more agitated. But she'd make him see. She knew what was best for them. And once he did, he'd go back to loving her the way he used to. She just needed to make him see. She had a few more ideas up her sleeve . . .

♋   ♋   ♋

Christian exited the 405 freeway and headed toward campus. It was a beautiful, sunny California day. He weaved in and out of traffic easily, but was caught at the second light before the turn to campus. Tapping his fingers on the steering wheel to an *Earth, Wind and Fire* classic, he surveyed his surroundings.

He was surprised to see McKenzie's jeep two cars ahead of him. She was flailing her hands about. He watched a minute, trying to figure out what she was doing. The light changed and she took off.

Christian followed closely. McKenzie looked like she was having a dramatic conversation with someone. She moved her head left to right, two counts on each side. She extended her right arm, palm up to the ceiling, as if sending a meaningful prayer up to the heavens. She held it there for a while—Christian imagined her, holding a long note—but to what song? She wasn't bobbing and weaving like it was a hip-hop song. Her movements were intentional, fluid, and slow. It had to be a slow song. *McKenzie? Listening to a slow song—by choice? Nah . . .*

She drove like a dude, weaving in and out of lanes and sliding in between cars. Christian easily followed suit. He smiled as he drove behind her. She continued to move to whatever song she was listening to, waving her hands about, when she wasn't making quick turns, in and out of the midday traffic.

He stayed three cars behind, watching her from a distance as she turned into campus. She slowly drove up and down the parking lot until she found a space close to the aquatic center. She grabbed her duffle bag and slid out of the shiny black jeep. Today's outfit consisted of a baby blue and grey nylon Adidas sweat suit, and matching blue, grey, and white Adidas tennis shoes. The corners of

Christian's mouth turned up as he reflected on her walk-in closet full of shoes.

McKenzie headed in the direction of the aquatic center. Christian watched her until she made it safely into the building. He scanned the quad, looking for the Major, before he took off to look for a parking space.

♋   ♋   ♋

McKenzie was on her way to the library when she heard her name being called from the food court area.

"Over here, Mac!" Christian stood and waved.

He was sitting at a table on the patio with a tall thin brotha with locks. She smiled and walked over to the table.

"Hey Christian, what's going on?"

"Aw, not much." He walked over and hugged her. "This is my Frat, TJ—Theodore Johnson. TJ, this is my classmate, McKenzie Batiste."

TJ stood and shook McKenzie's hand.

"It's a pleasure, sister. W-won't you join us?" He said in a deep, sexy voice. McKenzie smiled.

"Pleasure to meet you as well. Actually, I was on my way to the library. I don't want to disturb your male bonding time."

"Have a seat!" Christian said. "I see this negro every week."

"S-S-So, wha-what are you trying to say?" TJ said. "That bee-cause you see me f-frequently, m-m-myyy time isn't valuable?"

"What I'm saying is, McKenzie isn't interrupting. And that we would love to have her company—give me a break from listening to this bullshit you're kickin' over here." Christian said. They all laughed.

"W-w-well, let's ask the sister wha-what she thinks?" TJ scooted his chair up and faced McKenzie.

"Yeah. Go ahead. Let's get an unbiased person to tell you that's bullshit," Christian said, sitting back in his chair.

"Ho-ho-hold up, playa! Clearly you're tr-tr-trying to influence her be-be-fore she can even h-h-hear what a bruh has to say," TJ said.

"Oh, I have my own mind—you don't have to worry about me being influenced." McKenzie said crossing her legs. She was intrigued.

"Oh really? Lookie hear. Mi-miss Thing has her own mind, huh?" TJ said. "OK. T-tell me what you think." TJ looked over at Christian and winked.

Christian laughed and smiled at McKenzie.

"This brotha is m-m-mad because I called his ass bougie." TJ said.

Christian sat up.

"Can you believe that shit?" He said. McKenzie smiled.

"Shut up. Let me s-s-state my case. This brotha is bougie because h-h-his lifestyle says he's bougie."

"How so?" McKenzie said.

"W-w-well . . . he'll tell you, himself, he doesn't h-hang out east of the 110 freeway; he takes his car to the c-car wash; he has face and h-hair products; and, he gets m-manicures and pedicures."

McKenzie enjoyed the insights into Christian's personal life. She laughed at the basis for TJ's accusation.

"Is he b-bougie, or not?" TJ asked. Christian looked disgusted. McKenzie found it all hilariously funny.

"Well, I guess I define bougie a little differently, TJ."

""What?"

"Thank you!" Christian said.

"Wait! Wait! Listen!" She said, laughing. "When I think of a bourgeois person, I think of a snob—someone who thinks they are above or better than another person."

"Right! That's what I was trying to explain to this fool."

"Well, if you m-make it a point not to associate with f-folks who live east of the 110—what do you c-call that?"

McKenzie laughed. "You have a point there—unless, the reason why you don't associate with those folks is because you have nothing in common."

"B-black folks always h-have something in common."

"True. True. Stuff like our history . . . religion . . . culture, right?" McKenzie said.

"A-a-absolutely."

"But when it comes to lifestyles, there's a distinct difference, don't you think?" McKenzie said. Christian sat back and listened.

"What do you m-mean?"

"Well, you'd probably find Christian here at—what? A town hall with Farrakhan or a spoken word concert?" She looked in Christian's direction. "Where you'd probably find the folks east of the 110 freeway at a R. Kelly concert, or Ludacris concert or something? They probably spend most of their income on clothes, cars, and their hair. Where your frat here, probably has a diversified portfolio of investments. And I'm sure he owns real estate that has more equity in it than the depreciating value of his car." Christian clapped lightly and TJ nodded his head.

"An-and so you think the t-t-two lifestyles could never mix?"

"Sure, they could mix. They could do a BBQ or an event where they didn't have to engage much. But they definitely wouldn't make the best neighbors. But on being bougie . . ." She looked at Christian and said, "He thinks he's simple, *au naturel*—" McKenzie smiled. "But he's far from it." She looked back at TJ. "He is complicated, meticulous, he takes care of himself—his possessions. He might even be borderline pretty boy--"

"Hey, hey. I am not a pretty boy!" Christian said, rolling his eyes. TJ ate it up.

"Hush! L-l-let the woman finish." But McKenzie stood instead. "I am finished. You've known this brotha longer than I have. You know I'm right." McKenzie grabbed her book bag and swung it over her shoulder.

"I don't think he's 'bougie'. I think he's a good guy. Thank you for the chat, fellas. I really need to get to the library. TJ, it was nice meeting you. Christian, I'll see you in class, tonight."

The men stood. TJ shook McKenzie's hand. Christian hugged her goodbye.

♋   ♋   ♋

Professor Telfair wrapped up lecture early so the groups could use the last portion of class to meet. As the group filed into their seats, Christian happened to glance over at McKenzie and caught a panicked look flash across her face.

He moved in close.

"What's wrong Mac?"

McKenzie, quickly, regained her composure.

"Huh? Oh, nothing." She hesitated for a second.

"Are you sure?" Christian asked, watching her closely.

"Yeah—no. I forgot my fuckin' notebook in my truck. I'll be back." She stood up to leave. Christian figured the panicked look was probably McKenzie worrying whether or not she'd run into her stepfather on the way.

"Where's your truck? I'll go get it."

"What? Don't be ridiculous," she said, walking past him. Christian gently grabbed her elbow.

"It's dark outside, Mac. It's not safe. You know there's been a number of rapes reported this semester—just give me your key. I'll run and get it. It's no big deal." He didn't release her elbow.

McKenzie only paused for a minute. She handed him her keys. Christian could see the tension leave her forehead.

"OK. OK. It's parked in Lot 'C', about four rows east of the aquatic center entrance. I got lucky today," McKenzie said smiling.

"Cool. I'll be right back."

Christian left class and headed toward Lot 'C'. The sun was just about to set below the horizon. He started to jog so he could make it to the parking lot before the last of the light disappeared.

The jeep was right where she said it was. Christian pressed the remote to unlock the door. The chirp and click let him know the alarm was unmanned. He opened the door to a strong whiff of Jasmine. The truck was impeccably clean. He looked around for a second—there it was, on the floor, in the back. He grabbed it and closed the door.

Before he could get ten feet away, Christian remembered how intently McKenzie had been singing on the way in and stopped mid-stride. His curiosity got the best of him, and he headed back to the truck.

He opened the door, reached over the driver's seat, and inserted the key in the ignition. He had to know what song had her so entranced. He turned the key and started the car. The music blared out so loudly, Christian jumped back and hit his head on the door jam.

"Fuck!" He massaged his head.

Memories and distant refrain,
visions of the love we just made.

That was Teena Marie. Christian slid into the driver's seat and closed the door. *McKenzie was singing to a Teena Marie jam?* It was an old cut. But he couldn't remember the title. He listened to the lyrics.

Christian sat stunned as he listened to the words of the song. Teena was reflecting on making love . . . and if what she was feeling was really love? If her heart could do what her lover wanted it to do? Before he could actually process it all—possibly put it all together so it could make any sense, the song started over.

She has it on repeat?
Teena Marie crooned about feeling the fire in her lover's eyes, and tasting the fire for the first time. She compared his sweet lips to the taste of cherry wine. She said that his caressing her knocks to her to her knees, and he keeps her safe and warm - feeling like a quiet storm. Christian pulled the key out of the ignition, grabbed the notebook and jogged back to class.

"Did you have a hard time finding it?" McKenzie said as he handed her the notebook and keys.

"No. It was right where you said it was. You're right; you lucked up on a prime space." He smiled at her.

"I told you." She smiled back. "Thank you for going to get my notebook." McKenzie didn't want to admit it, but she was glad he volunteered to go get it. After the Major's appearance in the quad, she was nervous about him possibly lurking in the parking lot waiting for her.

"No problem." He smiled.

At home, later that night, Christian shuffled through his record collection until he found the album he was looking for. He slid the CD in his changer, clicked off his lights, and lay back in his bed. The room was dark with the exception of the green numbers on the CD changer. As the numbers started to increase, 01, 02, 03, 04, 05, the music slowly started to play.

Looking out my window today,
seeing nothing but your sweet face,
I wonder what this feeling can be, what's come over me? Can it be love?
Lying in your arms I have felt, a space and time that make my hear melt
I wonder what this feeling can be? What's this ecstasy?

This was where the song had come on in McKenzie's truck today. Christian listened to the words. His heart raced. His mind was going a mile a minute. He knew McKenzie didn't like mushy songs. Why was she listening to this song? And why did she have it on repeat? It must mean something to her if she kept singing it over and over? Christian sat up and pushed repeat on the changer.

He couldn't help but get excited. *Does Mac think she's in love with me?* It made sense; they had just made love. The thought made Christian warm inside.

165

CHAPTER EIGHT
Melvin

During the weeks that passed the Major didn't show up on campus. McKenzie had been extra careful though, changing up her routes home and watching to make sure she wasn't being followed. She didn't put anything past that man.

Tonight the group met up at one of Camille's favorite Karaoke bars for their weekly meeting. McKenzie walked in and scanned the room looking for her classmates. The hairs on the back of her neck bristled—she couldn't see him, but she knew Christian was close by.

Christian watched her scanning the room. He lay in the cut, in a dark area of the bar, sipping on an Apple Martini. He got there early to people watch. McKenzie walked over to the Karaoke machine and glanced through the titles. Christian crept up behind her.

"Are you going to sing for us, tonight?" He whispered into her neck, directly under her earlobe. McKenzie shivered. She closed her eyes and tried to compose herself. But it was too late, Christian saw her response.

"Only if you're singing with me?" McKenzie turned to face him, slowly rubbing her butt against him. Christian smiled.

"You better watch yourself, girl. Don't start nothing you can't finish."

"Oh, you know I have a spectacular finish," she said, running her fingers down his chest.

He looked--and smelled delicious! He had on a black V-neck sweater with a white t-shirt underneath. Some baggy blue jeans and black Kenneth Cole boots.

"Or have you forgotten already?" McKenzie said. Christian smiled, stepping back.

"I haven't forgotten. But there's someone else who's very interested in finding out." McKenzie looked perplexed.

"Really, who else?" She looked around the room.

"No one in here—well, actually with that outfit, I'm sure there are quite a few." He said, riffling through the list of Karaoke songs.

Her sheer burgundy blouse with bell shaped sleeves, plunged deeply to reveal caramel-colored cleavage. Meeting at the waistline to accentuate her hips and taut round ass in her tight blue jeans—the outfit screamed for you to check out her small, sexy figure. She wore a jean patch pageboy cap, big silver hoop earrings, and a suede burgundy choker. Beige UGG boots matched one of the patches in her hat and her suede-fringed purse.

"But it's TJ"

"TJ? Your Frat?" She smiled.

"Yes. He's been hounding me for your number." He watched her reaction.

"Really? He *is* a cutie."

TJ wasn't her type at all. But there was something about him that was very sexy. Maybe it was the shoulder-length locks? Or maybe it was his eyes? Or the musk-fragrance that seemed to slide off onto you after hugging him? She remembered smelling like him all day after they had hugged. And it was nice. Manly. Not too strong.

But he was hellah skinny. McKenzie was typically attracted to athletic-built men: muscular, running back or thicker. TJ didn't even have a basketball-built body. He was seriously lanky. And had *no* ass. That was no-no number one. But he was a beautiful bronzed brown—like the color of a Sugar Daddy.

And she got into his banter. He wasn't a punk. He was an intellectual. McKenzie loved an intellectual Black man. Clearly she was intrigued, especially after seeing Christian's annoyance.

"Give it to him" she said. Christian raised an eyebrow.

"Oh, OK. I'll give it to him the next time we talk" he said as he walked away.

McKenzie laughed to herself. By then, Camille, Henry and April had made their way into the bar. They grabbed a booth and started chatting, waiting for Melvin to arrive. Christian was at the bar, ordering another Martini.

Christian needed a drink to calm him down after his conversation with McKenzie. He knew he had no right to be irritated, but he was. Another drink would mellow him out and help him stay cool. The bar filled with music from the Karaoke machine. It was a bass filled song, led by drums. *Thump, thump, thump!*

The bartender handed Christian his drink. Christian reached for his wallet to pay the man when he heard the sultry voice come across the mic.

If I was your woman. And you were my man.
There'd be no other woman. You'd be weak as a lamb.

Christian turned to see McKenzie on stage singing a Gladys Knight oldie—with a definite twist to it. It was more hip-hop. It had more flava.

McKenzie didn't need to read the words on the screen. She moved off the stage to interact with the men in the audience—who were more than willing to be the focus of McKenzie's serenade.

Christian sat stunned. McKenzie's voice was amazing. It was a strong soulful alto. And it did put him in the mindset of a Lauryn Hill. He had assumed she'd sing with a high-pitched soprano voice since she was trained to sing classically. But there were no ripples in her voice. Nothing about the way she sang or moved implied tight, pristine, or classical. She was loose. And had such a presence about her that the entire bar had come to a complete stop to watch her perform.

McKenzie moved through the crowd and down the center aisle. She sang to a blushing white boy in his early twenties, two tables in front of the bar where Christian sat enjoying her work the crowd. He could clearly envision her as a superstar R&B singer on stage. She kissed the youngster seductively close to his lips, causing a ruckus in the crowd. Then, she turned and slowly and purposefully moved toward Christian. They locked eyes as she sang the lyrics. She told him that he's a part of her, but he just doesn't know it. She told him she's what he needs, but she's just too afraid to show it, but if she was his woman . . .

McKenzie bellowed, moving slowly in between Christian's legs. She sang into his eyes, touched his chest gently, and told him he's like a diamond but his woman treats him like glass. Her eyes pleaded. *You beg her to love you – with me you don't ask.* Christian flinched … Each word pierced his heart. They were so accurate.

McKenzie moved away backwards, never taking her eyes off Christian.

She turned and headed back toward the stage to finish the song. At the end, the whole bar went wild with applause. McKenzie bowed and moved toward the table where her classmates stood clapping.

"Oh, cut it out, you guys!" McKenzie said laughing.

"Girl, you are something else!" Camille said rubbing her back. "You dance, you sing. Just an original Janet Jackson, huh?"

"Except with real hair!" Furnell said. They all laughed. Christian walked up to the table.

"Here you go, Ms. Hill. I'm sure after that beautiful Alicia Keys rendition your pipes must be perched?" He said, smiling. He handed her an Apple Martini.

"Why, thank you, Mr. Malveaux. I certainly appreciate it." She said winking.

Melvin had entered the bar just as McKenzie started her serenade to Christian. Watching the two made him instantly angry.

That bitch and her self-righteous ass! Miss 'I'm Black and I only love the Black man' bullshit, Melvin thought to himself. On many occasions McKenzie expressed her personal philosophies about how wonderful the Black man is. And how he is the best creation God ever made—blah, blah, blah—on and on and on. It made Melvin sick.

Personally, all he saw in Black men were that they thought too much of themselves. They put too much stock in how they looked—their clothes—Oh! And those impeccable sneakers—like they were high-classed cars that had to be detailed every week or something. The way they walked--it was so stupid to him. Honestly, for McKenzie to be so damned smart, he couldn't understand how she could be so hoodwinked by the men in her race. It probably boiled down to those dicks. Everybody knew they had huge dicks.

And the way she and Christian always managed to be in each other's space spoke volumes. They weren't touching or kissing—or anything actually physical, but whenever they were close like this, it was very erotic: very sexy and sensual. And it unnerved Melvin to no end.

"Hey guys," Melvin said as he joined the crowd.

"What's up, Melly-Mel?" Christian said across the table.

"What up, Mel?" Furnell said pointing to his drink as if to say 'You want one?' even though Furnell had a beer on tap and everyone knew beer was beneath Melvin. He drank red wine.

"Yes, please. Traffic was horrible. And I had to travel across town today." He said as he pulled out his notebook.

"What's wrong Melvin?" April said. They had become really close since they became partners. Melvin sighed. Furnell ordered him a glass of red wine.

"My dad had to go to the hospital today." The group all turned their attention to Melvin.

"Aw, dude. I'm sorry," Christian said.

"Melly, is there anything we can do?" Camille said. Melvin hated how they all created him a nickname—some configuration of his actual name—that was usually longer than Melvin. That is, except McKenzie. If she used his name at all, it was always Melvin. Heaven forbid she implied in any way that she might like him. He knew she didn't. He knew if she had it her way he would simply disappear from the face of the earth.

"Uh, no. Thank you." Melvin managed a half smile.

April reached over and patted Melvin's hand.

April knew just how bad off Melvin's dad was. Spending time during their observations allowed her to see how the dementia put a strain on Melvin. Going to the doctors, administering the medications, making sure his dad was safe—primarily from himself--it was so much.

It made April see Melvin in another light, like his obsession with keeping a schedule made sense. His dad needed his medication at a certain time. Or, Melvin's inability to meet on certain days--his dad had to be at the doctor's office. His life really revolved around the care of his father who had no idea who Melvin was more days than not.

"Then let's get to organizing this presentation." McKenzie said. Christian threw her a sharp look.

What? She shot back at him. He just stared at her like a father reprimanding his child from across the room. McKenzie turned away.

"At least, let me buy you another glass of wine" Furnell said, motioning to the waiter to bring another glass of wine.

"Thanks, Furnell. That would be great. I certainly could go for another." Was all Melvin could muster without breaking down. He was horrible with expression.

"Well, let's give Melvin some time to regroup. In the meantime, the rest of us can review Professor Telfair's rubric to make sure that we all used the same criteria in our group observations. The last thing we need is to present an invalid study" McKenzie said. Everyone started pulling out notebooks and pieces of paper. They worked two hours on the criteria. As they started to wind down, Christian slipped away.

April turned to Melvin.

"Melvin, what are the doctors saying about Pete?" Melvin shifted in his seat.

"He's incoherent." He shoved his notebook in his backpack. "He's on a breathing machine." Before April could respond, everyone at the table started clapping and chanting.

"McKenzie, McKenzie, McKenzie!"

They turned to see Christian in the middle of the bar with his hands outreached toward McKenzie. April rolled her eyes. She had tried to engage Christian on several occasions but never got beyond a surface conversation. He was never rude, but he also never seemed to be taken by her. She couldn't believe he wasn't interested. That almost never happened with her and men. She figured she just needed some quality time alone with him so he could focus on *all* that she had to offer.

McKenzie tried to blow Christian off; she had had two Martinis and still felt buzzed. But her classmates wouldn't hear of it. They loved to see the two cha-cha, and practically pushed her onto the small dance floor.

Christian selected Luther Vandross for tonight's performance, "Bad Boy, Having a Party". McKenzie walked up and stepped into stride with Christian effortlessly.

"I figured this would be the only way to get a conversation in with you," Christian said.

"No, you didn't. You just like grinding up against me. If you can't be honest with yourself, at least be honest with me." She laughed. Christian laughed as well.

"Funny lady." McKenzie stepped in, held the extra beat so she could pivot and turn. As she turned, Christian moved in behind her. He grabbed her waist, and moved in close to her butt. McKenzie smiled. It was a smooth move. Christian started singing the chorus.

If you don't get here on the double,
you're going to be in trouble.
What in the world could be better
than getting together, yay yay.

McKenzie smiled. Christian had a nice voice.

"Sounds like we should've done that duet tonight," She whispered. Christian smiled.

"Uh, I don't think so. You've got some pipes on you Ms. Batiste. A brotha wouldn't want to embarrass himself like that." But Christian was being modest. The way he hit his notes let her know he knew a thing or two about voice control.

"I was impressed. Surprised really. I mean, I know you told me you knew how to sing--"

"But you thought what?" She turned to face him. "That I would sound like some Viking Opera singer?" She laughed.

"Uh. Yeah. I guess. But boy, was I wrong. You have a beautiful, rich, soulful voice."

"Thank you."

♋   ♋   ♋

PART TWO

"Always Come to Light . . ."

Christian eased out of the room to speak with the doctor about the extent of McKenzie's condition.

"She sustained some internal injuries. Her kidneys are bruised, so we want to keep her overnight for observation, make sure there's no internal bleeding or that her kidneys shut down. " Christian felt nauseous. "And she has a blood clot in her right eye.

We can't tell the extent of the damage to the left eye until the swelling goes down. Good news is the ribs are only bruised, not broken as we originally suspected. And the gash over her eye required six stitches that should heal just fine." Christian turned away from the doctor. The doctor paused.

"Well, if there's no bleeding and the kidneys heal on their own, the worst of it all will be the broken nose. We've set it, but she needs to see a specialist. We snapped her shoulder back into place. We've also stabilized her sprained wrist.

And of course, the bruising is going to cause her an enormous amount of pain for a while. But we'll give you some pain medicine to help ease that." The Doctor folded his arms, and rubbed the salt and pepper beard on his chin. "She's going to heal physically without a problem; she's young and physically fit—an athlete?"

"Yes, she's a swimmer. And she works out regularly."

"Yes. She's a beautiful woman. And physically she will no doubt return to her natural beauty. But you need to see to it that she gets some counseling to deal with those emotional wounds we, unfortunately, can't heal." He rocked back and forth on his heels watching Christian.

"I will. Thank you, Doctor. When can I take her home?" Christian said.

175

"So, if all goes well tonight, I'll release her tomorrow."
Christian stood motionless. The doctor placed his hand on
Christian's shoulder.

"I'm sorry you and your family have had to endure this
tragic ordeal. If you want, I can arrange it so you can stay the night
with her. Bunk in the bed next to her if you want?"

Christian looked into the doctor's eyes. He looked sincere.
Christian had no idea how he would explain to Jada why he was out
all night. As it was, she'd been blowing up his phone the last three
hours. He finally just turned it off.

"Thank you. Yes, I would like that. And thank you for taking
care of McKenzie." Christian said. He sighed deeply at what he had
to do next.

♋   ♋   ♋

"Hey Ahmad. It's Christian."

Christian tried to remain composed as he told Ahmad about
the assault. No details, just a high level account of the incident – he
didn't want to alarm him. But it didn't matter how composed or
calm Christian managed to be, Ahmad lost it on the other end of the
phone.

"What? I'll kill him. I am going to kill him." Ahmad
screamed into the phone. "Who is this bitch, Christian? Where is he?
I'm going to call Ty and the boys and he will be taken care of –
tonight."

"I already took care of him. Calm down." Christian said.

"Don't fucking tell me to calm down. That's *my* momma in
the hospital," Ahmad shouted.

176

"I know. I get that. I'm not minimizing this situation Ahmad. I'm asking you to calm down before you do something you'll regret."

"I don't care! I could give a fuck about what happens next, except that this punk bitch is eliminated from the face of the earth. Do you hear me?" Ahmad said, pacing back and forth.

"Yes. I hear you. And I need you to listen to me," Christian pleaded. "I took care of it already." There was a long pause.

"You killed him?"

"If he's not dead, he's knocking on Lucifer's door." Another long pause.

"You ain't fuckin' with me Christian, are you?"

"No, son. I wouldn't lie about this. I went over there before I came to the hospital. I have his blood all over my shirt."

"I'm on my way."

"How about you just come in the morning? She's resting. She won't even know you're here." Christian didn't want Ahmad to see McKenzie looking this way: Maybe 24 hours would reduce some swelling, help McKenzie look less scary.

"She'll know. And if she doesn't, I don't care. I'm coming, so stop trying to convince me not to, Christian. That's my mom. My mom's hurt and she needs me." Ahmad said in between sniffles.

"Yes, I know, young blood. It is your mom. And I need you to know I'm not trying to keep you from her. It's just that . . . She looks bad. And I know your mom wouldn't want you to see her like this. I swear that's it."

"I hear you. Will *you* be there or what?"

"Yes. I'll be here."

"Cool. I'll see you in few." Ahmad hung up the phone. End of conversation.

Christian paced the hallway, trying to process this crazy ass day. What would he say to brace Ahmad? What would he say to appease Jada? Christian was almost certain he had killed Melvin. What was he going to do about the consequences of that?

He walked to the restroom. Inside, he splashed cold water on his face. Christian looked into the mirror. He looked worn out. He *felt* worn out. What would he give to take that conversation back? To have let McKenzie just drive home and be safe. Instead, he coaxed her into the den of a rapist. How would he ever make up for this?

♋   ♋   ♋

"Where's my moms?" Ahmad said to Christian.
Christian decided to wait for him at the elevator. Crystal had driven him to the hospital.

"She's around the corner, room 1127. Hi Crystal."

"Hello Mr. Malveaux," Crystal said following Ahmad.

"Just brace yourself, Ahmad, she looks . . ." Christian got choked up. Ahmad stopped and watched Christian. "She looks pretty bad." Christian wiped his eyes.

"Broken nose. Internal bleeding. Her eye is swollen shut." He looked Ahmad in his eyes. "It's bad."

Ahmad was visibly shaken. His eyes filled with tears. He turned and walked toward the room. Crystal and Christian followed.

Ahmad lingered in the doorway. The nurse had dimmed the light, making it difficult to see any features on McKenzie. Ahmad walked in slowly and quietly, eyes locked on his mom's rising and falling chest. As he rounded the end of the bed, he stopped.

His face registered complete horror. His mouth dropped, his eyebrows arched. Ahmad covered his mouth with his left hand, and grabbed his stomach with his right.
He stood speechless for minutes. Then he moved in closer. He reached in to touch her face but couldn't find an area that looked

178

like it wouldn't hurt if he touched it, so he ran his fingers through her matted hair.

McKenzie stirred. Ahmad watched his mom's agony as she struggled to focus on his face.

"Uhmod?" McKenzie mumbled through swollen lips.

"Shhh. Don't talk. I'm here. It's me. I'm here." Tears streamed down Ahmad's face.

McKenzie reached out to touch her son. Two of her nails were broken and she had scrapes and bruises on her arm. Ahmad moved in closer. He slid his face into the palm of her hand and turned to kiss it. McKenzie smiled and closed her eyes. Ahmad cried into his mother's palm as she drifted off to sleep.

♋   ♋   ♋

Crystal went to the cafeteria to get them coffee. Christian and Ahmad sat in the waiting room. Christian gave Ahmad details about his role in the assault.

"I did this man. It was my fault. I should have just let your mom go home!" Christian pounded his fist into his hand. "She would have been at home, safe." He dropped his head in his hands.

Ahmad sat quietly, slouched in his seat, legs spread out in front of him. His eyes darted from side to side as he chewed the inside of his bottom lip. He let out a long deep sigh.

"Yeah, I guess. But how could you have known?" Ahmad said. They sat in silence. "And besides, my moms don't really come off as a damsel in distress, if you know what I mean?" The right corner of Ahmad's mouth inched up into a half smirk. Christian looked at Ahmad. He chuckled.

"True. But still."

"Yeah, I feel you." Ahmad said, standing up. "But it's hard to protect my mom."

Christian looked up at Ahmad. He had a serious look on his face as he paced the room.

179

"I try, but—"

"Whoa, whoa! Ahmad. I know it's been you and your mom. But young blood, you have to realize that that's a tall order to fill for a grown ass man, let alone a child." Ahmad shot him a look. "Hey, I get it. You're the man of the house. But you still are a child chronologically." Ahmad continued pacing.

"Yeah, whatever G. I am responsible for taking care of my moms. She's made so many sacrifices for me."

"That's what mothers do."

"Some. But my moms has had a rough life. And she's entitled to some happiness. She certainly doesn't deserve this."

"No, she doesn't."

"Do you know my mom has put me through catholic school since kindergarten?" He said full of pride. He looked at Christian. "Tuition for private school ain't no joke. But she does it. She says her son will be an educated Black man. He will have the best this life has to offer." Ahmad smiled when he said that. Christian laughed.

"I know it's hard. But she never complains. She makes so many sacrifices for me. My mom's don't bring men around, and she don't date—she don't even do shit on the D.L." Ahmad shook his head and returned to his seat.

"You wouldn't have problems with it if she did?"

"Naw. I ain't a kid no more. When I was young, I couldn't phase mom's hookin' up with some dude, you know—thinking about my moms doin' the do." He laughed and relaxed a little.

"Man, that would've drove me crazy. I can't say I'm all that comfortable thinking about it now. You know, that's my moms. She's gone always be my moms."

"But, I know she has needs." He paused and turned to face Christian. "When I was younger, I used to hear my moms crying late at night. Back then, I didn't understand. I thought all we needed was us. You know? But I'm older now. I know she gets lonely. Hell, everybody needs somebody to kick it with, to chill with every now and then. Everybody needs to feel loved and needed—and not like the love from a son. But like 'a woman needs a man' kind of shit, you know?" Ahmad looked strained.

"So, why doesn't she do it—date, I mean?"

"Man, she's on some superwoman kick, I think."

"What do you mean?"

"I mean, she says she don't need no man to make her complete. She says she's already whole. She says men only take you off track of your goal—and she's got a lot to accomplish. And that's good and all. But I know moms is just talking from the hurt."

"What hurt?"

Two uniformed officers, along with detective Anderson, walked into the waiting room. An officer approached Christian.

"Are you Christian Malveaux?"

Christian stood. He looked at detective Anderson who looked away.

"Yes sir, I am. What's this all about?" But Christian knew.

"Sir, you're under arrest for the attempted murder of Melvin Vaughn. Please turn around and place your hands behind your back." Christian did as instructed.

Ahmad jumped up.

"That son-of-a-bitch raped and nearly killed my mother, and you're arresting Christian? *Are you fucking kidding me right now?*"

The second officer rushed Ahmad, slamming him against the waiting room wall.
Christian turned with a force that threw the first officer off-balance, causing him to trip and fall.

"Hold up, officer! Wait!" Christian said. The first officer jumped up quickly and grabbed Christian.

"Everybody hold up!" The detective said. "Officers, stand down. This is going in the wrong direction very quickly. Let's just . . . let's calm down." The officers stepped back. Ahmad yanked free from the second officer and mad-dogged him. Christian moved toward Ahmad.

"It's cool Ahmad, just calm down. They're just doing their job."

"No, 'doing their job' would look like arresting the fucker who *raped* my mother. Not arresting the person who gave him what he deserved," he said, looking at the officers. The second officer started to move toward Ahmad. Christian jumped in front of him.

"I said stand down Officer Hill. I mean it." Detective Anderson said.

"Listen, Ahmad. I'm not happy about having to arrest Christian. But I have to," she said. "Hopefully, he'll post bail in a couple of hours and be back here at McKenzie's side before she wakes." The officers lead Christian out as Crystal was coming in with three cups of coffee.

"What's going on?" Crystal said.

"They're arresting Christian for attempting to kill the piece of shit that raped my mom." Ahmad and Crystal followed them out into the hall.

"Mr. Malveaux, is there anyone you want me to call for you?" Crystal said.

"No sweetie. Just make sure Ahmad stays calm, will you?" Christian said over his shoulder. "Ahmad, you have to stay calm so you can take care of your mom. Do you understand?"

"I got this C. I'm calm."

Ahmad turned to Crystal. "If I finish the job Christian started, they can't charge him with attempted anything," he said looking up in the air.

"Did you hear a word Mr. Malveaux said to you? You have to take care of your mom. You won't be able to do that from behind a jail cell." Crystal placed her hands on her hips. "Just relax. Let's go see your mom."

Crystal grabbed Ahmad's hand and led him to McKenzie's room.

Christian called his sister Kai, to post bail.

"Chris, what the hell?" Kai said when they were in the car. "Attempted murder?"

Christian begged Kai not to call Jada. He promised to repay her and explain everything – he just needed her to trust him and not involve Jada. Kai did as she was instructed.

"This makes no sense. The detective said you beat this man to an inch of his life over a woman?"

"My classmate, McKenzie," Christian said looking at his watch. "And I need to get back to her, Kai. Can you take me to Kaiser Cadillac, please?"

"What? Are you serious? Christian, please tell me what's really going on here? It seems to me that you should stay as far away from this woman as possible."

"Kai, stop. You don't know what you're talking about, so please, stop talking and drop me off at the hospital. My car is there," Christian said, looking out the passenger window.

"Are you going to get into your car and go home to your wife?"

"No. I'm going to go upstairs and check on McKenzie." The two rode in silence for several blocks.

"Listen Kai, she's in the hospital because of me. I sent her to that maniac's home and he raped her. So I went to his house—"

"With Jada in the car?" Christian turned to face his sister. "Jada called me as soon as she got in the house. She said some woman called, wouldn't give her name, and then the next thing she knew you were jumping in a car to go play Captain Save a Ho."

"McKenzie is not a ho!" Christian said. "She is smart, and funny, and warm, and strong. She's independent and thoughtful. McKenzie is talented and passionate about education in the inner city. She's a great mom—a single mom, who's made sacrifices to put her son in private school. She—"

"Whoa buddy!" Kai said smiling. "You are sprung on this woman!"

"What? No, Kai. I'm just saying. Jada is making this into something it's not. McKenzie is a beautiful woman."

"A beautiful woman that you're totally in love with." Kai said staring at her brother. I have never seen you lit up like you are now."

"I don't know what you're talking about. But, if I am lit up... "

"What?"

"It doesn't matter. McKenzie will probably never talk to me again after what happened to her."

"Uh, how about 'It doesn't matter because I'm married.' Uh hello?" Kai laughed. Christian looked at Kai and burst into laughter too.

"Oh yeah, huh?" Christian said. She socked him in the arm.

"*Oh yeah.* You are a hot mess Christian. A hot fucking mess."

CHAPTER NINE

Healing

Kai pulled up into the hospital parking lot.

"Christian. Are you sure about this? About being here?"

"Yeah, sis, it's probably the only thing I'm sure about right now."

"What are you going to do about Jada?"

"I'll deal with her later. Right now, I've got to get McKenzie situated," he said, opening the door. "Do yourself a favor. Turn off your phone." He kissed his sister and got out of her car.

Christian was exhausted. It had been a long 24 hours. He hadn't slept all night. The bed in the county jail cell wasn't comfortable. And even if it had been, Christian wouldn't have been able to sleep. He had too much on his mind.

He took the elevator up to the 11th floor. At the nurse's station, Christian inquired about McKenzie's release. The charge nurse said the doctor already signed the release papers and Nurse Constance was preparing her aftercare instructions.

"Do you want me to page her doctor?" the nurse said.

"Yes, could you please?"

"Sure, no problem."

Ten minutes later, Dr. Winslow approached the nurse's station.

"Good morning, Doctor Winslow. Have you had the opportunity to check on McKenzie yet?

"Yes, I have. I went by this morning."

"And?"

"And test results show there is no internal bleeding, and her kidneys are doing fine.

"Thank God" Christian sighed.

185

"Yes, she is lucky and strong. I'll sign the release papers so you can get her home. If you want, I can have the nurse call downstairs to the pharmacy to fill the prescriptions."

"Prescriptions? How many are there?"

The doctor paused. "Well, there are the pain pills, the sleeping pills, the antibiotics, and the PCP pill."

"The what?"

"The PCP—Post-Coital Pill--The morning after pill. We generally recommend it for rape victims, just in case--"

"That's fine." Christian cut the doctor off, disturbed by the thought. "If you could have her call the pharmacy, I'll pick everything up. As soon as that's done, I can take her home?"

"Yes, sir. You certainly can."

♋   ♋   ♋

Inside the room, the nurse was helping McKenzie get dressed. Christian had Kai stop at Wal-Mart so he could purchase McKenzie a sweat suit and some tennis shoes so she didn't have to wear anything that reminded her of . . .

Kai looked at him funny. But Christian couldn't worry about his sister's judgments right now. He had too much going on in his head, his court case, Jada, and McKenzie. Right now, McKenzie was his biggest concern.

"Are we ready?" Christian said, pushing the wheel chair into the room.

"I . . . am. I . . . don't . . . know . . . what you . . . are doing . . . with. . . that thing." McKenzie winced, trying to be flip

186

with her comment about the wheel chair. The nurse and Christian laughed. He rolled the chair over to the bed while the nurse helped McKenzie get up.

"Get in."

She stood and slowly moved to the wheel chair. He gently kissed the top of her head. "Very good." McKenzie rolled her eyes. The nurse laughed.

"We're . . . going . . . shit . . ." McKenzie paused and took a deep breath. Christian waited patiently. "We're . . . going . . . out the back?"

"Out the back?" Christian asked, confused. Was she afraid Melvin would be lurking in the front? "No, we're going out the front. Why?"

"Seriously? You . . . have me . . . in . . . a Wal-Mart Sweat suit." She was winded at the end of the sentence.

Christian looked at the nurse as if to say, *is she serious?* They both fell out laughing.

Christian stopped by the pharmacy on the way out. He wheeled McKenzie to his car.

"No, Christian. Take me . . . to my jeep. I can . . . drive . . . home."

"Get in." But she didn't move. "C'mon Mac, I'm driving you home. I'll come back for your jeep once we get you settled into your townhouse." But she didn't budge. Christian spun the wheelchair around and knelt down so they could be eye-level.

"What's up?"

"I'm not . . . an invalid." She sat, stone-faced. "I can . . . take care . . . of myself. *This much* . . . I can do." She broke down into tears.

"Look. No one thinks you're an invalid. Least of all me." He sighed. "I know you can take care of yourself. I just want to take care of you. Just for a little while." He leaned in and gently kissed her swollen lips. "You can take over when you get home. Can you just let me work off a little of this guilt, and at least get you home safely," he said, looking strained.

"Why are you . . . feeling guilty, Christian?" She said, in between grimaces from the pain. "Melvin . . . did this to me . . . not you. I'm not . . . some stupid . . . kid. *He* did this. . *He* made . . . that choice. Just like . . . I did . . . when I called you. I knew what

187

you'd do. . OK?" she said, standing up. She winced. "If I held you accountable . . . for anything . . . we were straight . . . the minute you inflicted pain . . . on him." She paused, looking him in the eyes. " I don't though. I mean it. Now let that shit go. Please." McKenzie slowly slid into the passenger side of Christian's car. *Old man car*, she thought.

Christian closed the door and walked around to the driver's side of the car. He took a deep breath in and slowly exhaled. He opened his door, slid inside, and made way to McKenzie's.

♋   ♋   ♋

Christian had called Ahmad from the hospital. He wanted to come up there to take his mom home, but Christian convinced him that McKenzie would be upset if he came up there. He asked him to get the house prepared and gave him a couple of tasks to complete for him.

"Do you think she even remembers me being up there last night?" Ahmad asked.

"Nah, young blood. I think they had her pretty heavily sedated. She recognized you last night, which I think brought her comfort when she needed it. You know what I mean?"

"Yeah sure, no doubt. It's cool. I just needed to be there for her."

"And you were. And you are. You're taking care of your mom. I am impressed Ahmad. You're a strong young man. And I know you love your mom. She knows it too."

When McKenzie walked through the door, Ahmad tried to keep a blank face. But she could see the shock all over his face. The bruises were darker, more visible. The swelling was still very prominent.

"Hey Ma, are you all right?" Ahmad said, moving in to kiss her lightly on the cheek. McKenzie attempted a smile.

"Yes baby. I'm fine." She moved toward the stairs.

"Here, let me carry you up Mac. Otherwise, it's going to take you a couple of hours." She paused, placed her hands on her hip and sneered at Christian.

"Ha, ha, ha funny guy. I've got nowhere else to go. So there." It took her only about twenty minutes. But she was exhausted by the time she made it to her room.

"Here, brought you some water." Christian handed her a bottle of cold water.

"Thanks." She took it and chugged the whole thing. "Christian, have you heard from detective Anderson?"

"Yes. She called me this morning. They went by Melvin's and arrested him."

"He survived the beat down?"

"Yeah, I guess so. She said he told the police he wanted to press charges against me." McKenzie sat up quicker than she should have.

"Ouch! Oh. Ooh." She frowned, grabbing her mid-section.

"Hey! Be careful. Are you all right?" Christian said, moving to her side.

"I'm fine. That asshole! *He* wants to press charges? You wait until I get through with his ass!" She lay back in her bed, crying.

Christian moved next to her. "Don't worry about any of it. Detective Anderson said she's been in communication with the D.A., trying to convince him to drop the charges. Not that I care." He ran his hands gently across her battered face. She turned away.

"Don't do that, Mac," Christian whispered. "The bruising is going to go away, the swelling is going to go down, and you'll be back to normal in no time."

"I've never been normal, Christian. What do you think I'll be returning to?" McKenzie replied. Christian pulled her into him. She lay quietly with his arms around her. She felt safe.

"Don't let him control you, McKenzie. Don't let him steal your belief in your worth, your value, your beauty."

"Melvin didn't take any of those things away from me. They were gone long before yesterday," she mumbled.

Before he could reply, he felt the gentle jerking of her body. Looking down, he saw a steady stream of tears cover her swollen cheek. He felt confused.

As long as he'd known her, McKenzie seemed to have self-confidence. She seemed to be sure about herself, demanding respect of her heritage—the very first day he met her, the way she checked the white girl. Her sexuality—the way she commanded his attention in this very room the day he watched her satisfy herself in the bathtub. Her intellect—the way she articulated her thoughts during classroom debates. What was she talking about? Did the rape have her confused and doubting herself?

"McKenzie. Do you think you'd be up to . . . I don't know, talking to someone about what happened?" He remembered what the detective and doctor kept reminding him—to make sure she got some help.

Her gentle jerks turned into sobs. She buried her face in his chest and held on to him tightly. He rubbed her back, unsure of where her bruises were.

"To tell them what? Can they change anything? They can't!" McKenzie screamed.

"They can't take it away, no. But they can help you work through the pain." Christian said

"Christian. There is no pain anymore. There is nothing inside. I stopped feeling a long time ago. I didn't feel anything yesterday. Don't you get it?"

Christian thought she was just responding to the shock of the trauma. But she was sounding very lucid.

"No I don't. Why don't you explain it to me so that I understand." McKenzie sniffled, wiping the tears from her face.

"Christian. Melvin didn't do anything to me yesterday that hadn't been done to me before—that's what I mean." Christian's eyes widened. "What are you saying? You've been . . . violated before?"

"That's what I'm saying."

"By who?" Christian's head was spinning.

"I told you . . . the Major." She said almost inaudibly.

"What? What, McKenzie! Your stepfather molested you?" Christian pulled her away to look her in the eyes. She screamed out in pain from the sudden movement.

"Oh, I'm sorry, baby!" Christian said as he released her, suddenly aware of the pain he was inflicting. "I'm sorry." He moved back.

"I thought he . . . abused you. I thought it was physical . . . I mean . . . I didn't realize he . . ." He pulled her close and kissed her head. The movement hurt, but she didn't scream out. She just let him hold her and pretended that nothing before this moment mattered.

"He used to come into my room late at night." McKenzie spoke as if she was talking to herself. "I tried to fight him. I didn't understand what he was doing. All I knew was that it didn't feel right." This was the first time she'd shared the details of her childhood abuse with an outsider. "I told him it hurt, and that I didn't like it. But it seemed like he got off on hearing that—on hurting me. He got rougher, more vile. It was like he was trying to find ways to hurt me. I couldn't understand it."

Christian's blood was boiling. He wanted to tell McKenzie to shut up. He was feeling nauseous. He had this man in front of him—he wished he had known what he'd done to McKenzie then; he would have ripped his head off! She was a child, an innocent child.

"Where was your mother when all of this was going on?"

"She was there. But she didn't do anything." She shifted in the bed, uncomfortably. "At first I didn't think she knew. And I was scared to tell her."

"Why?"

"Because she was so happy. She had this man to love her, and it seemed so important. I didn't want to be the reason it ended. You know?"

No. Christian didn't know. And he couldn't understand how she allowed herself to feel responsible for her mother's happiness— especially at her personal expense.

"You never told her?"

"I didn't have to. She knew."

"What do you mean? How do you know she knew? I mean, and she let it go on? For how long?"

"She knew. " McKenzie tensed up. Christian was incensed. How could her mother allow her husband to continuously abuse her own child?

"She left me alone with him. She went to women's bible study on Mondays, Choir rehearsal on Wednesdays. She was always out leaving me alone with him. And she knew." McKenzie said.

"He touched me, in ways that . . . that he shouldn't. He used to . . . He used to rub my clit. You know, to get me excited. And then when I did, he'd slap me and call me a filthy whore. He said I liked it. Then he'd say he had to punish me, and he'd get on top of me. And he'd be so rough." McKenzie was emotionless recounting the experience.

"I was so confused. He was doing these things to my body I couldn't control. He would take so much time . . . gently touching me, licking me, I would get so wet. I mean, it felt good. I was confused. My body was responding to his touch—and then, he just went cold. He turned so mean in an instant. It was the craziest thing."

Christian listened to the sick workings of the child abuser. He wondered how McKenzie managed to turn out OK. To him she seemed OK. But how could she be when the people she trusted the most had violated her so? Her mother, who should have protected her, allowed her to be abused by this maniac. A supposed Minister of God!

"After a while I just taught myself not to respond to any of it. Not to the touches that felt good. Not to the pain that followed. I just went dead. And he hated it. He would go into a rage because I would just lie there, no matter what he did."

Christian shifted underneath her. He thought about what Melvin had said to him yesterday—that she just laid there, not fighting him. She must've responded to Melvin instinctively, the way she had taught herself to respond to the Major.

"When my mother saw the bruises, she just ignored them. I mean, where did she think they came from?"

"And no one knew? And he was a minister."

"He got up every Sunday, in that pulpit and preached to his congregation. He counseled married couples. He baptized babies. He funeralized the dead. And at his house, he was having sex with his stepdaughter."

"And you're sure your mom knew what was going on?" Christian couldn't believe she'd live this incredulous lie. If her mother did know, she was sick. "Why would she let something so awful go on under her roof?"

"It wasn't her roof. It was the Major's. That was it. Before him, she had nothing. After she got married to this man of power, her life changed. She had security . . . prestige . . . she was the Major's wife--*The First Lady*. She lived in a big house."

"And? It was worth her daughter's innocence?" He felt sweat begin to form around his top lip and nose. It felt as if there was no oxygen in the room.

"You don't understand. She's from a different generation. She was a single mother. She felt honored to have a man of the Major's caliber to want to marry her—a widower with a child. Everyone made it a point to tell her, to tell me, how lucky we were."

"I don't give a fuck. She should have gotten a job— something. She just sacrificed you so she could live in a big house? I'm sorry, are you serious?" Christian was blown away.

"We played the part; at church, in public. But at home, it was a mess. I couldn't wait to get from under that roof. But he told me every day, '*You're mine. You'll always be mine.*' I hated it. I hated when he said that to me. I felt like I was being suffocated. I couldn't wait to get out."

"I joined everything I could at school. Cheerleading. Student government. Sports. Whatever would keep me away. But he would try and find ways to keep me home. He'd say it was disgraceful for a preacher's daughter to be kicking her legs up, showing her privates to everyone. Wearing that short skirt. It was 'worldly' he'd say."

"Eventually he'd get his way. My mother made me drop cheerleading. She made me drop out of student government. He did everything he could to make me miserable. Especially when he found out about Malik."

"Who is Malik?"

"Just a boy."

"A boy you liked?"

"I could have gotten to like him. The Major ran interference before we could really get to that point." McKenzie grimaced. "He was sweet."

"Did he know about the Major?"

"Yes. Besides you, he and Denny were the only other people outside the family that I told." McKenzie smiled thinking about him. "He made me feel normal. He was sweet and gentle. And I didn't feel dirty around him. I felt . . . so special." She closed her eyes. When she opened them she was crying again.

"That's good. You had somebody on your side. Somebody to help you through."

"Yeah. Until the Major got rid of him."

"How did he do that?" Christian wondered if he had him shipped off to another town or something. McKenzie pulled away from Christian. She slid out of the bed.

"What happened? Why are you moving away from me? Come back." McKenzie turned to face him.

"The Major got me pregnant. He blamed it on Malik." She lowered her head. Christian sat in silence. "Do you still want me to come back?"

Christian extended his arms. McKenzie slid into them. She looked exhausted. She felt like dead weight on his chest. She didn't cry; just lay there breathing heavily. Christian felt horrible inside. She had been through so much. He didn't know what to do. So he just held her and rocked her to sleep.

♋   ♋   ♋

Christian slipped out from under McKenzie once he felt she was sound asleep. He had been with her all night, and half way into the next day. Jada had been blowing up his cell phone so much he eventually turned it off.

He took the metro and two buses back to the hospital to retrieve McKenzie's jeep. When he got it back to the townhouse and made sure everything was straight, groceries, prescriptions, contacting McKenzie's job, he headed for the door.

Just then, the downstairs buzzer sounded.

"It's Auntee Denny!" Ahmad said to Christian.

One of the tasks he had Ahmad take care of was calling Denny. He knew he wasn't going to be able to be with McKenzie like he'd want, so he paid for Denny to come out for the week.

Christian went downstairs and met Denny. He helped carry her luggage inside.

"Does Mac know I'm here? Did you tell her I was coming?" Denny asked as she placed her carry on in the corner. "Thank you."

"No, thank *you*," Christian said to Denise. "I feel so much better knowing you and Ahmad will be here to help McKenzie this week. I'm not sure what's going to happen with court . . . but with you here, I know she'll be straight."

Denise watched Christian closely.

"I'm sure everything is going to turn out fine, Christian. And don't worry about McKenzie. I'll be here to wait on her hand and foot. I'll take good care of my friend," she said with a soft smile. Denny moved in and hugged Christian. Christian returned the hug. When they parted Denise headed up the stairs. Christian walked toward Ahmad.

"OK Ahmad, I gotta head out son." He reached for his wallet. "Here are a couple of bucks to tie you over until your mom gets on her feet. Just don't tell her I gave it to you. You know how prideful she can be." He handed him two twenties, smiling.

"Is my mom going to be OK?" Ahmad said. Christian saw strain and concern laced in between the young man's furrowed brows.

Christian walked back into the room.

"She's going to be fine physically, Ahmad. The injuries and bruises will eventually heal. The rest, we're going to have to get her some help. You know, for the emotional stuff." Ahmad nodded his head as if he understood.

"I thought after getting away from the Major, all this shit would be over." Ahmad said, sitting down. He rested his head in his hands.

"You know about the Major?" Christian said, sitting next to him.

"Yeah. My mom told me when I turned four. I didn't understand it all then. But we had to move to get away from him, and I was crying because I didn't want to leave my friends and school."

195

"What do you mean, get away?"

"She left when she turned 18, and was legally an adult. She was raring to get out of there."

"What happened?"

"She got a job working for one of the church members who let her bring me to work with her. She was making minimum wage and paying her rent, she didn't have enough for childcare too."

"Right, right."

"But the Major found out and had a talk with the lady's husband who immediately fired her."

"What? Why? Because 'the Major said so?'" Ahmad nodded his head.

"That's how we ended up back with them. But moms wasn't having that for long. She found something outside his control and we bailed. We snuck out one night, with nothing more than the clothes on our backs. We haven't been back since."

"What did she tell you? I mean--"

"I was four. She just told me we had to leave. It wasn't until I was seven that she told me he was hurting her. I didn't really know what she meant. It wasn't until I was 13 that she told me the entire truth. That he was my biological father, and--"

Christian was floored! Ahmad was the Major's son? He didn't know why it didn't click when she told him the Major had gotten her pregnant upstairs. He assumed he made her get an abortion.

Christian knew there was something about the Major that looked familiar that day. It was Ahmad that he saw in his face.

That man had gotten her pregnant, blamed it on Malik, and was walking around like he hadn't done a thing. And the mom knew?

"They sent her off to St. Anne's to have me." Ahmad said. "They told everybody that Malik was the daddy—even though he wasn't. And when she had me, they made it seem like they were doing the 'right' thing by letting her come back home. But when she came back, he started back up with her. Beating her because she was fighting back. But she was a minor and couldn't do jack. Grams didn't do jack to help her. So, she bailed as soon as she found a way to support us." Christian listened to Ahmad recount his mother's painful childhood.

"And how did that make you feel hearing that? Is that something you think she should have kept from you?"

"I mean. I was fucked up at first. You know. How do you think a 13 year old should feel? My dad is my grahams' husband. All my life he's been the Major—my gramps. That's some shit. But, I had to think about what my moms went through, you know? Living under that roof. And I just decided I had to be there for my mom, you know—to take care of her. And that's what I've been trying to do." He dropped his head in his hands and started to cry.

Christian was speechless. He rubbed Ahmad's back, truly feeling for this family. What a weight to have to bear so young. He didn't know if he would've shared that horrible information with his son. But he didn't have to live through the ordeal McKenzie had endured either. She did what she thought was best.

"I'm going to kill the mutha fucka who did this to my mom. You know that don't you C?" He said, calmly.

"I took care of him, Ahmad."

"Is he dead?" Ahmad looked him eye to eye.

"No. But I beat him so badly, he wishes he was. I put it on him, Ahmad. I promise." He stood up and headed toward the door. "You need to do what you said you were going to do, young blood. You need to be here for your mom." Christian stopped at the door. "You got it?"

"I got it," Ahmad replied. Christian winked at him and walked out the door.

♋   ♋   ♋

"Hey, baby." Denise said. McKenzie's back was to the door. She tried to turn, but stopped. It was too painful to move.

"Denny? Is that you?" McKenzie said and instantly started crying.

"Oh no! Don't try and turn. I'll come around honey!" Denise said, rushing around to the other side of the bed. When she saw McKenzie's face, she broke into tears.

"Jesus," Denise said, covering her mouth.

"I look horrible, don't I?" McKenzie said in between sobs.

"Yes. You look pretty fucked up," McKenzie laughed. If she couldn't count on anybody to tell her the truth, she knew she could *always* count on her Denny.

"Tell me how you *really* feel." McKenzie tried to sit up. Denise helped her. They laughed.

"Oh baby. It's physical. In a couple of weeks you won't have a trace of any of this," Denise said, more confidently than she felt. McKenzie nodded.

"It's not that bad. I only got a 'Jesus'. Not a 'Bless baby Jesus in the manger' or 'Bless 33 year old Jesus on the Cross.' They both laughed. "I would've been worried if you called on the 33 year old Jesus. You tend to call him when it's bad" They laughed hard and long.

"Who called you? How did you get here? Are the boys with you?" McKenzie fired off question after question. Denise waited patiently.

"Ahmad called me. He said Christian wanted to know if I could come right away and stay with you for at least a week. And, of course, I said yes. He paid for my ticket. I got the first flight out. And no, the boys are with my mom."

"Not surprising. Heaven forbid they stay with their dad. What did he say? That's what the bitch gets, I wish she had been killed?" They laughed.

"No, of course not." Denise said in horror. "You may not be his favorite person, but he wouldn't wish you dead. Cut that stupid talk out. Do they have you on pain killers?"

"Yep, Vicodin." McKenzie said pointing to the pills on her nightstand. "But I'm very lucid. You and I both know that Negro don't care a rat's ass about me. And it's so cool. I'm shocked, but very happy he *let* you come out to visit."

"Fuck you McKenzie Batiste. He didn't *let* me do shit. Just like he couldn't stop me from coming."

"I knew it! He did not want you to come, did he?"

"No, that's not it. He just didn't understand why I needed to stay the entire week," she said, casually. McKenzie hated Denise's husband. He was such an ass. And he didn't appreciate Denise at all. McKenzie would tell her, just get his ass a live-in Nanny, that's all he needs – someone to take care of him 24/7. Not a partner. He moped whenever he wasn't getting Denise's full attention. He moped even if she was giving the attention to his sons. It drove McKenzie crazy. But Denise functioned as if she didn't see shit.

"Well finally, something we both agree on. You don't need to stay an entire week. Not if you came to take care of me. I'm fine."

"Yes, as we determined 30 seconds ago. You look mah-veh-lous!" Denise teased. McKenzie laughed. "And so what? Now I have an excuse to come home, childless and kick it with my girl for 7 days!" She said, fluffing up McKenzie's pillows.

"Uh huh. Great. But bitch, you ain't gone be hovering over me like this all the time, are you? This is not going to work." McKenzie complained. "Move."

Denise moved to the end of the bed and sat.

"How about BITCH you failed to tell me how fucking fine Christian's ass was!" Denise blurted out. McKenzie laughed her first true happy laugh since leaving the hospital.

"Um, I think I did."

"Um, I think you didn't" They laughed.

"He *is* hella fine, ain't he?" McKenzie giggled.

"Let's just say . . . I might kind-of sort-of understand the whole adultery thing now." Denise smiled wide, that full-bodied smile –all teeth and sparkling eyes --that McKenzie had come to love.

McKenzie adored her best friend. She knew Denise did not approve of her relationship with Christian for so many reasons. But, as she always had in the past, Denise had found a way to accept her friend. She had a way of doing it that made McKenzie feel normal. But McKenzie knew that nothing about her was normal. But only around her best friend could she feel like she was.

♋   ♋   ♋

On the drive home, Christian had to pull over. He threw up all the nausea, anger, and disgust he had been holding in the past 24 hours. When he walked in the door at 5:00 pm, all hell broke loose.

"So, I just don't mean shit to you anymore. Is that it, Christian?" Jada said, as he entered the house. Christian's stomach was still sour. He couldn't tell whether or not he was going to throw up. His head was pounding. And he was tired.

"That's not it at all."

On his way home, he had tried to make sense of McKenzie's life. Knowing all she had gone through, he wondered how she could still have enough passion to want to teach—much less teach in their community where resources were limited and challenges were abundant.

She was brilliant. She could teach anywhere. Yet, despite her circumstances, she wanted to remain in South Central. She was adamant about giving their children a quality education. But more than that—before the past 24 hours—she had so much excitement, so much joy . . . despite everything . . .

"How could you drop me off on the fucking curbside and not call me to say 'Bitch, I'm alive.'" Jada said.

"I'm sorry for not calling you, Jada. I was wrong." Christian sat in his favorite chair, feeling depleted. He didn't have the energy to fight with Jada. But looking at her, he saw that fight was all she wanted to do.

"Damned right you were wrong. You were inconsiderate, selfish, and—"

Before she could finish the litany of adjectives, Christian stood up and walked over to her. He pulled her into him and held her close.

"I'm sorry, Jada. I know that doesn't excuse me. Or make up for the worry. But I am so sorry. I don't have more than that to give you right now. I'm sorry baby." For the first time in a long time, he felt tender toward her.

There was no love, as in romantic love, just a deep sense of protectiveness. He felt like he needed to keep her safe from the Majors and the Melvin's of the world. He needed to protect her— because he had not been able to protect McKenzie. She pulled away and stared up into Christian's face.

"You're not off the hook, Christian Malveaux. I have no idea who you were with or what you were doing. You think an apology and a hug is going to get you off the hook?" Christian paused a moment.

"Not off the hook, just a pass. I'm exhausted. I need to get out of these clothes and get some sleep."

Jada was furious. She wanted to know where Christian was and who he was with. But he looked so tired that she felt a temporary moment of tenderness. She just stepped back and let him walk past. Christian knew she would resume the conversation later.

When Jada walked into the room 15 minutes later, Christian was spread across the bed, half dressed—knocked out. She riffled through his pockets. All she found was a carbon copy of a prescription form. On the top of the slip was a name, McKenzie Batiste. There were several drugs listed, but the only drug she recognized was the PCP pill—*the morning after pill*. The blood in her veins ran cold.

♋   ♋   ♋

The next day, McKenzie was awaken by Detective Anderson's call.

"We've arrested Mr. Vaughn. We've sent the DNA samples to the lab for verification. He said he had 'consensual sex' with you---"

"Consensual!" McKenzie screamed. It ripped open one of the gashes on her bottom lip that was almost healed. "That mutha fucka raped me!"

"But when we showed him the photographs of your injuries, he recanted. The question is 'are you prepared to press charges'?"

McKenzie sighed, "Absolutely. Press charges, testify in court—the full nine." She rubbed her temples.

"Good."

"What? What is it?"

"I just want you to be prepared. His attorney has already insinuated that he's going to defend Mr. Vaughn by using his grief from his father's death and the alcohol as the reasons why he attacked you."

"I don't care if he says Jesus Christ came down from heaven and told him to do it. He's going to pay for what he did to me. He will not get away with this, Detective Anderson." McKenzie said, slowly and calmly.

"I understand. I just wanted you to be prepared."

"Melvin's the one who needs to be prepared. Detective Anderson, can you FedEx me copies of the police report and the photos, please?"

"Sure. I can probably get that to you by Friday. Is that OK?"

"That's fine. Thank you. Please call me if you need anything else."

"I hope all goes well with Mr. Malveaux in court today."

McKenzie sat straight up. "Ouch!" she said, grabbing her shoulder. Through winced eyes and clenched teeth, she replied, "Court? Why is Christian in court today, Detective?"

"If he didn't tell you, then it's definitely not my place--"

"He probably didn't tell me so that I wouldn't worry. I'm worried. Original purpose defeated. What's going on?" McKenzie slid out of bed and headed to her closet as the detective spoke.

"He's being charged with attempted murder Mrs. Batiste."

"What?" McKenzie grabbed the closet door. *Attempted murder?* She placed her hand over her mouth. "Oh my God. He's going to spend the rest of his life in jail because of me?" McKenzie whispered.

"Not necessarily. The evidence against Mr. Vaughn is overwhelming. I know the defense lawyer. I recommended him to Mr. Malveaux. He's shrewd and cunning. Trust me, he's in good hands." McKenzie smiled.

"Oh, thank you, Detective Anderson."

"Sure thing. I was amazed the DA even picked this one up. But it's re-election time. On the docket, the convictions only read 'convicted murderer'. Daniel's going to try to get it reduced to aggravated assault and battery with special circumstances."

McKenzie pulled out her navy blue Tahari suit and a pale blue blouse.

"Where's the court building located?" McKenzie said.

"Will the defendant, Christian Malveaux, please rise?" the bailiff said.

Christian and his attorney, Daniel Richmond, stood, two solid brothers in tailored suits: one, chocolate, one, peanut butter complexion. Christian wore a taupe suit, white shirt, with a rust, white, and gold striped tie, and matching rust belt and square-toed shoes. Daniel wore a navy pinstriped suit, a light blue shirt with thin navy stripes and a white collar and French cuffs, and black shoes.

"Mr. Malveaux, on the count of attempted murder of the plaintiff Melvin Vaughn, how do you plead?" Judge Mathieu asked.

"Not guilty, your honor." Christian answered.

"Your honor, in accordance with the United States Sixth Amendment, Mr. Malveaux would like to waive his right to a jury and request a speedy trial." The judge looked up over his glasses.

"Is this true Mr. Malveaux?"

"Yes, your honor."

"Very well then, the court acknowledges the defendant's request for a speedy trial and sets a trial date--"

The doors of the court swung open. In walked McKenzie, slowly, meticulously dressed in her blue two-piece suit, light blue blouse with matching earrings. Her face, still swollen, looked like she had been beaten with a bag of nickels. Her nose was bandaged, her bruises turning dark green and purple. Her arm was in a sling. And she used a cane to steady her gait. McKenzie tried her best to walk normal, but you could see pain register in her face with every step.

"May I help you? This is a closed proceeding," the Judge said. The bailiff moved toward McKenzie.

"My sincere apologies, your honor. My name is McKenzie Batiste." She stopped and took a deep breath, closing her eyes. "And I just learned today that Mr. Malveaux is being charged with attempted murder for protecting me against the criminal who raped me." She looked over at Melvin. "So, I had to come down to protest this injustice in person. Your honor, is this true?"

"Ms. Batiste, did you say?"

"Yes sir, McKenzie Batiste." She said, leaning on the wooden fence separating the peanut gallery from the official judicial proceedings.

"Mr. Malveaux has indeed been charged with attempted murder, and just entered his plea of not guilty." He eyed her up and down. "He will have ample opportunity to present his case in two weeks. " He flipped through a stack of papers then looked over his small square wire glasses to the two attorneys.

"Thank you, your honor." Mr. Richmond said.

"Works for me." Melvin's attorney chimed in.

"At which time, I'm sure, Mr. Richmond will allow you to testify on behalf of the defendant." Mr. Richmond smiled a broad smile and nodded. The judged banged his gavel twice.

"Until then, ladies and gentlemen, this court is adjourned." The judge stood, gathered a stack of manila folders and walked down off the bench. McKenzie turned to face Christian. They smiled at each other.

"Woman, what the hell are you doing here?" Christian said.

"Black man, where the hell else would you expect me to be?" McKenzie said.

"At home, recuperating."

"Not hardly." She extended her hand to the flawless attorney. "McKenzie Batiste." She flashed him her most gorgeous smile.

"So I've heard." Mr. Richmond said, taking her hand and shaking it gently. He smiled, leaned back, sat on the edge of the table, and crossed his arms over his chest. "Quite an entrance you made there." he said, jutting his chin out toward the court doors. They all laughed. McKenzie raised her cane slightly.

"No, I don't usually have visual aids."

"But, yes, she *always* makes an entrance." Christian said. McKenzie rolled her eyes.

"What the fuck, Christian? How come I had to hear about this from Detective Anderson?" McKenzie's brows were furrowed. She flung her left hand up in the air in exasperation.

"You weren't supposed to hear about this at all, thank you very much. The thought was to allow you to recuperate without worrying about anything else. And once it was all over then I'd tell you."

"See. This is why you don't get paid to think!" McKenzie said, pointing her finger at him. Mr. Richmond chuckled watching them go back and forth.

"Once it was all over? Once it was all over? So you had no intentions of having me testify either?"

"Uh, no."

"Again with the no thinking, Mr. Richmond?"

"Daniel, please."

"Daniel. Was this your idea? Because if so, no offense, but I'll be securing another attorney to defend Christian."

"Whoa, whoa! Slow your roll." Mr. Richmond stood, holding his hands up in a defensive stance. "First of all, no, that was not my idea. Christian will tell you himself that I said it was imperative that you testify. And secondly, just for the record pretty lady, you have no authority to fire me. That would have to come from my client, Mr. Malveaux."

McKenzie paused. She looked at Christian, who sat silently and watched the exchange between the two. Then she looked at the smirk on Mr. Richmond's face. He was looking quite amused with the situation.

"Well, good. As long as you and I are on the same page, because clearly this Black man ain't wrapped too tight right now."

Mr. Richmond glanced over at Christian who acknowledged it with a quick wink and broad smile.

☪   ☪   ☪

Outside the courthouse, McKenzie intentionally walked slowly so Christian could catch up with her.

"Hey, you didn't have to come up here today." Christian gently placed his hand at the base of her lower back as they walked side-by-side.

"Yes. I got that part, and that you actually preferred that I *not* be here today. Hence the failure to inform me that you had a court date. Oh! Wait! How about we go back even further – the failure to inform me that you had been charged, with attempted murder no less!" McKenzie was screaming. People on the street turned to look at her.

"*What*? What are you looking at? Mind your own damned business." McKenzie said to an old white woman standing on the corner. The woman quickly turned away.

"Stop it." Christian said. McKenzie rolled her eyes.

"You know I can't stand people all up in my business. Don't act like you don't know."

"Oh, I know darlin' - *and*, if you stopped screaming like a banshee, perhaps people wouldn't be inclined to turn around and get all up in yo business."

McKenzie stopped. She looked up into Christian's eyes.

"This is serious, Christian." He saw fear in her eyes. He gently grabbed her and pulled her into his chest.

"And I'm going to be fine. Daniel's game plan is tight. This judge has a reputation for coming down hard on sexual and domestic violence offenders. We're good. I promise you, if I thought I had anything to worry about, I would have told you."

And Jada. And his family. Christian hadn't told anyone except Kai about the charges. Least of all Jada. She would have had a complete meltdown. And the whole west side would have heard about it. She would have been the poor victim by the time she got to the end of the story, of course. No, Christian decided to wait. Especially because Detective Anderson had been able to arrange for him to turn himself in and had secretly helped him secure an attorney who arranged for bail.

Christian was very confident in Daniel's proposed defense. Nothing was airtight, but he felt good about it. And with McKenzie insisting on testifying, he didn't see the need to tell anyone now. No, he'd wait until he absolutely had to let folks know.

"You suck." McKenzie mumbled into his chest. Christian laughed.

♋   ♋   ♋

"When were you going to tell me, Christian?" Jada accused more than asked. Christian was washing his face in the bathroom when Jada walked in questioning him.

"Good morning to you, too." He replied as he returned the washcloth to the rack. He turned to face her. It was late morning and Christian had changed after court and slipped back into the house as if he'd been at his normal class all morning.

"Fuck you Christian. You don't get to act like we went to sleep last night on good terms. Did you completely forget that you spent the past 24 hours with some woman and never bothered to call your wife?"

"Well if I did, you certainly are doing a good job of reminding me." Christian said, walking past Jada.

"Stop trying to make me the bad guy here."

"I'm doing no such thing."

"Christian. You've been having an affair with this McKenzie bitch and got her pregnant. Is that where you were all night, holding her hand after she terminated your bastard child?" Jada seethed.

The accusation felt like a slap in the face. After all McKenzie had gone through in the past 24 hours, for Jada to come at him with this bullshit was just too much.

"Jada, you don't know what you're talking about." Christian said quietly.

"Yeah bitch! You thought you were so slick, huh you piece of shit!" She waved the prescription in his face.

"I know mutha fucka! I know about the bitch being pregnant! That's why yo ass jumped outta yo skin when she called my house, asking to speak to my fuckin' husband like she was runnin' something." She shoved the prescription in Christian's face. He grabbed her wrists.

"Let me go mutha fucka! Let me go!" Christian shoved her. Jada fell backwards. "Go be with that bitch then. You fuckin' her and making babies on me. Just go be with that ho!"

Christian stood looking at her. He remembered a time when he really loved her. When he would look at her and smile. Now, their time together created nothing but angst and anxiety for him. Obligation and responsibility kept him there, and even those two were beginning to lose their hold.

"I haven't gotten anybody pregnant," was all Christian said to her. He wasn't going to divulge McKenzie's personal information. If Jada thought he had gotten McKenzie pregnant then she'd just have to think it. He leered at her, then turned and walked out of the room.

Christian said he didn't get anybody pregnant. Jada didn't miss the fact that he never said he wasn't fucking her.

♋   ♋   ♋

McKenzie felt . . . ill. Not your typical 'body ache, fever, nausea' kind of ill, but more like an 'overall something just don't feel right' kind of ill. She slid out of bed and slowly climbed in the shower.

The water was piping hot. It stung the cuts and gashes that covered her body. She stood there allowing the pulsating sheath of water to cleanse her soul. It wasn't until the water started to turn cold that McKenzie realized that she had been standing in the shower crying for over 45 minutes.

She quickly soaped up—as quickly as she could—maneuvering around the tender spots, and stepped out of the shower. As she applied the Neutrogena Sesame Seed body oil to her bruised skin, she thought about what she could have done differently. McKenzie outlined each bruise. Some were a dark purple—almost black. Others were deep green. And she marveled at the two, one on her abdomen, the other on her clavicle, that were deep dark burgundy.

"Mom!" Ahmad shouted up the stairs. "Mom, can you hear me?"

"Yes, Ahmad, what's up, son?" She screamed back.

"Are you straight? I'm about to head out to school."

He waited at the bottom of the stairs. They had gotten into a huge argument yesterday when she came home. Ahmad wanted to stay home from school with his mom. "*Just in case you need anything*," he had said.

She replied, "*I'm not an invalid Ahmad. Whatever I need, I can get. You're going to school. Just call and check up on me at lunch or something, if that'll make you feel better.*"

"Yeah. I'm straight. Have a great day, baby. I love you!" McKenzie said.

"All right. I'll call to check up on you later. I love you too!" Ahmad said, heading for the door. "Oh yeah, Christian called while you were in the shower!"

And then McKenzie heard the door slam close.

Christian. She fell asleep on his chest last night and slept all through the night. She woke up, thinking about him and all that had transpired within the past 48 hours—him being charged with attempted murder!

She knew Christian felt guilty. But she really didn't blame him for this. She blamed Melvin. The hatred in his eyes during the attack let her know that Melvin was a ticking time bomb.

Christian had been there for her from the moment she placed that telephone call. But she wasn't sure what she was feeling right now. Hearing that he'd called warmed her inside. But there was something in the back of her mind that made her pause. If Detective Anderson hadn't told her about the court date she wouldn't have known anything about it or the charges until after everything had transpired.

As she lay there, thinking about what her real issue with Christian was, the telephone rang.

"Hello?" McKenzie said.

"Uh, y-yes. H-h-hello. May, may I speak with M-McKenzie, please?" said the baritone voice on the other end of the telephone.

"This is McKenzie, speaking," she replied, trying to figure out the voice.

"Is this the Ph-philosopher in the f-flesh?"

"Well, I don't know about all that . . . With whom am I speaking, please?"

"Y-you certainly knew a c-couple of weeks ago. W-what happened between then and now?"

The last past 48 hours flashed before McKenzie. She absent-mindedly rubbed the bruise on her inner thigh. "Nothing."

"This is Theodore, by the way. Christian's fraternity brother. I-I met you on the qu-quad—"

"Yes, I remember you. You're the sexy brotha with the locks?"

"Y-you think I'm s-sexy?" McKenzie could hear the smile across the telephone.

"Absolutely."

211

"W-well thank you k-kindly sistah. I th-thought you were p-pretty damned t-tasty myself." Theodore replied with excitement in his voice. McKenzie smiled. She wondered if he would think she looked tasty right now, all banged up.

"Well, thank you. And what do I owe the honor of this call?" McKenzie said, shocked because this call meant Christian gave Theodore her number. *Hmm. Interesting.*

"Oh, a b-bruh was just calling to ch-check up on a sis."

"I appreciate that."

McKenzie paused a moment in complete fear that Christian had told Theodore what had happened.

"Have you spoken to Christian recently?"

McKenzie closed her eyes and stopped breathing. She gripped the phone tightly in anticipation of TJ's reply.

"Y-Yeah, last week we spoke on the ph-phone. But I haven't s-seen him since I was up at your c-campus." TJ said. McKenzie let out a deep sigh. *He didn't know!*

"W-well. I w-was wondering if y-you wanted to g-go out f-for lunch sometime?" McKenzie smiled. She liked the idea of Theodore being attracted to her. Today—for more reasons than one.

♋   ♋   ♋

McKenzie didn't talk to Christian for weeks. And he didn't push. He thought she needed some time to herself. Plus, he still felt guilty. And to keep it really real, he'd been trying to stay close to home to keep Jada quiet. They had argued for four hours the day he came home from court.

The morning after pill consumed hour number one. She swore that baby was Christian's. You would've thought she had walked in on Christian butt-naked and mid-pump on top of McKenzie the way she went on and on about what she *knew*. Because he didn't want to get into McKenzie's business he just ate that one.

The rehashing of him playing on her in college consumed hour number two. *He was a liar and a cheat. She had sacrificed so much. She didn't trust him, couldn't trust him, wouldn't trust him EVER! He hadn't changed. He was ripping the wound off a painful scab, pouring alcohol on it, making it bleed. Blah, blah, blah. On and on and on.*

The last two hours were the ones he actually engaged in. She informed him that she had called his father and told him what Christian had done. He went off.

"You did what?" Christian screamed.

"I was distraught. What else was I supposed to do Christian?"

"How about you call *your* father, not mine?"

"Mr. Malveaux is like a father to me. And someone needs to talk some sense into you."

"That wasn't your place."

"Of course it was my place. I'm your wife. And besides, Dad agreed it was just disgusting what you did to me. He said it was awful and disrespectful," she said with a venomous smirk across her face.

"Did he say actually that?"

"Yes, he did. He said he was going to talk to you because he didn't raise you this way."

Christian tried to draw analogies during the four hours to help Jada understand how she had crossed the line, but she wasn't hearing any of it. Every time he'd make the comparison, she'd lie and say:

"I'd be fine with you calling my mom about that." Or she'd say, "That's not the same thing – this is different." But it wasn't.

It was all about respecting boundaries and respecting his relationship with his blood family. And if the shoe was on the other foot Christian knew that Jada would be livid if he had crossed those lines. But if she got it, Jada would die before she'd admit to being wrong.

So, for two hours they went around in circles. And at the end of it all, Christian was exhausted and still a lying, cheating, never to be trusted, good for nothing mutha fucka, sorry son-of-a bitch who was ungrateful for the wonderful woman he had.

So, for the next two weeks he stayed close to home. He attended functions he normally was "too busy" to attend. He even had sex with her twice without making her beg for it.

Jada threw in jabs about the situation as often as she could. Her goal was to milk it for as much and as long as she could. This was the way their relationship worked. Jada guilted and Christian gave in.

Intellectually, He knew this wasn't healthy, but emotionally, he just didn't have the energy to argue with her. As the four hour and countless other arguments proved, there was no space for compromise in their relationship. It was Jada's way or no way.

McKenzie hadn't pushed to see him. Christian felt the distance might be good for her. He still felt terribly guilty about his role in her rape. He felt she could use this time to heal, and not really have him in her face reminding him of what he had caused. He missed her of course. Wondered what she was doing. How she felt. But he gave her space and for the most part, let her be.

McKenzie had become a recluse. She stayed in the house, in her bed most days. Christian still sent the emails every morning—the one thing that didn't change after the rape. Everything else seemed so . . . out of whack.

As much as she tried, McKenzie couldn't bring things back to the way they were before. And she was pissed. As she had shared with Christian, it wasn't like she hadn't spent the majority of her life being violated. Why couldn't she shake this? Why couldn't she blow it off and just go back to the way things were?

During this time, she had been talking to TJ almost every night. He was a welcomed distraction. And he was funny. His humor was crass most times, but McKenzie wasn't your average female. Most things he said would have offended most women—but McKenzie either checked him, or blew him off. Either way, their conversations covered a wide variety of topics and stretched to three and four o'clock in the morning.

"W-when you gone let a b-brotha show off h-his culinary skills?" TJ asked one night.

"What. You can cook? Naw, I don't believe it!"

"Y-y-yeah, hell yeah I can cook! W-what kind of c-cuisine do you p-prefer?"

"I'm easy."

"I l-love to hear those w-words!" They laughed.

"You wish!" she said laughing. "Just include shrimp on the menu and I'm good to go!"

"Th-then let's set a date."

"You want to cook for me Dr. Johnson?"

"I-I-I just told y-yo ass I d-did. Wh-what? I w-wash my hands after I pee."

"You are such a nasty bastard, Theodore Johnson. I swear!" McKenzie said into the telephone. They laughed. She promised to check her calendar and call him with a date for their dinner.

♋   ♋   ♋

"What's up with McKenzie?" Camille asked Christian at the beginning of class. The group knew about what had happened between Melvin and McKenzie. They were all stunned and offered to testify for the prosecution at Christian's impending trial.

"I don't know really. She hasn't been in contact with me much," Christian confessed. Besides the morning emails and a couple of text messages, they hadn't had too many conversations. He hadn't seen her face-to-face at all.

Christian looked sad. Camille rubbed his back.

"She's going through a rough time. She'll bounce back. She's a tough kid." Camille said, smiling sympathetically. Christian had shared with Camille his guilt over sending McKenzie back to Melvin's. "It wasn't your fault, honey. Melvin is one sick puppy. End o' story." Camille paused.

"You know that punk had the audacity to call April and ask her to be a character witness for him?"

"Are you kidding me? She said no, right?"

"Of course. She flat out refused. It was no secret she and McKenzie would never be best friends, but April told him unequivocally there was no excuse for what he had done," Camille said. "She told me she used to talk to him quite often about her goals of creating her group home for girls and was offended that he would think she'd testify for him knowing her position on young girls' self-esteem and empowerment."

"Melvin only cares about himself." Christian said. "For him to think about how another person feels means he'd have to stop being a victim. And right now, that's his position: he's a victim of his circumstance. And McKenzie happened to show up at the wrong time while he was grieving."

"Well that's some bull shit if I ever heard any. I don't know what that nut was thinking, but he's got another thing coming if he thinks he's broken McKenzie's spirit. She's strong Christian. She's going to bounce back, you'll see. Stronger than ever."

Everyone thought McKenzie was tough. But Christian had seen the fragile side. He held her until she fell asleep. He had heard the fear in her voice, saw it in her eyes, felt it in her clutch. She was tough. She had endured the unfathomable. But Christian knew that deep inside she was hurting a pain so horrible, she didn't even allow herself to feel it.

Christian smiled at Camille. "Thanks."

April slid in close to Christian. She rubbed his back. Camille rolled her eyes. April was not in Christian's league. She had nothing up in that head of hers. She thought her body could get any man. But Christian preferred a smart'n'sassy woman. Someone who kept him captivated first in the mind. And, he was a man—he loved the chase. April advertised. She let you know all she had to offer was sex. That wasn't enough to get Christian's attention. It certainly wasn't enough to keep him.

"You look so sad, Christian. Is there anything I can do to help?" April said, sliding her boobs into his space. Christian shifted. He couldn't help but feel the double D's damn near in his chest.

"Uh, no April. Thanks. Hey, and thanks for not being a character witness for Melvin. I know you two had gotten pretty close during your observations."

"Yes, we did. But that doesn't mean I turn a blind eye to justice." April said, theatrically. She moved in closer and placed her hand on Christian's chest. "I said no to Melvin, and I meant it. And I'm saying yes to you Christian, and I mean it."

"What the hell?" Camille said.

"Ahem. What I mean by that is," April said, rolling her eyes at Camille, "I am here for you, unlike Melvin." She patted his chest gently. "Day or night. You can call on me anytime. I'll always make myself available for you whenever you need me."

Christian wasn't stupid. He knew when a woman was pushing up on him. He just wasn't interested. April made it clear on more than one occasion that she was interested in him. He knew for a fact he could hit it if he wanted to. He just didn't want to.

"Thanks, April. Really. But, I'm cool."

"Are you sure? Because I don't mind--"

McKenzie walked into the room. And just like that, April was nonexistent.

CHAPTER TEN

The Show Down

Christian stood up. "Hey Mac! What are you doing here?"

He pulled her into him for a long, heart-felt hug. If she didn't know better, she'd swear he missed her.

McKenzie returned the hug. The bruising was gone, so she held onto Christian tightly. They held the hug for a moment. She felt odd, because over the weeks she made herself stop obsessing over Christian. After her testimony in court she didn't see him again until the reading of the verdict "Not guilty". Christian had to rush off to some Sorority or family event with Jada right afterward – which she found so retarded.

"What if they had found you guilty, Christian? What would you have done?" McKenzie asked him. She had invited him out to celebrate, but he declined, telling her about his plans.

"Then, I would have had to tell her and everyone else." But he didn't. And he had managed to go through a possible life-altering trial without his wife, family *with the exception of Kai*, or closest friends having a clue.

After that day, she wouldn't see him again until this evening.

She found comfort in her morning emails that she religiously looked forward to reading over a hot steaming cup of coffee and waffles. But he was a safe distance away. Connected only by optical fibers and t-lines.

Feeling his arms around her waist, holding her so tight, brought all those feelings back. McKenzie closed her eyes and pretended nothing had happened all those weeks ago. She slowly pulled away.

"I'm here for the group presentation, of course." McKenzie smiled weakly.

McKenzie hadn't been to class or a group meeting since the assault. Camille looked at Christian in surprise. April stood up in feigned protest.

"You haven't been here in weeks, and you think you can just walk up in here and do the presentation?" April shouted.

McKenzie felt hurt. She came because she didn't want to let the group down. She wanted to keep her end of the bargain. Carry her weight of the project like she promised. McKenzie's stunned look registered across her face. Christian jumped to her rescue.

"Of course she can. She knows the material like the back of her hand." He grabbed her hand and walked her inside the group. "And I'm sure she can handle presenting our partner observation without a hitch." He eyed April who returned to her seat.

"No. April's right. That was very presumptuous of me. I'm sure you've prepared to present without me." McKenzie smiled. "I apologize."

She ran her hand through her curls, a little flustered.

"And I apologize for leaving you guys in the lurch these past couple of weeks." There were no physical traces of the attack besides the stitches over her right eye that she camouflaged with a scarf, and the red eye—the busted vein that was still healing—that she hid behind sunglasses. It was a glamorous "Hollywood" outfit that only McKenzie could pull off.

"Nonsense, McKenzie!" Camille said. "Stop apologizing. You didn't do shit. Now, let's talk about who is going to do what in this presentation tonight. And that includes you Missy." Camille said with a smile, grabbing McKenzie's hand.

McKenzie loved Camille. There was something about her that was so genuine, so warm. And she was so happy Camille always interjected with the perfect words at the right time.

♋   ♋   ♋

Jada watched Christian from the back of the class, through a crack in the rear door. She had been there, waiting. And she saw the reception he gave "Mac" when she walked through the door. She watched Christian holding her like he didn't want to let go. Christian lead her to the center of the group like she was some lost child and he was her savior. Jada saw his smile, bright, brilliant, and genuine. She couldn't remember the last time Christian smiled at her genuinely.

Jada closed the door behind her, slid into a seat in the far back corner, and waited. Watched, listened, and waited.

McKenzie held her own during the presentation. Christian thought she was magnificent. She didn't have a huge part, but he felt it was enough to make her feel like she added value.

After class, McKenzie stopped by Professor Telfair's desk and handed her the "Incomplete" form for her to sign. They had talked earlier in the week and Professor Telfair told her she had missed too many days, too many assignments, and the final. It would be too much for McKenzie to try and make up.

She tried to slip out of class without talking to anyone but Christian was on her heels as she left the room. McKenzie turned the corner into the hallway.

"McKenzie, I'm sorry about what happened. But you can't be serious."

It was Melvin. He looked scrawny, unkempt. He hadn't shaven and a scraggily red beard covered his face. His wrinkled beige Dockers and an olive t-shirt looked like he slept in them last night.

McKenzie jumped back, startled to see him. She grabbed her heart as if it threatened to stop beating. All Christian could see from his angle was McKenzie's response. He rushed out the door to end up face-to-face with Melvin.

"What the fuck are you doing here?" Christian screamed between clenched teeth. He grabbed Melvin's shirt and slammed him up against the wall. Melvin's face registered complete fear.

"I . . . I . . . just came to apologize."

McKenzie slowly walked over to them.

"I don't want your apology."

"No. You want to ruin me!" Melvin said. Christian banged his head against the wall. "Ouch!"

"You shut up!"

"It's not enough that you pressed charges against me," he said to McKenzie, "But you had to get me thrown out of school too?"

Melvin reached into his pocket and pulled out a crumpled piece of paper. McKenzie grabbed it and read it. Melvin had been expelled from the University based on corroborated evidence that he had violated the school policy on assault and rape. McKenzie smiled, dropped the piece of paper, turned and walked out of the hallway.

"You bitch! You self-righteous bitch!" Melvin started screaming and kicking—trying to get free of Christian's hold. Christian socked Melvin in the stomach, knocking the wind out of him. The silence was deafening.

Melvin slid down the wall to the floor. Christian stooped down to eye him.

"You don't want to fuck with me. I *will* kill you this time. And nothing would happen to me – double jeopardy. You remember that the next time you get another one of these brain-haired ideas." He stood and started to walk off. "Stay away from McKenzie. You understand me? Don't try to talk to her. Don't get within 500 yards of her. You hear me?" Melvin nodded.

By this time, the rest of the students had filed out the classroom and watched in silence. Christian didn't see Jada wedged in the crowd. He went looking for McKenzie.

McKenzie sat crying at a table in the quad area. Seeing Melvin made her cave in like a baby.

"Are you OK?" Christian whispered behind her.

"Yeah, I'm fine. Thanks." McKenzie whispered back, wiping the tears from her face.

She stood up and turned to face him. He looked concerned. She smiled.

"Really. These are tears of anger. The nerve of him coming up here."

She folded her arms across her chest. Christian walked up behind her and held her. She leaned back into his chest and they stood there silent, in the pitch-black night.

"How cozy." came a female voice from behind them.

"Would you like to introduce your classmate to your wife?" Jada said.

McKenzie pulled out of Christian's embrace to face his wife. They stared each other down, both sizing the other up.

"McKenzie Batiste." McKenzie said. Jada walked up closer to McKenzie and spoke as she glared at Christian.

"Do you always stand, holding your classmates under the stars, or is that reserved especially for . . . what's your name again?" Jada turned to face McKenzie.

McKenzie smirked. She knew Jada knew her name and was just trying to make her feel uncomfortable. She laughed out loud.

"Yes. Well, Christian, I'll talk to you later." McKenzie said, looking at Christian.
She started to walk off.

"Don't leave on my account." Jada said, leaning back on the table.

McKenzie looked her up and down, slowly shook her head from side to side, and let out a quick laugh. The look enraged Jada.

"Fuck you, bitch! You don't get to fuck my husband and look at me like I'm the ho' here. I am the wife." Jada said pointing a finger in McKenzie's face.

McKenzie stared her in the eyes. She smiled.

"You have the title. I could care less about a title." McKenzie turned and walked off.

"You'll never have him, bitch!"

Over her shoulder, McKenzie said, "I have what I want--his heart. And you know it. Because if you thought otherwise, you wouldn't be sneaking around following him."

Jada turned to face Christian. He met her stare with a look of disgust. Jada knew McKenzie was right. She knew that woman had her husband's heart.

McKenzie pulled out her cell phone. She couldn't believe her night. First, the embarrassment in class, then Melvin showing up, and then Christian's wife. What fucking luck did she have?

"Hello? Hey you. I'm hungry."

"W-well bring yo ass over s-so a bruh can feed you." TJ said.

I was beginning to think y-you didn't want to h-hang out with a bruh." TJ said placing a spoonful of turkey spaghetti on McKenzie's plate. She smiled slowly crossing her legs.

"Great things come to those who wait. You've heard that before, right Dr. Johnson?" McKenzie said twirling noodles around her fork. He poured them both a tall glass of red wine. "What, are you trying to get me drunk?"

"O-oh, don't tell me you're a l-light-weight."

"I drink socially. What about you? Looks like you have a high tolerance?"

"I'm n-not a drunk, if that's what you're asking. I-I drink. More than a lightweight. But not to the p-point where it's a problem." He said dabbing some French bread into the spaghetti sauce.

"Mm. This is delicious," she moaned with a mouth full of food.

"C-careful over there, g-girl. You g-getting a bruh w-worked up over here." TJ shifted in his seat. She laughed. He blushed.

"Seems like it doesn't take much," McKenzie said with a coy smile.

"Not when there's a f-fine ass sistah sitting across from me it d-doesn't."

McKenzie closed her eyes and enjoyed her food. She chewed slowly and intentionally, taking in the flavor of the sauce, the seasoned meat, the fresh hot, buttered French bread, and the constant adoration from the man across the table. It all felt so good.

♋   ♋   ♋

What's up, Black? Where you been?" Christian said. "You're in-cog-negro these days. What's been keeping you so busy?"

"N-not what. W-who?" TJ said, with a wide grin.

"Whoa! The Meister's in the house! Who's the latest victim?" Christian said.

"The l-lucky lady is none other than M-Ms. McKenzie Batiste!" TJ beamed. Christian nearly choked.

"Whoa! What? I didn't know you guys were kickin' it?"

"Y-yeah. We've been kickin' it p-pretty tough since you gave me her number. We h-hung out for the first time l-last night."

Christian tried calling McKenzie last night, but she didn't answer. Now, he knew why. She was with TJ. His head started to pound. His mouth became dry.

"Oh, yeah? I'm sure you had fun." Christian wanted to know, but at the same time he didn't.

"Aw m-man, it was nice. She's a c-cool sistah, you know?" TJ sat up excited.

"Yeah. Yeah, Mac is way cool," Christian whispered. "What. Um . . . Did you guys go out?" He found himself asking before he knew what he was doing.

"Naw. We k-kicked at my house. She s-stayed the night," TJ said, smiling. "I c-cooked her dinner, we h-had wine. You know, two g-grown folks, h-hanging out."

"Right, right," Christian said. "So—" He took a deep breath. "You diggin' her?"

"Man, am I! I k-know it's way early. And I know it's going to b-break a slew of women's hearts—b-but I think this girl may c-cause the J-Meister to turn in his Playa card."

☙ ☙ ☙

226

"Hey, McKenzie. How you doin' pumpkin'?" Camille said.

"I'm good. How are you?"

"I'm fine. Listen, I was calling to personally invite you to our graduation."

Because of the incomplete, McKenzie couldn't walk this semester. She would have to retake the class and reapply for graduation in the fall.

"Everyone thought it was a bad idea to invite you. But I know better. You're coming, right? It wouldn't be the same without you."

"What? Does everyone think I'm falling apart at the seams, Camille?" McKenzie was incensed.

"No, that's not it. They just know how hard you worked for this degree. And it's not your fault you're not walking, so they just didn't want to seem insensitive."

"And I will get the damned degree. In the fall." McKenzie said. "But I'm thrilled for the rest of you. And I wouldn't miss being there to cheer each of you on when you walk across that stage."

"I knew it!" Camille screamed. "So you'll be there? And you're coming to the party too, right?"

McKenzie laughed. "Yes, Camille, I'll go to the party."

"The gang is going to be thrilled." Camille sighed. She knew McKenzie would want to be there. She meant it when she said this kid was a winner. She knew McKenzie had gone through some shit in her short life, but she also knew she'd come out on top. Camille could see it in her eyes.

I just want to know if you're fucking her." Jada said.

"No, you don't. You want me to make you feel secure about our relationship." Christian replied.

"And what's wrong with that? I shouldn't feel secure about our relationship?"

"I shouldn't have to convince you over and over and over."

"If that's what it takes, then you should convince me. And you shouldn't mind doing it if it means making me happy."

"I wouldn't mind—IF I didn't have to do it all the time, Jada. It's old already."

"Maybe if you lit up when *I* walked in a room. Maybe if you nearly knocked over a room full of people to get to *me*. Maybe if you coddled *me* and handled *me* . . . maybe I wouldn't need you to do it over and over. Because I'd know."

Christian didn't reply. How do you do any of those things when you don't feel them? He knew, as her husband, he should. And heaven knows he'd tried. But he just didn't feel that way for her—his wife.

The most he could do was go through the motions; being polite; being a gentleman; opening the door, pulling her seat out; paying for the bill; doing for her the same things he'd probably do for a stranger on the street.

Jada told him she had watched them in class. She cried as she described how he looked at McKenzie . . . how he held her close. He felt bad. But he couldn't change the way he felt for McKenzie. All he could do was to do the right thing by Jada. And that's what he was doing.

"Maybe so, Jada," Christian sighed. He scratched the back of his head. "But if that's not the case—because it hasn't been the case in a long while, and it's not going to be the case in the foreseeable future—then what?" He looked tired.

"Then, we need to do what it takes to get back to that place. To get that intimacy back." She cried.

"Jada, you are who you are. And I am who I am. All the counseling in the world isn't going to change those fundamental truths." He looked at her, resolute in his assessment.

"What is wrong with you? You got this girl on the brain and you've lost all hope for us?" She sobbed.

"One doesn't have anything to do with the other—and you know it."

"I don't know it. What I know is that you promised to love me until death do us part. And you're not keeping the vows you made before God."

"Have you ever thought about that Jada? 'Til death do us part?"

"Of course I've thought about it! Shit, I'm fighting for it!"

Christian stared at her. He really looked at her closely. This was the woman he used to be in love with. This was the woman everyone said was perfect for him. *What happened?* Christian thought to himself. He didn't dare ask out loud. He knew what the answers would be if he asked them out loud: *You stopped touching me, You stopped kissing me, You stopped holding my hand.* There would be a litany of things that *he* did, that caused this relationship to go to shit. It was all *his* fault. And he was tired of hearing it.

He couldn't deny that most of the accusations were true. He did stop doing those things. The feelings he used to have that made him want to do any of those things had been replaced with deep seeded anger, resentment, and on some occasions, hate.

Christian knew Jada hadn't thought about that phrase. He knew she hadn't contemplated the basic simplicity of "'til death do us part,' because if she had, they wouldn't be having this conversation. They would've stop having these types of conversations years ago.

They would have decided to just make this arrangement work. It could look however she wanted it to look in public. Christian had gotten accustomed to playing the role. He knew the right words to say. He knew how long to hold her hand, or stand next to her while she hugged him, so that no one would suspect that anything was wrong. Hell, he could kiss her on the lips all day long. The closed-lip pecks didn't make him flinch. But they were public and intimate enough to give the impression to others that intimacy still dwelled in their house.

But the truth was the truth. And whether Jada would admit it or not, this relationship was dead. And in his mind, that's what this infamous bible verse meant. If you've tried all you can, done all you can do, and there simply was no life left in the relationship, and it'd run its course, then you need to decide to just go your separate ways.

Staying in a miserable relationship couldn't be pleasing God. He couldn't want people wasting their lives, getting absolutely no fulfillment out of them because they're doing the 'morally' right thing and staying with someone who does nothing for them. Christian just couldn't see that. But Jada, and all the other self-righteous, self-appointed religious right would adamantly disagree.

"You get everything you want. You wanted a big ring; you got a big ring. You wanted a big wedding; you got a big wedding. You wanted a big house; you got a house. You wanted a new car; you got a new car. You wanted to travel; we travel. You get every damned thing you want, Jada. To anyone looking at us, they'd think we have the perfect marriage. That's all you really wanted, right?" He smirked. "I'd say I've kept my end of the deal."

"I want you to be in love me. I want your heart, dammit!"

"Oh, we're long beyond that."

"You are a bastard! An asshole! You are a cruel, insensitive mutha fucka Christian!" she screamed. "All I want is a happy marriage. Where my husband loves and adores me. Where he is *in love* with me. And wants me. Is that asking for too much?"

"Did you ever think *I* might want something in this marriage?"

"I used to think we wanted the same thing, Christian."

Christian laughed. He knew before they got married they didn't want the same things. He just didn't know those differences would create such discord in their lives.

♋   ♋   ♋

"Ladies and gentlemen, please put your hands together in helping me to congratulate California State University, Long Beach's graduating Class of 2010!"

The crowd sent the Pyramid ablaze with screams, shouts, and blow horns. The graduates tossed their hats and filed out into the waiting crowd to greet friends and family.

The Education department hosted a reception for the graduates after the ceremony in the Niner's Loft. The graduating class and their guests slowly filled up the brown and gold decorated room.

Furnell stood in front of a table and waved over everyone from their study group.

"I've got these three tables reserved for us," he said with a wide grin. He had a shoe on one table, and jacket on the other as placeholders.

"You are so ghetto," Camille said pulling up a chair at the table.

"It must be the company I keep." Furnell said pushing Camille's chair in behind her. They laughed.

"Hey guys!" April screamed as she made her way around the table, hugging and kissing everyone. "We did it. We finished this fucking program!"

"And not a day too soon!" Camille said, giving April a high five.

Christian followed Jada into the room. Furnell waved them down. Christian pointed in the direction of the group.

"This way Jada. Looks like Fern and the gang have seats for us over there." Christian said.

"Why do we have to sit with them? Why can't we find our own table? Shit, you spent the last two years with them. You can't have your goddamn graduation party to yourself?" Jada said. Christian's stomach tightened. He walked ahead of her to the table.

"What's up Graduates?" Christian shook Furnell's hand. He kissed Camille and April on their cheeks as Jada stood glaring.

"Camille, April, this is Jada."

"His wife." Jada said.

April's mouth dropped open. Camille rolled her eyes. Furnell turned his head away, so as not to look at Christian. Christian pulled out Jada's seat. She sat, watching everyone's different expressions. She enjoyed seeing the discomfort on their faces. She hated this little group. They thought they were so important the way they hung out all the time. She was annoyed by the constant calls "about school." No one was happier than she was that this day was here. Finally, she would get her husband back.

"It's nice to finally be able to put the faces with the voices after all this time." Jada said smiling and batting her eyes.

"Look who's here." Christian said.

Christian waved to get TJ's attention. TJ saw him and walked over to the table. "What's up TJ? Thanks for coming man."

"Aw, man. You k-know I wouldn't miss your g-graduation bruh." TJ replied, giving Christian a half-hug. He reached down and kissed Jada on the cheek. "Hello pretty lady." Jada smiled.

"Hey TJ. What's going on?" Jada perked up, happy to have someone at the table she had some history with.

"Aw-aw, not m-much." TJ replied. Christian introduced him to everyone at the table.

April took off her robe only to find Jada staring at her boobs. She hesitated, not sure if she should put it back on or what. She placed the robe on the back of the chair. Jada glared at Christian accusingly.

"So, where's your family April?" Jada said.

"Oh. They're coming."

"Really? Do you have a boyfriend or husband to celebrate this special day with you?" Jada said.

But before she could answer, Camille stood and shrieked "McKenzie! You look gorgeous!" And she did.

Christian stared as McKenzie made her way across the room in a cute, little black dress. It was a spaghetti strap, knee-length dress underneath a chartreuse colored shrug. Her curls were gone! Her hair was straight. It was styled in a short tapered haircut, with golden bronze highlights. They added flare, style, and dimension to the boyish haircut that would have probably looked boring on any other woman. And . . . McKenzie had on heels! Except for the boots she occasionally wore, McKenzie never wore heels. She looked amazing . . . feminine . . . elegant.

She made her rounds hugging everyone, congratulating them. As she made her way toward Christian, he noticed her impeccably made up face. Christian had never seen Mac in anything other than lip-gloss.

"TJ!" McKenzie moved over to give him a hug. "How are you?" She asked, placing a kiss on his cheek—a little too close to his lips for Christian's comfort.

"O-oh, n-not nearly as g-good as y-you. D-dayum McKenzie, y-you look g-gorgeous!"

"Well thank you Mr. Johnson. You're looking mighty dapper yourself."

"You like that?" TJ said, tugging at his suit lapels.

"Absolutely."

TJ blushed. Christian tried to remain emotionless even though he was slightly irritated at the way they were going on.

McKenzie saw Jada watching closely, daring her to do anything with that penetrating stare. So, of course, McKenzie sashayed over to Christian and gave him a huge hug.

"You did it! I'm so proud of you!" Christian returned the hug.

"Thank you Mac. You know you'll be walking across that stage soon." Christian whispered in her ear. She smiled and pulled away. She turned to Jada.

"Jada." Was all she said.

"McKenzie. What are you doing here? I thought you weren't walking this semester." Jada said with a smirk plastered across her face. Christian shot her a look. Camille started to reply, but McKenzie didn't miss a beat.

"I came to congratulate my classmates." McKenzie said, turning to face them. "I came to share in this special moment with them. They worked so hard for this day."

"And it wouldn't be complete without McKenzie here." Camille said, looking at Jada.

"I'm just saying. This party is for the graduates and their family members." Jada said.

"And McKenzie is a part of our family." April said.

McKenzie smiled, surprised at her response.

"Of course she is." Christian said. "She came to wish us well, just like we'll be here to wish her well next semester." He smiled. McKenzie smiled.

"Um, excuse me. I'm going to go congratulate Henry and the others." McKenzie said and left.

Christian sat with his back to Jada, talking to TJ at the table. Eventually, he would have to engage in conversation with her; but for now, he was too pissed off to even look at her.

After the Department Dean addressed the graduates, the DJ started playing music. The folks in the room were mixing and mingling, taking pictures and exchanging hugs. McKenzie was talking to one of her classmates when she heard someone calling out her name. She turned to see Furnell waving his arms about.

"Mac! Mac! C'mon!" Furnell said, motioning up to the ceiling referring to the music. McKenzie paused and listened. It was a Frankie Beverly and Maze song. "Golden Time of Day."

There's a time of the day
When the sun's going down
That's the golden time of day

McKenzie tossed her head back and laughed. The entire group was flagging her down. It was show time. And she had a score to settle. Or, at the very least a 'tit' she was going to 'tat'. She walked over to the table and stood behind Jada and Christian. She darted in front of Jada.

"Mrs. Malveaux, you don't mind if I borrow your husband for 2 minutes and 20 seconds do you?" McKenzie said, grabbing Christian's hand and pulling him up out of his seat.

"Excuse me! What are you doing?" Jada started to protest.

"I'm going to cha-cha with your husband, with your permission of course." McKenzie paused. She looked at the group as if to say, 'C'mon guys.'

"Of course it's OK, right Jada?" Camille said.

"Sure Mac, you have her permission." Furnell said.

"Hurry up!" April said. "The damned song is going to be over in a minute." Everyone eyed Jada.

"I can cha-cha with him." Jada started to get up. April pushed her back down in her seat.

"Oh, anybody can cha-cha with Christian. That's not the point." Camille explained. "It's tradition. The way these two cha-cha is an art form. And today, they need to cha-cha to commemorate our graduation."

"Yeah," Furnell said. "It wouldn't be complete without these two cuttin' it up on the floor one last time."

Everyone watched Jada. She searched for the words that would prevent the two from going out on that dance floor and keep her from looking like a bitch.

McKenzie saw her brain working. She smiled. She took Christian's hand and headed toward the dance floor.

"Jada, I know you don't want to be a killjoy. I promise to bring your husband right back."

Before Jada could respond, the group was clapping and cheering the two on to the dance floor. Jada sat seething.

They fell right in step the moment they hit the center of the dance floor.

"You know that move just cost me two weeks of peace Miss Thang?" Christian said. McKenzie threw her head back and laughed.

"Actually . . . you probably lost that the moment I walked into the room tonight." Christian laughed. She was probably right. He twirled her around, and they fell back into step as she finished the spin. The room went wild. The perfectly choreographed routine was smooth and effortless.

"I love this song." Christian said, singing along with the words.

Christian twirled her around again. This time, McKenzie stopped next to him. They cha-cha'd side by side a few beats before Christian dipped, paused, turned and waited for McKenzie to step in front of him. He looked deeply into her eyes as he sang the next verse.

When you feel deep inside
All the love you're looking for
Don't it make you feel OK

Everybody was on their feet, clapping and singing along.

Christian and McKenzie left the floor to claps and cheers. Christian walked over to the table where the group sat. McKenzie pointed toward the bar to indicate that she was going to get a drink. The truth was, she didn't feel like getting into another tiff with Jada.

She'd come to celebrate her classmates' graduation. And she had. She was done with all the juvenile bullshit. It did nothing for her. She hesitated for a minute. She didn't really want a drink. She wanted to leave this place. McKenzie turned to head for the door and ran into TJ.

"Whoa! W-where are you in a hurry to?"

"Oh, I'm outtie TJ." McKenzie said, heading toward the door. He grabbed her arm.

"Already? D-did you say bye to everyone?"

"Uh, no. Are you going back that way? Can you tell them I said goodbye?"

"J-just come say goodbye."

"No, really. I gotta go." she said grabbing his hand. "Can you please just tell them for me? Please."

"Sure . . . Are you OK? I-I can drive you home if you want."

"No, TJ, I'm fine. Thanks. I'm just tired of all the drama at the table."

She stared over in the direction of the table. TJ knew she was referring to Jada. She had a tendency to show her ass every now and then. It wasn't the first time he'd witnessed her insecurity. Most folks just ignored her.

"W-well. OK. Then how about you c-come over to my house and h-have that drink?" TJ said. McKenzie hesitated.

"You'll tell the gang I said good bye?"

"Y-yep. And I'll meet you at m-my house?"

236

"OK." McKenzie agreed. TJ practically skipped over to the table.

"H-hey guys. I saw M-McKenzie on the way in. Sh-She asked me to congratulate you one l-last time and say goodnight." They nodded and continued to socialize. TJ pulled Christian off to the side.

"Did Mac look all right?"

"Oh, she's f-fine. Sh-she's meeting me b-back at my place for a d-drink." TJ winked and patted Christian on the shoulder. Christian froze.

"Are w-we still on f-for brunch tomorrow?"

"Uh. Yeah. Sure. Unless you got other plans?"

"N-naw. I'll see you tomorrow." TJ said on his way out.

Christian watched him practically float out. He was going to meet McKenzie. He knew why TJ was on cloud nine.

♋   ♋   ♋

"Red or chardonnay?" TJ asked as he made his way to the kitchen.

"You have any White Zen?" McKenzie said, taking off her heels and shrug. "May I use your restroom?"

"S-sure. Go ahead," TJ called from the kitchen.

McKenzie washed the make-up off. It had been working her nerves. She wanted to scratch her face all night.

"W-White Zen? That's Kool-Aid. I forgot y-you're not a real d-drinker. I-I can go out an-and get some?"

"No. Chardonnay is fine, TJ, really." She said walking back into the living room.

He walked in with a glass of Chardonnay for McKenzie and a glass of red wine for himself.

"Here you go." He handed her the wine. McKenzie took the glass and took a long slow sip. *Mm.* She'd had a hard day. She put on a good face, but it hurt her deeply that she wasn't able to graduate with her cohort. Then, being in the same space with Jada. . . She needed something to relax her. She closed her eyes. TJ moved behind her and slowly started to massage her shoulders.

"Mm." McKenzie moaned. "Careful Black man. Don't start nothing you can't finish."

TJ gently kissed her neck. McKenzie jumped, surprised. He waited a few seconds and kissed her again. This time, she sat quietly. TJ took that as a sign of approval.

McKenzie felt a rash of emotions. Anxiety. Fear. But for the first time in weeks, she felt desired. And she loved the feeling. TJ didn't know about the rape. To him, she was just a woman he wanted. Not a damaged woman he felt sorry for. He slowly pulled her straps off her shoulders . . .

"What up, Black?" TJ said as Christian took his seat. They met at TGI Fridays for brunch.

"What's up? How's it going?" Christian said pulling up a chair.

"Aw, a b-brotha doin' all right—c-considering." TJ said.

"Good afternoon, gentlemen." The young waitress said. "Can I get you started with something to drink today?"

"Are y-you even old enough t-to serve alcohol?" TJ said. The waitress placed her hands on her hips.

"Yes, I am. I'm 22 years old, as a matter of fact." They all laughed.

"I'll just have a diet Coke with a lemon wedge, please." Christian said.

"I'll h-have an ice tea, please." TJ said.

"You mean, you went through all that and you're not going to order any alcohol?"

"Uh n-no. We're straight. We were just t-trying to find a reason to converse with a b-beautiful sistah—that's all." TJ said. The girl blushed.

"He was trying to find out if you were jail bait." Christian said. They all laughed and the waitress walked off to get their drinks.

"Why you t-trying to bust a brotha out?" TJ asked Christian. Christian just laughed.

"Just calling a spade a spade, Black." Christian said, leaning back in his seat. He watched TJ, still annoyed with the fact that McKenzie went by his house last night for a drink. He knew he didn't have the right to be—but still.

"I'm n-not interested in that tenderoni. I got a real w-woman I'm completely devoted to." TJ announced proudly. Christian's stomach tensed. He knew he was talking about McKenzie.

"Devoted? The Meister? Never."

"Yes, I know. B-but it's true. Dog, M-McKenzie is remarkable. I told you I-I was d-diggin' her."

"Yeah, there's a difference between diggin' a woman and being completely devoted to her. What, are you whipped?"

"I-I think I might be." Just then, the waitress brought their drinks. Not a minute too soon. Christian's mouth went dry. He couldn't believe what he was hearing

"Tell me about it."

"Christian, m-man, McKenzie is the one. If I d-didn't know it before, after last n-night, I'm certain." He sipped his ice tea.

"What happened last night?" Christian's curiosity got the best of him.

"You k-know I don't k-kiss and tell—but . . ." TJ scoped the restaurant to make sure no one could hear him. Christian felt queasy. He gulped his diet coke and chased it down with his ice water.

"We slept together." TJ blushed. Christian choked on his water. He couldn't believe what he was hearing. How could McKenzie do this to him? How could she sleep with his best friend?

"Really?" Was all he could say.

"Yes. It was n-nice, Christian. Not like h-how it's been with the other w-women I've s-slept with." TJ struggled with his words.

Christian felt he understood what TJ was trying to say. He had experienced McKenzie's passion, her sexuality, and her ability to make a man feel . . . like a man. She had made him come alive with her kisses and the way she gave herself to him so completely.

"I mean, she's a r-reserved lover." Christian was taken by surprise. *Reserved? Mac?*

"What do you mean by reserved?"

"Well . . . S-she's just not a f-freak—I guess."

Christian was really confused. McKenzie was the freakiest woman he'd ever made love to. Maybe she was struggling with intimacy after the rape.

"But that's O-OK. I think that w-will come in t-time. You know what I mean?"

"Oh yeah. Definitely. Sex, um, always gets better . . . with time."

"Yeah. T-that's right." TJ scanned the menu. "Man, what are you having? I'm starving."

Christian pretended to scan his menu. He knew he wouldn't be ordering too much today. After this unexpected revelation, he had completely lost his appetite.

♋   ♋   ♋

McKenzie lay in her bed, confused about what she was doing. She had sex with TJ last night. It wasn't shit to write home about. But still. She knew the code. And what she had done, you just don't do. You don't sleep with your girl's man *past, present, or the one she's feelin' –even if he ain't feelin' her.* And you don't sleep with your man's best friend, distant friend, homie, brother – blood or fraternity.

"He's not my man. He's married, remember?" McKenzie said to Denny.

"It doesn't make what you did right. You knew Christian was married when you slept with him. Now you're mad because you want to be with him so you sleep with his friend and say it doesn't matter cuz he's married?" Denny said. "Seriously Mac? That's weak."

"Then it's weak. Cuz I've already done it. Can't take it back." McKenzie lay on her back, phone to her ear, filing her nails.

"You broke the code."

"Ain't the first time I broke something, Denny."

"Why are you being such a bitch right now?"

"Why are you being holier than thou? You're the one always telling me I need to find somebody available. Someone who adores me and appreciates the woman that I am."

"And I meant it. But you mean to tell me out of 11 million people in Los Angeles, you couldn't find anybody else but that man's best friend?"

"Honestly, I didn't try. What's wrong with TJ and me being together?"

"Let's see. He's best friends with Christian. So if you do end up in a serious relationship you'll be in his face, and his wife's all the---Bitch, that's what you want?" Denny screamed into the phone.

"What?"

"Don't *what* me, like you're all innocent. You're trying to hurt Christian by being with his best friend. You want to be up in his space, rub your relationship in his face, don't you, Satan's little Black love child?" McKenzie laughed hard.

241

"You going to hell, McKenzie."

"In gasoline draws Denise."

There was a long pause.

"Do you even like him?"

McKenzie thought a second. She thought about last night. The earth didn't stop spinning on its axis. Sex with TJ wasn't anything compared to sex with Christian.

"He screamed and moaned like a 7th grader bustin' a nut for the first time." McKenzie chuckled to herself thinking about how he called out her name.

"No way!" Denny said laughing.

"Oh, McKenzie! Yes! Yes! Ooh, girl. Mm, you feel so good! Shit baby!" McKenzie changed her voice to try and sound like TJ's. They both laughed. "But TJ is sweet. He's the kind of man you know will take care of you. And he is diggin' me, big time. I can tell. He tried to play like he was hard. Giving me a hard time, arguing with me and shit. But in the end, he always found a way to concede, or give me what I wanted." McKenzie whispered. "He is the type of man your momma told you to look for--smart, kind, and considerate . . . a provider. TJ is all that."

Sigh.

"But your heart still beats for his fraternity brother?" Always the objective observer, truth sayer. *Bitch.*

"Doesn't matter. He is married, Den. Jada made sure everyone knew he was married."

Sigh.

"So I'm not going to sit around and pine for a married man. Not when I have a perfectly good man in pursuit of moi!"

"Especially when that married man isn't making any attempts at leaving his completely miserable marriage?" Denny pointed out.

"Yeah, fuck him."

CHAPTER ELEVEN

The Proposal

"How long you been dating?" Christian said.

"A couple of months now." TJ replied, looking over the menu at Lucille's. "H-have you tried the t-tri tip salad? Is it g-good?"

"Uh, yeah. It's cool." Christian replied, careful not to sound too anxious.

Even though it had been a couple of months, it felt like just yesterday when TJ told him he and McKenzie had slept together. Christian wouldn't have admitted it to anyone, but he was so hurt. But at the same time he knew he didn't have the right. He was a married man. And he hadn't made any attempts at leaving his marriage.

His commitment—the right thing to do, he told himself—was to step back, get out of the way, and let two beautiful people find happiness. He wouldn't be selfish and come between that.

Although it was hard, Christian did all he could to be supportive of their relationship. He wasn't really reaching out to McKenzie via email anymore. He felt it was disrespectful. Not that he ever said anything out of line to McKenzie in the emails. It was just that most of the songs he'd send her were laced with subliminal messages he didn't have the courage to tell McKenzie himself. So, he felt that was disrespectful to TJ, even though no one but himself knew what he was doing.

"And you still think she's the one, eh?" Christian said. TJ smiled broadly.

"Yeah, man. A-actually, that's why I suggested we have b-brunch at Lucille's today."

Christian looked confused. "Why?"

"M-man." TJ paused. "I-I'm going to a-ask McKenzie to m-marry me, an-and I was h-hoping a bruh, would h-help me pick out a—you know, r-really nice ring. S-since you've already d-done it b-before. Th-there's a R-robin's Bros. Next d-door."

Christian went silent. His head was throbbing and he couldn't get a word out for a long time. He coughed to kill the silence.

"Um, uh—yeah dog, of course!" Christian forced a smile.

"Cool! I kn-know a bruh got n-nice taste and all. J-Jada's ring was n-nice and c-classy."

"Thanks." Christian's mind was going a mile a minute. "Has she . . . I don't know. Seemed like she wants to get married? I mean, have you guys talked about it—you wouldn't want to just spring something like this on Mac—"

"W-we've talked in th-theory. You know, like 'if I were to get married . . . or my husband or wife would have to . . .' k-kind of shit. I-I have a pretty g-good feeling about it."

"And you think she's ready to be serious?" Christian said, unwilling to believe she'd be serious about marrying him.

"Y-yes. Christian, I k-know you're worried. B-but I'm serious. My hoin' days are o-over." TJ replied. Reading into Christian's line of questioning. "H-hey, I read that t-the ring is s-supposed to c-cost three months of a b-brotha's salary?"

"Fuck that shit, Ted. The ring ain't supposed to have a brotha selling his nuts on e-bay to pay for that bitch!" They laughed.

Christian was torn. He wasn't feeling the idea of TJ proposing to Mac. But at the same time, he knew he didn't have the right to object—he was a married man. And he knew Robins Bros. didn't have the caliber of ring to suit McKenzie. But he honestly struggled with whether or not to hook TJ up with his jeweler just because he was jealous.

"Teddy, we can go check out Robins Bros. But, seriously, I doubt that they'll have what you're looking for. Something nice, and affordable." Christian said, refusing to give in to his personal feelings. "They've got overhead to account for, being here in Torrance. They've got to cover salaries for all of those sales people. Import/Export charges for the huge inventory they have to keep."

"Well, w-what do you recommend?"

"I'll hook you up with my jeweler. He's got some beautiful pieces, reasonably priced. And he has a craftsman on site. If you don't see anything there you like, he can help you design your own setting."

TJ looked excited. "Cool! You know you my dog, right 'C'?" TJ hugged Christian who felt like shit.

"Yeah 'T', man. I'm gone always have your back."

Christian spent the rest of the afternoon with TJ and his jeweler picking out the perfect ring for McKenzie. TJ decided on a two-carat marquis cut ring set in 14 carat gold. Christian knew he was wrong for doing it, but he allowed TJ to settle on that ring although he knew it was not the ring for her.

Christian had picked out the perfect ring for Mac. It was not quite a carat, princess cut, with two beveled diamonds on each side—white gold. It was understated elegance, and it reminded him of her, small, petite, but classy. He honestly thought the ring TJ got her was way too gaudy. But TJ insisted on spending at least three months of his salary—and he did.

It just went to show that TJ didn't really know McKenzie. She loved nice things, but she wasn't flashy like that. If he had paid any attention to her at all he would have noticed that the jewelry she wore was quality. They were unique pieces, but very simple. She wore them with her athletic gear and with her professional attire. And they were silver. Christian knew McKenzie would hate that ring.

"So, Theodore," Christian said, slapping TJ on the back as they made their way out of the jewelry store "Are you satisfied with your purchase?"

"Man, y-yes! And I-I know McKenzie is g-going to love it. Thanks bruh. I-I certainly appreciate your h-help."

"Not a problem. Not a problem at all." Christian said, feeling a little guilty. "So, when are you going to pop the question?"

"This w-weekend. A-after dinner on S-Saturday."

ॐ ॐ ॐ

"Thanks for meeting me." Christian said to McKenzie as they took a seat in the quad. The last time they were there she and Jada had exchanged words.

"No problem." McKenzie replied, running her fingers through her damp curls. She had just finished her afternoon swim. "What's up? It sounded pretty important." She looked concerned.

"It is. There's no easy way to put this, so I'm just going to tell you." Christian looked McKenzie in the eyes. Her stomach knotted up at his words.

"OK then, tell me." She braced herself for the worst.

"TJ is going to propose to you this Saturday."

McKenzie sat staring at Christian for a moment, processing what he just revealed. She ran her hand through her curls.

"OK . . . and you felt the need to share this with me because?" She replied slowly and intentionally. Christian looked shocked at her response.

"Uh, I guess so that you would know what he had in mind."

"But why?" McKenzie said.

"What do you mean why Mac?" Christian shot back. "You know why."

"No. Actually I don't know why. Why don't you tell me why? Why did you feel compelled to tell me that TJ is going to propose to me Saturday? Those things are usually—oh, I don't know, surprises." She said, but Christian quickly cut her off.

"C'mon McKenzie. You know why I'm telling you."

"No. I honestly don't. But you can just tell me if you're so inclined." McKenzie replied, crossing her legs.

"Because. He is going to ask you to marry him. And—" Christian shouted.

"And what?" McKenzie screamed back.

"And you need to know so that you're prepared to gently tell him 'no' come Saturday!"

McKenzie's head snapped back. Her eyes furrowed and her lips were pursed.

"And why would you think I would reject his proposal?" McKenzie asked in an even whisper.

"Because you're not in love with him—for one. And secondly—he doesn't know you!"

Christian stood up and paced around the table. All kinds of thoughts flashed through his head. TJ's revelation about how timid McKenzie was during sex with him. The fact that he didn't have a clue about the type of ring she would like. The list went on and on in his head.

McKenzie was livid.

"What's that got to do with anything, Christian?"

"Everything, McKenzie. Why would you go into a marriage knowing you don't love a person, and that the person doesn't know you?"

"Probably for the same reasons why you'd stay in one." She glared at him. They stood there looking at each other while the words penetrated.

"Fine. If that's what you want McKenzie--"

"Since when did it matter what I want Christian?"

"It's always mattered. What are you talking about?"

"I'm talking about the same thing you're talking about, a relationship: Yours and mine; Yours and Jada's; Mine and TJ's."

"This has nothing to do with me and Jada." Anger creased the center of his forehead, although he knew he was lying.

"You can't tell me you would marry a man you're not in love with—my Fraternity brother. I introduced you, McKenzie! Do you think I want to see you fuck him like that?"

247

"First of all, Christian . . . this has everything to do with you and Jada. Because the bottom line is you don't want me to marry your fraternity brother because you're in love with me. But you won't tell me that, will you?" She stared him dead in his eyes. "You won't tell me that because that means you'd feel like shit for fucking over your frat, right?"

Christian started to reply, but before he could answer she continued, "That means you'd have to finally be honest about that fucked up marriage you're in—the one where *you're not in love with your wife,* and *your wife doesn't know you?"* McKenzie enunciated each painful truth.

"The truth is, Christian, you thought I'd always be here—waiting for you to decide to leave your wife. And now that someone has figured out that I'm a damned good woman, and wants to make me happy, your ass is running scared that you're going to lose me." McKenzie crossed her arms and watched Christian move around nervously.

"You can't have it both ways. Either you're going to do what it takes to keep me. Or, you've got to stand by and watch as you lose me. It's just that simple." McKenzie stood and watched the myriad of emotions flash across Christian's face, anger, confusion, and then . . . resignation.

"That's what I thought." McKenzie said, grabbing her things to leave. "You don't want me, but you don't want anybody else to have me."

"That's not true." Christian said in a low whisper. He wanted her more than anything. "It's just not that simple."

"Nothing ever is Christian. Life is hard. That's what being an adult means. Making hard decisions." Christian sat there watching her in silence. Searching for the right words to say to try and explain this whole situation.

"I am going to accept TJ's proposal." McKenzie said as she started to walk off. "I may not be in love with him." She paused, looking at him longingly. "But I will love him. I am not going to fuck over him, Christian. I will make him happy," she assured him. Then she paused before saying.

"I would never hurt him. He's the first man in my life that's truly made me feel special and loved. I'll honor that. I'll be the best wife he could possibly have." And she walked off.

Christian sat and watched McKenzie walk away. He wanted to cry but it'd been so long since he'd done it his tear ducts didn't know what to do. Inside, it felt like his heart was screaming out in protest to what was just set in motion. But the only things that could hear it were his lungs. And they were collapsing under the pressure of not receiving any air.

McKenzie couldn't sleep. She spent the entire night tossing back and forth, regurgitating her conversation with Christian the day before. *The nerve of him,* she thought.

She was tired. She turned on her computer and checked her email. There was a message from Christian.

Hey Ma,
I was wrong. You were right.
I wish you all the happiness in the world. TJ is a wonderful person, and no doubt will love you the way you deserve to be loved. I wish you a lifetime of happiness. And I hope you can find it in your heart to forgive me.
* -Christian*

There was an attachment. It was a song. She clicked on the icon and the mp3 started to play. Will Downing sang, "Before We Say Goodbye." McKenzie turned up the volume on her speakers so she could hear every word. She knew Christian took time to select the songs he sent her. And after yesterday's ugly conversation, her heart was racing, wondering what he had to say to her. McKenzie lay back on her bed, eyes closed, concentrating on the lyrics.

Here we are again
Thinking of how to mend
Our broken hearts

The song read more like a letter. Will's deep sultry tenor voice recounting how he and the love of his life fell in love so easily, but now it seems as if they can't work things out. McKenzie listened intently. She imagined Christian singing the words of the song to her. He tells her to relax tonight because it doesn't matter who's wrong or right as long as they both gave it their all to save the love they shared.

McKenzie paused the mp3. Christian hadn't given it his all. He was in a loveless marriage, and was trying to prevent her from being happy. She sucked her teeth and hit play. Will crooned, asking for a simple kiss before they said goodbye. He talked about looking back over the years, shedding some tears, but always making it through. He didn't know exactly where they went wrong but he was sorry that they were moving on.

He said he was sorry that they couldn't seem to work it out.

McKenzie rolled her eyes at that sentence. *"Couldn't seem to work it out?" This song was so Christian: so passive aggressive.* If you listened to the words as if they were coming from Christian, you might think he really put forth an effort to be in a relationship and it just 'didn't work'. But McKenzie knew the truth. And if Christian was being honest with himself, he knew it to.

Christian hadn't tried to make things work with her. Not from what she could tell. He stayed in that relationship with Jada for whatever reasons. Now that his ass was coming to the realization that she wouldn't be sitting on the sidelines twiddling her thumbs, pining over his ass, he was nervous. He thought that half-ass attempt at an intervention was going to stop the train from moving on the track.

The truth was, so had she. McKenzie wanted Christian to tell her he loved her and he didn't want her to marry TJ. She didn't even want him to say he wanted to marry her. She just wanted him to have the balls to leave that loveless marriage and give them a chance. But he didn't. Instead he took a punk ass approach and tried to come off all holier than thou. How dare he make it seem like she wouldn't be happy because she didn't love TJ. *What did love have to do with it? Isn't that what He was doing? Ain't that the pot calling the kettle black?*

The song faded out on the words "It doesn't matter who is wrong or right, my love, as long as we both know we gave it all to save the love we shared my love."

"Shit," she mumbled as the song softly faded into silence.

Her stomach was in knots as she fought the tears pressing against the back of her eyes.

McKenzie grabbed her pillow, pulling it into her for comfort. "Shit, fuck, fuck!" Was all she could say.

♋　　♋　　♋

McKenzie opened the black velvet box TJ nervously handed to her after dessert on Saturday.

"W-would you do me the h-honor of making me the happiest m-man on earth by being my w-wife?" TJ said, his voice shaky, his eyes lit with excitement.

McKenzie had been practicing her reply all week since Christian shared with her TJ's intentions. And as she'd practiced, she placed her hands over her mouth and smiled brightly.

"Oh TJ!" She opened the box to find the most horrid ring. But she had prepared herself for that moment too.

During practice, she'd created a stone face—in case she didn't like the ring. This would allow her to quickly switch to the 'Oh my God! I love it!' response. And that's exactly what she did.

TJ beamed with pride as McKenzie slid on the gaudy ring. She held it out and admired it in front of him. She reached over and slowly and gently kissed him.

"I would love nothing more than to be your wife, Theodore Johnson."

♋   ♋   ♋

"What kind of nasty shit is this?" Jada said. She was waving an envelope around in Christian's face.

"You and TJ sharing hoes now?"

Christian ignored her. TJ had asked him to be his best man. He was experiencing too many conflicting issues to have considered informing Jada sooner.

"TJ is marrying McKenzie? What, has she got the pussy of gold? Is she a ripper? What?"

"Has it ever occurred to you that you might have jumped to the wrong conclusion?" Christian said.

"About you and that bitch?"

"Stop calling her a bitch, Jada."

"Stop defending her, Christian—if she ain't your bitch. And no, it never did occur to me that I jumped to anything wrong because I SAW YOU, Christian! How you looked at her, how you held her—have you forgotten, mutha fucka, because I haven't! She stood there in my face and told me she had my husband's heart, and my husband did not deny it!" She was up in his face screaming, spit flying everywhere.

"And that means we were fucking?" he said, without flinching.

"Don't try and play me, Christian. I'm not stupid." She started shuffling papers around on the desk next to her. "I didn't catch you in the act, but you two were way too comfortable with

252

each other. The way you protected her and held her that day is proof enough. And I haven't forgotten about the morning after pill."

Jada had told Christian that there was a gentle intimacy between them that made her blood pressure rise whenever she thought about it.

"You're paranoid Jada. And I've always told you that you jump to conclusions way too quickly. You don't want to know the truth, you just want to be right." He looked at her with resentment.

Christian knew how to shake her confidence: tie in accusations from the past that supported his point, poke holes in her reasoning, and say it all with gentle ease. He shook his head.

"So, once again you've come to a conclusion? Now, look at this situation. Does any of it make sense to you? Do you really think TJ and I would be involved with the same woman? C'mon now, we're brothers." He gave her a pathetic look that he could tell made her uncomfortable.

Jada hesitated. *Had she jumped to the wrong conclusion?* She knew what she saw. But it didn't make sense that TJ would be involved with McKenzie if Christian had been. Shit! She didn't know anymore. She hated when she got mixed up like this.

Jada looked exasperated. She took the invitation and shoved it in the kitchen drawer. She didn't want to think about the situation anymore. Christian looked relieved. For very different reasons, she imagined he didn't want to think about it either.

♋   ♋   ♋

"Sweetie?" TJ said, flipping through his chart.

"Yes," McKenzie replied, without looking up.

She was putting the remaining "Love" stamps on the last of the invitations. She had become completely immersed in planning this wedding—something she never imagined herself doing. McKenzie was practical, pragmatic, and very reasonable. She would have preferred spending this money on a house. Instead, she had conceded to a production of a wedding, with bridesmaids, flower girls, a puffy white gown . . . and a church.

TJ insisted. He wanted McKenzie to have the wedding of her dreams. The problem was, this wedding was not it. But he seemed so happy about all of the unnecessary bullshit, like a big puffy white dress that she went along with it. McKenzie would have preferred a simple cream-colored slip dress, Denny as her bridesmaid, and a beach.

But she wanted to make TJ happy. A small sacrifice, considering . . .

"I d-don't see your p-parents' names on the chart." He flipped back and forth scanning the pages. "D-did we misplace a p-page?" TJ looked worried.

McKenzie froze. She hadn't discussed her past with TJ. He knew nothing of her childhood, the abuse by the Major, or her strained relationship with her mother. She had gotten really good at changing the subject when it came time to talk about her family.

"Uh. No. I believe all the pages are there." McKenzie hesitated for a moment. "I . . . um . . . I don't think they'll be able to make the wedding honey." she said, gathering up the invitations and shoving them in a big box. TJ turned to face her.

"What? Why not?" TJ had assumed her stepfather would give her away. He hadn't met them yet, but he had assumed they would go out to dinner or something soon.

"I . . . he . . . I think they told me he'd be stationed out of the country around that time, sweetie."

TJ had been a sweetheart these last few months. He'd tried very hard to make everything perfect for her. He had asked Ahmad to join him at a weekend conference in San Diego so they could get to know each other. He asked him to be a groomsman. Christian would be the best man, his brother Raleigh would be the other groomsman.

TJ had practically planned the entire wedding on his own. He picked out the cake, ordered the flowers, hired the photographer and videographer, the DJ, and caterer. They had spent every weekend putting down deposits, tasting food, and smelling flowers, picking arrangements and packets for this or that.

He was so excited and so happy. McKenzie enjoyed watching him. His joy somehow made her happy. He loved her, and she could feel it. It was warm, patient, and comforting. McKenzie rationalized every day that it was better to be safe than to risk it all for a whirlwind romance. Not that the whirlwind romance was even an option at this point.

"Well, d-did you tell them the d-date?" A deep frown formed in the center of his forehead.

"I'm s-sure they have enough t-time to work something out with their schedule. He has to b-be there to walk you d-down the aisle." McKenzie almost gagged. She cleared her throat instead.

"Uh . . . um . . . No, no he doesn't TJ." She said standing. "I'm a grown ass woman! I have a grown ass son for heaven's sake!" She grabbed the box and walked toward the door. "I am a Black woman rooted in reality. Not some silly young white girl trying to live out some American dream about her daddy walking her down the aisle on her wedding day!"

Hurt and confusion covered TJ's face but he didn't utter a word. McKenzie fled the house. Outside, she stopped to catch her breath. The thought of those two at her wedding made her nauseous. On her way to the mailbox, McKenzie thought long and hard about how she would get around that situation.

♋   ♋   ♋

"And then what did she say?" Christian asked, practically on the edge of his seat.

"Nothing. She just grabbed the invitations and stormed out the house." TJ answered. He shook his head and searched Christian's face for an answer.

Christian paused. McKenzie hadn't told TJ about the Major. *What the fuck was she thinking?* She hadn't told him about the rape either . . . but for some reason; Christian understood why she wouldn't share that with him right away. But not telling him about the abuse—and the full story about Ahmad?

Christian was stressed out listening to TJ go on about their recent blow up, knowing full well why McKenzie was reacting the way she was. He couldn't understand why she would hold back on telling her soon-to-be husband about her painful past.

"Man, weddings and funerals bring out the worst in people." Christian said, covering for McKenzie. A part of him felt like shit because he didn't like keeping the truth from his Brother. But another part of him felt . . . good. Because it confirmed what he had been thinking all along . . . McKenzie wasn't in love with TJ. And they weren't close—not by a long shot.

♋   ♋   ♋

"Hello, may I speak with McKenzie, please?"
Christian wanted to talk with McKenzie. They hadn't spoken since the scene on campus. He had tried to smooth things over with an email. But she never replied. He just wanted to hear her voice—even if that voice was cussing him out.

"I'm sorry, she's not available. May I ask who's calling?" Ahmad said.

"Aw, what's up young blood?" Christian said, smiling into the telephone. Ahmad laughed lightly.

"What's up 'C'? Where you been man?"

"Oh, here and there."

"Yeah, right. I've been wanting to talk to you. But I didn't want to ask moms for your number."

"Oh yeah. What's up? Everything a'ight?" Christian asked. Worry coated his throat. He really liked Ahmad. He was a smart kid, well mannered, and he had lots of personality.

"I mean, if my mom marrying your best friend when she's obviously in love with you is all right—then yeah, everything is gravy."

Christian was quiet. "You know young blood. I just gotta be honest with you." Christian started to explain.

"Oh, please do." he said, sitting down on the arm of his sofa, waiting for Christian's explanation.

"Life ain't that simple. When you're an adult, shit gets screwed up real quick and easy like. You know what I mean?"

"No. Why don't you give me the 'Why Adults Fuck Up, for Dummies' version real quick? —cuz, uh, that's what this wedding fiasco is—a Fuck Up. And you, my mom, and everybody--but clueless Theodore—knows it. That nut is on cloud nine about this wedding." Ahmad replied. Christian could hear the disgust in Ahmad's voice. He wanted to laugh. Ahmad had jokes. But more to the point—he was right.

257

"Aw come on, Ahmad. TJ loves your mom." Christian said in his defense.

"Oh, no doubt. He loves her dirty draws. I have no doubt about that at all 'C'. My observation is that McKenzie ain't feelin' ol' boy the way he feelin' her. Why? Cuz she still jonesin' for yo crusty butt!"

"For weeks, my mom woke me up to that Jill Scott "You Love Me" groove. I know *every* beat, pause, symbol, chord and moan in that song. Every morning, I had to hear about 'your smile, your hand, your intelligence.' Three minutes and 24 seconds. That's how long that damned song is. And she'd sing to the top of her lungs. I could hear her smiling when she sung. Because she was singing about yo butt. So, I never said a word. I just woke up to Jill Scott. Every morning. For weeks. You know what she gets dressed to now?"

"No. What?" Christian was eager to know.

"Rap."

Ahmad sighed. "We're back to rap and hip hop. Now you know I'm a hip-hop fien, that ain't it. It's what she's feeling in her heart. Rap? C'mon 'C'! A bride to be ain't supposed to be vibin' with no cat on no rap and hip hop level. She should be kickin' that mushy Jill Scott—you love me from my hair follicle to my toe nails crap—and you know it."

Christian paused. "TJ is going to take good care of your mom."

"My mom can take care of herself. What she needs is to be with a man she loves—who can love her back, even though she got attitude and mouth for days." They both sat silent for a couple of seconds. "That ain't TJ."

"Yeah well . . . that was your mom's decision." Christian sighed.

"Uh huh, and I'm sure your situation did quite a bit to make that decision—what would you say --easy, or hard?"

As soon as Christian hung up the telephone with Ahmad, he ran to his entertainment center, flipped through his CDs until he found the Jill Scott, and slid it in the player. He'd heard the song a billion times on the radio, but with this new information he wanted to listen to the words more closely.

You love me, especially different every time
You keep me on my feet happily excited
By your cologne, your hands, your smile, your intelligence
You woo me, you court me, you tease me, you please me

      Christian had heard Jill flow hundreds of time. This cut was number one on the airwaves for weeks. But today he listened intently. He listened from the perspective of McKenzie speaking the words to him directly. As the words oozed off Jill Scott's lips like melted butter Christian tried to think of examples where he did the things she sung about. "You school me, give me some things to think about" Christian thought for sure this could be her introduction to the 'Classic R&B Songs' he shared with her. She used to call them mushy love songs, but over the months during their discourse he knew she had come to view them in a different way.

      Jill became McKenzie as she softly said to Christian that he was different and special in every way imaginable. He blushed. His body tingled as she said with certainty that he loved her from her hair follicles to her toenails. Damn! He laughed out loud. That's some deep shit right there. Christian chuckled even though he'd heard the phrase a thousand times before. He knew the words like the lines from a movie he'd watched a hundred times on HBO. He smiled knowingly at the way she described how he had her feeling: like the breeze, easy and free, lovely and new. He understood that feeling down to his core. That's exactly the way he felt about McKenzie—how she made him feel inside.

      A part of Christian was happy listening to the words. But the other part was fucked up. Knowing all that McKenzie had been through in her life, he felt that her having these types of emotions had major implications. He didn't want to be the person to make her give up on love. But at the same time, his hands were tied.

      He pressed repeat and lay back listening to Jill fuck the shit out of some lyrics. She loved her man. Christian imagined McKenzie singing the words . . .

"Is this fine?" The waitress said looking at the table

"Yes thank you." McKenzie replied, smiling at the cute Puerto Rican girl. TJ pulled out McKenzie's chair and sat across from her.

"Are you hungry sweetie?" TJ said scanning the menu.

"Yes, I'm starving! And I haven't had Thai food in ages." McKenzie said grabbing her napkin and placing it in her lap. TJ couldn't concentrate on the menu. He was nervous about what would take place in a few minutes. The server came by.

"Hello, I'm Jen and I'll be your server today. Can I get you started with drinks and appetizers?" she said in an upbeat tone.

"I'll have a coke with lemon—" McKenzie said, when a voice from behind cut her off mid-sentence.

"She'll have a water," the deep baritone voice said. "McKenzie, how many times have I told you that soda is bad for you?"

McKenzie's mouth dropped. She turned to find the Major and her mother standing there, full of smiles. She quickly turned to face TJ whose face was lit up like a kid on Christmas day.

"Surprise!" TJ shouted.

McKenzie sat frozen in her chair, unsure of how to respond. The Major pulled out her mom's chair and sat across from her.

"I'd say so." The Major replied, eyeing McKenzie closely. "You're getting married—and your mother and I haven't given our blessing."

"Because obviously I don't need it." McKenzie said. She glared at him, but TJ missed the look trying to flag down Jen.

"Absolutely you do. That's why this young man invited us here today, isn't it Theodore? For our blessing?" The Major demanded of TJ.

"W-well actually S-Sir . . ."

Normally, TJ's stuttering didn't bother McKenzie. But today, watching the Major's condescending look as TJ struggled in his nervousness, it irritated and embarrassed her. McKenzie was already irritated at the fact that TJ had gone behind her back and invited them here today. But in his defense, she knew it was an innocent act of love on his part. This was all her fault for not telling him the truth. But the fact still remained that TJ was spitting, clicking and clacking trying to get his words out and McKenzie was mortified.

The Majored sneered. All McKenzie could do was hold her breath and try to will his words out.

"I-I w-was ho-hoping w-we c-could j-j-just t-talk." TJ paused to catch his breath. "An-and get t-to know e-each other."

"TJ." McKenzie said as sweetly as she could muster. "Baby, I know you meant well. But this *family* already knows each other as much as we ever will." McKenzie shot her mother, who continued to sit there quietly, a piercing glare. "There was a reason I didn't plan an introductory lunch or invite them to our wedding." McKenzie stood up from the table. Jen arrived with their drinks.

"OK folks, here are your drinks. I'll just get the other couple's drink orders, and give you a few minutes to decide on what you're having to eat today."

"Don't bother." McKenzie cut the Puerto Rican girl off. "We're not staying." McKenzie grabbed her purse. TJ stood.

"Sit down McKenzie." the Major said. "You haven't seen your mother in months. It won't kill you to spend a few hours with her today." But McKenzie didn't fall for the guilt trip.

"I'm leaving." McKenzie looked at TJ who moved in her direction. "If my mother was concerned about seeing me or spending a few hours with me, she would have made it a point to do so." McKenzie eyed her mother who sat and studied her menu attentively, never looking up, and never commenting. The Major slammed his hand down on the table.

"I said sit!"

Everyone on that side of the room turned their attention to the table. TJ paused in mid-stride.

"Hold up!" TJ said facing the Major. "I don't know what the hell your problem is, but you don't talk to McKenzie like that. Not ever!" he said, clearly, lucidly, and without stuttering or stammering over one word. The Major glared at him. He started to stand. But TJ politely placed his hand on the Major's shoulder.

"You're fine right where you are." TJ nodded at McKenzie who walked briskly out of the restaurant. He addressed McKenzie's mother.

"Ma'am, I apologize f-for any disrespect--"

"None taken, son," She whispered, finally looking up at him.

"N-no ma'am. N-not for t-today," he said, pulling out three 20's and placing them on the table. "F-for the fact that I-I am rescinding your in-invitation to our w-wedding." He looked directly at the Major. "Y-you're n-no longer welcomed t-to attend." He walked out the restaurant.

♋   ♋   ♋

McKenzie sat in silence all the way home. TJ watched her through his peripheral vision. She stared straight ahead the entire time. As they turned the corner to his house, TJ tried to apologize.

"McKenzie, b-baby, I'm s-sorry--" he started. McKenzie held up her hand for him to stop.

"Don't apologize. This was my fault. I should have been more clear about my expectations. I thought you caught the hint with that whole invitation incident. But, obviously I should have just told you that I don't get along with my parents and would prefer that they not be invited. I'm sorry."

TJ pulled up to the curb in front of McKenzie's house and turned off the car. He leaned in to kiss McKenzie but she quickly jumped out the car.

"I don't feel well TJ, I need to rest. I'll call you later."

♋   ♋   ♋

TJ woke up to a searing pain in his lower back. At 36, he had his share of body aches. What started off nearly a year ago as occasional stiffness in his upper thigh, gradually turned into common stiffness in hips, and now pain in his lower back.

Not the athletic type, or the type who spent his days pumping iron in the gym, TJ feared his body was slowly failing him and he was being punished by the body gods for not doing a better job at taking care of his temple, as his grandmother commonly referred to their bodies.

He made a mental note to schedule a doctor's visit as soon as he returned from their honeymoon. Now that he had a family to take care of, he had to be more responsible about his health care. He self-diagnosed himself with a premature onset of rheumatoid arthritis, or Arthur, as his grandma called it; since it plagued several members of his mother's side of the family.

But today, the sun was shining, the birds were chirping, and he was the happiest man alive. Since McKenzie had accepted his wedding proposal everything seemed right in the world. Of course he wouldn't admit that to anyone, especially his boys—but in his heart, that's how he felt.

They had spent the past six months planning the perfect wedding, getting through sticky moments like meeting her parents, and just getting to know each other. And the next 48 hours would bring all of their planning into fruition. TJ was a happy man. And he vowed to himself to make McKenzie the happiest wife a woman could be.

That's some corny sounding shit, TJ said out loud to himself. *Brothas don't say bullshit like that.* He looked around the empty room and smiled. *That's why you're saying that whipped shit to yourself.*

But he knew in his heart that's what he felt. For years he'd been the odd man out-- all of his boys were in serious relationships or married. He dated often, and had a steady stream of fuck partners, but nothing serious. His boys always admired him for his bachelor lifestyle, and he did his best to play the role like it was all that. But the reality was that TJ wanted to be married. He wanted a family. *Now, he was happy.*

"Ooh shit," TJ moaned.

He tried to ease out of bed but the stiffness in his hip stopped him mid-stride. TJ paused and waited for the pain to subside. Lately, it had begun to take longer for the pains to go away.

♋   ♋   ♋

McKenzie lay in her bed thinking about her life. How things had been with Christian, before . . . Melvin. And how they seemed to have dissolved into nothing. How she ended up engaged to his best friend – *what the fuck! What the hell was she doing? Allowing a good man to love her.*

"Ugh! You sound just like your pathetic ass mother!" she said out loud to herself. And she did. "Humph!" Her mother would say. "If a good man wants to love me and take care of me, I'd be stupid to refuse. I'm going to allow a good man to love me. Better than letting a piece of shit just fuck me and give me nothing but a hard time."

McKenzie rolled over and pulled the covers over her head. She tried to convince herself that she was different than her mother. That this marriage would work. That she loved this man. That she was doing the right thing.

But McKenzie's heart ached. And that was enough to let her know that no matter how hard her mind tried to convince her she was doing the right thing. Her heart knew better.

♋   ♋   ♋

"So, has the sex gotten any better?" Christian asked TJ.

Since their confrontation before the proposal, Christian hadn't spoken much to McKenzie. Most of his information came unwittingly from TJ. Before, Christian didn't want to know. But since McKenzie accepted TJ's proposal Christian found himself obsessed with trying to find out if she was really in love with him—and why.

"Yeah. I think you were right. I was just anxious." TJ said.

That was not what Christian wanted to hear. Secretly, he was pleased that McKenzie hadn't given TJ all of her. He knew he was wrong for feeling that way, but it was the truth.

"So, she's a freak?" Christian said, trying to sound casual. TJ contemplated for a moment.

"No. Definitely not a freak."

It took all of Christian not to smile. TJ's answer meant McKenzie was still holding back.

"She tries to please me. And I like that. But she doesn't moan, or get buck wild, you know?" TJ said thoughtfully.

"Are you OK with that?"

"Yeah. I ain't tripping. I love the way she holds me and kisses me when she cums." TJ said smiling.

"What do you mean?" Christian said, thinking about the times they had sex, trying to remember how she held him, or if she kissed him when she came.

"I don't know. It's just nice."

"What does that mean, though?" Christian said. He wanted to know.

"Well . . ." he paused, embarrassed, "she just holds me tight right before, and kisses me right after. And I like it."

Christian snorted. He thought about the times they were intimate. How wild and nasty McKenzie was. He started to wonder which one was the real McKenzie? Which mode meant she was feeling good . . . wild and sexy or soft and demure. It drove him crazy not knowing.

♋   ♋   ♋

At the rehearsal dinner, everyone slowly milled in the restaurant, stopping to chat and catch up. McKenzie stood next to TJ, holding his hand, and smiling. She couldn't wait for tomorrow to come and go. All the hype, the showers, the planning, and decision-making--was just too much for her. She just wanted to fast forward to the Cayman Islands and honeymooning.

Denny had gotten into a huge argument with her husband about leaving her family – i.e., HIM -- *again* to go be by a friend's side. She said they had argued for hours. At first, Jermaine said it was the money. But Denny pointed out that Christian had paid for her ticket the last visit. TJ offered to use his miles to fly her out, he was determined to give McKenzie the perfect wedding and that would include having her best friend standing next to her.

Then Jermaine went on a tangent about *how disrespectful it was to have 'all of these men' flying her across the country. What are you doing that they're so willing to pay for your tickets left and right?* Stupid ass said.

"What the fuck was he implying? That you're giving up the booty for airline tickets?" McKenzie couldn't stand him. He was ignorant, plain and simple. Finally, McKenzie told her to forget it. "It's not worth all of this."

"It's your wedding." Denny said. "I'll be there for you."

"You have been here for me, *I* don't have to live with the bastard. If being in my wedding is going to cause him to question your fidelity then it's not worth it." McKenzie said, even though she knew nothing would stop Jermaine's insecurity but psychotherapy.

Denny cried on the telephone, "Are you sure?"

"I'm sure. It's going to be a small quick ceremony anyway – then we're off to the island to honeymoon. You'd just be in for the rehearsal, the ceremony, and back home in two days – why get into a tiff with shit for brains over a two-day stay?" McKenzie said.

"That's just it, it's only a two day stay – and it's my best friend's wedding!" Denny said. McKenzie could hear her sniffling.

McKenzie was angry that Jermaine was being such a dick. Who makes a person chose between her best friend and her husband? It's a wedding. That's when friends are supposed to step up. He was such an asshole. But Denise would stay home. She'd feel guilty and hurt, probably even start to harbor resentment for her husband. But she wouldn't tell him how she truly felt. She'd continue to do whatever it took to keep her family together "for the boys." The boys, who were watching their father treat their mother like shit. What were they learning?

"Denny, listen honey. I know you'd be here if it were up to you. Don't worry about it. I'll be fine."

A part of her was relieved that Denise wouldn't be there. She didn't think she could handle Denise's scrutiny in person. McKenzie knew if Denise saw her with TJ, she'd know something wasn't quite right, just like she knew something was off when Denise married Jermaine. This way, she could get through the wedding without any stress. Bam, bam, done!

♋   ♋   ♋

267

"Hey Camille!" McKenzie said, running toward her friend.

"Hey Mac!" she said equally as excited. McKenzie kissed TJ and joined Camille at a table off to the side.

"And how's my maid of honor?"

"She's doing fine. How's the beautiful bride?"

"Doing beautifully!" McKenzie laughed.

"Well, tomorrow's the big day. Are you ready?"

She and McKenzie got along well during their Master's program. They had easy conversations—but she was somewhat shocked when McKenzie called her a few months ago and, over lunch, asked her to be her matron of honor.

"I'm ready for it to be done and over with." McKenzie confessed.

McKenzie smiled, looking around at all the folks filing in, but Camille could read the underlying emotion in her face.

"This . . . all of this is for TJ. I would have been happy with a justice of the peace ceremony."

"Girl, then why are you doing it? It's your day too. If you didn't want all of this-- McKenzie grabbed her hand.

"It'll be over tomorrow. TJ will be happy. And then we can move forward with our lives. That's all I'm looking forward to. Being happy--"

The hairs on the nape of McKenzie's neck stood on edge. She turned to scan the room. Camille watched McKenzie's expression change as she stopped speaking mid-sentence. She turned to see what caused the pause. Christian. He and Jada had walked into the room. McKenzie quickly regained her composure. Camille watched her switch reels, and go from frazzled to back in control in less than 6 seconds. Her party smile was back on her face, looking as if Christian had never entered the restaurant.

"I'm sorry, what was I saying?"

"How you were looking forward to being so happy."

During their lunch, she tried to confront McKenzie about her feelings for Christian. But McKenzie shut her down. Camille spent a semester watching the chemistry grow between those two. She didn't know how the situation got to the point where McKenzie was marrying Christian's best friend, but something in her gut told her it wasn't over between those two.

"That's right." She said smiling brightly. "This is TJ's dream. He's so sweet. He wants me to have a perfect wedding—in his mind, this is it." McKenzie waved her hands referring to all the hustle and bustle of the wedding. "If it makes him happy to believe he's making me happy with all this—then I'll just smile and enjoy it all, right?"

McKenzie had justified her actions, just like she had justified marrying TJ tomorrow.

"You know, there's a saying in my family." Camille said, grabbing McKenzie's hand. "How the marriage starts, is how the marriage ends."

After dinner and the rehearsal, McKenzie slipped away to the restroom. She had played the role of the happy bride to the tee, but the truth was she was drained. Walking up the aisle on Ahmad's arm with Christian's eyes on her, she could barely concentrate. She tried focusing her energy on TJ's beaming smile. She smiled and willed herself to believe it would all turn out right. And she was convinced it would, as long as she didn't make eye contact with Christian.

She splashed cold water on her face and dabbed it dry. Jada walked in as McKenzie started to reapply her lipstick.

"Oh!" Jada said, a little taken aback by McKenzie's presence.

They had managed to stay out of each other's way the entire night. McKenzie didn't flinch. She continued to apply her lipstick as if Jada had never walked into the restroom. Jada walked up to McKenzie.

"Well, congratulations McKenzie!" Jada said smiling politely. "I wish you and TJ all the happiness in the world. He's a great guy."

Much to McKenzie's chagrin, Jada spoke as if they had never had a confrontation in the quad. As if she had never called her a bitch or a whore.

McKenzie grabbed a napkin, faced the mirror, blotted her lips, ran her fingers through her curls, turned and walked out the restroom.

♋ ♋ ♋

Knock. Knock.

"Come in." McKenzie said.

"Hey. Ooh, you look beautiful!" Camille said.

McKenzie turned to face the full-length mirror. *Who was this woman?* She thought. Wearing this puffy white fairy tale dress, so inappropriate for her--someone so far from being pure.

"Thanks. I think I'm getting nervous." McKenzie paced.

"Second thoughts, kiddo?"

McKenzie just stared at herself in the mirror. *I can do this. I will do this. I will marry this man, and make him happy.* She turned to face Camille and shot her a picture perfect smile.

"Nervous about tripping over all this fucking material Camille." McKenzie grabbed the bulk of the dress and moved toward the door. "That's all." She smiled. "Can you grab the back and help me make it to the got damned altar? I'm ready!"

♋ ♋ ♋

270

It was 3:00 p.m. and the wedding was starting. TJ said, come hell or high water, their wedding was going to start on time. He hated that Black folks couldn't seem to start anything on time and refused to be a part of the stereotype.

The hosts started seating the family members. The intro music began to play, and the female vocalist began to sing. Christian turned to look for the singer, but didn't see anyone.

I used to cry myself to sleep at night
But that was all before he came
I thought love had to hurt to turn out right
But now he's here, it's not the same, it's not the same

Camille entered the church, followed by the ring bearer, and the flower girl. They marched in as practiced the night before, only this time to the soulful sultry voice filling the church telling them how this man fills her up, and gives her more love than she's ever seen. All heads in the church looked about for the songstress with the powerful voice that commanded the room and made you believe that this man was all she had in this world, and was all the man she needed.

During the instrumental part of the song, McKenzie entered the church. Everyone stood. She walked up to Ahmad who ushered her down the aisle. Midway down the aisle, Ahmad stopped and McKenzie took the rest of the walk by herself. To the crowd's amazement, McKenzie began singing.

And in the morning when I kiss his eyes
He takes me down and rocks me slow
And in the evening when the moon is high
He holds me close and won't let go
He won't let go

     TJ was floored. Everyone watched as he struggled to keep his eyes from welling up. Christian knew it was McKenzie singing when the music first started. He'd heard her sing countless times and knew her voice anywhere. He watched her glide down the aisle looking magnificent in that horrid dress that wasn't her style at all.

     He watched her singing her heart out to TJ and his throat started to tighten. The air in the church started to thin, and he began to sweat profusely underneath his tuxedo. Christian watched TJ as McKenzie approached the altar. He was so happy. Christian's heart understood TJ's. He looked at McKenzie wistfully and knew if he was the one standing in TJ's place he'd feel the same exact way. Like he was floating on top of the world. Mac had a way of making you feel like that.

♋   ♋   ♋

Clink, clink, clink!

"Excuse me!" Christian yelled into the microphone. "Excuse me ladies and gentlemen! It's time for the toast." The crowd settled down. "Please lift your glasses and join me in wishing the happy bride and groom a lifetime of happy moments, an abundance of prosperity, and above all an eternity of the love that abounds in their eyes today."

Christian turned to face McKenzie and raised his flute of champagne. The crowd raised their glasses and cheered.

"Here, here!"

McKenzie caught Christian's underhanded dig. She smiled brightly and raised her glass. The guests began clinking their glasses and the bride and groom obediently moved in for a slow kiss in response. Christian grabbed another glass of champagne and turned away from the kiss.

"Painful?" Camille said. Christian turned to face Camille who was watching his response.

"What?" Christian said gulping down another glass of champagne. "The toast? Old hat. I've been in more weddings than I can count on both hands."

Camille smiled. She didn't reply. But the look in her eyes told Christian that she knew he was struggling. Unfortunately, Camille wasn't the only one who noticed. Jada was on watch all day. TJ wasn't the only one struggling for air in the church. She watched Christian's expression as McKenzie sang her way down the aisle and thought he was going to pass out. Jada couldn't tell who was the groom, TJ or Christian—the way they both were so damned emotional. You'd thought they'd never heard a bitch sing before, got damn!

"You all right honey?" Jada said, walking up behind Christian, rubbing his back. She eyed Camille who seemed to be a little too engrossed in conversation with Christian.

"Huh? Uh, yeah. Fine." Christian said reaching for another glass of champagne. Camille grabbed it before he could get to it.

273

"I think you need some water to chase that dry chicken down, don't you, big guy?"

"I'll get that." Jada said eyeing Camille.

"Then I'll be on my way. Let's get together soon Christian. So we can finish this conversation with less interruptions." She turned and left before Jada could reply.

"Old ass white bitch!"

"What?" Christian said. "Camille is cool people. Why you trippin'?" He started to walk off, but Jada quickly jumped in front of him. She was determined to be the center of his affections tonight. With McKenzie wrapped up in TJ she didn't think it would be a problem.

"Listen." Jada said, pointing up to the ceiling. Christian paused to listen to the music. "Let's go dance." It was a Frankie Beverly and Maze cut. The one that he and McKenzie cha-cha'd to during his graduation. Christian smiled and looked for McKenzie. She and TJ were walking around the room thanking guests for coming.

He watched as TJ tapped McKenzie on the shoulder . . .

McKenzie and TJ were wrapping up the last table, thanking the guests for attending their wedding when she heard the music. Instinctively she smiled. Before she could register it McKenzie felt a tap on her shoulder. She turned quickly, expecting to see Christian asking her to dance, but was stopped in her tracks to find TJ, hands stretched out smiling.

Her smile dropped. Christian caught the quick glint of disappointment cross her face. As soon as it registered in her brain, McKenzie quickly splashed a huge smile across her face and grabbed TJ's hands. TJ led her to the dance floor.

"Surprise." TJ whispered in her ear as he hugged her long and hard.

McKenzie found herself staring into Christian's eyes. She forced herself to smile when she really wanted to scream.

TJ stepped back and waited for McKenzie who waited for TJ. They stood uncomfortably for a few seconds.

"The man usually takes the lead." McKenzie finally said.

"Oh. I'm used to the woman starting. That's how I learned." He said. Already frustrated, McKenzie stepped in to take the lead. TJ stiffly followed.

274

"One. Two. Cha, cha, cha." TJ whispered out loud as he moved back. "Three. Four. Cha, cha, cha," he said as he moved forward. Christian stood watching.

"Hello!" Jada said. Christian turned to face his wife. "Can we go dance?" She tried to sound enthusiastic. Trying not to notice that Christian's eyes were stuck on the middle of the dance floor.

Christian walked over to the dance floor and began dancing with Jada. She turned her back to him and started to cha-cha. Reluctantly, he moved in behind her and fell in step.

McKenzie looked over at Christian and Jada. She looked back at TJ who was still counting out his steps, so there was no way she could turn and shove her butt into him. It would throw him off. He wasn't that advanced.

McKenzie smiled at TJ. He'd gone out and learned how to cha-cha just for their wedding. That was sweet. Just sweet. TJ looked down at McKenzie and smiled.

"Having a good time?"

"The best."

McKenzie looked over at Christian who had been watching them. He smiled. She smiled back. McKenzie knew Christian felt as stifled as she did, dancing on the same floor together, but with different partners. Their bodies had learned to move together, and right now cha-cha'ing with someone else felt . . . wrong.

Well too bad, McKenzie thought to herself. *This is who you're going to be cha-cha'ing with from now on, your husband.*

As the music faded, the guests eagerly clinked their glasses. The happily married couple leaned in for a long passionate kiss.

"I love you Mrs. Johnson." McKenzie stood on her tippy-toes, slid her arms around his neck, looked him in his eyes and said, "I promise to always honor that love, Mr. Johnson."

The guests cooed at the PDA and clapped at the tender moment. Jada looked affectionately at Christian, remembering their romantic wedding day. She smiled and moved in to give him a long passionate kiss. He reciprocated with a closed-mouthed peck, a fake half-smile, and casually walked off the floor. Jada tried her hardest not to burst into tears on the dance floor. Instead, she rushed to the bathroom where the tears gushed out as soon as she hit the door. Camille walked out of a stall as Jada ran in the restroom.

"Jada, are you OK?" Camille said. Jada looked devastated. Quickly dabbing at her eyes, she tried to compose herself and reply casually.

"Yes. I'm fine."

But, she wasn't. Her husband was going through the motions in their marriage. And she wanted passion. She wanted connection. Fuck! All she wanted was a simple tongue kiss! But he was so cold.

It was just a few hours ago Jada was calling her an old white bitch—she heard her—but, at this moment, Camille felt sorry for her. Camille paused at the door for half a second, contemplating whether or not to say something. *Some lessons can only be learned by banging your head against the wall enough times to figure out that that shit hurts,* she thought to herself.

Knowing it would probably fall on deaf ears, Camille simply said, "You know Jada, the definition of insanity is doing the same thing over and over but expecting a different outcome."

And like the last time, Camille walked away before Jada could reply.

♋   ♋   ♋

CHAPTER TWELVE

Duty and Obligation

The searing pain in his back woke TJ from a comfortable and peaceful sleep. He moved slowly, so as not to wake his wife. *His wife.* He smiled at McKenzie who slept soundly next to him.

TJ had to literally bite his bottom lip to keep from screaming. The pain was excruciating. But he managed to ease out of the bed without waking her. By the time TJ made it to the bathroom he was completely drenched in sweat.

TJ grabbed a towel and wiped the sweat from his face. He moved to the toilet lifted the seat and stood. He hoped relieving his bladder would ease some of the pressure he felt inside. He stood there a while, focusing, trying to force the pee to come. It was morning time and his bladder was full. But despite the fullness he felt in his bladder, he couldn't pee.

"Fuck it." TJ placed his penis back inside his boxers.

He turned on the faucet and splashed his face with cool water. He felt warm and achy. TJ reached for his bottle of Aleve, popped two pills, and cupping his hands under the faucet, slurped some of the water to force the pain relievers down.

"Good morning, sunshine," McKenzie whispered as she entered the hotel bathroom behind TJ. Warmth replaced the aches inside him. He turned to greet McKenzie whose curls were all over her head. She stood naked in the doorway.

"Good—heeeeey there!" He pulled her into him.

"Wait, no! Yuck TJ, I have dragon breath!" McKenzie said, turning her head away from his persistent attempts at kissing her. They laughed as she reached for her toothbrush.

"How are you feeling, M-mrs. Johnson?" TJ said wrapping his arms around her waist and kissing her neck. His locks cascaded over her shoulder. The rich, deep musk oil scent fill her nostrils. She loved the way he loved her: openly, lovingly, completely.

"I'm a little sore." McKenzie said. "But other than that—" She spit the last of her toothpaste into the sink and turned to face him. She slid her arms around his neck and kissed him slowly, "I'm in heaven." She smiled. TJ looked worried.

"Are you s-sure you're ok? M-maybe we shouldn't have . . ." He said, guilt all over his face. "I m-mean, you didn't w-want to . . ."

"I did want to." McKenzie reassured him. "I was just, you know, nervous. I'm fine. Really." She lied. "Now, go order us some breakfast." McKenzie said shoving him out of the bathroom. TJ reluctantly turned to leave.

"We d-don't have to d-do it again, baby." TJ said. McKenzie smiled and kissed him.

"Did you like doing it?" She said. TJ paused, then slowly nodded. McKenzie smiled. "Then we'll do it as many times as you want. I don't have no little Dick Willie." She said, grabbing his crouch. "I just have to get used to it. That's all."

"Did y-you like doing it?"

"Yes." She lied. "I loved the way it turned you on especially." That was the truth. TJ's worried look relaxed. "We're learning each other, baby. That means you learning what I like and me learning what you like. That may mean a little discomfort in the beginning. But once we become familiar with each other and what we like, it'll become old hat. Right?" McKenzie rationalized out loud. TJ leaned down and kissed her.

"N-no, you're absolutely right. I just d-don't like knowing I h-hurt you. I don't ever w-want to hurt you."

McKenzie smiled. "I said I was sore. I didn't say you hurt me."

"Now, after last night's workout, I'm starving! Can you please call room service and order me some bacon and eggs—scrambled soft with cheddar cheese and onions, some wheat toast with strawberry jelly, hash browns, and a tall orange juice with ice—please, baby? Your wife is hungry." McKenzie playfully whined as she shoved him into the bedroom and shut the door.

TJ laughed, "OK, OK!"

McKenzie sat on the toilette to pee. She grabbed paper off the roll and wiped herself. As she reached her butt, she caught her breath and grimaced.

"Ouch!" she whispered to herself as she turned to look down at the bloody tissue in her hand.

"Hey, mom!" Ahmad said grabbing McKenzie's bag and laying a kiss on her lips. "I missed you."

Things seemed so out of whack lately. The wedding, the move into TJ's house—it was a disruption Ahmad quietly went along with, but internally wasn't feeling. McKenzie had sat down and had a conversation with Ahmad the day after Christian told her TJ would be proposing. She couldn't have accepted if Ahmad wasn't on board—it was just that simple. No man came before her son. Ever.

But Ahmad was 16 years old --17 in three months. And in a year, attending a University somewhere on a scholarship. He figured he wouldn't make any waves since he'd be out the picture soon. He had his opinions about his mother marrying the best friend of the married man he knew she was really in love with—but hey, that was grown folks' business, and he would just stay out of it.

Besides, Ahmad didn't want to see his mom grow old and be by herself. TJ seemed to be crazy about his mom. Maybe she could learn to love him? Crazier things have happened.

"I missed you too, baby. Everything all right while we were gone?" She said, placing her purse on the dining table.

"Yeah. Everything was cool. Hey TJ, you guys have more bags in the car?" Ahmad said heading toward the door.

"Yeah, a c-couple. Thanks." TJ's back and thighs were on fire. He slowly moved to the couch. McKenzie saw the look on his face.

"TJ? Baby, what's wrong?"

"T-talked too much shit about b-breaking your back, momma. L-looks like it went the o-other way," He tried to joke. He painfully stretched out on the couch. "My l-lower back and th-thighs . . ." He tried to finish his sentence but the pain seared the words in half. "Ow! Shit!" McKenzie moved to his side.

"Hold up TJ! Just lay down baby. Let me get you some ibuprofen and a heating pad. I'm the queen of dulling pain."

"Oh. This shit h-hurts real bad." He moaned. And to top it off, he needed to pee. He moved to get up from the couch. "Fuck!"

McKenzie returned with the pills. "Will you lay down?" Irritation registered in her voice and the scowl across her face.

"J-just as soon as I piss." McKenzie helped him up and to the bathroom. "Thanks baby." While he handled his business, McKenzie went to get the heating pad from their bedroom.

"You all right?" She didn't hear anything. "TJ? Baby, you OK in there?" She said tapping on the door as she entered. She opened the door to find TJ sitting on the toilette with a pained look on his face.

"Oh, I'm sorry! I thought you had to pee." She turned to leave.

"N-no, it's OK. I'm n-not taking a dump. I just h-had to sit down. My b-back was killing me. Now, my ass c-can't even piss!"

McKenzie walked to the kitchen and ran him a glass of water.

"Sounds like you probably have a kidney infection. Here, drink some water. Those mothers of fuckers ain't no joke! I had one, once and didn't know it. And, because I let it go so long it got so bad I couldn't walk."

He drank the water. She filled the glass again from the sink and handed it back to him.

"Drink it. My back was all swollen and shit. I bet that's what it is. And you probably have a urinary tract infection, which is why you can't pee. Those typically accompany kidney infections." McKenzie tried to reassure him.

"Damn. This s-shit is painful." He shook his dick down in the toilette to try and get it flowing. Nothing. "What did they do?"

"Just give me some antibiotics and told me to drink a gang of fluids. C'mon, let me help you up. We can go to emergency."

"Naw. I-I would rather go see m-my primary physician." He said as he stood up. "Dr. Barrow. The ibuprofen feels like it's kicking in. I'll be cool." He said as he walked passed her.

"This could be serious TJ. You promise to call your doctor?" McKenzie called behind him.

"Promise. Th-this shit ain't the k-kind of shit I want to fuck with."

♋   ♋   ♋

TJ woke up feeling good. It had been days since he woke up with no pain. *Man, it feels good not to hurt.* He thought to himself. He was supposed to call his doctor today. But he thought he'd stop by his Granny's while he was feeling good. He could always call him when he got back home. TJ jumped out of bed, showered, and headed to Compton.

"Hey, Nanny." TJ said kissing his grandmother on her cheek as she opened her screen door to let him in.

"Hey, baby. How ya' doing today?" She said, looking him up and down.

"Fine. Fine. W-what you cook?" TJ said as he headed toward the kitchen.

"You are such a Negro." came a high-pitched voice from the back room.
"First thing out of your mouth is 'what did you cook?' not 'do you need anything?' or 'can I fix something for you gramps?' Just 'what's in here to eat?'"

"Sh-shut the hell up, Tamara Marie." TJ said rummaging through his grandmother's kitchen. "Y-you don't know w-what I do for granny on the regular. So, ch-check yourself and l-let that guilt sit right w-where it should. With you—c-cuz this is one grandson t-that does what he's supposed to f-for his grandmother. Ain't that right, Nanny?" TJ shouted.

"What's that?" Granny shouted back. "I got some cobbler at the bottom of the fridge. Just made it yesterday."

"Oh s-snap, some cobbler!" TJ did the happy dance.

"Fuck you Theodore. Fuck you--you dread head!"

TJ laughed. Tamara, or Me-Me as everyone called her, lived with his grandmother. She was supposed to be taking care of her, so she was getting the in-home care check. But everybody knew she wasn't doing shit. TJ stopped by his grandmother's once or twice a week and made sure she had the things she needed. Between him, his mom, and his brother Raleigh, Granny didn't want for anything.

He knew Me-Me was feeling guilty because she wasn't doing shit. The front door slammed shut and TJ heard Raleigh's voice.

"Hey, Nana! Why you lookin' so sexy today—yo' boyfriend comin' over?" He kissed his grandmother. She whacked him in the back of his head.

"Boy! Hush yo' foolishness!" Granny laughed.

"What? You broke up with your boyfriend—you breakin' hearts at seventy-five?" He turned to swat her on her bottom.

"Boy, I'ma hurt you. Stop playing with me. You know my playing days is over." Everyone in the kitchen turned to look at their grandmother.

"What?" They all said and broke out into laughter.

"What the hell did your granny say?" Raleigh said to TJ. He grabbed his bowl of peach cobbler out the microwave and started eating it.

"Naw, dude, w-what did *yo Nana* say. You know t-them hoin' jeans c-came from Granny's s-side of the family. T-they always want to blame it on the m-men. But the women in our family g-got it locked down." TJ said giving Raleigh dap.

"Shut up talking about my grandmother like she's some cheap ho." Me-Me said. She socked Raleigh and walked out the kitchen.

"Retired ho . . . that makes a difference. And granny had ass—she wasn't cheap, trust me. Niggas had to pay *just for sho'tie bang bang to look their way!*" Raleigh said laughing. He knew he was annoying Me-Me. He enjoyed it. He looked at TJ and winked.

"What up, bro. Where your skinny ass been?" Raleigh opened the freezer in search of some vanilla ice cream.

"Aw, m-man. I been l-laid out!" TJ explained his pains and McKenzie's thoughts on what it could be.

"It's possible." Raleigh said. "You know, I still have my antibiotics from my strep throat if you want them? They're in my car."

"You didn't finish them?"

"Naw." Raleigh said handing him the cobbler a la mode. TJ eyed the spoon suspiciously. Raleigh caught the look.

"Fuck you TJ! I'm fine. You ain't gone catch nothing." He snapped walking toward the front door. "Bitch, you want the pills or not?"

TJ laughed. "S-shit. How the fuck w-would I explain getting s-strep throat to McKenzie?" TJ said. Raleigh laughed.

"True. True."

"Yeah, I'll take them. T-thanks.

"Ma! Ma!" Ahmad called.

"Boy, what are you screaming like a mad man about?" McKenzie came out the back room looking worried.

"Mom!" Ahmad was jumping up and down, waving a white envelope.

"I got it! I got in!"

"Howard? You got into Howard?" She started jumping up and down with him.

"Yes! I got in!"

He was so happy. They stood there for a moment and hugged each other. Howard was Ahmad's first choice but he had applied to five other colleges and universities across the country—at his mother's insistence.

"I knew you were going to get in son." McKenzie whispered in his ear.

"Uh, yeah right. That's why you made me apply to sixteen other schools, because you knew I was going to get in. Right?" Ahmad said.

"I made you apply because you have to always have a Plan B, and C--and shit, a D and E won't hurt. Life is so uncertain, you have to be ready for whatever comes your way." She smiled. "Howard University." She said smiling big. "My baby."

"That's right! And don't be turning my room into no office the day after I leave. Because your *Baby* will be back!"

♋   ♋   ♋

"Hey baby," McKenzie said kissing TJ as he walked in the door.

"Hey." he said returning the kiss. "What's this?" He hugged her and pulled her in close.

"This." she said wrapping her arms around his neck "is your wife . . . " She slid her tongue slowly inside his mouth ". . . kissing her husband." They kissed for a while.

"Mm. I c-can handle t-that" He said smiling. "I l-love you, too."

McKenzie pulled away. "Guess what?" She clapped her hands and grinned from ear to ear. TJ laughed at her unexpected exuberance.

"What? W-what's got my baby all smiles?"

"Ahmad got into Howard!" McKenzie jumped up and down. TJ grabbed her and swung her around.

"That's great! W-where is he, we n-need to celebrate!" TJ moved toward Ahmad's room. "Hey, Ahmad!"

"Oh baby, he's with Crystal. He was so excited." McKenzie informed the disappointed TJ. She reached up and stroked his cheek. "But we definitely can celebrate with them this weekend."

"This is a m-monumental moment McKenzie," He moped. "Celebrating t-two days later is like, c-celebrating your birthday t-two days afterward."

McKenzie smiled. She knew TJ wanted to get closer to Ahmad; he'd been trying so hard. She loved the fact that he was trying to win Ahmad over. TJ told her that he wanted Ahmad to come to see him as his dad. Given their situation—she thought that was the sweetest thing. Even though TJ still had no idea about her past.

McKenzie grabbed his hand and led him toward their bedroom.

"Well then, let's you and I start celebrating tonight."

A huge smile formed across TJ's face. "I love you M-Mrs. Johnson."

McKenzie kissed him long and hard. She slowly undressed as he watched. She saw love in his eyes. She felt his adoration. She forced a smile. But deep inside, she wanted to scream. It had been months and she didn't feel the way she should about her husband. He told her almost every day that he loved her. She'd kiss him or change the subject—but she didn't tell him back. She couldn't. She just didn't feel it.

"How much?" McKenzie said unzipping his pants.

"This much." TJ picked her up, flipped her over, and kissed her down her back. McKenzie closed her eyes.

♋　　♋　　♋

In the morning, McKenzie grabbed a bowl of Special K cereal and sat in front of her computer to check her email.

Her heart raced. "Christian Malveaux" greeted her in her 'In Box.' She stopped chewing. It had been months since she'd received an email from Christian. The "Good bye" email was the last one to be exact.

There weren't any attachments. He sent it last night at 10:30 p.m. He was still using his Cal State account. McKenzie sat and stared at the name for about 10 minutes before she opened the email.

> What's up Mac?
> Hope all is well in your world.
> You look happy every time I see you. You look good every time I see you. Marriage suits you.
>
> I've never seen TJ happier. I am happy for you both. Maybe we can kick it sometime?
> -Holla back

McKenzie read the email about 20 times before she replied. She was happy that Christian thought she looked happy with TJ. She was even happier that he thought TJ was happy, since in the beginning he was so convinced that she was going to fuck him. She was going to make sure TJ was happy and didn't regret marrying her. But more than that, she was going to make sure she proved Christian wrong.

She read the email one more time. She didn't overlook the sentence where he said she "looked good every time he saw her." She especially loved that sentence. The few times she'd been around Christian, he acted as if she wasn't even in the room. Although she had to admit, she tried her best to act as if he wasn't in the room either.

> Hi Christian.
> I'm great, thanks for asking. Married life is wonderful. TJ is a great guy, but you know that already, right? ☺
>
> Sure, we can kick it. Just let TJ know and we can set it up. How's everything going in your world? How's Jada? (JK)
> - Mac

Before she could move away from her computer, Christian replied.

> Aren't you full of jokes this morning? Jada is Jada. Nothing's changed.
> Are you free this Sunday? If so, why don't you join me and TJ for breakfast? I'd love to see you.
> - Christian

It irritated her, but she smiled reading this email. If anyone had called her on it, she'd deny it as if her life depended on it. But she was extremely thrilled to hear that "nothing's changed" between him and Jada. She knew what that meant. They were still miserable. She knew she was supposed to wish that they'd work out their differences and reach an amicable place of harmony in their lives—and intellectually, she did. But her heart wasn't as forgiving. She was happy to know Jada still didn't have Christian's heart. In McKenzie's mind, she didn't deserve it.

She was a married woman. She had no right to be wondering . . . but she wondered who had Christian's heart now? It didn't matter. She didn't care! McKenzie smiled. She rolled her mouse back and forth so her screen lit back up. She read the sentence again. "I'd love to see you." She smiled. She frowned.

"Shit!" she said to herself. She shut down her email.

"What's up dog?" Christian said extending his hand.

"Hey, what's up Black?" TJ said slapping it.

"You got it. You got it." Christian looked around. No McKenzie. He was disappointed.

"Where's your lovely wife?" Christian felt anxious. He really wanted to see her.

"Oh no, s-she wasn't feeling well. She's at h-home in the bed." TJ said grabbing the menu. He didn't need it. They ordered the same thing every time they went there.

"Is she all right?" Christian said concern brushing his eyes.

"Yeah. Yeah. She's j-just a little under the w-weather. She'll be fine," TJ said smiling.

"So. How is married life treating a bruh?"

"Oh, I w-was made for m-marriage man." TJ said smiling. "I'm l-loving it. Mac is m-more than I imagined."

Christian smiled. "That's good, man. I'm happy for you. For you both." Christian cleared his throat.

"W-Well, you know w-what I mean—right?"

Christian paused. No he didn't know what he meant. Christian wasn't in marital bliss like TJ and McKenzie. He was miserable. And he'd never been at the point where they were in their relationship—euphoria, giddiness, lovey dovey. Never had a meeting of the souls. That is, not with Jada . . .

"Actually, Teddy, I don't." Christian cleared his throat and turned away. TJ looked up and saw the pain in Christian's eyes.

"Hey Frat. What's going on?" They sat silent for what felt like a long time.

"Man," Christian said dropping his head in his hands and rubbing the back of his neck. "Jada left. We're getting a divorce."

TJ sat blinking. He knew Jada was over the top. He had witnessed more than a few public episodes during the course of their relationship – the latter ones more 'out there' than earlier years. But Christian managed to keep it all in stride, downplay them. TJ thought they had a perfect marriage, he'd said it a couple of times before. Nobody was perfect, but they did a good job of putting on a show in front of their family and friends. Goes to show you what you really know about people. Even people you consider your closest friends.

"C-chris. Man, I'm sorry. Do you think you just need a little time? You know, some *absence makes the heart grow fonder* shit?"

"Nah Frat. It's over. It's not a temporary separation. It's final"

"Y-you two got history. H-how can it b-be over l-like that?"

"It can, and it is." Christian motioned for the waitress to come over. "She said she deserved more."

"Yes, how may I help you?" The waitress said.

"A mimosa please?"

"M-make that two."

"Go ahead." TJ couldn't believe what he was hearing.

"Jada said she deserved more, and she's right, she does."

"More than what? You gave her everything! A big ring, house, new car—"

"Things have been dead between us for a long time TJ man. Some of the shit Jada did to me--all the guilt and manipulation, the ultimatums. I literally lost who I was trying to bend and twist into who she thought I should be. But instead, I just became angry and resentful. And it had an impact."

"I mean, I know she became super insecure after ol' girl in grad school." The waitress returned with their mimosas.

"Thank you." Christian said to the waitress.

"No problem." She said as she turned and walked away.

"Yea, that was the underlying issue – distrust, insecurity. But it got worse. It became about me making her happy. And dude, the one thing I will walk away from this relationship knowing is that happiness comes from within. It drove me crazy that she made me responsible for her happiness and blamed me for her sadness."

"I-I mean, we can make a p-person happy though, c-can't we? McKenzie has me f-floating on Cloud 9—I- I'm so happy."

Christian frowned. TJ wasn't following his explanation.

"You should be, bruh. McKenzie is independent. She doesn't rely on anybody to define her, or demand you to be a certain way or do specific things just to make her happy." Christian explained. "Jada had this idea of what I should be, do and say at all times, in order for her to be happy. That's not my role. My role as her husband, her partner, was to enhance her--to support her, to love her with all I have."

"And you didn't?"

Christian thought for a while. "No I didn't. She wouldn't allow me. She spent too much time trying to control me. Trying to make me wrong. Trying to blame me for everything under the sun. It was just exhausting TJ. And then, I just didn't want to. I was too angry."

"M-man Christian. I s-swear, I never knew it was this bad. I just k-kinda thought, you know, s-she was high m-maintenance. But I never k-knew it was all this."

Christian smiled. "I know dude. We weren't very public." He paused. "And in all fairness TJ, she left me because I wasn't emotional and affectionate with her."

"You did it intentionally?"

"Not at first. At first I was just too mad and hurt to be affectionate. Then, I guess . . ." Christian scanned the room "I guess I started punishing her."

"P-punishing?"

"Yeah. Jada was so good at manipulating a situation. Calling Kai or my dad. She was a mastermind at getting her way." Christian picked up the mimosa and swirled it around in the glass. "But she couldn't make me kiss her, or hug her, or any of the sensual things I knew she loved and craved. The things that made her feel special – I withheld." Christian looked away, unable to meet TJ's eyes after his confession.

"W-wow man. That's deep. But I-I think I u-understand."

"Do you?" Christian said. "Because honestly, I don't know if I do."

"W-what do you mean? Who can continue t-to live like that? Y-you bogged down with the responsibility of b-being someone's everything and her not g-getting the love she needs?"

Christian didn't tell TJ that Jada compared everything he wasn't with her to everything he was with McKenzie.

"I want that! I want what you gave her!" Jada screamed at the top of her lungs. It would be their last argument. "I deserve to be loved, not tolerated, Christian. I am your wife," she said sobbing.

Christian looked her in the eyes. "I don't have that to give to you."

Jada charged him, swinging and cursing. Christian grabbed her hands and held her tight. He felt horrible, but he wouldn't make another promise that he knew he wasn't going to keep.

293

"Look," Christian said into the top of her head as he held her. "We can agree to stay in this marriage knowing exactly what it is and what it isn't. But you won't continue to manipulate me into being something I'm not."

"Manipulate you?" Jada yanked herself free. "You mean to tell me that you expect me, after 17 years of sacrifice, after staying with your lying, cheating ass – you expect me to accept that my husband is never going to light up when I walk into a room? He's never going to show me tenderness and affection? Christian, you can't hold me for more than 10 seconds without pulling away. I stood there and watched you wrap your arms around another woman, nestle your face into her neck and stand there forever! And you think I'm going to agree to go on with this marriage *knowing exactly what it is and what it isn't*? Sheeeeee-it! No chance in hell. Fuck you, Christian. Yo dick ain't in me long enough for that--"

Christian rolled his eyes. He had hoped it wouldn't get ugly. But he knew Jada. If she hurt, you had to hurt worse. "This isn't about that Jada and you know it."

"Oh but it is mutha fucka. It's about *that* and more. If I have to beg you to fuck me – let's keep it real, you don't make love to me. You pump two times and call it grace. If I have to beg you to fuck me every time we do it, it's about that. If I have to be the one to grab your hand, every time—it's about that. If I have to sit in my house like I'm here alone, and you're right next to me, it's about that."

"Right, Jada. It's *always* about *you*. It's always about what you're not getting, where I'm falling short. Has it ever occurred to you that I have some wants and needs?"

"Of course, why do you think I try to be there for you? I try to have sex regularly because I know a man should want sex often."

"You're missing the whole point. "I" have needs. You never bother to ask me what I need. You assume you know. But the truth is you don't know me, and the bigger truth is you don't care to know me. You just want me to do what the hell it is you want – when you want, how you want. And I'm not a robot Jada."

"What do you want? McKenzie?" Jada said getting up in his face. "She's married to your best friend." Christian looked down into her face.

"What I want is a woman who is genuinely comfortable with herself. Someone who takes responsibility for her own happiness and doesn't blame me and the rest of the world for everything that happens in her life. I want a woman who doesn't see me just as her provider, her fix-it man. I need support too—and no, I haven't allowed you to give me any in a long time, but it's because it always comes with a price."

"A price. What does that mean?"

"It means you always throw it up in my face."

"I don't know what –"

"The time I cut my finger on the lawn mower, and you drove me to emergency. I had to hear about that for months. 'I'm driving your ass to emergency.' Like it was some major feat. You're my wife; you're supposed to do it. You should want to do it. But anything you do for me is an opportunity for you to hold it over me – so I've made sure I don't need you for anything. And so what's happened is I have come not to need you for much of anything. It's intentional."

Jada cried. She wiped her face with the back of her hand. "Well, if you don't need me for much of anything Christian, what am I doing here?" Christian just stared at her with a blank expression on his face.

"Do you love me?"

"Sure, I do. I don't want any harm to come to you. I want the best for you."

Jada laughed. "I ain't no rescue puppy at the pound Christian. I'm your wife. Do you love me like a man is supposed to love his wife? Are you in love with me and want to grow old with me?"

Jada had never asked Christian these pointed questions before, primarily because deep in her heart she knew the truth. She just never had the courage to hear it.

"No, Jada. I'm sorry; I'm not in love with you. And I don't want to grow old with you." Tears streamed down Jada's cheeks.

"What do you have when the man you love don't love you? What do you have?" Jada sobbed. She looked up at Christian. "I don't want your pity. I want to be loved. I want to be cherished."

"I know. But I don't have it to give. There's just been too much damage. We've tried counseling, recommitting and starting fresh, vacations to rekindle the romance--it's just gone."

"Well, you can forget me living the rest of my life like this. I won't"

"I understand," Christian said quietly.

"No you don't. You don't understand shit, definitely not me. If you did, you wouldn't be breaking my heart right now. After all I did. After all I put into making us work. If you understood you'd be fighting for our love, not throwing your hands up like I'm not even worth the effort!"

Christian looked her in her eyes. "I *understand* that you refuse to live the rest of your life in a marriage where you're not getting your needs met." He said softly.

"And that's it? What about fighting for us Christian? What about our future?"

"What it is, and what it's not Jada. If we agree to stay in this, that's what it's got to be." Christian stood firm.

"And what does that mean? That we'd be in some kind of open relationship? You get to fuck other women?" Jada stood and placed her hands on her hips.

"If that's what we decide. I don't know. But it can't be this. This isn't working for me or you."

"And it won't be that! You've been hanging around them white folks too long. That's some white people shit—open relationship. Fuck you, Christian." Jada sat back down and cried. And cried and cried.

Christian watched as his wife's limp body, jerk over and over. He wanted to feel sad/bad. But he literally felt nothing for the woman in tears in front of him. He felt empty, detached, disconnected. Of course he didn't want her to hurt, but on the flip side, he didn't feel compelled to comfort her and reassure her like she wanted and needed.

"It's over Christian," Jada finally said.

"It's been over for a long time."

"Fuck you. And shut up." She said rolling her eyes. "You're so cold, so matter-of-fact. So OK with our marriage ending." She glared at him. "I hate you."

"I'm sorry you feel that way."

"No you're not. You don't care."

Christian just looked at Jada. He wouldn't engage in Act IV of The Fight. Actually, he did what he always did at this point of The Great Inquisition. He looked at his accuser, knowing full well that it didn't matter what he said next. He would be beheaded. So he held his silence. He knew he wouldn't win the war, but he would win the battle, if in no other way than by maintaining his pride.

♋   ♋   ♋

"How was breakfast baby?" McKenzie asked as TJ walked into the room.

"Um . . .Weird."

He pulled the headband from around his locks and let them fall free around his shoulders. He slid in bed and nestled in behind McKenzie. He wrapped his arms around her and lay quietly, resting his face on her neck.

"Weird?" She sat up suddenly scared. "Is something wrong? Is Christian all right?"

"Huh? Oh. I g-guess—I don't k-know," he said pulling her in to kiss her. McKenzie was annoyed.

"What do you mean, you don't know? Did you see him? What happened, what did he say? That makes absolutely no sense."

"Y-Yes, I saw him. W-we talked. I was j-just thrown by what he told me is all."

McKenzie was livid. "Well, what is it TJ? Is this some Fraternity secret? Why can't you just tell me what's going on?" McKenzie screamed.

TJ paused and stared at her. He'd never seen her so angry. "Christian and Jada are g-getting a divorce." TJ said almost inaudibly. "They've been s-separated for a few weeks." He watched her struggle for a response.

McKenzie sighed. She didn't know what TJ was going to tell her, but before she could control herself she had worked herself up into a dither.

"Oh. Um" She said, flustered. "That is—too bad."

McKenzie knew TJ was watching her. She felt caged. She took several deep breaths to help her regain her composure. She smiled and turned to face TJ. She leaned in to kiss him, but he turned his face away.

"Look TJ. Have you forgotten that Christian and I were friends first? When you came in this morning, you looked so— weird. I thought something was wrong. I thought maybe he was sick or something." McKenzie tried to explain to TJ; tried to explain to herself.

"Don't be mad at me. I can't stand it if you're mad. I'm sorry for snapping at you. I was just worried. That's all."

She sat staring at TJ waiting for his reply. TJ was thrown by McKenzie's response. But after listening to her explanation it made perfect sense. Christian and McKenzie had been close friends before they got married. TJ thought they would all hang out, the four of them, after settling in. But it never happened. Christian and TJ continued to hang out like before but McKenzie seemed to always have something else to do.

"N-no, I understand. Of course you w-were worried." He assured her. "Come here." McKenzie slid into his arms. "Y-you have every r-right. Christian is your f-friend too. T-that's why we've g-got to be there for h-him now. He's r-really going to need us M-McKenzie." McKenzie remained quiet. *They finally did it. It's finally over. Why did he wait so long? What caused them to finally call it quits after all this time?*

"Sure. Of course."

♋   ♋   ♋

"Ahmad!" McKenzie said. "Ahmad, you're going to be late, son!" She grabbed her purse and headed for the door.

"Stop all that primpin' and simpin' and let's go!"

Ahmad came out looking handsome in his suit. McKenzie paused to take a good look. She smiled broadly.

"Oh Ahmad, you look so handsome son."

Ahmad did a 360. At the end of his slow turn he stopped and posed. Chin slightly turned up, arms folded across his chest—as if he was deep in thought, or looking up to God in heaven. McKenzie laughed.

"Oh come on! You're such a ham." McKenzie said throwing his cap at him.

"Hold up! Hold up! You're going to mess up the clothes." Ahmad said straightening out his tie. His mom walked over picked up his cap and placed it on his head.

"There. Perfect. My scholar." She kissed his forehead. "I am . . . so proud of you Ahmad."

"Thanks mom." He grabbed his gown. "Hey, Christian's coming, right?" He headed toward the door. "I mean, he said he was when I called to invite him. Have you spoken to him?"

"I haven't spoken to him son. I'm sure if you personally extended the invitation then he's going to come." She smiled.

"I hope so."

"Really, why?"

"I mean, you know. Christian is cool."

"Uh huh. And?"

"Well, and—we've kept in touch over the past year. And . . . you know. We talk and hang out." Ahmad quickly glanced her way to see her response.

"Really? No, I didn't know you hung out and talked to Christian regularly. Why would I know that?"

"Well, I guess I thought he told you."

"No. He didn't." McKenzie headed for the door. "But, hey! I don't have to know everything that's going on in my son's life, right?" Ahmad couldn't tell if his mom was hurt or pissed.

"No, just the important stuff. You always know the important stuff mom."

Hanging out with Christian was insignificant? Ahmad knew TJ wanted more than anything to have that type of relationship with him. Not that he was ever mean to TJ. He was just—cordial. TJ wanted to be close to him. He wanted to do the things that obviously he was doing with Christian.

"Right." was McKenzie's reply. "Let's go before we're late to your graduation son."

♋   ♋   ♋

The sun was beating down on the crowd cramped inside the football stadium. McKenzie had given her seat to an elderly lady who looked like she was going to pass out. There were about five men sitting around her. She was undone that none of them had the decency to offer the woman their seat. Her cell rang. It was Christian.

"Hello?" McKenzie said into her cell. Her heart was racing. She instantly became annoyed with herself.

"Hey. Where are you?"

"On the east side of the score board; near the 30 yard line. Probably about 10 or 15 bleachers up. I'm near the aisle.

"Do you have on a spaghetti strapped sun dress?" Christian said in a low sultry voice. McKenzie looked around. "Burnt orange. That color goes really well with your complexion, McKenzie Batiste." McKenzie smiled.

"Where are you Mister Malveaux?" she said smiling, still looking around for him.

"You don't feel me?"

"No. So you can't be close." She said before thinking it through. Christian smiled.

"Close enough to know you have on orange panties."

"Obviously not. I'm not wearing any panties." The man sitting to her right turned to look at her. She rolled her eyes at him. Christian laughed.

"OK. You busted me out! I'm across the field. I'm checking you out through my binoculars." McKenzie laughed and tried to scan the crowd across the field.

"I can't see you."

"That's fine. As long as I can see you, we're good," He said quietly.

"And what about that makes it fine?" She said frowning.

"Stop frowning." He said. She straightened out her forehead.

"What kind of binoculars do you have that you can see my frown?"

301

"The good kind. I want to make sure I can see Ahmad." He said, his tone serious.

"He was worried that you might not be here today."

"I wouldn't miss today. I'd think he know that."

"I think he knew. I think he just . . . really wanted you here." Christian watched her face.

"I'm going to always be here for Ahmad. He is a really good kid. You did a wonderful job raising him Mac. Really." McKenzie smiled.

"Half as good as you, Mister Malveaux?" She whispered, remembering. Christian smiled. It seemed like so long ago since they'd had that conversation. But he remembered.

"Twice as good Miss Batiste." There was a pause. "Here comes your husband. I'll talk to you later."

The phone disconnected. McKenzie stood looking over at the crowd. She wanted to see his face.

"H-hey honey. Why are you s-standing?"

"That woman wasn't looking too good so I let her and her husband have our seats." TJ watched her. She looked like she was miles away. "Where have you been?"

"Parking." The truth was he was in the restroom trying to pee. He felt like he really had to go but once inside the restroom he barely got a trickle. And his bladder still felt full.

He had gone three months without any back pains. He took Raleigh's antibiotics and thought they had cleared up whatever his problem was. Now he was having problems with his urine.

"Yo ass is just getting' old and breakin' down!" Christian had said to TJ the last time they hung out. TJ was filling him in on his wonderful life and fucked up health.

"You'd better go to the doctor man. It could be something simple. You don't want it to turn into something serious. You know your fucked up family has a history of all kinds of diseases—high blood pressure, diabetes, cancer, and—what does Granny have?"

"Rheumatoid arthritis."

"Uh, yeah, dog. You need to get on that right away."

TJ was worried. It seemed as if his life was finally on track. He was so happy with McKenzie. He couldn't fathom having to deal with a serious illness. Not now.

"It's going to be a mess getting out of here isn't it?" McKenzie said, jerking TJ back into the present.

"Yep. A complete mess." He said to no one in particular.

The hairs on the back of McKenzie's neck started to bristle. But, before she could turn to see him, she heard him.

"Congratulations Crystal!" Christian said walking up behind McKenzie. He squeezed her elbow as he walked past her. TJ was on her left taking pictures.

"Hello Mr. Malveaux! I did it!" Crystal said.

"Yes, you did, Miss Magna Cum Laude!" Christian beamed, kissing her on her cheek. He handed her a card and turned to face McKenzie and TJ. "Where's the man of the hour?"

"H-here he comes, b-behind you!" TJ said, pointing behind him. Christian turned to see Ahmad running up to him.

"What up 'C'?" They hugged.

It was a long sentimental hug that everyone in the group paused to witness. When Ahmad pulled away they were both in tears. McKenzie was confused. *Tears?*

"What's up, Ahmad?" Christian said, standing back and looking him up and down—with pride. "Man, you lookin' good," he said smiling brightly.

"Did you see me walk across the stage?"

"Yeah. I saw you." They laughed. "I saw you."

He grabbed Ahmad around the shoulder and they stepped off to the side and exchanged a few words. TJ paused. McKenzie watched him observe Ahmad and Christian's moment. She was certain she detected hurt flash across his face. She felt bad for him. TJ was such a good guy. But Ahmad and Christian had bonded. She didn't know if it was as a result of the time they spent together during her ordeal or what. But today demonstrated the depth of that bond.

"C-Crystal. Come stand n-next to McKenzie." TJ said, turning his back on the little love fest. "Smile!"

♋   ♋   ♋

McKenzie was brushing her teeth when TJ called out from the bedroom.

"McKenzie, w-what do you think about c-checking out St. Lucia?"

"I've always wanted to go to St. Lucia." McKenzie spat out the toothpaste. "When were you thinking about going?" McKenzie ran her fingers through her curls as she slid in the bed next to her husband.

"Um, next month," He said flipping through a travel catalog. McKenzie looked up at him.

"Really, why so soon? What's up?" She hugged him around his waist.

He kissed the top of her head. He contemplated for a minute before responding.

"Nothing's up. I just t-thought a trip before the summer ended w-would be nice. And . . ."

"And what?"

"And C-Christian's divorce is finalizing. He's b-been so depressed and w-withdrawn." He said, worry consuming his voice. "I d-don't know. I t-thought it would b-be nice if he came along. J-just to get away. And, you know, b-be around friends." He looked down at McKenzie. "W-what do you think?"

Everything in her screamed 'No!' McKenzie forced a smile. "I think it's a great idea," she said kissing him. "He's lucky to have you as his friend."

"To have *us*. W-we're going to h-hang out, and help him forget about how f-fucked up shit is for him r-right now."

McKenzie laid her head on TJ's chest. Anxiety welled up inside of her. Her mind was racing a mile a minute trying to figure out a way to get out of this trip.

♋　　♋　　♋

"Aw, Teddy—man, that's . . . That's really generous of you. I appreciate the thought. But--" TJ interrupted him.

"M-man, fuck that b-bullshit. You're going! I-I already paid for y-your ticket." TJ said smiling triumphantly.

"I'll reimburse you." Christian protested.

"And then w-who is going t-to come with us? This trip is about us. F-friends."

Christian felt heavy. He had done everything by the Friendship Code. He was the best man in the wedding. He did breakfast with his boy on a regular. And most importantly, he had managed to do a decent job at staying away from his best friend's wife.

"Teddy, man—I ain't trying to be no third wheel, dog. Seriously."

"'C', man—as many t-times as I've rolled out with ya'll m-mutha fuckas. You better not e-even go there. Besides. This ain't no c-couples thing. For real, we're g-going to hang out as f-friends. Like h-how we were when we f-first met. Remember? That w-was cool, right?" TJ defended his position.

Christian was not feeling this trip. But TJ was dead set on it. He had bought the tickets, made the travel arrangements—and had a reply for every argument Christian tried to pose.

"Yeah Frat. It was cool."

"S-so, you're going to go, right?" TJ eyed Christian.

"Yeah, man. Thanks. I really appreciate this." Christian forced a smile.

"Man, you are my b-boy. E-everything I got is yours. T-that's on the shield."

CHAPTER THIRTEEN
St. Lucia

TJ preferred the window seat, Christian the aisle, because of his long legs, leaving McKenzie in the middle. She felt stuck. Claustrophobic. Sandwiched in between the lie and the truth—both clueless.

On the flight to St. Lucia, McKenzie thought long and hard about her situation. *Situation? What Situation?* She thought to herself. *You're married to a wonderful man who adores you. What situation is there? Oh there's a situation when the close proximity of the truth on the left has you dripping wet in your seat. Shit.*

McKenzie flipped through the magazines she brought to keep her occupied. She was reading an article in Essence about women finding their soul mates. It said that relationships start off challenging. First of all, two people who are raised totally different, enter into these pacts (relationships) with people who, because of their upbringing, culture, family traditions and expectations, and baggage from previous relationships, go into the relationship expecting the other to know and abide by their values, rules, and expectations. And being able to work through those differences, those expectations, and reach a middle ground—a place where both people are happy and thriving—is a major feat in itself.

But when you find your soul mate, there seems to be less of a struggle. This person seems to gel with your quirks. It said that there is a natural balance in the relationship—both people are happy, not just one person.

"What do you think about that?" Christian said.

"What?" McKenzie said. She had tuned both of them out and was in her own zone.

"The article. What do you think about that? I read it last week."

McKenzie smiled. "You get Essence?"

"Well, Jada had a subscription. So . . ."

She couldn't tell if Christian was the sad, hurt, divorcee TJ made him out to be. She thought maybe TJ was transferring. That maybe TJ thought Christian *should be* sad and hurt, and because *TJ* would be devastated if *they* divorced, he assumed *Christian* was devastated. He didn't know the truth about Christian and Jada's relationship. He thought they were a perfect couple, just like everyone else thought before they split.

"Um. I think it's pretty much bull shit."

Christian laughed. "Really, why?" He shifted so he could see her face.

"Because I don't believe both people can be happy in a relationship. Happy is relevant. But the way they describe it, it's this euphoric—I don't know, mushy, blissful place." McKenzie frowned. "And I don't think that's real."

"Then, what's real?"

"Real is compromising." she explained. "Real is not doing what you want all the time because you're in a relationship with another person. And if you love that person, sometimes you do things you don't want to do so they can be happy sometimes. And besides, when you're paying bills, and working, you don't have time for all this bullshit they're talking about in this article."

"Really? I thought it had some good points. You make a good argument, of course. But, what about the point they made about feeling happy inside when you're around your soul mate?" McKenzie didn't reply. "When your spirit feels lighter when you're in that person's presence, versus not feeling anything at all? There's this, I don't know—magnetic pull." Christian paused for effect. "I think when you respond to a person spiritually like that, it makes dealing with reality a whole lot easier. That's just what I think. I could be wrong of course."

McKenzie remained quiet. She knew he was talking about them. And it was true her insides had been doing flip-flops the entire flight, just being next to Christian. Every time he was in her space she felt lighter—happy. But he wasn't getting that confession from her.

"Well, I guess. It just seems so unrealistic to me. What are the odds of you running across this soul mate?"

"The odds are probably very slim." Christian whispered. "Probably once in a life time—if you're lucky."

♋   ♋   ♋

They arrived in St. Lucia around two in the afternoon. They agreed to unpack, eat an early dinner and retire for the night. It was a long uncomfortable flight. Both Christian and TJ complained about being cramped in the airplane.

TJ had booked them a couple of tours of the Island, a booze cruise, and some late night dancing. McKenzie had pre-programmed herself to have a splendid time in St. Lucia. This was an island she had been dying to visit! She would simply ignore Christian and focus all her energy on either the island activities or her husband. It was just that simple.

And even though her body had already begun to betray her programming efforts, she put on a good face and no one was the wiser.

"H-he looks like he's r-relaxed already, don't you t-think babe?" TJ said unpacking. McKenzie smiled. TJ really cared about Christian. She had to admit this man was a good friend.

"Yes, he does. I think this was a wonderful idea. The tropical tranquility will do him some good," she said smiling in his direction.

"W-what about you?"

"What about me?"

"Y-you seem, I don't know. D-distant. Are you ok?"

McKenzie walked over to TJ taking his hands in hers. "I am perfect as long as I am with you." She said smiling. It was a sincere smile and it warmed TJ's heart.

"I want you to have a good time too. This isn't all about Christian. It's for all of us to just relax and have a good time, 'k?"

"Of course. And we will, I promise."

They met in the hotel lobby. They were staying at the Ti Kaye Village resort in Castries. TJ had made dinner reservations at the Rainforest Hideaway Restaurant on the north shore of Marigot Bay. The twenty-minute drive to the ferry went fairly quickly. The driver gave them a local's overview of the history of the island.

Christian engaged in conversation with him all the way to the ferry. The driver explained the island's history, from the Arawaks, the Caribs who worshipped the volcano, to the battles between the French and English. St. Lucia changed hands fourteen times during the eighteenth and nineteenth centuries.

He talked about the ruins of the slave prison and graveyard, softly telling tales of the former slave trade on the island.

Christian was always very social—he could talk to anyone, anywhere, about anything. McKenzie remembered how he was the peacekeeper in their cohort because he had this skill.

They left Castries at the perfect time. The three-minute ride on the boat was peaceful, made even more beautiful by the setting sun. McKenzie walked over to the rail and closed her eyes. The warmth of the sun felt good on her skin. A cool gentle breeze brushed her face.

The ferry whisked them to the alfresco restaurant, which was perched on a dock. They were greeted with complimentary champagne, live jazz and by friendly staff. They were seated in the bar area with their drinks while they waited for their table.

It was a lovely atmosphere, an open-air restaurant situated by the water. The nighttime had crept up on them and the blanket of stars in the sky overhead illuminated the warm tropical evening.

The food was outstanding, wonderfully presented, so fresh and tasty. TJ ordered fresh-caught fish, Christian ordered a succulent steak, and McKenzie ordered tenderly prepared shellfish for dinner. The rich sauces, exotic vegetables, and excellent wines blew them away.

"This was a perfect find TJ" Christian said.

"It is p-pretty damned good, huh?" TJ said with a nod.

"Man, this is nice! The food." Christian waved his hands around. "The music. The ambiance---it's perfect."

They made light conversation over dinner and dessert.
Afterward, McKenzie excused herself with her glass of white Zen
and took a leisurely stroll out on the veranda. St. Lucia was a
beautiful place. She leaned on the railing and looked up into the star-
blanketed sky. No thoughts filled her mind. The white Zen had
traveled to that place in her mind where her thoughts resided and
conveniently flicked the "off" switch for the night. She was at peace.

"Are you r-ready baby? The f-ferry's here to take us b-back
to the hotel." TJ said walking up behind her.

She turned to face him. He was a handsome man. Still a little
thin for her taste but he was sexy and kind and sweet. McKenzie
smiled. She didn't want to ruin her perfect mood by flicking that
"On" switch.

"Yes, I'm ready." she said laying the glass on a table as she
made her way to the ferry. There would be plenty of time for
thinking.

In the room, McKenzie lay in bed waiting for TJ. Before she
knew it, her thoughts were consumed with Christian. He looked and
smelled so good. He wore a sexy salmon colored linen suit and a
pair of brown slide–in sandals. It was a perfect outfit for the island:
sophisticated in a relaxed, comfortable way. And his cologne was
sexy. Not too loud, but just enough to tantalize the vagina into a
moist response.

"What are you t-thinking about?" TJ's voice scared her back
into reality.

"What?" She said, feeling the guilt consume her.

"You h-had the sexiest smile on your f-face. I was just
asking w-what you were thinking about?" He slid into bed next to
her.

"You have to ask? I was thinking about our evening and how I couldn't wait to feel you inside of me." TJ smiled. He leaned in to kiss her, but her lie and guilt caused her to turn away. She slid down under the sheets to shield her guilty face. *Dammit Christian!* She thought to herself. *Get out of my head. Get the fuck out of my head!* McKenzie grabbed TJ's dick inside her hands and slowly started to massage it.

"I thought you w-wanted to feel me inside you?"

"Later." Her goal was to take his mind off of her, that look, and the inconsistencies of their current conversation. She knew one sure way of doing that was to give him head. TJ loved the expert way she blew him. McKenzie didn't care for it. The Major had "helped" her craft her technique.

When McKenzie learned that the Major wouldn't have sex with her on her period she conveniently bled for 7 to 10 days to keep him off of her. After a few months of these, he made her give him head every day she was on her period. He'd hit her when she didn't do it just the way he liked so she became an expert at it relatively quickly.

But tonight, she slid down on TJ with the ease of a pro. He moaned and groaned so loudly McKenzie had to look up from under the sheets to make sure he was OK.

"You all right up there?"

"Oh shit, baby yes! D-damn, that feels so good!"

As McKenzie moved up and down his shaft she imagined Christian's dick inside her. She tried to shake it, but eventually gave up and went with it. TJ didn't know. Shit, the way he was screaming, she doubted very seriously if he'd care.

McKenzie had never given Christian head. He'd expertly been between her legs. He'd licked her until she came all over his face. The thought caused her to close her eyes. She could tell TJ was on the brink of a climax so she grabbed his balls in her right hand and squeezed gently. With her left hand she massaged the area between his balls and asshole and waited patiently for the thick, warm juices to shoot to the back of her throat.

A few minutes later, she lay in a fetal position. TJ was fast asleep against her back snoring in her neck. She adjusted her body to slide from under him. TJ rolled over snuggled into his pillow and resumed his snoring.

Despite herself, McKenzie started thinking of all of the intimate times with Christian. She slid her hands between her legs, parted her engorged walls, and gently caressed her clit.

Tears gently glided down her face as she quickened her strokes. She turned her face inside her pillow as she climaxed. She wanted to cry out. She wanted to call his name. But she muffled her voice. She shook with a veracity she hadn't felt since . . . she was last with him—Christian.

Her body felt light. But her heart felt heavy. She wiped her cum on TJ's back, rolled over and willed her mind to shut off so she could find sleep.

♋   ♋   ♋

Good morning!" Christian said.

He was bubbly and full of energy in his teal green shorts and white wife beater t-shirt. He wore a pair of white low-top K-Swiss and white footsies.

"What's up 'C'?" TJ replied as they half-hugged and palmed each other their greeting.

TJ was wearing a pair of beige linen shorts and a printed button down shirt with browns, oranges, and greens. McKenzie couldn't tell for sure because the shirt was so damned busy but it looked like the print could've been flowers . . . or maybe birds?

"'Morning." McKenzie moved toward the breakfast area where the handsome blue-black chef in his crisp white uniform was making omelets.

She was pissed off at Christian about last night. And even though she knew it didn't make sense—that he had absolutely nothing to do with her thoughts—a small part of her seriously believed that he did. It was that part of her that made her short with him this morning.

"Man! All of these choices! I'm going to be a fatty when I leave this island!" Christian joked, trying to lighten the mood he picked up on. But McKenzie didn't reply.

TJ chimed in "Shit, I can s-stand to put on a pound or too. But if t-they keep serving it up like this, *I* might j-just be a fatty when I leave too!" They laughed. McKenzie walked over to the coffee decanter and poured herself a nice hot mug.

"Isn't it too hot for coffee?" Christian said.

"If it's too hot for you, you don't have to drink it." She walked off to find a seat in the sun.

She knew neither of them liked sitting in the open sun and would probably find a cozy shaded seat under one of the misting verandas.

Christian was thrown by her clearly agitated tone. He walked off with his plate of waffles and hash browns, thinking hard about what he had done to cause such a reaction. He grabbed a seat next to TJ in the shade.

"How did things go last night?" Christian asked TJ.

"Man! I t-think this tropical air got to McKenzie l-last night!" TJ chuckled like a little kid with a secret. He looked around to see where she was before breaking his 6-second silence.

"I don't usually k-kiss and tell, but damn man! I m-married a ripper!"

Thrown by TJ's confession, Christian just shoved a corner of his waffle in his mouth. He chewed for a moment then replied, "You just got lucky all around with that one didn't you?" He looked in McKenzie's direction.

"Man, d-did I!"

McKenzie turned to find Christian staring at her. She inconspicuously flipped him off. His shocked looked brought her enormous joy. She knew he was confused but she couldn't help it. She was pissed off at him.

TJ motioned for her to come sit at their table, but she pointed up at the sun, placed her sun glasses down on her face, and moved to one of the folding chairs near the shore and ate her breakfast.

"I'm sorry." came a sultry voice from behind her.

McKenzie continued to chew her food and watch the tourists splash around in the clear aqua-blue water in front of them.

"I don't know what I did, Mac, but whatever it is, I repent, and ask humbly and mercifully for your forgiveness." Christian said pulling up a chair next to her.

He watched her ignore him. She focused on the crowd in front of them and on the bacon she intently crunched as he watched her.

Christian couldn't help but soak in her smooth caramel legs that led up to her luscious thighs. Thighs he'd rested his face in between. She lay back in her sexy two-piece, all-white, crocheted, bathing suit. Her flat stomach and full, small breasts didn't give away the fact that she had a 17-year-old son. She looked exotic. He smiled—and she saw him.

"Don't patronize me. You know I'm not a dumb bitch Christian." He turned all of his attention to her piercing eyes.

"You are absolutely right. I do know that. And I wasn't trying to patronize you. It's just that I honestly don't know what I did in between last night and this morning to warrant such wrath from you." He frowned. "That cold greeting, that fucked up reply at the coffee station—what? What did I do Mac?"

McKenzie struggled for a sensible reply. But couldn't find one. She became instantly irritated with herself for acting so childish.

"C'mon Christian. Don't act like you're just getting to know me," she said rising up from the chair.

She looked down at him, watched him shift in his seat, uneasy about her body so close to his. Her midsection was directly in front of his face. She got an immense amount of pleasure in that moment. It somehow evened the score for her torment the night before.

"I told you when I first met you I had issues." she said as she walked off.

♋   ♋   ♋

"So, what's on our itinerary, today?" McKenzie asked in such an upbeat tone that it caused Christian to do a double take. She was sliding on a pair of white nylon cargo shorts over her bathing suit.

"Well, I h-have reservations for w-water activities if anyone's g-game? Then I thought l-lunch—a nap, and then t-there's the Booze C-cruise, followed by d-dinner and dancing or K-karaoke." TJ read down his list of stuff to do.

"Sounds like a full day." Christian said.

"W-well, it's a list of p-possibilities. What we a-actually decide to do d-depends solely on us." TJ said. "So, w-what do we want to do?"

"Let's do it all!" McKenzie said with a coy look on her face. TJ looked at her then at Christian, who smiled.

"Christian?" TJ asked smiling—as if a challenge was put out there.

"I'm down." Christian replied eyeing McKenzie—who winked at him. He laughed, shook his head, and walked off in the direction of the main road.

McKenzie knew she was wrong. But, for the life of her, didn't care. She had done what she was supposed to do. She was being a good wife to TJ. He was happy. She didn't want to come on this trip with Christian. He threw her equilibrium off. So, if she had to deal with the aftermath—Christian was going to deal with it too.

The day started off with a tour of Soufrière. They visited the Volcano and the Botanical Gardens in the morning. Then, they dropped anchor at Anse Cochon, a magnificent deserted beach that was made just for snorkeling, and snorkeled for hours in the afternoon. On the way back to Castries, McKenzie sat on TJ's lap as Christian watched the loving couple.

"Are you ready for your nap, Daddy?" She ran her fingers through his locks sniffing in deeply. She wrapped them around her fingers and brushed them affectionately across her face.

Christian stared. His gut instinctively tightened up. He tried to turn away but his eyes remained glued on the ease of their intimacy.

"Man am I?" TJ sighed. "Y-you know I have to g-get my naps in every day—ain't that r-right 'C'" TJ leaned over McKenzie's shoulder to include his friend in on the conversation.

"Teddy's got to get his nap in e'ry day!"

"That's right!" TJ laughed.

Christian tried not to feel jealous as he watched TJ tenderly rub McKenzie's ass. But he couldn't help it. He turned to look outside the window and focus on the beautiful St. Lucian woman walking up the road.

Instead of admiring them he found himself ripping them apart. One was too fat. One was too short. One was too dark . . . but the fact remained that he was comparing them all to McKenzie. They were fatter, shorter, and darker than McKenzie. Christian sighed.

♋　　♋　　♋

TJ stirred from his nap in excruciating pain. It was so painful he started to cry. The pain in his back felt like someone had kicked him with steel-toed boots. He lay there motionless praying the pain would subside.

Raleigh had been his local pharmaceutical hook-up the last past six months. He provided him with everything from antibiotics and heating/cooling creams to muscle relaxants and sleeping pills. Although he hadn't had any serious painful episodes in weeks, TJ had packed away his stash just in case. This evening was definitely a "just in case" moment.

He crawled out of bed, grateful that McKenzie wasn't there. He rummaged through his luggage to find his bag of "goodies." TJ popped two naproxens and lay back down to give them time to kick in. By the time McKenzie came in with two hands full of shopping bags the pain had subsided.

"Hey sleepy head!" McKenzie called out as she walked into the room. "Are you rested? You slept long enough." McKenzie said as she opened and closed drawers looking for something to wear to dinner.

"I think all that h-heat wore me out." TJ eased out of bed and picked out some clothes for dinner. "W-what about you? You're n-not tired?"

"Naw! I love this heat. It's like, I come alive in the sun. I'm sure my ancestors must have come from a part of Africa where the sun was scorching hot!" She said as she busied herself with matching her accessories to her outfit.

"Wouldn't that b-be every part of Africa sweetie?"

"Nee-gro, you know what?" McKenzie shot back. "Clearly there are *some* people who prefer the shade. *I*, on the other hand, really enjoy being in the sun. That had to come from somewhere don't you think?" She said turning on the shower.

McKenzie had been out most of the afternoon shopping. She purchased souvenirs for everyone she could think of. TJ shouldn't have to buy any unless he just wanted to.

319

She had been so frazzled by Christian's presence that she was excited to be away from both of them. By herself, she felt light and at peace. She was in a very good mood.

"T-the crazy Africans, I guess. W-who in their right m-mind would want to toast to a m-mutha fuckin' crisp?" But McKenzie didn't hear him. She was in the shower, letting the hot water wash off all the sweat and dust from her body. She stood there motionless and tried not to think.

"C-can I join you?" TJ asked stepping into the shower.

McKenzie would have preferred to shower by herself, but of course she didn't say so.

"My shower is your shower." she replied and smiled. TJ grabbed the soap and began washing McKenzie's back. She stood there while he gently soaped and rubbed every part of her body.

She rinsed off standing directly under water. TJ washed her hair, massaging her scalp. McKenzie closed her eyes. TJ kissed her. She instinctively opened her mouth and he eagerly slid his tongue inside.

They stood kissing and groping each other. McKenzie reached down and grabbed his dick in her hands. She stroked it hard and bent over for him to enter her. TJ shoved himself inside her and started to pump. But mid-stride he slowly lost his erection. Embarrassed, TJ pulled out. McKenzie stood and turned to face him.

She smiled reassuringly and grabbed his hand as he tried to leave the shower.

"Don't walk away from me Theodore." He turned to face her. She slowly and tenderly kissed him.

"I love you," she said staring him in the eyes. In times like these, desperate times called for desperate measures. She had to pull out the big guns. "You do know that, right?"

"Yes, I do know that."

"Then you also know I'm not trippin', right?" But TJ didn't reply. He just stood there, staring into her eyes.

"I guess I'm tired."

"Of course you are. We had along exhausting day today. You'll loosen up on the Booze Cruise tonight. You just need to unwind honey." They stepped out of the shower, got dressed in silence, and made their way to the shore.

The boat held about forty people including the workers. There was a DJ, a captain, and two bartenders who also helped with the sails.

The music was blaring and the two locals were working hard to keep up with everyone's drink orders. Christian and TJ tried to make conversation over the music. McKenzie, glad for the break, milked her Smirnoff Ice and stared off into the beautiful tranquil blue water.

TJ was slamming drinks left and right. Before the boat set sail he was lit. Christian was buzzed and feeling nice. The white people on the boat were pissy drunk, dancing *if you want to call it that* around the deck. The DJ was bumpin' one jam after another. McKenzie was starting to feel nice. She bobbed her head to the music and sang along with the old school jams.

"Nice music, huh?" a Caribbean girl said.

McKenzie raised her right hand to shield her eyes from the glare of the sun. The Caribbean girl was standing in front of her gyrating her hips to the LL Cool J song the DJ was blasting.

"Girl, he is doin' the damned thing!" They clinked cooler glasses.

"I'm going to ask him for a mixed CD, before we get off this boat tonight."

"Good idea. I am too!" Montel Jordan's "This is how we do it," blared across the speakers and everyone shouted, "Haaaaaaaay!" And stood up to dance.

McKenzie was on her feet shaking her ass to the funky beat. The Caribbean girl smiled and followed suit. They danced with each other screaming the lyrics out loud.

McKenzie watched the ease in which the girl moved her pelvic area. It was intoxicating---or she was just majorly intoxicated! Her hips moved as if they had their own mind, swerving and dipping, bumping and grinding. McKenzie kept in step, but she couldn't help but admire the girl's fluidity of motion.

TJ watched McKenzie dancing with the exotic looking local. The girl couldn't be more than twenty-two years old, twenty-four tops. Her smoked almond complexion was smooth and flawless and was accentuated by the thick beautiful black hair that hung mid-way down her back. She wore make up that she obviously didn't need and was scantily dressed with a lavender sarong and a lavender, white, and green bikini top.

The girl moved in close on McKenzie. She danced and swayed with her with an intimacy and familiarity that made TJ uncomfortable. McKenzie was on her third drink and was oblivious to the encroachment of her space by this local beauty.

The DJ expertly blended the one time famous hip hop song into an equally *one time famous* white song, "Louie, Louie" at which point the white people jumped up and started their wild and crazy dancing.

McKenzie moved to the edge of the boat and found a seat. The Caribbean girl sat down next to her. They struck up idle conversation for a few minutes until the girl motioned that she was going to get another drink. She asked if McKenzie wanted another.

"Nah, I'm cool."

Christian and TJ were still engrossed in conversation. McKenzie was fine right where she was. Well, she was, until she stopped moving. Sitting still, McKenzie felt the cold from the evening winds. She grabbed her drink and made her way downstairs to the warmth of the cabin below.

Christian watched McKenzie make her way down the stairs and motioned to TJ to follow. They carefully descended the narrow staircase to find McKenzie in a corner, staring off into space.

"A penny for your thoughts." Christian said.

McKenzie forced a half-smile. *Why couldn't they stay upstairs and leave me the fuck alone?* She thought.

"L-let's do one b-better--" TJ slurred. "L-let's play 'What If!'" he said, turning to face Christian who walked over to the table in the center of the room and sat shaking his head.

"Yeah, I don't know about that one dog." Christian said sipping on his beer.

"Yeah, niggah. L-let's play. Shit. Fuck it!" he said as he stumbled to the table.

"What's 'What If'?" McKenzie said as the white folks started to make their way downstairs.

"It's a game we used to play in college." Christian said.

"W-we need some l-liquor!" TJ yelled. "In order t-to play this g-game right, we n-need some got dam liquor!" The boat rocked and TJ went stumbling over a chair.

"Christian, get him please!" McKenzie said.

Christian walked over and picked TJ up. "I'm f-fine dog. What's up? Yo s-scary ass gone play, or what?"

"What's the object of the game?" McKenzie said to Christian.

"T-to be the last one s-standing." TJ said.

"Basically it goes like this, someone asks you a question. Like, 'What If your mother and your only child were drowning in a lake, and you could only save one—which one would it be?' We all have a shot waiting. You give your answer, you say 'your child.' Whoever gives the same answer doesn't have to drink. But those who answer differently do. The object of the game is to see who will be left standing—literally."

The white people started gathering around passing out shot glasses and filling them up with tequila.

"Let's do it!" one Blonde slurred.

"You in 'C'?" TJ said.

Christian looked at McKenzie. "Yeah I'm in."

"F-first question is yours." TJ said to Christian.

"OK." Christian said, raising his shot glass. "Who wants to answer?" He waved his glass around the room.

"I'll answer." A dark haired white boy in his mid twenties moved to the center. His face was red and peeling from the sun. He was shirt-less, and had on flowered swim trunks and flip-flops.

"There's this sistah--" Christian smiles "An African American woman--"

"I know what a sista is!" the white boy said.

"OK, OK! You hip to the Ebonics. All right then."

McKenzie laughed. TJ shook his head. The Caribbean girl just watched McKenzie. TJ watched her watching McKenzie.

"So, there's this sistah you been feeling for a while. She's super sexy, and—you've never been with a sistah before . . ."

Christian looks over at McKenzie and winks. She rolls her eyes knowing he's trying to get up under her skin.

"But if ever you were going to taste, she'd be the flava you'd want to try." The group laughed.

"Where's the question, Mr. Malveaux?" McKenzie shouted

"OK. OK. So, you get up the nerve to ask her out and she says yes. You go out and you have the best time, right?" Everyone was nodding.

"So, your parents are racist." The group shouts and hoots. "Ah man!" and "Ah shit!" Christian continues "and you have a trust fund."

"Not a trust fund!" one guy shouted.

"Drop her ass!" another yelled out.

"Love over money!" a girl screamed.

"Just keep her on the side—they don't have to know!" another shouted. The room was loud with screams, shouts, and side conversation.

"OK, OK. So you see where this is going?" Christian laughs. "Whatcha gone do bruh? You gone give up the trust fund for this hottie? Or are you going to say 'Bye, bye' to the best relationship you've ever had for financial security?"

"Shot glasses up!" TJ screamed. Everyone lifted their glasses while the white boy contemplated.

"Man! That's fucked up. Money or good pussy, huh?" the white boy said swaying with the motion of the boat.

"Not just good--" McKenzie said. "The *best* you've ever had!" she said laughing. The group picked up on the inference and started shouting out instructions again.

"What's your decision?" Christian said, shot glass up in the air. The white guy raised his shot glass.

"Fuck it, I'm practical. I like a nice easy life. I say TRUST FUND!" He slammed his drink and took it to the head.

Some people booed him; others clapped and cheered. McKenzie rolled her eyes at the white boy and then at Christian.

"What?" He laughed. "I didn't say it!" She stood with her arms folded across her chest waiting to see which way he would go.

"O-kay! Time t-to drink. L-let's go!" TJ said and took a shot.

McKenzie took a shot and eyed Christian. He laughed and downed his drink. He winked at her and chuckled knowing he'd gotten under her skin.

"My turn to ask!" McKenzie said. "Christian, you answer!"

"Wooo!" someone in the crowd said. "She's pissed off, look at her face!" The Caribbean girl filled McKenzie's glass.

"So, there's this sistah—"

"What's up with all the Black woman questions?" a white chick said.

McKenzie instantly turned to face her. "Are you fucking serious?" the white girl hesitated, not knowing how to respond. "You're on an island populated by Black folks. You don't like us, yo ass should've gone to Europe to vacation!"

"Shiiiiit!" one blonde guy said.

"Careful. She might beat yo ass!" one white girl tried her best to speak Ebonics. The girl sat in silence. McKenzie rolled her eyes. The Caribbean girl smiled.

"Anyway—like I was saying," McKenzie continued. Christian shook his head. He thought of the first time they met in class.

"There's this sistah you've been feinin' for, for like forever. You've played the role like you're her friend or whatever. But you're really, really diggin' her. But she's got a man!"

"Don't they always?" one guy shouted.

"And the problem would be . . .?" another guy shouted. The room fills with a burst of laughter.

"OK, OK . . . and?" Christian replied, uneasily.

"And . . ." she said with a twisted smirk on her face "her guy breaks up with her." The boat goes wild.

"You're in there!"

"Comfort her, like a good friend would!"

"So!" McKenzie shouted over the crowd. "She's devastated. Depressed. You haven't seen her at work in a week. You go by her apartment to find that she hasn't showered the entire time!"

"Naaaaasty!"

"Uggggh!"

McKenzie laughs. "But because she's so distraught. You have this one window of opportunity. It's now, with the tart twat, or never. Do you take it?"

"Oooo! That's a good one!"

"Do it to her in the shower!" a red head called out.

"No, it's right there in the living room. No showers, no baths. Rank, funky, and hot." McKenzie said laughing as everybody in the room made a disgusted face. "Deep sea diving all the way!"

"Fuck it. Do it!" an Asian guy screamed out. Everybody turned to look at him. "What? This is his only opportunity for God sakes!"

"It ain't that serious, dog," a guy shouted.

"Pinch your nose and dive in."

McKenzie slammed her glass and shouted. "Glasses up!" Everyone lifted their glasses. "Well, Christian, what is it? The woman you've been dying to sleep with. This is your only opportunity—after this, that's it! Are you going to go for it, or what?"

Christian stood as the Caribbean girl filled his shot glass. He scanned the crowd with a serious face.

"Hell the Fuck yeah!" He said taking the shot to the head.

The boat went wild with screams and laughter. People were re-filling their glasses when Christian caught TJ whispering in the Caribbean girl's ear. The conversation was brief. And he watched her make her way back by McKenzie.

"OK, OK. Who's next?" the Blonde chick screamed, almost falling down.

"I am." the Caribbean girl said, standing. "And this question is for the sistah here." She said turning to McKenzie. McKenzie was buzzin' off the tequila. She turned to face the Caribbean girl and fell into her. She and two other girls grabbed her and sat her down.

"Go for it!" McKenzie slurred. TJ watched intently. Christian was taking in the entire situation.

"What if . . ." The Caribbean girl paused, as if she were contemplating the question. "OK, what if your husband wanted you to participate in a ménage trois?" The men on the boat went wild. Some of the females did too.

"Two guys and a girl!" The women were chanting.

"Two girls and a guy!" The men were screaming.

The Caribbean girl held up her hand for silence. "That type of stuff don't really float your boat. But your husband wants you and another woman at the same time." she said seductively.

The men were whistling, giving each other high fives, and screaming, "Yeah!"

McKenzie wasn't into that type of stuff. She was just about to slam her drink when she looked over at TJ who mouthed "For me?" as if to ask her if she would do that for him? McKenzie's head was spinning. She couldn't tell if it was from the tequila or TJ's question. Christian watched in disbelief. The boat filled with chanting.

"Do it for your husband. Do it for your husband!" TJ sat back smiling at McKenzie. McKenzie slammed her drink.

"No part of my mouth would touch her—but I'd do it, for my husband." she said unconvincingly. The men went crazy.

"Can I get a wife like that?" one guy shouted.

"I guess that's what they meant by for better or for worse?" one female said. McKenzie downed her drink and stumbled over to TJ. He pulled her down on his lap. She kissed him. Christian walked away.

They stumbled off the boat and to the hotel. TJ was sloppy drunk and kept falling down. McKenzie couldn't walk at all. Christian had to carry her to their room. Inside, he placed her on the bed and waited for TJ to come out of the restroom.

"She's fucked up man. She's out for the night," Christian said looking over at McKenzie.

"All-all right man. I g-got it from here. My d-dog." TJ slurred. He gave Christian some dap at the door as he left.

Christian's room was right next-door. As he entered the stuffy room, Christian heard TJ outside stumbling over patio furniture and cursing. A couple of minutes later, Christian didn't hear him so he assumed TJ had gone back inside and finally passed out.

Christian opened his patio door too, to let the cool ocean breeze fill his room. He took off his clothes and decided to jump in the shower to get the day's sticky off of him.

There was a knock at the door. TJ walked over and opened it up.

"Hey"

"Hey, what's up, momma?" TJ stumbled backward. She caught him and helped him rest in a chair next to the bed.

"She's asleep."

"It's all-all right. S-she's a light s-sleeper. Go ahead."

She hesitated. "I thought you said she wanted to?"

"T-trust me. S-She does. S-she's just a l-light weight. S-she's fucked up. Here, l-let me wake her—" TJ started to get up. But she pushed him back in his seat. He was so drunk he couldn't fight.

"That's all right. I'll wake her, my way," she said pulling McKenzie out of her fetal position. McKenzie didn't stir.

"This is light sleeping to you?" she said as she pulled McKenzie's shorts and bikini bottoms off. She lifted the t-shirt over her head and untied the bikini top. TJ watched the woman undress his wife. He reached down and started rubbing his dick.

"O-once you t-touch her, she'll w-wake up. T-rust me."

The woman slowly spread McKenzie's legs a part and began kissing her inner thighs. Disoriented, McKenzie started to stir. The woman continued kissing up her thigh. By the time she reached her vagina McKenzie was barely getting her bearing.

McKenzie turned to find TJ sitting in a chair next to the bed. *What?* She thought, confused. *Am I dreaming? If TJ is there, then . . .* McKenzie looked down to find a mop of black hair between her legs. She pulled herself up. The girl sat back on her hind legs surprised at McKenzie's reaction. She looked over at TJ.

"What's going on?" McKenzie stared hard trying to focus on the familiar voice—it was the Caribbean girl from the boat! "What the fuck is going on here?" McKenzie screamed trying to pull the cover over her body.

"J-just relax baby." TJ said looking at McKenzie. "I got you a p-present. You like it?" He smiled.

For some reason McKenzie couldn't process this situation.

"What are you talking about TJ? What present? Why is this woman in our bed? Why am I naked? Why was she in between my—" The sentence caught in her throat.

"Now, j-just lay back, a-and enjoy." he slurred stroking his dick. "We h-have her all n-night." McKenzie was stunned.

"TJ. I ain't into this." McKenzie said, trying to move off the bed. But TJ jumped up and blocked her. He kissed her softly.

"Ok. I-I understand. But you s-said you would do it f-for me?"

"What?" McKenzie jerked back away from him. "I never said any shit like that!" she screamed. She looked at his accusing face. Then turned to look at the woman sitting on her haunches on the end of her bed. *The drinking game on the boat!* McKenzie massaged her temples. Her head was throbbing. She couldn't focus.

TJ pulled her face into his chest and stroked her curls. He motioned for the Caribbean girl to come close. She moved up behind McKenzie and slowly kissed her neck, then her shoulders. She rubbed her back while TJ held her in his chest. McKenzie closed her eyes.

TJ got up in the bed, turned McKenzie around, and laid her on her back between his legs. He kissed her forehead and motioned for the Caribbean girl to move forward.

She spread McKenzie's legs a part as she had before. She tenderly sucked her toes and kissed her feet. She licked her legs and kissed her knees. McKenzie lay motionless, expressionless. She didn't move, didn't say a word. She turned her face and focused on the hotel wall . . . how the pattern seemed to take the shape of a tidal wave.

She left the room. In her mind, she was in the ocean riding that wave. It was taking her high, the crisp blue backdrop was the sky, and she was so high she saw herself riding a cloud instead of a wave.

The Caribbean girl parted McKenzie's lips. She looked up to see McKenzie's reaction but received none. She was disappointed. She was dripping wet just from touching her body—she had hoped McKenzie would be excited too.

When McKenzie walked on the boat she instantly gained her attention and affection. She tried to find a way to engage her in conversation. The music was a perfect segue.

After the light conversation the Caribbean girl was more intrigued than ever. She watched McKenzie dance on deck and everything in her wanted to reach out and touch her. Kiss the soft, shiny, supple lips. Kiss the sparkling chestnut brown eyes. Kiss the peanut butter skin.

When they went below she was trying to connect . . . to start another conversation but McKenzie was only cordial and showed no interest at all. TJ had approached her during the game and asked her to ask McKenzie the question about the ménage a trois. He said they had talked about it before and she would be down.

It was obvious to the Caribbean girl that McKenzie wasn't down. But she was so attracted to her; she went along with her husband when he invited her over after the boat docked. He offered to pay her to please his wife while he watched. She would have done it for free . . . but she'd gladly take his money.

"Look at her." The Caribbean girl frowned. "She doesn't want this. I'm not into rape." She started to get up.

"S-she's always like this at f-first. She h-has to be w-warmed up. W-warm her up with your t-tongue. She'll respond. T-trust me." TJ said.

McKenzie wasn't a passionate lover with TJ. He always had to get her going. Her body would always respond. She'd get wet, she'd eventually wiggle, sigh and cum.

The Caribbean girl hesitated at first. But she so wanted to be inside McKenzie, to taste her juices. And he spoke as if this behavior was normal. Like she was rigid. The Caribbean girl spread McKenzie's lips and slowly, gently licked her labia. She took her time. She kissed her clit, over and over. McKenzie didn't move. TJ watched her face. Nothing. He whispered in her ear.

"I l-love you McKenzie Johnson." He kissed her forehead then turned her face and kissed her. Mechanically, she kissed him back.

"I am s-so blessed to have you as m-my wife. You make m-me so happy. I just w-want you to be happy," he whispered in her mouth. "A-are you happy?"

"Yes." McKenzie obediently replied.

She turned her face back to the wave on the wall. She focused on the crest and imagined herself riding the wave back into the safety of the shore. The beautiful warm white sand caressing her toes as she walked along the crashing waves . . .

The Caribbean girl slowly slid her finger inside McKenzie and moved it back and forth as she sucked on her clit. McKenzie flinched. Her body responded. The Caribbean girl was filled with joy. McKenzie was getting wet and she began to twitch underneath the woman's mouth.

"Um!" McKenzie moaned. TJ watched her respond to the woman's devices. She began to gyrate slowly.

TJ felt himself growing hard. McKenzie's head still rested between his legs. The Caribbean girl kept her pace even though McKenzie was moving faster. He wanted to flip McKenzie over and shove himself inside her and pump back and forth as fast and hard as he could. He wanted to her to feel all of his dick inside her. This woman's slow and steady pace was annoying him. He felt she should have increased her pace with McKenzie's movements.

"P-put on your strap-on," he said instructing the Caribbean girl. "Fuck her in the ass." he said coldly. McKenzie froze. The girl could feel her go frigid.

"No, we're good."

"P-put it on. I'm p-paying you."

The girl got up. She looked at McKenzie's face. That was not a face that enjoyed anal sex. She walked over to the corner of the room, opened her backpack, and pulled out her dildo. She strapped it on and slid back on the bed.

TJ turned McKenzie over on her stomach. He ran his fingers through her hair. "I'm going to t-take care of you." He whispered into her hair.

He looked up at the Caribbean girl and motioned for her to begin. The girl pulled McKenzie's ass in the air and rubbed her butt. She gently kissed each cheek trying to get McKenzie to relax. Impatient, TJ instructed her to start.

"I t-told you, once you s-start she'll g-get into it." he said agitated.

But the Caribbean girl wasn't buying it. She knew McKenzie wasn't receiving any sexual pleasure from her husband. He didn't read her body. It was all about him.

The Caribbean girl flicked the tip of the dildo across McKenzie's butt, gently rubbing it across her anus hole. McKenzie tightened up. The girl tried to gently slide it inside her but couldn't because of the tension.

"Go ahead!"

He was annoyed. The girl was taking too much time. He wanted to see the pleasure on McKenzie's face. He was always behind her when they had anal sex and he wanted to see the look on her face. The girl slid on top of McKenzie. She kissed her back, her shoulder, and her neck. She whispered in her ear.

"Don't worry Miss Lady. I won't violate you. I only want to bring your body pleasure. OK?" she kissed McKenzie's neck. "Just relax. I am going to love your body."

With that, the girl slid back on her knees and gently slid her tongue inside McKenzie. She licked her until she became moist again. The girl got back up on her knees. This time though, she slowly moved the tip of the strap-on in and out of her vagina. She'd slide the tip in, wiggle it around a little, and then pull it out. Each time she went deep inside McKenzie's canal until McKenzie relaxed.

Her walls were wet again. The girl finally slid the dildo all the way inside. McKenzie moaned. TJ stroked her hair and watched as her eyes rolled to the back of her head. The girl slowly pumped. McKenzie started to move with her. Each time the girl would go deeper.

The girl pulled out, slid her fingers inside and felt how wet McKenzie was. She unlatched the strap on, and flipped McKenzie over. TJ watched the girl move expertly. She placed her head between McKenzie's legs and began lapping.

"Oh!" McKenzie said. "Oh shit!" She arched her back as the woman plunged deeper inside her. She felt tingling in her toes and started to break a sweat.

"Oh! Um! Oh!" McKenzie panted. She tried to pull back but the Caribbean girl's arms were wrapped tightly around her hips holding her down. The tingling sensation was traveling up her calves. The girl unhooked one arm and slid her fingers inside McKenzie again while she gently sucked on her clit.

"Oh shit, oh shit!" McKenzie screamed. "It . . . it feels, sooo good!" Her head was spinning.

McKenzie's body was on fire. She was oozing, her walls were so slippery it was hard for the Caribbean girl to keep a slow methodical pace.

"Oh . . . yes!" McKenzie was confused. Her body was in ecstasy, but her mind was a whirl of emotions. How could TJ do this to her? But she did say in front of everyone that she would do this for her husband. It's just . . . she never thought he would.

She didn't know what the Caribbean girl did, but all of a sudden, the tingling feeling shot up her thigh and traveled to the space between her panty line and navel. It dove down like a crashing wave and exploded!

"Ohhhhhhhhh!" McKenzie screamed as she shook violently.

The Caribbean girl pulled back and slowly rubbed McKenzie's clit as she continued to cum. This extended her orgasm and sent her reeling for another two minutes. She moved back and forth so hard she shoved TJ back into the headboard, banging against the wall over and over.

TJ watched McKenzie. He had never seen her move like this. Never heard her scream out in ecstasy. Never saw her body glisten from the act of sex. Never saw her body rise and fall in response to his tongue. He never saw her back involuntarily arch in pleasure from his touches. She never clawed the sheets or grabbed his hair like she did with this woman. She never lay panting from exhaustion after making love to him. Never.

His head was spinning.

♋   ♋   ♋

Christian stepped out of the shower and towel dried himself. He applied a thin layer of oil all over his body, brushed his teeth, his hair, and walked out the bathroom.

He grabbed a bottle of water and lay down in his bed naked. The cool breeze from the patio felt good against his skin. He reached for the remote and turned on the television. He flipped through the channels but nothing caught his attention. After twenty minutes of not watching the television he started to doze off.

"Um!"

Christian stirred. He paused and listened.

"Oh!"

The sounds came from . . . from the patio. Christian sat up in his bed and tried to focus. He reached over and grabbed his bottle of water. He chugged the rest of it.

"Oh shit!" Came the moan from the patio. Christian slowly slid out of his bed and moved toward the patio.

"Oh, Um Oh!"

It was McKenzie panting! Christian was glued to the spot on his patio. Their patio door was open and he was listening to McKenzie and TJ making love!

His knees felt weak. His mouth was dry. Intellectually, he understood that McKenzie and TJ *had* sex, but . . . to actually *hear* it . . . wow! And . . . obviously she had moved from being—how had TJ described her? A docile lover. She was moaning and screaming . . . like how she had with him.

"Oh shit! Oh shit!" McKenzie screamed. *"It feels so good!"*

Christian peeled himself from the patio and walked back into his room. He closed the doors behind him. He felt like he'd just been sucker punched in the gut. He tried to talk himself through his emotions. *You fucked up Christian. Why are you trippin'? McKenzie deserves to be happy . . . to be loved . . . to have passionate sex.* Christian walked to the bathroom and splashed his face with cold water. He couldn't handle the thought of McKenzie sleeping with another man. Even if that man was her husband. Christian paced the room.

"*Ohhhhhhhhhh!*" came through the walls.

Christian reached for the remote control and turned up the volume. The infomercial was blaring, --*and for the ridiculously low amount of $330, this one of a kind tennis bracelet could be yours! It's perfect for an anniversary, birthday, or Christmas present. Or if you're smart, get a head start on that Valentine's day present!*

The headboard started banging against the wall. Christian turned up the volume again. *With flex pay payments of $15.00 a month, you can't beat this deal!* The host said enthusiastically. Christian slid on some shorts and a t-shirt, grabbed his room key and wallet and left the room.

♋   ♋   ♋

McKenzie slid out of bed. She walked to the bathroom, splashed her face with cold water, grabbed her tankini and shorts off the shower rod and slipped into them. She didn't look in their direction, didn't utter a word, she just slid into her flip-flops by the door and left the room.

The door clicked shut. The Caribbean girl got dressed and grabbed her bag. TJ was pouring some liquor into a glass. He tossed it back and poured him another. The Caribbean girl stood and watched.

"I didn't know I m-married a fuckin' lesbian." TJ said slamming back yet another glass. The girl looked at him in disbelief.

"A what?"

"A f-fucking lesbian. My w-wife is a fucking lesbian!"

He pulled the scrunchy from around his locks and let them fall before pouring another shot of liquor.

"Your wife is definitely not a lesbian."

"The h-hell she ain't! The way she m-moved and moaned." He stumbled over to a dresser drawer, opened it, and pulled out a manila envelope. He turned to face the girl.

"S-she ain't never did that s-shit with me! S-she's a fucking c-cunt sucking lesbian!"

"First of all, she only participated because you made her."

"Y-yeah right. She l-loved every minute of it. I saw her f-fucking back arch. I-I was in the g-got dam room remember?" He pulled out a wad of money from the envelope and counted out $500.

"She was responding to her body being touched the right way. Trust me. Your wife is *not* a lesbian," the girl snapped.

TJ poured the last of the dark brown liquor into his glass and tossed it back.

"I f-fuck my wife all the t-time and she has n-never . . ." TJ said pointing his index finger at the Caribbean girl. He stumbled forward and grabbed the back of a chair to catch his balance. "N-never came like that b-before." He threw the five hundred dollars in the girl's direction.

The bills floated to the floor. Enraged at his arrogance and stupidity, the girl grabbed her bag and headed for the door.

"Hey! Your m-money! You forgettin' your g-got damn money. Y-you fuckin' earned it." he slurred. "You m-made my wife purr l-like a fucking kitten. He said moving toward her. "You m-made her move like s-she was fucking on f-fire, like . . . like. Y-you" He stood in front of her pointing his finger in her face.

"You've never made love to your wife before. You've fucked her you stupid asshole. She only responded to your selfish ass." TJ's face registered shock. "Stop blaming her for your fucking short comings as a man. There's absolutely nothing wrong with her, except she's never been loved."

She gave TJ the most pathetic look she could muster, shook her head, and walked out the door . . . leaving the money and TJ's ignorance behind without a second thought.

♋   ♋   ♋

Christian walked around the hotel aimlessly. His mind was a blur. He heard McKenzie's moans and groans over and over in his head.

It was a perfect tropical night with the sporadic breezes teasing the perfectly landscaped trellises. Christian found a vending machine and purchased three bottled waters. He chugged the first one, tossed the empty bottle, and meandered aimlessly around the hotel.

He walked through the opening where they held the banquets and special events for tourists. The other night, they featured a cool steel drum band. There was a buffet and an open market with local vendors selling their handmade merchandise.

Christian turned right and followed the tree-lined walkway to the center of the hotel. He heard a subtle splashing in the pool and decided to walk in that direction. He grabbed a lawn chair and carried it toward the pool. He gently placed the chair down so as not to disturb the swimmer.

Her strokes were smooth and easy. She swam the length of the pool effortlessly. She touched the edge of the pool and flipped. She pushed off the wall and glided a nice distance before beginning the breaststroke. Christian stared. After the third lap, the swimmer came up for air. He knew it was McKenzie.

McKenzie swam for nearly an hour before exiting the pool. The cool water soothed her soul. The calculated strokes cleared her mind. One, two, three—breathe. One, two, three—breathe. The monotony of the motions, listening to the swoosh from her strokes, and listening to herself breath kept her mind from going to that dark place.

She raised herself out of the pool. Christian walked over and handed her a towel. McKenzie looked shocked to see him.

"Oo! Oh hey Christian. I'm sorry. You scared me." She grabbed the towel and dabbed her face dry. "I didn't expect to see anyone here. It's late."

McKenzie stepped out of the pool. He wrapped a large towel around her and gently dried her body. She let him. When he was through, he walked back to his lawn chair.

He sat and stared out at the illuminated pool. She walked over and sat next to him. They sat silently for about ten minutes.

"What are you doing up?"

Christian held up a water bottle. "Couldn't sleep. Went out for a drink," he replied.

"Too hot to sleep?"

Christian sighed. "Noisy neighbors." He tapped the bottle on the arm of the chair.

"Were they drunk?" McKenzie said.

Christian rolled his eyes.

"They had been drinking. But no, they were just fucking." he said in his most condescending tone.

"Who would be up at this horrid time of morning--" McKenzie started to say, but mid-sentence she realized who Christian was talking about.

It was her! His room was next door to theirs and the patio door was open. McKenzie was mortified. She was too embarrassed to look at him. And didn't quite know how to make a graceful exit. She wanted to just get up and run.

"Must've been pretty good?"

McKenzie sat motionless and silent. Recounting the incident made her nauseous. Christian couldn't have been further from the truth.

"Look. Just drop it."

"I think you already did quite a bit of that, huh? 'Drop it like it's hot?'"

"Fuck you Christian!"

"Do you have any in you left after tonight—I mean—" he started to say. But McKenzie burst out into tears.

"Shut up! Shut the fuck up Christian. You have no idea what the fuck went on tonight. Stop sitting here acting like you know, because you don't, OK? You don't know shit!"

She stood up and ran out the courtyard. Tears flooded her eyes to the point where she could barely see. She pushed through bushes that lined the walkway. Christian was shocked. He jumped up and gave chase.

"Mac, wait!" he shouted. The echo reverberated through the courtyard. "Mac, I'm sorry! Will you wait a minute?"

McKenzie didn't stop. She weaved her way in and around the courtyard until she hit the beach. On the sand he quickly caught up with her. He grabbed her by the arm. "McKenzie, stop!" he screamed at her. She was crying hysterically. "Mac, what happened? What the fuck is going on—you're scaring me. What happened?" His heart was racing. *What the fuck! Why was she crying?* McKenzie fell to the ground and buried her face in her sandy hands.

"Shit!" She said as the sand stung her eyes. "Fuck!" She said. Christian removed his t-shirt and gently rubbed the sand out of her eyes.

"Be still. Let me get it all out."

McKenzie sat still while he removed the sand. She calmed down and caught her breath. Christian watched her. The tears didn't stop flowing.

"Look," Christian said. "I'm sorry about what I said. I was out of line back there." He said softly.

McKenzie didn't reply. He pulled her into him and rubbed her back. She leaned in and rested her head on his chest.

"What happened tonight?" He whispered into her curly wet hair.

When McKenzie told Christian what had happened he exploded.

"What?" he screamed into the warm midnight air. He paced back and forth rubbing his head. "Why would TJ do that?" He stared down at McKenzie, confused.

"I guess it's . . . What, one of his fantasies? I don't know Christian."

"Well, why would you go along with it McKenzie? You do have a mouth, a mind—why didn't you just tell them both *fuck no*. I mean, if you really didn't want to participate." Christian didn't let up. It seemed simple to him. They didn't hold a gun up to her head.

McKenzie sat there looking dejected "What was I supposed to do Christian?" She whimpered. "That's my husband."

Christian stared at her in disbelief. "What?" he said sitting down in front of her. He lifted her face to his. "What did you say?"

"TJ. He's . . . he's my husband. And . . . he . . . he . . ."

Her words were drowned in her tears. Christian couldn't believe his ears. This wasn't the self-confident McKenzie he knew.

"So because he's your husband, he has the right to violate you? To manipulate you into doing something you wouldn't

341

normally do?" Christian said, lifting her chin so her eyes would meet his. McKenzie stared at him blankly. She didn't say a word. Christian had seen this look before. McKenzie had disassociated. She was disconnected.

"McKenzie!" She looked at him. "What's going on with you two?" None of this was making sense. "What happened? Did something happen?"

McKenzie wiped her face. "Nothing. I mean, it wasn't a big deal. I don't even know if that was it Christian." she said sniffling "Earlier that day, he couldn't get it up."

"His dick? He couldn't get an erection? That can't be it. Shit, everybody goes limp every now and then." He stood up and paced back and forth. "Has this been going on for a while or something?" Christian was concerned. He loved TJ. He had been there for him through many trying times in his life. And certainly nobody was perfect. *But this? This was outrageous.* Especially given McKenzie's sexual abuse history.

"Yeah, a couple of times. But I downplayed them."

How do you down play ED Mac? That's some serious shit for most men, He thought to himself. Christian sighed. He walked back over to her.

"Why did you do it Mac?" he said softly.

"I felt I had to Christian. I don't know how else to explain it," she mumbled.

McKenzie scratched her head. She rubbed her eyes, tired from everything that had happened tonight. She looked up at him with a dejected look on her face.

Christian extended his hand to her. She grabbed it and he pulled her up. He held her tight.

"It's OK. I understand." He kissed her salty curls.

"You do?" She asked into his chest.

Because she didn't. She didn't understand why she didn't protest. Why she didn't storm out of the room. Why didn't she curse them out? Why didn't she tell TJ, *No! I don't want to do this?*

"Yes. And you *are* a good wife." Christian said, looking down at McKenzie as they started walking toward the hotel.

She smiled feebly as if Christian's affirmation made her feel better. They walked slowly back to the hotel.

"Hey Mac," Christian said as they entered the hotel lobby. Why don't you stay the night in my room tonight?" He paused. "I'll get another room or something. You don't have to worry about me--"

"I'm not worried about you," she said cutting him off. She smiled and walked with him to his room.

Inside, McKenzie took a hot shower and washed off the chlorine and sand. She grabbed a towel and walked into the room. Christian sat in the chaise chair and stared blankly at the television. He had laid out a t-shirt for her to sleep in.

McKenzie grabbed the Neutrogena oil off the dresser and walked over to Christian. She handed him the oil, dropped her towel, and climbed in the bed on top of the covers. Christian moved to the bed and gently massaged the oil into her body. He massaged her legs, her back, and her shoulders.

McKenzie loosened up under his touch. His heavy hands worked the kinks out of her tensed shoulders. She was exhausted. She lay on her stomach and watched as the night sky turned from dark to light over the patio railing. She felt safe. A security she only seemed to feel in Christian's presence.

They didn't talk. Christian just rubbed her all over until she slowly drifted off to sleep.

♋　　♋　　♋

Christian woke early the following morning with McKenzie's arms wrapped around his waist, her head buried in his chest, and her legs intertwined with his. It felt so comfortable. He pulled her in close and buried his head in her curls that smelled like his shampoo.

He didn't remember them coming together in the early hours of the morning. After McKenzie fell asleep, he gently lifted her and pulled the covers over her. She didn't stir. He got under the covers and consciously stayed on the right side of the bed. Before he knew it, he had dozed off . . .

He eased out of bed, untangling their bodies. McKenzie still didn't wake up. She had had a long night. Christian threw on his t-shirt and shorts from last night, grabbed his key card, and walked to the balcony. He climbed over the railing and entered their room.

TJ was sprawled across the bed, fully clothed. A bottle of E&J was his bed partner. Christian spotted a brown prescription bottle sitting on the nightstand. He walked over and read the label—Raleigh Harris. *Sleeping pills*. He reached down and shook TJ. TJ lay motionless. Christian shook him harder. Nothing. Rage built up inside him. Christian grabbed TJ's lanky body and lifted him to his feet. Groggy, and slowly coming to, TJ opened his eyes.

"Stand up Bitch! Wake up!" Christian said slapping TJ extra hard in his face.

"What? What!" TJ blurted.

"Oh shit, fuck, TJ—go wash your funky ass mouth man. Damn! Yo shit smells like something crawled up in there and fucking died. Shit man!" Christian said dropping him back on the bed. TJ rubbed his eyes and slowly started to focus.

"Man." TJ said sitting up. "What the fuck time is it?" He sat on the edge of the bed rubbing his temples. "My h-head feels like a j-jack hammer is in there going c-crazy."

Christian stared at TJ.

"Go brush your teeth."

TJ moved slowly toward the bathroom. He washed his face and brushed his teeth. He dried his face and walked back into the

344

room. Christian pulled open the curtains to let the rising sun and fresh air in the musty room.

"Damn man. I f-feel like a vampire this m-morning. You t-think you could c-chill out on all the s-sun?" TJ mumbled. After last night, the statement unnerved Christian.

"Wake up. Hurry up and wake up. We need to talk."

"Talk about what?" For the first time TJ noticed that McKenzie wasn't in the room. "Where's McKenzie?"

Tight-lipped, Christian replied. "Down at the breakfast buffet."

TJ scratched his chest. "Shit, I need some c-coffee. My h-head is pounding."

"No, what you need to do Teddy is figure out what the hell is wrong with you." TJ turned to face Christian.

"Wrong with m-me? What are you t-talking about?"

"Have you forgotten about what happened last night? What you did to your wife. How you fucking violated her? Are you crazy man—what the fuck is wrong with you?" Christian got up in TJ's face and hollered.

TJ paused, watching the anger shoot across Christian's face. Then, he remembered. He remembered what the Caribbean girl said to him before she left. He remembered drinking and drinking . . .

"Y-yeah man. I-I—" Christian shoved him. TJ flew back onto the bed. Christian stood over him.

"I-I-I my ass!" Christian said. "What in the fuck is wrong with you?"

TJ rolled over on his side and started crying like a little baby. Christian could not believe his eyes. TJ was sobbing, practically screaming.

"Christian, man. I-I don't know w-what the f-fuck is wrong w-with me." TJ sobbed. "M-mcKenzie is the b-best thing th-that's ever h-happened to m-me. And, I-I fucking k-know it!" he cried. Christian just watched him in disbelief.

"I introduced you two Teddy." Christian paced the room, rubbing his head. "I won't let you fuck her man. I just won't. You have to understand that."

"No man. I-I understand. I-I've been f-foul. I-I don't know what's g-gotten into me. Shit." He lay there crying silently for a few minutes. Christian just stood there and watched his best friend come undone.

"'C', man. I j-just got worried man."

"Worried about what? What could worry you so much that you could force your wife to have sex with another woman?"

"M-man, I know it s-sounds f-fucked up. But at the t-time, it made s-sense."

"Oh, you got to explain how that shit made sense to you."

"I've b-been . . ." TJ sat up and ran his fingers through his locks. "I ain't been a-able to k-keep my dick h-hard man." TJ held his head down in shame.

"Teddy. EVERY man has technical problems every now and then. Shit! It's normal." Christian tried to sound compassionate but his nerves were wearing thin.

"Y-yeah, I know. A-and probably if i-it was any other w-woman, I wouldn't give a fuck. B-but, I r-really love M-mcKenzie."

"And you think doing what you did demonstrated love, how?"

"I-I was trying t-to make s-sure her needs were b-being met."

"With a woman? Against her will? Come on Theodore, I ain't buying it bruh."

"N-no, seriously. I thought I-if we h-had a ménage a t-trois, then s-she could get off--"

"And you could get off on one of your twisted ass fantasies? Is that what that was?" Christian couldn't believe this shit.

TJ was silent for a moment. The redness quickly covered his cheeks. "B-but then 'C', when it w-was all g-going down, I-I couldn't handle it. M-mcKenzie was m-moving in ways I ain't never s-seen. S-she was m-moaning, and g-groaning, and g-getting' into it and s-shit--"

"And what, yo dumb ass got jealous?"

"M-man, I g-guess. B-but I felt angry."

"Angry? Angry at what—at McKenzie? Bitch, you should be angry at yourself for creating that situation. That was on you!"

"I-I know. That's w-what the C-caribbean girl said w-when I s-said M-mcKenzie was a l-lesbian."

"You said that?" Christian shouted. He was livid. Here Mac was, trying her hardest to please TJ, doing things she wouldn't normally do just to keep this bitch happy—and he gets angry with her for doing what he wants. And now she gets labeled a lesbian!

"Y-yeah, to the g-girl before s-she left l-last night."

"What did she say?"

"S-she said M-mcKenzie wasn't gay. S-she said s-she was just responding to b-being loved right, or some s-shit like that. B-basically, she s-said I wasn't f-fuckin' my w-wife right. C-can you believe t-that shit?"

Christian wanted to say "yes" because he knew Mac was a passionate lover. But of course he couldn't.

"Well bro, I don't know about all that. But the woman was a professional. And based on what you've told me, she got Mac to respond to her in ways you haven't been, right?" TJ nodded reluctantly.

"Then, at the very least, you need to take that shit into consideration."

♋   ♋   ♋

McKenzie stirred from her peaceful sleep to find Christian gone. She was disappointed. She remembered feeling his hands all over her body and loving it. She remembered waking up and watching him sleeping so peacefully. She kissed his eyes and slid her arms around his waist. He wrapped his arms around her shoulders, slid his legs in between hers and pulled her into him. She was in heaven.

McKenzie slid out of bed and put her bikini back on. She needed coffee bad. She found her flip-flops and flipped and flopped her way down to the buffet for a hot cup of coffee before she had to deal with her reality.

McKenzie sat in the sun slowly sipping her coffee and nibbling on her cheese Danish when the hairs on the nape of her neck began to bristle. She turned around to find Christian and TJ walking up along the pathway. Her face went blank.

"Good morning!" Christian said.

"Hey." McKenzie replied.

"G-good morning b-baby." TJ said softly as he attempted to kiss her lips. McKenzie turned her face so his kiss landed on her cheek. TJ paused-- taken aback by her dis. Christian caught it, but moved over to the orange juice carafes and poured himself a tall glass. TJ sat next to McKenzie.

"L-listen McKenzie, don't b-be that way." he whispered.

She just looked at him and rolled her eyes. She raised the mug of coffee up to her lips and kept it there to intentionally block her view of TJ. Christian watched it all from a distance and chuckled to himself. He knew first-hand how much of a bitch McKenzie could be. TJ was in store for a brutal punishment.

"Leave me alone Theodore Johnson." McKenzie said. TJ looked around nervously.

"For how long?"

"For as long as I feel repulsed by your presence." McKenzie said staring straight ahead.

TJ flinched at her words. "I'm s-sorry McKenzie. I was w-wrong."

"What part of 'leave me alone' don't you understand? Don't you have a doctorate degree?" McKenzie said still not making eye contact.

"McKenzie?" he begged.

"Go."

TJ got up and walked away. He sat on the other side of the patio. He made eye contact with Christian and nodded for him to go sit with McKenzie. Christian grabbed some fruit and sat next to McKenzie.

"How are you?"

"Thank you for last night." she said so softly Christian's breath caught in his throat.

"No problem, no problem." he said lightly. She sipped her coffee and smiled at him.

"Why is he sitting across the way in time out?" Christian looked over in TJ's direction.

"I told him to leave me alone. I don't want to see him right now." McKenzie picked at her Danish. "I mean, I know last night was my fault--"

"Whoa, whoa, whoa! How was last night your fault?"

"Well, that's what you said, isn't it? I went along with it. I should've walked out, said no—well, I said no—but I should've screamed it or protested more. That's what you meant?"

"I didn't say it was your fault, because I didn't mean it was your fault. I was just trying to understand why you went along and I understand." he said gently. "TJ should have never asked you to participate. And after you let him know, quietly or otherwise, he should've sent the girl packing." Christian scooped up a spoon full of fruit and chewed quietly. McKenzie didn't reply. She just sat there staring out into the sunny day.

"What are your plans for the day?" Christian asked breaking the comfortable silence.

"I'm going to the Spa today." McKenzie smiled.

"Here in the Villa?" He saw the advertisements posted in the hotel lobby last night while he was walking around.

"No. I'll be at the Royal St. Lucian Spa, actually. I'll be putting some distance between me and your best friend today."

"Why? You don't think he'd impose on your privacy do you?" Christian replied, surprised at her inference. He didn't think TJ was the stalking type. But he never figured TJ the type to do what he did last night either.

McKenzie just stared at Christian in a way that told him that's exactly what she thought. "I'm going to a place that will hopefully help me forget about the past 24 hours. I just hope I can find some hands as strong and sure as yours to work out all of these kinks in my neck." She looked Christian in the eyes.

Christian couldn't tell if McKenzie was flirting or being kind. He smiled. He wanted to say, *if you can't, you're more than welcomed to come back over to my room.* Instead, he lifted his glass of orange juice and chugged it down.

♋   ♋   ♋

Christian felt bad about how things ended up today. Clearly McKenzie took his questions to heart and was taking a stand. Having talked to them both about the situation, it seemed like they both contributed.

Christian knew McKenzie's history must have caused her to react the way she did. Helping her to see that she didn't bring that situation on herself was a good thing in his opinion. But TJ looked miserable. It was 11:00 a.m. and already he was drunk.

"You're drinking already?" Christian said.

"It's 3:00 p.m. somewhere in the world. And wherever that is, that's the time zone I'm functioning in." TJ said.

But TJ wasn't even functioning. He was trying to drown his sorrows. He was trying to escape. And Christian knew he was trying to escape more than this situation with McKenzie, he was also running from his past—his childhood hurts.

♋   ♋   ♋

McKenzie checked in to the Royal St. Lucian right after breakfast. Located Six miles north of the island's capital, the Spa was nestled in magnificent gardens overlooking a wide sweep of golden sand on Reduit Beach.

It was truly a world-class hotel in paradise. Her walk through the luxurious hotel to the day spa illuminated tranquility and relaxation. It was exquisite: the perfect setting for a dream wedding, a romantic honeymoon or just a relaxed blissful holiday.

"Welcome to the Royal St. Lucian Ma'am." the caramel colored lady behind the white and grey marbled counter top said.

"Thank you." McKenzie smiled. "I have a reservation for McKenzie Johnson please."

"Yes ma'am." She typed McKenzie's name into the computer. "I see here that we are starting you off with a Thalassic bath, followed by a shiatsu massage, a spirulina wrap, and ending with an aromatherapy facial?"

"Is that the Royal Package?"

"Yes ma'am, it is."

"Then yes. That's what I'll be having today."

"Very well. Do you have any preferences for your masseuse?" the woman said as she typed the data into the computer.

"Uh, yes. Can I have a nice, heavy-handed man who knows what he's doing? Who can really work out the kinks in my neck and shoulders?" McKenzie said rubbing her neck.

"Yes ma'am. Tyler fits that description perfectly. He's a favorite at the St. Lucian . . . he's our most seasoned masseuse." She smiled.

"Great." McKenzie felt relaxed already.

♋   ♋   ♋

Christian knocked on TJ's door loudly.

"Theodore!" Christian screamed over and over, until TJ opened the door. TJ was groggy and disoriented.

"What?" he mumbled rubbing his eyes. Christian pushed him aside and walked into the room—rank with funk and alcohol.

"Damn man! What the hell is going on? It's funky as hell in here"

Christian yanked the curtains open and opened the patio door. TJ followed behind him and shut the doors and curtains.

"It ain't none of your business. Just go on Christian. I don't have the energy for you right now."

Christian turned to face TJ and saw the bottles of E&J around the room.

"Shit, with all of these empty bottles, I wouldn't think you'd have energy for much of anything."

"Fuck you, Christian. Fuck you and get out. I didn't ask you to come here." TJ said grabbing the prescription bottle, opening it, pouring two pills in his hands, and popping them in his mouth. He grabbed a glass of clear liquid and chased it down.

"Are you mixing alcohol and pills man? What are you trying to do, commit suicide?" Christian said.

"It's water." TJ said walking toward the door.

"Where's Mac?"

"I don't know. I haven't seen her since this morning when she instructed me to leave her alone." TJ said opening the door.

"Well you've drank—and slept the day away. It's 6:00 pm. Why don't you shower and we can go get something to eat?"

"I'm not hungry. Why don't you go find McKenzie and have dinner with her? Seems like she's not repulsed by your presence." TJ walked back to the bed and climbed in. He pulled the cover over his head and didn't say another word.

Christian walked out the room and pulled the door close behind him.

♋   ♋   ♋

McKenzie spent the afternoon shopping for an outfit to wear to dinner. She was totally relaxed from her day of pampering. And after speaking with Tyler about the amenities at the Royal St. Lucian, wanted to extend her day. He told her about the award winning beachside L'Epicure Restaurant that offered excellent buffet breakfasts and themed dinners.

McKenzie found a sexy turquoise off-the-shoulder peasant dress. She splurged and purchased shell and turquoise beaded accessories and a pair of strappy sandals. The outfit was simple and carefree. And she loved it. She'd have dinner and make her way back to the hotel to pack. They were leaving the island tomorrow.

♋   ♋   ♋

Christian sat at the hotel bar sipping an Apple Martini. This trip had turned out to be a mess. TJ did a thoughtful thing inviting him along to 'help' him 'get over' his divorce blues. The truth was he hadn't thought much about Jada since they arrived. Most of his thoughts were about McKenzie. Just like now.

Right now, he was worried about her. She had been gone all day and no one had heard a word from her. TJ had no idea where she was. But she'd told him she was going to the Spa at another resort, the Royal St. Lucian.

Christian sat there for 15 minutes contemplating what he should do. Then he chuckled and decided to do another 'stalking' move—just to make sure she was ok.

He recalled their conversation this morning and felt bad that Mac was so certain TJ would stalk her but never suspected he would. Given the fact that he'd made a habit out of stalking her, he felt a slight twinge of guilt--but not enough to keep him from flagging a taxi down to take him to the Royal St. Lucian.

♋   ♋   ♋

A wall of rainbow colored sails adjoined L'Epicure to the Mistral Lounge where soft piano music filled the room. McKenzie sat at a candle-lit table by herself, relaxing with a delicious tropical cocktail as she gazed upon the dawning Caribbean beyond.

Directly behind her, Christian strolled through the lush tropical garden of the hotel.

He had walked through the Royal St. Lucian day spa earlier looking for her. The young lady behind the marble counter was helpful in providing him with ideas as to where he could probably find her.

The garden was colorful and fragrant and softly lit by votive candles floating on the pond in rotund glass vases. Tea lights were strewn around tree trunks and trellises and all around the open area. The natural landscape included indigenous tree species, exotic flowers and fruits, and its paths were sprinkled with tiny bromeliads, wild orchids, hibiscus, and mushrooms.

He scoped out the restaurant to the right of the garden, La Nautique, and didn't find her there. He walked further up the path to the lounge and spotted her sitting at a small table by herself staring aimlessly off into the setting sun. She looked so peaceful and relaxed he didn't want to interrupt. He waited awhile then flagged down a waiter to announce his arrival.

"Excuse me madam?" the waiter said, handing her a note. He smiled and walked off. McKenzie looked around and opened the folded piece of paper.

> *Do you know how to dance? I mean besides the cha-cha?*
> *I realized tonite, I've never danced any other way with you.*
> *May I have the honor?*
> *--Christian*

McKenzie lit up like a light bulb and immediately turned to look for Christian. She looked and looked. And finally found him perched comfortably on a boulder in the garden. He was grinning from ear to ear—obviously getting a kick out of her response. She walked outside to where he was.

"Funny guy!" she said socking him in his shoulder. He laughed.

"What happened, you got kidnapped over here or something?" Christian said grabbing her around her waist. She easily followed suit sliding her arms around his neck. They slow danced to the jazz music playing over the PA system in the garden.

"I thought you were just getting a massage?"

"Isn't it beautiful here?" McKenzie said dreamily, gazing around them.

"Yes, it is amazing."

She tightened her arms around his neck and rested her head comfortably on his chest. They danced through two songs in silence. It was a comfortable silence. McKenzie was light on her feet and followed Christian's lead with little effort. He held her close resting his hands on the top of her butt.

"I love your dress." Christian said into her curls. Her hair smelled like the tropical flowers in the garden.

"You do?" She replied. "What do you like about it?"

"Hmm, let me see." Christian said spinning her around. "It's very elegant."

"Elegant huh?" McKenzie said smiling. "That wasn't the look I was going for; but I'll definitely take it."

"Were you going for exotic and sexy?" he whispered in her ear. "Because you are definitely those as well." McKenzie giggled.

"Why Mister Malveaux, you're making me blush!"

Christian chuckled. Talking about her appearance started to cause a physical reaction in his pants. So he pulled away.

"Thank you very much for the dance. I was worried your repertoire only included the cha-cha. I see you got some skills young lady."

"You know what?" she said, placing her hands intently on her hips. Christian laughed. "I am full of surprises and unexpected delights!" She said in an animated voice. "You better watch out."

Christian laughed heartily. "Is that right? Well I hope I get to see a couple. Personally, I think you're full of shit." Christian said tickling her. McKenzie screamed and ran away from him. They headed back to her table.

"They took my drink." McKenzie frowned.

"Just order another. What were you drinking?" Christian said motioning for a waiter.

"A Bahama Mama."

"One Bahama Mama and a hurricane please."

"After we get our drinks, do you want to walk over to the restaurant and have dinner?"

"Sure. Do you know what's on the menu?"

"No, just that it came highly recommended."

Christian didn't overlook the fact that McKenzie hadn't mentioned TJ once tonight. She was in a very light and easy mood. He loved it. She seemed relaxed and happy. It reminded him of the time back in school when they'd first started hanging out.

He decided not to bring TJ up. Instead, he'd let her decide when and if she wanted to talk about him. Until then, he would do his best to be good company and show her a good time tonight, their last night on the Island of St. Lucia.

The drink orders came and they walked through the garden and over to La Nautique. A waiter sat them immediately.

McKenzie threw her hand up in delight.

"What a beautiful view!" The waiter sat them in a cozy little private corner with the view of the ocean.

"Yes ma'am." the waiter replied. "This table is reserved especially for lovers." he said and walked off. McKenzie blushed. Christian pretended to study the menu.

"So, what do you have a taste for tonight?" Christian asked, scanning the menu. "Or did your highly recommended referral suggest a 'must try'?" he said as he continued to browse. McKenzie decided on a mango shrimp dinner. Christian chose chicken curry.

"Cheers!" the crowd roared in the room behind them.

"Sounds like they're having fun."

"Sure does." McKenzie replied in a near whisper.

Christian looked up at McKenzie. "Everything OK?" He asked, worried by the sudden mood change. He turned to face the direction McKenzie was staring. *The crowd.* It seemed to be a wedding reception. And they all really seemed to be having a ball.

"Reminiscing?"

McKenzie ran her fingers through her curls. "About my wedding day? Hardly. I'm enjoying my last night in paradise," she said taking a long deep gulp of her drink.

Christian watched her thoughtfully. He looked over to the crowd behind them. They were having a good time doing the electric slide.

"Are you?"

"Am I what?" McKenzie replied focusing back on Christian.

"Are you enjoying your last night in paradise?" He said as he stood up.

McKenzie looked up at Christian. He extended his hand to her. She took it and stood up.

"Yes I am." McKenzie replied. She flashed a huge smile.

Her evening so far, was very nice. She always enjoyed Christian's company. He had this way of always making her feel at ease.

"What's up? What are we doing?"

"Trust me," he said leading her down a narrow path. "I'm going to make sure you enjoy your last night in St. Lucia. How about that?" His tone was so sweet McKenzie's heart melted.

"Christian, that's not your responsibility." She followed behind him. "Anyway, I told you already that I am."

They entered the room off the garden where the wedding crowd was still dancing. Christian pulled McKenzie onto the dance floor and into the middle of the crowd. McKenzie started laughing. But they did the electric slide with the room full of folks.

"OK ladies and gentlemen, boys and girls!" the DJ said. "We're going to take it back, just a little bit." He smoothly mixed in an old school jam.

Cutie pie, you're the reason why . . .

The crowd went wild. "Heeeeeey!" they screamed. The few who were seated ran onto the floor. The rest of the folks who were already on the floor started dancing.

Christian and McKenzie did their screaming as well. Christian leaned in and shouted in McKenzie's ear.

"You don't know nothin' 'bout this!" McKenzie threw her head back, spun around so her dress flared out and laughed.

"Man, what are you talking about? This song was written especially for me!" she said batting her eyes up at him and pointing to the ceiling. She placed her hand up to her ear with the free hand as if to tell Christian to listen. He was dancing but pretended to stop and listen.

Cutie pie, You really pick me up
Till I can't, Hardly get enough
You're the girl who makes me feel so good
Cutie pie

McKenzie smiled broadly. She moved in close.
"Do I pick you up Mr. Malveaux?"
A huge smile swept across his face.
"Til I can't hardly get enough."
They laughed. They danced. They enjoyed the partying crowd. The DJ was bumpin' all night. He played hit after hit; and did a wonderful job at mixing in songs from the 80s, 90s, and current day. They were on the dance floor all night. When they finally sat down for a breather, one of the family members tapped Christian on the shoulder,

"Hey, we was tryin' to figure out who ya'll related to? Lisa or Damon?"
The older man slurred. The lady sitting to his right leaned in.

"I told his drunk ass you was Lisa's cousin. You can see it in your nose," she said waving her hand in front of her nose. "You got Harry's nose—don't he Porshay?" She nudged the lady to her right.

"Is Larry fine?" she said spitting in the lady's face. "Cause this brotha is fine as fuck. Is this yo man? I ain't mean no disrespect sistah," she said holding up her hands in apology to McKenzie. McKenzie saw Christian grimace when the woman suggested interest in him. He leaned in and hugged McKenzie.

"None taken sistah." McKenzie replied.
McKenzie looked him up and down and smiled brightly. "He *is* fine as fuck."

They all laughed. The man coughed an uncomfortable cough and tried to resume his conversation. "Yeah, fuck all that bull shit .. . who is yo peoples?" he asked again. The women looked on.

"No, actually I'm here with her." Christian said pulling McKenzie in close. McKenzie perked up, pinching Christian's thigh under the table. He jumped and laughed.

"Uh yeah. He's here with me . . ." McKenzie said kissing him gently.

An electrical current shot through her the moment their lips touched. Christian closed his eyes and opened his lips, instinctively receiving the very intimate kiss. They opened their eyes and looked at each other for a moment. McKenzie turned to the people watching them like they were a Soap Opera.

"And Damon's my peoples."

The man screamed at the women,

"I told ya'll them wasn't Lisa's peoples! They too damned citified. Lisa's peoples is 'hood, all of 'em!" McKenzie raised her eyebrows. Christian forced a fake smile.

"A'ight! A'ight!" The DJ announced. "This next one is only for the Grown n' Sexy folks! No perpetrators tonight! I got an oldie but goodie with and added twist for you. Check this out!" MC Lyte's sultry voice piped across the sound system

Yeah, I'm ecstatic for love Fanatic of love
And if I'm not around It's you I'm thinkin' of
I'm gonna make it real for you Whenever I deal wit you
I do do do do anything

"Oh hell no." Christian said in McKenzie's ear. McKenzie turned to look at him.

"What?" she watched him closely.

Christian grabbed McKenzie's hand and yanked her onto the dance floor. They fell in step naturally like they were breathing from the same lung. He pulled her in close as he passionately sang the Bobby Caldwell classic in her ear.

I guess you wonder where I've been
I searched to find a love within'
I came back to let you know

Got a *thing* for you and I can't let go

Christian intentionally turned McKenzie so she would face him. He looked her in the eyes as he told her that his friends wonder what is wrong with him because he's in a daze from her love. McKenzie tried to pivot and turn. She was totally embarrassed by the sincerity in Christian's eyes. But he wouldn't let her turn. Instead he slid his hand around her waist with his left hand, and moved her arm up around his neck with his right hand. She gently clasped her hands around his neck. He smiled as he confessed how he came back to let her know, that he's got a thing for her and he can't let go.

McKenzie stepped back to look in his eyes. They were somber and sincere. But they sparkled like she'd never seen before. Her heart melted. She spun around, dipped, and came back to that place . . . that space and time that seemed to belong exclusively to her. It was inside his space. It was a comfort zone she seemed to always find . . . that he seemed to always provide . . . that they seemed to always share.

Some people go around the world for love
But they may never find what they dream of
What you won't do, do for love
You've tried everything but you don't give up
In my world only you make me do for love
What I would not do

Once again, McKenzie felt as if they were the only people in the room. They moved around the floor with Christian crooning in her ear. He stepped back so he could face her. His eyes seemed full of pain. His words were strong and steady. But his eyes told a different story. The thought gripped McKenzie and left her breathless. All of a sudden she couldn't breathe. The room became extremely hot. She felt as if she was suffocating. She jerked away from Christian and ran out of the room. Surprised, he ran after her.

"Mac, wait!" Christian called after her. "Mac!" But she didn't stop until she'd reached the garden. She took several deep breaths.

"Are you ok?" He said walking up behind her. He gently slid his arms around her waist. McKenzie pulled away and walked to the other side of the garden.

It was beautiful. The night sky was pitch black and alive with twinkling stars. The garden was softly aglow from floating tea lights and tiki torches strategically placed around foliage and furniture. Christian followed her.

"I'm sorry Mac. Did I do something wrong?" he said trying to recall what he could've done.

McKenzie turned to look at him and quickly walked away. She crossed a white bridge that traipsed over a running brook. It was much darker on the other side.

"C'mon, talk to me. It seems as if you're always running away from me. What's up with that?" Christian pleaded. He followed her across the bridge. But McKenzie didn't stop.

Directly in front of them was a beautifully lit, cascading waterfall. The water crashed loudly over smooth rocks. She finally turned to face him.

"I'm sorry." she turned to face him. Tears were streaming down her face. Christian's heart sank. He reached out for her but she pulled away.

Frustrated, Christian threw his hands up in the air. "What? What are you sorry for? Why are you crying?"

"You looked so sad . . . and you seemed so sincere singing those words . . ." she said looking up into his eyes.

"I mean . . . That song said a lot about how I feel. But I wasn't sad." He moved away from her. "I think I felt more like, I don't know—remorseful."

"I don't want to make you feel remorse or sadness Christian. I don't want to make anybody feel fucked up," she whispered. "I know how that feels. I never want to make anyone feel that way."

"You don't."

But McKenzie walked off. He watched her run her fingers through her curls. He smiled. She turned to face him and gave him a half smile.

"I do. Despite the fact that I try as hard as I know how, and do things I hate doing!" She burst into tears.

Christian eyes widened. "What are you doing that you hate?"

McKenzie stood silently crying. Christian walked up behind her and pulled her into his chest. She didn't pull away.

"What is it Mac? You can tell me." Christian tightened his hold around her waist. She felt warm, safe.

"It's not a big deal, really."

"Well if it's not a big deal, then tell me."

McKenzie rested her head on Christian's chest and closed her eyes while she spoke. "It's about TJ. Well, when we have . . ." McKenzie felt uncomfortable. She paused and Christian waited patiently. She took a deep breath and blurted "anal sex." She buried her head in his chest like a child who was . . . embarrassed . . . afraid.

Christian was speechless. After last night, and first-hand knowledge of TJs history in college, he wasn't surprised. But he was taken aback. Based on their conversations Christian got the impression TJ really loved McKenzie. He just assumed he would be treating McKenzie like the jewel she is—and not disrespecting her by making these twisted sexual requests.

"He forces you to have anal sex?" Christian said his anger slowly rising. McKenzie shifted.

"No . . . he doesn't force me. I guess I've just gone along with it . . . but I hate it." she tried to explain.

"You go along with it? Like you went along last night?"

McKenzie pulled away. She looked wounded. "What are you saying?"

"I'm not *saying* anything. I *am* asking . . . why do you go along with this shit if you hate it so much. You're being violated, disrespected—my God, McKenzie, you're a brilliant woman! You are smart. I've heard you rip people apart for so much as looking at you the wrong way." Christian said pacing back and forth. McKenzie held her head down. "Why have you lost your backbone Mac? Why are you going along with all of this shit?"

"What else did I have to give him Christian?" She screamed.

"What? What are you talking about?"

"What else did I have to give my husband, Christian?" she repeated through clenched teeth. "I couldn't give him my virginity.

My stepfather took that!" She stood up and walked toward the bridge. Christian was speechless. "I couldn't give him my heart," she said staring him in his eyes. "You have that." They stood there for a few minutes letting the truth permeate the fragrant air. She lowered her head. "He married me Christian." she whispered, "I wanted to give him something."

Christian ran his hands over his head. He couldn't believe what McKenzie was saying. Intellectually, he followed her line of reason because he knew about her past. He just thought she was too confident in herself, too proud and sure of all that she was to allow herself to do anything she didn't want to do. But he watched her and he saw the façade crumbling.

"You did, Mac," he said walking to her. "You gave him you. That was more than enough." He pulled her to him. "You are enough, baby. You are something special. Don't you know that?" She tried to pull away. But Christian wouldn't let her run.

She laid her head on his chest and he wrapped his arms around her tightly. She closed her eyes and cried. He rubbed her back slowly and tenderly.

"You . . . are . . . enough." he whispered in her curls. "Just . . . . you . . . alone . . . if you never do another thing. You're enough, Mac. Do you hear me?" McKenzie didn't respond. "Do you believe me?" She didn't reply. She just held on tight.

"Mac?" Christian stepped back so he could look her in her eyes. She tried to turn away, but he gently held her chin so she couldn't look away.

"That's sweet Christian . . . I think you mean well--"

"But you think I'm lying to you?"

"Christian, my stepfather raped, copulated, sodomized, and did whatever his sick mind could imagine to me--until he got me pregnant."

"So. That's on him. He was the sick bastard. You were an innocent victim."

"I'm no innocent victim. I'm nothing. I've always been nothing." She walked and stood near a table. She dropped her face into her hands.

"What?" Christian shouted. "You are a Queen. A beautiful Nubian Queen, remember? What happened to that?" he said moving toward her. He sat down on the table.

"It's a lie." McKenzie wore defeat in every part of her body, her face, her shoulders as they slumped. The tears rolled down her face. "And you know it."

"I know--"

"Just like Melvin knew it." She stared at Christian.

"Melvin was a stupid piece of shit," he screamed. He was so frustrated.

"Funny how all the pieces of shit find me. What am I, a shit magnet?"

Christian saw where she was going with this.

"Do I count as a piece of shit?" Of course he felt like he did. If he had left his situation sooner, she would have never married TJ.

"No." McKenzie touched his cheek. "You . . . are . . . the finest man I know." She smiled weakly. "So kind and loving." They stared into each other's eyes. "That's why . . . after, Melvin . . ." McKenzie shifted uneasily. "That's why I pulled away." Christian watched her.

"Why? Because I--"

He looked confused. "I thought it was because you probably still harbored some anger at me for sending her over there. I thought you needed time to heal, to regain your identity." McKenzie shook her head.

"Because you were too good for me--or, because I was not good enough for you. I don't know which one," she said shaking her head.

"That's bullshit Mac, and you know it."

"Do I?"

McKenzie's head was throbbing. She was tired of crying. Christian knew all of her dirty little secrets. Why would he want her? He didn't. And she knew it. She also knew he was just too nice to tell her. But his actions said all that she feared. She wasn't worth him leaving his wife for. He didn't love her the way she loved him: *because she wasn't good enough.*

But she wasn't angry at him. She understood why. It was too much to expect any man to accept. That's why she didn't tell TJ. In his eyes she was enough. And if she wasn't, she was determined to do whatever it took to be enough.

How could she refuse anal sex or a threesome with her husband? It's not like her body hadn't already experienced worse . .

. in her mind, she would have been a hypocrite to say no. At least she knew TJ loved her. At least she knew that these sacrifices meant something. She would be getting something out of this. She'd finally be getting the love she deserved.

"Yes, you do!" Christian said grabbing her arms. "Look at me and tell me you honestly believe that shit?" he shouted.

"I honestly believe that shit," she said almost before he could finish his sentence. "I honestly believe it. Honestly I do." She repeated over and over. Tears covered her cheeks.

Christian pulled her in between his legs. He covered her mouth with his. He slid his tongue inside her warm mouth and explored the inside like an untraveled cave. His heart exploded into a frenzy of erratic beating. He kissed her long and passionately, eyes closed, and arms wrapped around her . . . holding her close . . . feeling her chest rise and fall, her breath, heavy and warm.

She kissed him back, finding that perfect fit—her lips with his; Her movements with his; Her arms around his neck, his around her waist. Everything just fit; Her chest next to his. She didn't know how to explain it; she just knew that it felt like a perfect fit.

With TJ, she had to turn and adjust to get their mouths in position to kiss. She had to adjust to hug him and get into a comfortable position. It never just fell into place. It never felt like a perfect fit.

Tonight confirmed her annoyance. She was annoyed that she had to make things work with TJ. She was annoyed that she had to work so hard. But she didn't know why she was so annoyed. Everyone knew you had to work at a relationship--that nothing and no one was perfect.

Now she knew why she was so annoyed when he touched her. It was because his touch didn't soothe her or ignite anything in her. She was annoyed because TJ was not Christian. And he didn't make her body feel what she was experiencing this very moment.

It felt like they had been kissing for hours but he didn't want to pull away. He felt hungry for her mouth . . . her kisses . . . the simplicity of her arms around his neck, her hands gently rubbing his chest and the lower portion of his back. His body was in heaven. His mind was a ball of emotions.

Christian lifted McKenzie and placed her on his lap. She opened her eyes and they stared at each other. Christian smiled and

McKenzie smiled back at him. She placed her hands on both of his cheeks and pulled him to her. She kissed him long and hard. Christian's dick was hard and throbbing. McKenzie felt the growth beneath her and slowly began to grind him.

"Mmm" he said.

Eyes closed, all Christian could do to contain himself was to try and focus on something else. But he kept losing his train of thought. All he could think about was how good McKenzie felt, how good he felt—how badly he wanted to be inside her.

McKenzie threw her head back and began to grind Christian harder. Her gyrations were slow and sexy. Christian licked her neck.

"Ooo" she moaned.

Her nipples were poking through her peasant dress. Christian pulled the dress down off of her shoulders and hungrily took the right nipple in his mouth, sucking it like a starving baby who needed to be fed. McKenzie grabbed the back of his head and pulled him into her. She squirmed on his lap out of control from all the sexual stimulation.

Christian moved to the left nipple and sucked it gently, blew on it, then kissed her areole in a slow, circular motion.

"Oh shit Christian . . ."

"You . . . OK?" But before she could answer, Christian felt a gush of wetness against his dick.

"Oh!" she said shaking.

She held on tightly to his head as her body gently went into convulsions. Christian smiled. *That was some sexy shit!* And it turned him on. He slipped his hand underneath the flowing turquoise skirt, only to find an uncovered bush, soaked in warm juices.

"Fuck Mac! Are you trying to kill me woman?"

She just smiled and spread her legs open wide. Christian lifted her and gently laid her on top of the table and slid two fingers inside her hot velvety walls.

"Um" she moaned, grabbing the sides of the table.

"Oh shit!" Christian said, amazed at how wet she was. "Mac, you're soaking wet . . ."

"It's you . . . you get me so hot . . . I can't control it." She panted as she pumped her hips, trying to get all of his fingers inside her. "Chris, oh! I'm about . . . baby, I'm about to . . ." But before she could get the words out her body began to shake again. "Oh! Yes!

Oh, fuck!" she screamed. Her body shook and she arched her back as the last wave passed through.

Christian raised her dress up to her hips. He slid his linen pants down to his ankles. McKenzie spread her legs open as she watched him move closer to her. He grabbed his dick and brushed the tip gently across her clit.

"Uh!" Her body jolted at the touch. "Stop teasing me" she ordered. Christian ignored her.

He brushed the tip up and down the insides of her vagina. McKenzie grabbed the sides of the table and bit her bottom lip. Her body was extra sensitive. Anything he did sent electrical currents racing through her body. She reached down to touch herself but Christian moved her hand.

"I got this." He pulled back. McKenzie quickly opened her eyes, searching for her lover.

"What are you doing? Where are you going--" Worry covered her face.

"Shhh" he said watching her face. He rubbed his hands up and down the insides of her thighs. She lay back and relaxed.

"I got this."

He pulled McKenzie to the edge of the table. He leaned over and kissed her slowly. It was the sexiest kiss she had ever felt in her life. When he pulled away she had to take a deep breath in. He smiled down at her. She smiled back at him. They locked eyes as he slowly slid inside her. McKenzie closed her eyes.

"Tell me." Christian said, as he gently moved in and out of her warm and silky walls.

She turned her head to the side and bit her bottom lip. Her nipples were tingling, her thighs were on fire, and her heart was beating a mile a minute.

"Tell me Mac." He said bending down over her.

McKenzie was breathing hard, almost panting. Her eyes were rolling; beads of sweat covered her top lip and the top of her nose. Every part of her body was responding. He nibbled on her earlobe.

"Tell . . . me."

"Ooh. . . OK . . . I . . . I . . . love you." she whispered. Christian turned her face so he could look her in the eyes. He smiled.

"That sounds so good. Tell me again baby." He said grinning from ear to ear. She laughed.

"Oh does it?" She said socking him in the shoulder.

She tried to push him away but he shoved himself deeper inside her.

"Oooh!" She said jumping. They laughed. He grabbed her ass and pulled her into him. She bit her bottom lip, closed her eyes, and moved with him.

"Does it feel good?" McKenzie purred. She moved her hips around and around. Christian's eyes rolled to the back of his head. He dropped his head on her shoulder.

"Oh, fuck yes. It feels good. You . . . feel good Mac."

He increased his speed, pumping with a force that let McKenzie know how much he wanted her. "Mmm. Shit baby, you . . . feel, sooo . . . good."

"Tell me." she demanded.

Christian continued to pump faster and faster. His face was buried in her neck, her legs wrapped around his waist.

"I Love You. I Love You, Mac!" He grunted in her ear. She grabbed his face and kissed him passionately. They kissed, and kissed, and kissed.

McKenzie moved with a passion and energy she hadn't felt in months. Christian fit her perfectly. His lips, his hands, his dick—they all fit her perfectly. She slid from up under him.

"What? . . . " Christian looked perplexed.

"Wait a minute."

She pushed him back on the table. McKenzie kissed him and threw her leg over him. She pushed up on her knees, grabbed his dick, and guided him inside her. She slid down on him.

"Ohhh." He grabbed her hips and moved her up and down. They moved together.

"Ooh yes." McKenzie sped up, moving up and down on his hard, throbbing dick. "You like this?"

"Mmm hmm."

His head was filled with a humming sound. His breath was constricted and his toes were tingling. He couldn't remember the last time his body felt this hypersensitive. He felt like he was about to explode.

"Good. Brace yourself . . . I'm about to really blow your mind." McKenzie leaned forward, grabbed his chest, and began thrusting her hips.

"Oh shit Mac." Christian whimpered. "What are you doing to me?" McKenzie laughed.

"Shhh." she whispered. "Don't talk. Shhh. Just feel me . . . all around you. Just feel me. Loving you." McKenzie closed her eyes. Christian held on.

She rode him long and hard. When she felt him grab her hips and pull her down harder and faster, she sped up . . . and let go. Her breath became shallow, faint pants. She moved faster, enticed by Christian's moans and groans.

"Oh . . . Mac . . . I'm . . . I . . ." He pulled her into him. She let go, and her body began to shake violently.

"Ohhhh! Oh . . .Christian . . ." she moaned. Her convulsions took over her. She shook.

He tightened up. Eyes closed. His body jerked. She fell on top of him, exhausted. Full. Happy. Christian held her close. He kissed her neck and rubbed her back. They lay there, on the table, half naked, holding each other.

"It's getting late Christian. We should probably go." McKenzie said into Christian's chest.

He was gently rubbing her back. She got up, adjusted her dress and walked over to the flowing waterfall. She wrapped her arms around her shoulders and rocked back and forth.

Christian sat up and watched McKenzie rocking. He slid his clothes on and walked over to her. He wrapped his arms around her waist and pulled her into him. He knew she was probably thinking about everything, this trip, TJ . . . them, where they would go from here. He felt so good inside. He was happy. But he knew that things weren't as simple as them making love. Things were complicated.

"I'm sorry," he said in her hair. "Shit is just so fucked up Mac."

"I know."

They stood there watching the water crash against the rocks. Over the P.A. a Ruff Endz cut started to play.

I bet you that I could read your mind
And tell you everything you're going through

372

Baby, I could try to find a thousand reasons why
You're alone and acting so cold

David and Dante took turns as the lead. McKenzie couldn't distinguish the two if you paid her. It was scary how on point the lyrics were in describing the woman she had become. But David didn't judge her. He wasn't discouraged. He wanted to know how long she'd been this way? He asked if maybe he could open up her heart. McKenzie hugged herself. Her eyes filled with tears. He told her he's been waiting all his life for someone just like her, and he knew she'd been waiting to, *for someone to love her.*

Christian pulled McKenzie close. They slow danced to the song. Their movement, like their heartbeats, were in sink. The night air filled with the words. Christian held McKenzie tightly as she cried into his chest.

All you need is someone who cares (For someone to love you)
Someone who will always be there (Mmm...mmm...)
All you need to say is that you want me to be with you
Girl, I know you've waited so long
For someone to love you

Christian sang along, almost inaudibly. But he gently rubbed McKenzie's back as they effortlessly glided around the garden. He kissed the top of her head and sang into her curls.

Baby, I wish I could be there for every time you ever shed a tear
Baby, I hate to see a pretty girl like you going through the things
that you do, yeah
Girl, I think you've gone too far too long without a good man to
make you smile
How can I appeal to you and make you understand that I'm here,
when you're ready for someone to love you

♋   ♋   ♋

They took a cab back to the hotel. On the ride over, Christian held McKenzie close.

"What are you going to do Mac?"

"I don't know Christian." she replied, knowing exactly what he was asking. "I made vows." She looked miserable. She knew in her heart she'd never feel for TJ the way she felt for Christian. She also knew TJ loved her and that she couldn't just walk away. It wasn't that simple.

The cab pulled up to the curb in front of the hotel. Christian felt like his throat was closing. He couldn't breathe and his heart felt like someone had it in their hands and was squeezing all the blood out of it. He forced a smile.

"Of course. I understand." he said as he stared into her eyes.

McKenzie couldn't smile. In fact, she fought back tears. She gently ran her hands across his face.

"No matter what happens Christian, I love you."

She kissed him passionately. To Christian it felt like a kiss goodbye. He pulled her in close and returned the kiss.

"No matter what you decide. I love you. I'll always love you." He replied.

They sat there for a minute and took each other in. Then McKenzie opened the door and got out of the cab. Christian paid the cab driver and watched McKenzie walk into the veranda of the hotel. He just stood there, closed his eyes, and replayed the night over in his mind. He didn't know how he would do it, but he had to have that woman in his life . . .

♋   ♋   ♋

McKenzie walked into the hotel without ever looking back at Christian. With every step she felt like she was walking away from her only hope at happiness. It was 3:00 a.m. when McKenzie opened the door and walked inside the hotel room. TJ was sound asleep.

The room reeked of alcohol and hot stuffy tropical air. McKenzie opened the patio door and started packing.

By 4:45 am McKenzie had all their things packed. She sat quietly in the chaise lounge watching TJ sleep. She thought incessantly about the week and all that had transpired. She wasn't even angry with TJ. As a matter of fact, she was angrier with herself than anything. Christian was right. She had allowed TJ to do those things to her. *But no more.* That much she knew.

TJ stirred. He was groggy and disoriented. After a few minutes of trying to focus he recognized McKenzie. He sat up and rubbed his eyes.

"Oh . . . McKenzie . . . baby . . . hey. I'm sorry. Honey. Will you forgive me? I was h-horrible. I was a c-complete asshole. I am so sorry."

"I know." McKenzie smiled.

She got up and walked over to him. She handed him a glass of water. He grabbed a bottle of pills and opened it. He shook out two pills, grabbed the water and tossed them in his mouth. McKenzie watched him lay back on the pillow.

"How are you feeling?" She said feeling his forehead. He was warm. "You have a fever TJ." She looked worried.

"Like shit. L-like a big piece of w-worthless shit." he said looking embarrassed. He grabbed McKenzie's hand and kissed it. "I swear, I'll n-never . . . treat you like that . . . l-like that again." McKenzie pulled away.

"I know." she said barely above a whisper. She walked over to the chaise and grabbed his clothes. "Here, go get dressed. We need to head back to the states."

He grabbed the clothes and went into the bathroom to change. McKenzie took the luggage down to the lobby while TJ dressed.

Christian walked up with his luggage. McKenzie was coordinating their shuttle to the airport when he walked up.

"Hey Mac, good morning." He searched her eyes.

"Good morning Christian." she said, her voice strained.

The shuttle driver motioned for McKenzie and she walked away. Christian watched her the entire time. He watched how she took care of business and how she held everything together even when her world was crumbling down around her. It was a game she played well.

"What's up 'C'?" TJ said walking up behind him. Christian turned to face his best friend for the first time after making love to his wife the night before.

"Oh hey. What's up Teddy?" They hugged.

"I'm s-shit-faced man. T-thanks for taking care of McKenzie l-last night. I a-appreciate that." McKenzie and Christian locked eyes for a split second.

"Oh, no problem." Christian said and walked off.

♋   ♋   ♋

CHAPTER FOURTEEN
Life and Death

Ahmad greeted them at the door. He grabbed McKenzie's bags.

"Hey mom!" Ahmad said. He kissed her and hugged her tight. McKenzie's tension quickly dissipated. Ahmad always had a way of making her feel so special.

"I missed you."

"I bet you did. You didn't have any parties up in here, did you Ahmad Aquil?"

"Nope! No parties at all. Nu uh, not even one." he said laughing. They all laughed.

"Did Stephanie see Crystal any this week?" McKenzie said hanging her jacket up in the hall way closet.

"Once or twice. You know, when Cris needed some money." Ahmad said laughing.

He and Crystal were headed in different directions after the summer, so they spent every moment together that they could. Crystal had been accepted to UNLV on a full basketball scholarship. They had decided not to do the long distance relationship thing.

"How was the trip?" Ahmad directed the question to TJ who was returning to the living room after placing the luggage in the bedroom.

"Aw, it-it was nice. S-St. Lucia is a b-beautiful island. D-don't you think M-McKenzie?"

"It is indeed," she said walking over to Ahmad. She grabbed his face in between her hands and kissed his lips.

"I missed you so much my heart ached. I saw the St. Lucian women there with their children playing in the water and I thought about us." She stroked the top of his head gently "Remember our day trips to the beach?"

"To Zuma beach? Yeah. But the water was far from clear."

"I know. But it wasn't about the water, baby. It was more about the fact that you and I were together . . . enjoying each other's company. We were happy, just the two of us—dirty water and all."

"Yeah, they were some fun times." Ahmad said noting the nostalgia in her voice. He looked over at TJ who was looking uncomfortable with the conversation.

"Did something happen over there that I should know about?"

"Just that your mom realized what was really important in her life." She got up to leave. She paused and turned to face Ahmad. "You are the most important, the most precious . . . I love you son." She gave him a big hug and kiss.

Ahmad became worried. "I love you too mom."

Ahmad looked at TJ who smiled warmly. He looked back at McKenzie but she had already left the room.

McKenzie was in the study flipping through an Essence magazine and talking to Denny on her cell when TJ stuck his head in the room. McKenzie turned her back to him and threw her legs over the back of the chair. TJ took heed to the message and walked away.

"Well, if you had such a good time why aren't you talking to your husband?" Denny repeated.

"Because he's an asshole."

McKenzie had shared with her best friend some of her most shameful secrets but she couldn't find it in herself to tell Denise about St. Lucia. After listening to Christian, McKenzie felt embarrassed about her role in the ménage trois. But not enough to forgive TJ for instigating it. And just enough to not give Denny the details.

"Hmph. Sounds suspicious. Yeah, doesn't make sense to me McKenzie."

"Does it have to make sense to you? I saw a side of my husband that I didn't care for. Does that make sense to you? I'm sure you can relate to *that*, right?"

There was silence on the other end of the phone. McKenzie tried very hard not check her friend hard and low; but sometimes Denny acted like McKenzie didn't know the full story about *her* husband.

"Yes, of course I can relate to that. I think it's probably safe to say most married women, and men for that matter, can relate to that." Denny's voice trailed off. "After awhile, you get to see all sides of a person, good and bad . . . shit you really don't care to see."

"Yes, well that's all it was dear."

"And did you get to see that side because you happened to be in close proximity to a certain Fine Deep Dark Chocolate someone all week?" Denny said. "And being that close made you see the flaws in your husband that you didn't care for?"

McKenzie smiled. *Denny thought she was smart.* "You know what bitch. Stop playing Sigmund Freud over there and just ask the question. 'Was I comparing Christian to TJ, and in doing so, did TJ come up short?'"

"OK, well were you?"

"First, I didn't need to be hemmed up on an island to do that." McKenzie snipped. "But No, that wasn't it. TJ almost ruined a perfectly beautiful trip because he was trifling, insecure, and incorrigible. Didn't have shit to do with me or Christian for that matter."

"OK. OK. I'll leave it alone. I think it's a beautiful thing what you guys tried to do for Christian. And I'm happy you were able to have a good time despite your husband's shortcomings."

McKenzie didn't reply. She saw in her peripheral vision TJ pass by the study three more times. "Yes, me too. Listen, Denny, I gotta bounce honey. I'll call you later OK? Love you mama."

As she hung up and turned to face the door TJ walked in.

"Are w-we going to t-talk about it?" TJ said. McKenzie flipped through the pages of the magazine.

"And say what?" She said looking up at him. "You've already apologized. You said it wouldn't happen again. I think we're fine. Let's just keep it moving." She returned her attention to the magazine. TJ stood there for a minute.

"I love you McKenzie. I know y-you may q-question that n-now, but--"

"I know you love me TJ," she said placing the magazine on an end table. "And all marriages have their rocky moments. It doesn't mean you can't work through them, right?"

"Right." TJ replied, hope filling his voice. "It's j-just that y-you seem so distant. I-I didn't k-know if you w-wanted to w-work through them or n-not."

"I'm distant because I need to find my way back to you. You can't slap a person TJ, and then turn around and hold your arms out to them and expect them to run into them just because you said I'm sorry." A flicker of anger seeped into her voice. She quickly smoothed out her forehead. She took a deep breath. "So, give me my time Theodore. Give me my space."

TJ didn't reply. He watched his wife flip through the pages of Essence magazine. He analyzed her face—every part of her body. He couldn't put his finger on it, but something about her was different. He turned and left the room, giving his wife her requested space. But something about the way she was caused a deep-rooted fear inside him.

Two weeks had passed and TJ hadn't heard from Christian. He knew Christian was angry with him about what had happened in St. Lucia. Hell, he was disgusted with himself. He didn't know what had come over him. He tried to rationalize that it was the alcohol and pills, but he knew he had to take responsibility.

He watched McKenzie retreat deeper and deeper into isolation. Every day she had some reason not to be in his presence. And even though he tried to honor her request it was making him nervous. He called Christian to see if he would run interference.

"C-can you just t-talk to her f-for me man?" TJ pleaded with Christian.

They met at TGI Fridays. Christian listened as TJ described McKenzie's behavior. He hadn't heard from her and had assumed she was trying to work things out in her head. He had hoped she would leave TJ, but listening to him repeat what McKenzie told him sent Christian into a downward spiral.

"I don't think I should get involved Teddy. I probably interfered too much as it is."

"N-no man, you were r-right to check me. I-I was foul in St. Lucia. B-but she t-trusts you 'C'. She'll c-confide in you." TJ pleaded.

"And what is it you want me to do?" Christian was agitated. "I think you already know what the problem is. She told you, she just needs some time. What can I do?"

"I d-don't know." TJ said stroking his locks. "She's d-different. And it's n-not the s-shit that happened on-on the island. I j-just think it's something else. A-and I think y-you could get it out of h-her."

"Naw dude. I'm going to pass on that one." Christian said feeling heavy and blue. He just wanted to get out of there. Hearing McKenzie wanted to work things out with TJ felt like a kick in the stomach. He no longer had an appetite. "As a matter of fact" he said, grabbing his briefcase "I'm going to have to pass on lunch. I'm running late for an appointment bruh." Christian reached over and shook TJ's hand. "I'll holla though. She'll come around man. Just be patient."

Christian walked quickly through the restaurant. He practically slammed the front door open, trying to quickly get out to the parking lot and into the fresh air. Outside, he paused and took in a deep breath.

His head was reeling from what TJ said. *McKenzie had decided to stay with TJ.* After all that happened in St. Lucia he never thought McKenzie would stay with him. He thought she would take some time to gently and rationally tell TJ she was leaving him. The news that she was staying with TJ came as a shock. And he felt like his world had stopped spinning on its axis.

Christian jumped into his car and drove aimlessly around the city. His thoughts were a fog. He contemplated calling McKenzie but he had no idea what to say. *I thought you said you loved me? I want you to leave TJ. Don't let your past make you ruin your future.*

He threw a lot of phrases around in his head. But none of them seemed to adequately convey what he was feeling.

He was feeling lost and so sad. For a while on the island he had felt alive again. He thought Jada had zapped all the life out of him. He fought so hard to maintain his sanity with her that he felt he had depleted himself of all emotion.

But McKenzie proved him wrong. When he was with her he came alive. And he felt she came alive too. He didn't know what to do right now.

Christian drove for hours, and before he knew it, he found himself parked in the public parking lot of Zuma beach. The sun was just beginning to set just like it did the day McKenzie brought him out here.

He adjusted the radio and pulled the lever to let his seat down. Christian stared at the ceiling as if he might find a solution up there. The radio announcer came on the airwaves.

"It's the end of the summer folks, and we're reporting sudden and unexplained rain showers traveling through southern California." Christian frowned at the announcement, *Rain? Now? What the hell?*

"I don't know about ya'll, but when it's 93 degrees in the summer and it starts pouring down rain, I think God is trying to tell us something." the announcer said. "For all you praying folks, ya'll better get prayed up. For all you unsaved folks, you better find Jesus and accept him as your Lord and Savior today." Christian frowned at the radio *What is this, the Billy Graham Evangelical hour, or what?*

"And for those of you who just don't give a damn, here's a Carl Thomas cut for ya' that I think is perfect for such an occasion." Before the first note played, little speckles of water slowly covered his windshield.

"What the--" Christian said sitting up in his seat. The keyboard music began playing. Carl painfully described Christian's heavy heart and the weird weather storming outside:

The rain that keeps him home. Quiet conversation that makes him warm.
Summer rain, sweet rain whispers me to sleep
And wakes me up again, my rain
Sometimes I swear I hear her call my name, I swear, I swear
To wash away the pain, my summer rain

Christian's throat tightened listening to Carl Thomas painfully and metaphorically describe his feelings about the woman he loved. He turned the Bose system up high and got out the car. The rain started to trickle down lightly. Christian walked over to the brick wall and leaned against it, watching this spectacular natural event unfold in front of his eyes.

The sunset, a perfect back drop, showed off deep purples, midnight blues, and dark magentas that gently kissed the ocean's surface while soft white clouds peacefully drifted over a sky that splashed across it a layer of colors resembling Gouda, American, and Sharp cheddar cheeses.

In the forefront, the sporadic sprinkles had unceremoniously turned into a soft sheeting blanket of rain. Christian sat there in the pouring rain singing a duet with Carl Thomas.

In the middle of the night when I'm alone
I feel her kisses on me even when she's gone
Can't wait 'till she gets home

The pain welled up inside him like the thundercloud hanging overhead. Alone on the beach Christian was free to let the tears surface. He dropped his head in his hands and sobbed. He cried a guttural cry, the pain coming from deep deep inside. He stood and screamed the lyrics at the top of his lungs.

McKenzie thought she could do this. She thought she could will herself to get beyond St. Lucia. But as the days passed, she found herself thinking more and more about Christian. She'd lie in her bed for hours crying into her pillow. Her iPod only played one song these past two weeks, a soulful Aretha Franklin-sounding song by Mary J. Blige, "I Found My Everything."

McKenzie curled up in the corner of the couch, knees up to her chest, clutching a pillow that felt the intensity of her sadness and caught the stream of her tears as she reminisced about Christian and their time together in St. Lucia. Like a third person's POV, she saw herself, happy, smiling. Mary J. said it all . . .

Can't you see, look at my face it's glowing. And it's all because of you.
Everything about ya, ya see I need. And I thank God for sending you through. Ya see I found, my everything in you.

McKenzie lipped sync'd the next line *"Ooo, the way you kiss me it's like a real man, Mmm."* She cried into the pillow. *My life is so fucked up. What is wrong with me? Why can't I just have a normal life? Why am I so screwed up? Seriously? Falling in love with a married man. Marrying his best friend. What normal person does that?*

McKenzie reached for a Kleenex from the box on the nightstand beside the couch and blew her nose. She couldn't understand how deeply she loved Christian. He understood her, or at the very least, didn't judge her. He had a way of making her feel . . . safe. And desirable, like she wasn't damaged goods. She couldn't explain it, but Mary J. Blige understood her. "You define me now, my world feels so free." That's exactly how she felt about Christian when she was with him, so free. But now . . . now she felt caged and she didn't know what to do.

And as the days passed, McKenzie found herself slipping deeper and deeper into depression. Ahmad was spending most of his days and nights with Crystal and TJ was trying his hardest to give her the space she requested. She could see on his face the worry and frustration. But she didn't care.

She missed Christian. She missed his kisses, the way he looked into her eyes. The way he held her, listened to her, kissed her . . . filled her up inside. The perfect way all of their imperfections seemed to balance life out . . . McKenzie pushed "replay" on her iPod, buried her head in her pillow and cried.

♋   ♋   ♋

After the third week of returning from their vacation, TJ woke to a searing pain in his pelvic area. The pain was so bad he screamed out. McKenzie ran into the room.

"TJ, what happened?" She rushed to his side. He was curled in a ball, grabbing his hip and crying.

"TJ?" She was looking all around the room to try and figure out what could have happened. *Did he run into something? Did something fall over on him, what?* But nothing was out of place in the room. And TJ was in a fetal position with an excruciating look on his face.

"I'm going to call 911!" McKenzie said running for the telephone.

"No! . . . Don't!" TJ managed to say. "Just . . . just give me a minute." he said breathing hard. McKenzie sat next to him and rubbed his shoulder. She felt so helpless.

After about ten minutes, TJ motioned for her to hand him some pills out of his nightstand. She got up, opened the drawer and grabbed the pills. The prescription was made out to Raleigh. She turned to him.

"Why are you taking Raleigh's pain pills?"

"To ease this p-pain I've been in." he said, agitation filling the room.

He sat up and grabbed the bottle. He poured the pills in his hands and tossed them in his mouth. He dragged himself into the bathroom, turned on the faucet, cupped his hands and drank water from the sink.

"Obviously." She rolled her eyes. "But why are you taking your brother's medication? I thought you were going to the doctor—TJ, you never went to the doctor?" she yelled at him.

TJ walked back to the bed and lay down. "It was getting better with the pills. "Obviously not." McKenzie walked over to the closet and started pulling clothes out. She threw a polo shirt and a pair of jeans on the bed.

"Get dressed Theodore."

"Where are we going?" he said slipping obediently into the clothes.

"To urgent care." she said grabbing her purse and keys.

♋   ♋   ♋

In the urgent care at Kaiser, TJ underwent a series of blood, urine, and x-ray tests. The doctor frowned listening to TJ describe his symptoms. He asked several questions about the length of time TJ had been experiencing them and about his family medical history. He jotted notes down in his chart and took a deep breath in before speaking.

"Well Mr. Johnson, we won't know anything for sure until the test results are in. But what you're describing to me sounds like symptoms of an enlarged prostate."

TJ looked at him in disbelief. "Prostate cancer?"

"Not necessarily." The doctor walked over to a large poster of the male anatomy that was posted on the wall and began explaining.

"An enlarged prostate – known as benign prostatic hyperplasia or BPH – is caused by an overgrowth of prostate cells. This enlargement constricts the urethra so the flow of urine is reduced making it increasingly difficult to empty the bladder." He pointed to the walnut sized gland located just below the bladder that surrounds the urethra.

McKenzie watched TJ sink into the chair as the doctor continued to explain BPH. He looked like he was going into shock.

"One of the main functions of the prostate is to produce an important liquefying component of semen which allows the sperm to move freely. The gland is divided into three zones, peripheral, transitional and central. With BPH, it's the central part where overgrowth of cells takes place." The doctor spoke slowly and maintained eye contact between both McKenzie and TJ.

"BPH is very common, affecting about one third of men over fifty. Although it isn't prostate cancer, the symptoms of BPH are similar to those of prostate cancer. We will have to wait for your lab results before we can make a diagnosis."

McKenzie began with a litany of questions while TJ sat stoically in his chair. At the end of the conversation, TJ was given a date the test results should be back. He was to schedule an appointment with his primary physician to go over the results.

McKenzie thanked the doctor then she and TJ made their way home.

After a quiet drive home, TJ slowly walked into the house and headed straight for the den.

"What's up mom?" Ahmad said walking into the living room.

McKenzie filled her son in on the morning's happenings and asked him to steer clear of TJ for a while. Ahmad hadn't been at home much lately, so staying out of TJ's way wouldn't be a major problem for him.

McKenzie automatically dialed Denny.

"Hello?"

"Hey." McKenzie said.

"What's wrong?"

"I didn't say anything but 'Hey' damn." McKenzie laughed.

"All I need is one note. I can name that tune, darlin'. What's wrong with my friend?"

McKenzie shared with Denny her fears about the diagnosis, her anger about TJs procrastination, and his current disposition after the doctor's visit.

"Well, honey. Don't take this the wrong way, but everyone doesn't respond to tragedy like you do."

"What the hell does that mean?"

"Um, let's see . . . where most people crumble, McKenzie Batiste laughs, rolls up her sleeve, bobs and weaves, ducks, and comes up swinging! And when most folks are going down for the count, McKenzie Batiste is serving her most grandiose knock out punch." They laughed.

"Are you a writer? Cuz if not, you ought to be. That is some creative shit right there."

"I'm just trying to say that everybody responds differently to life's punches. Be gentle with your husband. Give him time to process this. And when he's ready, help him to see the value of being proactive about his health issues versus procrastinating with dealing with them." Denny heard McKenzie snort. "Regardless to the outcome McKenzie, he's going to need you. Obviously, you're the strong one."

McKenzie sat for a while thinking about what Denise said about TJ. She was angry that he'd self-medicated for so long. But Denny was right. There was nothing she could do about that now. All she could do is make sure that from now on things got handled. That's what a good wife would do. And McKenzie would be that good wife.

McKenzie let TJ be by himself for a couple of hours before she went back to check on him.

"Hey, are you hungry?" She asked sitting next to him.

"No, d-don't have m-much of an appetite. T-thanks though."

"No problem. Do you want to talk?"

TJ stared straight ahead in silence for a long while. "I-I don't know w-what to say." McKenzie slid her hand over his and rubbed it gently.

"Then don't say anything."

She looked him in the eyes and smiled a warm, loving smile. TJ smiled and reached for her. She let him pull her into him. She let him hold her tight and kiss her. She let him feel like she cared about him out of love, even though she was only going through the motions out of obligation.

"I love you so m-much, McKenzie." TJ said into her neck. She couldn't say the words back to him although she tried.

"I will always be here for you TJ. You don't have to worry about that. OK?" She said instead. "For better or worse."

"For b-better or worse." he whispered.

Everyone seemed to be on pins and needles the next week. Waiting for the results of the test had been harrowing. But McKenzie was relieved to some degree because the focus was now on TJ's prostate and not her. It was easier to sneak away and stay lost. TJ was too busy on the Internet or lying down resting to notice that McKenzie had unceremoniously slipped back into her depression mode.

Nothing was making sense to her. *She couldn't have Christian because she had a husband. Now her husband may have a fucking fatal disease! What the fuck was that?* McKenzie struggled to understand her dilemma and how it was all playing itself out in her life.

For the past four weeks her life had seemed like an unbearable cross she had to bear. She hadn't spoken to Christian until this morning when she called to tell him about TJ. She thought for sure he would have told Christian, but when she found out he hadn't she made the call.

"Hello?"

"Christian?" Silence. "Hello?"

"Uh. Yeah, I'm here." he said, clearing his throat. "I'm here. What's up, Mac?" He said softly. She smiled.

"Christian, TJ is sick. I think he's going to need you."

Twenty minutes later, their call came to an end. She'd stretched out the explanation about TJ's prostate as much as she could. She didn't want him to get off the telephone.

"So, I don't know if it's pride, pity, or remnants from the trip that you've been MIA. But you are his best friend and he's going to need you now more than ever."

"His best friend is in love with his wife." McKenzie's mouth dropped open. She quickly regained her composure and shook her head.

"Christian, now's not the time for this." she said pacing the room.

"No, I know that. The time to say it was at Zuma beach, or any number of times I held you on a dance floor. Maybe it was when I was inside you at your townhouse . . ."

McKenzie closed her eyes and listened. She envisioned every one of the intimate moments he described.

"Well, those times have come and gone Christian. TJ needs our support. We owe him that much--don't you think? We've violated our most sacred trusts to him: your brotherhood and friendship, and my matrimony." McKenzie had thought the deception through all month. She knew its ins and outs. She knew the moral breach, and the social statute that would indict her despite how much her heart ached to be with Christian.

Christian sat silently.

"Of course I'll be there for him Mac."

McKenzie closed her eyes. A deep part of her wanted him to protest. Wanted him to defy her and fight for their love.

"Thank you Christian." McKenzie whispered into the telephone. "Good bye."

"Good bye Mac."

Christian lay back in his chair, grabbed his remote and pushed play. Babyface would once again serenade him with the lyrics of the *Loneliness* he'd been singing on demand over and over all month. It was prepped and ready. Christian pressed play.

I'm sitting here, Thinking bout
How I'm gonna do without
You around in my life and how am I
I'm gon' get by

Christian lay back as the tears filled his eyes. His heart felt as if it were breaking into a million pieces as Babyface described perfectly his situation. He didn't have days, just lonely nights. He could've said to McKenzie the same words he was mouthing, if she

393

wanted the truth, *he wasn't all right: he felt out of place and out of time, he thought he was gonna lose his mind.* The chorus was a back and forth between Babyface and his lost love.

So tell me how you feel (I'm lonely)
Are you for real (so lonely)
Do you still think of me (I think of you)
Baby still (are you lonely)
Do you dream of me at night (like I dream of you all the time)
So let me tell you how it feels (its like everyday I die)

Christian stared at the ceiling as the tears flowed down his face. He closed his eyes, and wiped away the evidence of his sadness. Babyface crooned in the background that he wished he was dreaming but it's real, how it feels when he opens up his eyes, and doesn't see her pretty face . . . that he thinks he'll never love again. Christian sighed deeply. The words pierced his heart because they understood his soul. He missed McKenzie's face, and her kiss. He even missed the arguments. He missed her standing by his side, and he was dying because it's clear to see that there ain't no her, God knows there was no him. He nodded in solidarity as Babyface said, "Don't wanna live, I wanna die, If I can't have you in my life." He felt the same despair and hopelessness; In particular, because he couldn't tell if McKenzie felt the same way.

She fell silent when he told her he was in love with her. But she didn't say she felt the same. Instead she said they had to be there for TJ—something he knew and understood, but if she had just said she felt the same way too . . .

After that conversation, McKenzie almost became a complete recluse. She'd check on TJ, make sure he ate and took his medicine. But for the most part, she was out of sight.

What did I do? McKenzie said to herself all week, thinking about her last conversation with Christian. She wanted so badly to call him and tell him she was in love with him too. But she knew he already knew that. She just didn't have the courage to leave her husband to be with him. It wasn't that simple. It wasn't that easy.

McKenzie felt ill. *It must be all the stress and strain from this situation* she reasoned. She was sad, lonely, and now her body must be internalizing the stress. Her stomach was a mess. She walked to the refrigerator to get some milk to settle her stomach. She poured a tall cold glass and drank it down.

"McKenzie?" TJ called out.

"In the kitchen TJ." McKenzie gulped down another glass of milk.

"I just got a call from Dr. Hansen. The test results are in." She turned to face him. He looked scared. McKenzie placed the glass down on the counter.

"Well, go put on your shoes TJ. And let's go find out what's going on with you so we can get you better babe." she said. She gently stroked his cheek. TJ smiled.

♋   ♋   ♋

McKenzie had been TJ's rock through this whole ordeal. He was petrified. But during the doctor's visits McKenzie had asked the questions, questioned the answers, and taken care of everything-- from scheduling tests, follow up appointments; pharmacy and prescription pick ups—all of it. She made sure he ate and got plenty of rest, and she gave him his space.

TJ knew he loved McKenzie, but during this scary experience he'd come to love her even more. *This was the stuff good marriages were made of* he thought to himself. Despite all the shit he had put her through she remained by his side.

At the doctor's office, Dr. Hansen dealt them a devastating blow.

"Preliminary results show possible cancerous cells."

"Cancer? Are you certain?" McKenzie screamed more than asked.

TJ sat stunned. McKenzie grabbed his hands and instantly went into question mode. "How do you know it's cancer Dr. Hansen?"

"I don't know for sure McKenzie. We need to do a biopsy to be certain. But I systematically ruled out everything else. We checked him for kidney infection. Negative. Gall stones, kidney stones, gall bladder problems. Negative. The x-rays didn't show anything that would cause the back or hip dysplasia."

"The last appointment, I did a digital rectal examination (DRE) and found some nodules with abnormal hardness in your prostate. These indicated the need for further testing to see if there is cancer. So, these last series of tests I did a thorough blood work up and administered what's called the PSA test. It stands for Prostate Specific Antigen. When prostate cancer develops the PSA level usually goes above 4. TJ's PSA level is above 10." Dr. Hansen said lowering his head.

TJ moaned. McKenzie's eyes filled with tears but her voice was level and calm. "But there's still a possibility that it's not cancer . . . Dr. Hansen?" McKenzie asked pleading with her eyes.

"With a PSA reading so high--" Dr. Hansen said but saw the tears fill up in McKenzie's eyes and the top of TJ's head because he was staring down at the floor. "It's . . . recommended that we get a biopsy to be sure."

"There's always the case of false negative readings. And . . . and then there's the possibility of benign prostatic hyperplasia, or BPH, something many men have, as they grow older. It can also increase with prostatitis, an infection or inflammation of the prostate gland." Dr. Hansen tried to sound encouraging. "Any one of these could be possible," he said, although years of experience told him otherwise.

"OK then." McKenzie said squeezing TJ's hand.

He slowly lifted his heavy head.

"Let's do the biopsy." McKenzie said.

They both looked at TJ who was looking lost and confused.

"TJ, dear. Did you hear Dr. Hansen, baby? It could be that your glands are swollen, honey. Go do the biopsy. If that's the case, he can give you medicine—or you'll undergo treatment." McKenzie said looking at Dr. Hansen as she threw out possible treatment options. Dr. Hansen nodded his approval as she tried to encourage TJ. "To get the swelling down and under control--"

"What if it's cancer?"

396

"Well honey, if it's cancer . . . then we need to know so we can aggressively attack it and get rid of the shit. Baby, it's just that simple."

"It's simple because it's not your prostate. It's simple because you weren't just handed a possible death sentence. It's--"

"It's my life too, TJ." McKenzie snapped. "It's your prostate, but got dammit, it's my life too: My fucking life with you. If your stubborn ass had come in when you first started having these pains, maybe you'd get some sympathy from me. But you didn't."

"So stop with the fucking pity party already, take the fucking biopsy, and let's get a handle on this shit. OK?" McKenzie said. "We can't fight this unless we know what the hell it is. If it's cancer, TJ, then it's just fucking cancer. If your gland is swollen, then the shit is just swollen. But if you keep your head stuck in the mutha fucking sand, thinking that's going to make the shit go away, well then shit is just going to get worse. We've seen that happen." McKenzie took a long deep breath.

She stared TJ in the eyes.

"Today is all we have. Today, you can do what you can to fix this situation. Knowing what the problem is, is half the battle. I'm not going anywhere TJ. I will be by your side through it all. If they let me in the room, I'll hold your hand the entire time. I promise baby. I ain't going nowhere."

Dr. Hansen was initially taken aback by McKenzie's profanity. But it worked. TJ took a deep breath, stood up and said:

"You heard the lady. Let's take the fucking biopsy."

TJ was mentally exhausted. He went straight to their bedroom and got in the bed. McKenzie tucked him in, kissed him, and left the room. Half way down the hall she felt her stomach turn. She ran to the bathroom and for the next 10 minutes paid homage to the Porcelain God. Her offering, two cups of 2% milk—that right now, felt more like half a gallon of hot buttermilk.

397

The following morning didn't show McKenzie much mercy. She found herself jerking over the toilet, relieving her body of excess bile, as she had nothing else in her body to regurgitate. After brushing her teeth and washing her face she went to the kitchen to make herself a cup of chamomile tea.

McKenzie sat in her kitchenette and slowly sipped the steaming hot tea. She thought about TJ and the looming news that lay ahead in a week. She was angry with him for lally gagging around and not going to the doctor sooner. She was angry at him because he needed her. She couldn't leave him now, even if she had the courage to.

She prayed silently that TJ didn't have cancer. Not so much for him, but more so for the hope of somehow finding a way to be with Christian. She felt fucked up about even thinking that way. But only she and God knew what fucked up thoughts occupied her mind and dominated her thoughts. *Forgive me God* she prayed.

But God must have known the insincerity in that prayer because before the *Amen* could pass her lips she was up and running to the bathroom to sacrifice the herbal chamomile tea.

♋   ♋   ♋

McKenzie lay in the den, wiped out from vomiting all day. She drank her water and stared aimlessly out the window as she talked to Denny on the phone. Water seemed to be the only thing she could keep down and helped to rehydrate her from the day's abdominal over activity.

"When was the last time you ate?" Denny said. "You're already as thin as a rail. You need to eat. How about some broth?"

McKenzie got nauseous *thinking* about trying to eat.

"Naw. I'm cool. I'ma sip on this water. I think I'm just dehydrated."

As she reached over to grab her water bottle she brushed her arm against her breast.

"Ouch!"

"What happened?"

"Fuck, my titties feel extra tender."

McKenzie placed the water bottle down on the end table and gently felt both breasts. They were tender to the touch.

"Bitch, you're pregnant!" Denny whispered. McKenzie sat silently for a moment.

"Fuck you Denise Byrd. Hold up." McKenzie placed the phone down.

Slowly McKenzie got up from the couch and walked to the armoire in the corner. She rummaged through the top drawer until she found the calendar she was looking for.

Back on the couch, she frantically flipped through the pages of the calendar . . . calculated days . . .

"Shit." McKenzie mumbled to herself as she picked up the phone.

"What? What bitch, what?"

McKenzie sat motionless. It hit her like a ton of bricks. The last time she vomited uncontrollably for days on end and had tender breasts—*was when she was pregnant with Ahmad.*

"Denny. I *am* pregnant."

399

McKenzie held the Sav-On bag close to her as she entered the house. She slid into the guest bathroom and removed the pregnancy test from its package. She read the instructions, placed the dipstick in her urine stream, and stressed the hell out for the next ten minutes.

When the indicator flashed a happy face, McKenzie sat on the toilette in complete disbelief. She knew before she took the test that she was pregnant. But seeing the happy face just made what she already knew real.

As the reality of her situation sunk in . . . McKenzie became overwhelmingly excited. She gathered the pregnancy test instructions, box, dipstick, and tied them up in the Sav-On bag. She splashed her face with cold water and patted it dry. Staring in the mirror she looked long and hard at herself. She slowly and gently rubbed her flat stomach, the reality of the life growing inside her becoming real. Unconsciously, the corners of her mouth slowly started to turn up.

You're carrying Christian's child.

♋   ♋   ♋

Later that night, McKenzie prepared a beautifully romantic meal for two. Ahmad was away, as usual, and McKenzie took the opportunity to lay out a fantastic spread for TJ.

Still a little under the weather, TJ reluctantly attended the candle-lit dinner. She had all of his favorites: chicken Marsala, creamed spinach, fresh garlic bread, and red wine.

"This is b-beautiful McKenzie." TJ marveled. "What's t-the occasion sweetie?" he said pulling out her chair.

"We are." McKenzie said smiling broadly. "It's been so stressful around here, I thought we'd celebrate! Bring some joy back into this house. Bring some romance back into this marriage." TJ reached down and kissed his wife. She pulled him in and gave him a long and sexy tongue kiss.

"Whoa! Y-you better b-be careful woman. We m-might end up s-skipping dinner and h-heading straight for d-desert!" he said pulling out his chair.

McKenzie stood and sauntered over to him. "I'm not opposed to that." She poured him another glass of wine and straddled him in his chair. She watched him as he drank the glass of wine. Smiling, she took the glass and filled it up again. She kissed him slowly and gently. TJ began to caress her back.

"I-I hope my hip w-won't be a problem." he said, stress rising in his voice.

McKenzie handed him the glass of wine.

"It won't. We won't let it," she said as he finished another glass.

His eyes were glistening and she knew he was getting buzzed. He loved red wine and she'd always had to monitor him when he drank it.

"Besides." she whispered in his ear "There are too many positions out there for us to try for that to be a problem." She said kissing TJ's neck. She could feel him rise underneath her.

"W-well, shit. In t-that case . . ." But McKenzie handed him another glass of wine.

"Are you feeling good baby? I want you to be relaxed."

"S-shit, McKenzie . . . a-any more relaxed a-and a brotha w-will be laid the f-fuck out." McKenzie detected a slight slur on the tail end of his sentence.

"Don't worry about that baby. I'll be doing all the work tonight." She unfastened his belt buckle and unbuttoning his pants. She pulled his dick out, slid her panties to the side, and slid down on top of him.

"Oh s-shit McKenzie!"

She rode him gently, conscious of his hip and back. She anchored herself on the base of the chair and lifted herself up and down, so as not to place any of her body weight on him. McKenzie moved up and down until a few minutes later he reached an orgasm.

"Oh shit, oh fuck. Mm. Whoo! Girl. Damn!"

She slid back on the table and he gently rested his head on her chest. She poured him another glass of wine. He took it and eagerly gulped down the burgundy elixir.

McKenzie ran her fingers through his locks, inhaling the masculine musk and oil fragrances. She planned to give him more of where that came from in their bedroom but she had to make sure he remembered cumming at least once that night.

She grabbed another bottle of wine, took TJ's hand and led him to their room. She poured him another drink and went into the kitchen to blow out the candles. By the time she returned TJ was knocked out.

McKenzie smiled as she slowly undressed TJ and pulled the sheet over him. She gently kissed his head and stared at him. She turned, rubbed her stomach and walked out of the room.

♋　　♋　　♋

"I'm sorry, TJ, McKenzie . . . but the biopsy results did show that you have cancer in your prostate." Dr. Hansen said sitting on the edge of the desk in front of them.

TJ sat completely still and McKenzie grabbed his hand. She leaned over and kissed his cheek.

"Oh baby" McKenzie whispered quietly into his face. "It's OK. You're going to be OK. Right, Dr. Hansen? He's going to be OK? Now . . . now that we know. All we have to do is, what? Aggressively treat it now, right?" McKenzie insisted more than asked.

Dr. Hansen pulled out a tabletop flip chart. "Prostate cancer has four stages." He flipped to a chart of the male anatomy. There was a picture with lines pointing from various parts of the chart. They were labeled T1, T2, T3 and T4.

"Stage 1: the cancer is very small and completely inside the prostate gland which feels normal when a rectal examination is done; Stage 2: the cancer is still inside the prostate gland, but is larger and a lump or hard area can be felt when a rectal examination is done; Stage 3: the cancer has broken through the covering of the prostate and may have grown into the neck of the bladder or the seminal vesicle." He paused, looked at TJ, and then continued. "Stage 4: the cancer has spread to another part of the body. Prostate cancer tends to spread to the bones rather than any other organs." Dr. Hansen paused uncomfortably. "I'm sorry, TJ. It appears as if you are at Stage 4."

McKenzie jumped up. "What? How is that possible? Dr. Hansen—that's the worst stage!"

"I'm dying? A-am I dying, Charles?"

"You're in a critical stage TJ. But with aggressive treatment—and we're going to refer you to an oncological specialist, of course—research has shown that the majority of men survive this cancer, and/or live another ten to twenty years."

TJ got up and walked out of the room. McKenzie started to go after him but Dr. Hansen grabbed her hand.

"I know you want to go after him McKenzie. But he's at a critical stage. Both of you can't afford to be emotional if you're serious about prolonging his life" he said walking around to sit behind his desk. "Now, there are certain things that must take place. And you're either going to have to make Theodore do them, or you're going to have to do them yourself." He handed her a stack of papers and for the next hour they discussed treatment options, medical insurance, and support groups.

♋   ♋   ♋

Six weeks had passed and TJ was starting his treatment. Radiotherapy. The oncologist felt this was the best treatment option as it was commonly used as a palliative measure in advanced cases of cancer to treat symptoms, such as the pain caused by spread of cancer to the bones—which was the case for TJ.

He explained that radiotherapy involves the exposure of parts of the body to radiation, beams of high-energy X-rays, gamma rays or particles to destroy cancer cells that grow abnormally, rapidly, and in abnormal sites. The cancer had advanced so quickly within the undetected time that it had metastasized to his pelvic and hipbones.

TJ was receiving treatment three times a week, and as an inpatient because his response to the treatment was so severe. He had obtained mouth ulcers, was weak, nauseas, was constantly vomiting and had diarrhea. His specialists believed he could receive the best care in the hospital where nurses could attend to him 24 hours.

McKenzie's morning sickness had subsided. She'd gone to her doctor to start prenatal care. She knew the day she had

conceived and was preparing for the birth of her second child--
Christian's child-- alone.

During the entire vacation, TJ never reached the point of
ejaculating inside McKenzie. The two times he tried he was in so
much pain or lost his erection, so it never came to pass. She knew it
was Christian's baby. And everything in her was elated. She
beamed.

Even though she understood the complexity of the situation,
McKenzie was so happy to have a piece of Christian growing inside
her. Their child had been conceived in love. Adulterous love, but
she didn't care. She had figured out how she would make this
situation work. And despite TJ's current circumstances, McKenzie
was moving forward with her plan.

She thought about telling Christian. But ruled it out right
away. She knew he'd want to be an active part of her pregnancy and
the child's life. With TJ undergoing radiation, it just wasn't a good
time to create unnecessary drama in their lives. She rationalized that
she'd tell everyone the truth once he went into remission. He'd be
stronger and things wouldn't look so fucked up.

If she told him now she'd look like the worst wife--sleeping
around with his best friend—and then, getting pregnant while her
husband was fighting for his life, battling cancer. No, she'd wait.

And honestly, McKenzie was perfectly fine with her secret.
She hadn't been this happy in months.

TJ was home recuperating from therapy. Ahmad was
miraculously home preparing to leave in a couple of days for
college. McKenzie walked into the living room and made her
announcement.

"We're having another addition to our family!" She smiled
brightly as she gently rubbed her belly.

TJ sat up in disbelief. He tried to get up, but just didn't have the energy. McKenzie walked over and sat on the arm of the chair. She kissed him on his forehead while he leaned in and gently kissed her stomach.

"This is a blessing. A true blessing." he cried.

McKenzie absent-mindedly stroked his locks. When she re-focused Ahmad was staring at her in disbelief.

"You're going to have a little brother or sister Ahmad. What do you think about that son?" Ahmad stood up and walked out of the room.

"Yeah mom, whatever. Like it matters at all what I think."

TJ tried to get up but McKenzie gently nudged him back down. "L-let me go t-talk to him. H-he can't be f-fuckin' talking to you l-like that!" TJ said, angrier that Ahmad was responding to his child like that than he was at the way he spoke to McKenzie.

"No. He's just jealous." McKenzie assured TJ. "He's been my only child for 18 years. Within the past year he's gotten a new stepfather, he's moved into a new home, he's leaving for college in a couple of days, and now a new baby?" She rubbed his hand. "C'mon. That's a lot to have to adjust to. If I know my son at all, he's thinking I'm trying to replace him or something." She chuckled. "I'll give him a few minutes and then I'll go talk to him."

TJ smiled brightly. "T-this couldn't have h-happened at a b-better time McKenzie. Ooh, I-I-m so happy about t-this baby." TJ beamed. McKenzie felt a twinge of guilt.

"I am too baby. I am too."

♋   ♋   ♋

Christian stopped by the hospital on his way from work. He had managed not to run into McKenzie all of the times he'd come by to visit TJ. He knew it was by design. He only came after work and McKenzie would conveniently be "away" running an errand.

Today, when he walked in he was surprised to see McKenzie there.

"Hey Mac!" Christian said.

He walked around TJ's bed and gently placed a kiss on her cheek. She smiled and hugged him.

"Hey stranger. How've you been?" McKenzie said. Christian watched her. There was something about her that caught his attention and made him stare. He couldn't put his finger on it . . . she looked beautiful. But she always looked beautiful.

"Been doing OK and yourself? You're glowing McKenzie," he said. TJ and McKenzie giggled.

"Y-you're so observant 'C'" TJ said.

"What do you mean?" Christian said looking at the two of them.

"S-She's glowing because s–she's pregnant! You're going to be a g-godfather!"

Christian was silent. He looked back and forth at TJ and McKenzie who were grinning from ear to ear.

"Well shit man! Congratulations!" Christian walked over to give TJ a hearty handshake. TJ beamed with pride.

"Thanks man. It-it's terrific news. C-couldn't have come a-at a better time."

"And you, Miss Lady" Christian said extending his arms. McKenzie moved effortlessly into them. "Congratulations mommie." He hugged her gently.

"Why, thank you, thank you."

When they pulled away Christian ran his hand across her stomach. McKenzie jumped and quickly moved away.

"Uh, excuse me fellas. I have to go to the restroom. I'll, uh . . . be right back." She disappeared into the hallway where she leaned against a wall and caught her breath. *Shit.* She didn't anticipate that. Christian rubbing her stomach . . . touching *their* baby . . . she didn't know if it was her hormones or what, but that small act literally brought her to tears.

"Mac, are you OK?" McKenzie turned to see Christian approaching her.

"You raced out of there so quickly, I wondered if everything was all right?" Christian said worry written all over his face.

McKenzie tried to wipe the tears from her face and quickly regained her composure. "Um, as well as can be expected, given everything that's going on." McKenzie hoped he wouldn't press the topic.

"Of course." Christian said wiping the tears from her cheeks. "You're going through so much. You're to be commended for being so strong. TJ's told me how you've practically carried him through this entire ordeal."

"Well Christian. It's what I do. You know that," she said walking away. "I'm the strong one." She sniffled. She felt Christian walk up behind her. He wrapped his arms around her waist, resting his hands gently on her stomach.

"I know you try to be. But don't forget, you're going to have to let some of that stress and shit go . . . you're carrying precious cargo now." he whispered sweetly into her curls. She leaned back into his chest.

"Babies are resilient Christian. She'll be fine."

"She? You know what it is already?" He sounded surprised.

"Well, it's too soon yet to know. But I hope it's a little girl." she whispered.

"That would be nice." Christian winced.

"Yes. TJ needs this baby Christian." she said almost apologetically. "He's been fighting so much harder since we found out I was pregnant. It's like he has something to live for now."

"And having you isn't enough to live for?" Christian, brows furrowed.

McKenzie chuckled a nervous laugh. That statement made her uncomfortable. She pulled away from Christian. Looking in his eyes she could tell he still thought she was a prize, truly something special. But she knew better.

"You know what I mean Christian Malveaux. Why do you always have to be so difficult Black man?" Christian smiled the most beautiful smile. It reminded her of the first day she met him.

"Difficult? You think this is being difficult, My Queen?" McKenzie blushed. Christian turned to walk away. Over his shoulder he said "It's because of you I've been easy. Easy like Sunday Morning."

All through McKenzie's pregnancy TJ underwent radiotherapy. In her last trimester, he was in remission long enough to gain enough strength to actually help deliver the baby: a 7 pound, 7 ½ ounce, 21 inch girl named Madison Angelique.

Born a month before her due date, little Madison was as healthy as a full term baby—no complications and no extra hospital stay. The naming was a concession on both parents' part: TJ wanted the first name to be Angel, the middle name Madonna.

"What?" McKenzie screamed in horror. "She is a Black baby! What's this Mexican-catholic sounding shit?" She wanted her named Morgan Taylor.

"Is she a girl or a boy? With that name, no one would know!" TJ said.

The concession: Madison Angelique.

Ahmad came home for the birth of his baby sister and stayed for Spring break. The entire time he walked around holding her, cooing to her, talking to her. They were inseparable from the very beginning.

"Ahmad won't let me hold my own child McKenzie." TJ complained. She laughed and nudged him.

"Fuck TJ, you can't have it both ways. You were ready to take his head off when you thought he didn't want her to be born, now that he's loving her to death, you want to take his head off—which one is it going to be?"

"I want to hold my baby." TJ whined. McKenzie socked him in the arm.

"Let him bond with his sister. He'll be headed back to school in a couple of days." she laughed.

McKenzie was happy. Her baby was healthy, TJ seemed to be doing fine, Ahmad was in love with his baby sister, and she . . . well, she couldn't ask for things to work out any more perfectly than the way they had.

Because she didn't tell her doctor when she had really conceived the baby, no one made a stink about her being born early. Everyone assumed the stress from TJ's cancer caused her go into premature labor. But the baby's healthy weight and bright disposition helped everyone to move on to celebrating and not thinking about "other possibilities."

"Are you going to invite your parents to the Christening?" TJ said.

"No. Your parents, our friends, and immediate family are fine." McKenzie said standing up. She looked down at TJ who just stared at her.

"Don't you think they'd want to see their granddaughter McKenzie?"

"Do I care what they want Theodore?"

TJ dropped the subject. There were very few times McKenzie used his full name. The last time was when she "told" him he was going to undergo radiotherapy:

"Oh, you will be taking the treatment, Theodore Johnson. Or you will find yourself without a wife. You decide and you decide right now dammit!" She said.

McKenzie walked out of the room. She paced the kitchen. "Dammit, dammit, dammit!" she cursed under her breath.

She knew a time would come when she'd have to tell TJ the truth about her past. She just kept hoping that time wouldn't be now. Every day was a now she didn't want to come.

McKenzie ran her fingers through her curls. She rehearsed her lines over and over. How she would tell him about her sordid past. How she would explain why she waited so long to tell him. Why she felt—

"Ahhhhh shit!" came a scream from the living room, followed by a loud thump. The baby starting crying. McKenzie ran into the room followed closely by Ahmad who came dashing from his bedroom.

"What happened?" Ahmad screamed, running for Madison.

He quickly picked her up and gently coaxed her into a calm silence. McKenzie ran to TJ's side.

"TJ, baby--" She watched the excruciating pain shoot across his face.

She followed his hand down to his groin area; he was gripping it tightly. Her heart sank.

We're going to start him back on the radiotherapy, McKenzie," Dr. Hansen said walking outside TJ's door. "It's metastasizing at an alarming rate." he said, his eyebrows furrowed.

"What are you talking about Charles? He was just in remission his last visit. What the fuck is going on here?" McKenzie shouted in between tears. Ahmad stood to the side holding Madison. Christian was at McKenzie's side.

"Could someone have, I don't know, read the results wrong?" Christian tried to offer and explanation.

"Cancer doesn't operate on our intellectual consciousness. It does what it wants. All we can do is respond—aggressively."

McKenzie just turned and walked away. She walked down the hall and out of the hospital without saying a word to anyone.

♋   ♋   ♋

Madison was just barely starting to walk on her own when TJ's battle with cancer finally ended. For nine long months he underwent every treatment, every surgery, took every medication known to man. But in the end, he told McKenzie he was tired.

"Just . . . l-let me go McKenzie." he said one quiet spring morning during her visit in the hospital.

"Nonsense TJ, you're going to be fine." She straightened out his cover. He grabbed her hand and made her look him in the eyes.

"I've taken care of everything for you and the kids. James came in last month and finalized the paperwork," he whispered in between labored breaths.

In these last weeks, TJ's stuttering wasn't as prominent. It was odd. She missed his clicks and clacks and stammered sentences.

She didn't think he could get any skinnier than what he was, but he had shriveled down to a skeleton of a man. A mass of dried up dreadlocks with no luster. His crown and glory, an outward reflection of what his almost lifeless body had slowly become. Worn out from the battle.

"Please. Just let me go."

McKenzie lay on his bony chest and cried. She felt as if God was punishing her for all of her sins. She didn't know how to make it right. She didn't know what to do.

"Baby . . ." she pleaded. "I know you're tired." She cried. "But I'll be your strength."

TJ smiled weakly. "That's just it . . ." he gasped. "You have been my strength." He rubbed his mangled fingers through her curls. "I've been fighting for you and our children. I haven't been doing this for me." Tears trickled down TJ's cheek. "I'm tired." He groaned. "I'm tired of this life, here in the hospital. I'm tired of the medications—being picked, poked, and prodded." He sat up and grimaced, pain covered his face. "This is no life."

"It's temporary Teddy. Until you go into remission again baby. Just hold on." McKenzie begged.

"It's not . . . this is it . . . this emaciated body won't return to the sexy man you fell in love with ever again." he forced a weak smile. McKenzie was in too much pain to joke. He watched the pain take over her face, her body. "I'm no good for you or Madison like this." He sighed. "This is not a life and you know it." TJ started to cough. The phlegm filled his lungs and almost sent him into cardiac arrest. The nurses rushed in and administered some medicine and in a few short minutes TJ was resting peacefully.

"He wants me to let him go Priscilla." McKenzie said to the head nurse who she had come to know all too well. Priscilla smiled knowingly, jotted down TJ's vitals in his chart and turned to her.

"He asked you to let him die?"

McKenzie nodded her head. The nurse paused. She walked over to McKenzie and hugged her tight.

"You've been a good wife." Priscilla whispered in her ear. "Now be a good human being. Give the man peace." She said, hugged her again and walked out of the room.

McKenzie watched TJ sleep. She wrestled with the demons in her mind. Guilt rode her like a wild stallion running free in an open range. She needed TJ to live so she could make right her wrongs. As he lay there, she knew she never really loved him. She never gave her heart to him. She cheated him out of his last years and his birth child. She felt like shit and didn't know what to do to make it right.

"Christian?" McKenzie's voice was barely audible. Christian forced himself woke. He rolled over and looked at his clock. The green-boxed numbers read 3:23 am.

"Mac? Is that you?" he called out. But there was silence on the other end of the line. "Mac! Baby, what's wrong?"

"TJ is dead," she sobbed.

♋   ♋   ♋

The days that followed were a blur to McKenzie. People coming and going, asking stupid ass questions like "How are you?" and "Is there anything I can do?" She wanted to scream *I'm fucked up! I'm a fucked up Bitch who never loved her husband, who slept with his best friend, who let him die thinking his best friend's child was his own!* But instead she smiled and shook her head "No" to every question anyone asked and tried to make it through each day.

The night before the funeral, TJ came to her in her sleep. He called her all kinds of ho's and tramps. He told her she was good for nothing and that her lies killed him. He said her poisonous ways infiltrated his body and caused him to slowly deteriorate.

An image of TJ's emaciated body danced around the room taunting her: "Slut!" "Worthless tramp!" It flew to the center of the room, pointing his finger down at her, taunting, jeering, accusing, "You were never raped! You got what you deserved! Look at you! You weren't innocent! You caused everything bad that ever happened to you!"

McKenzie jolted up from her sleep. She was drenched in sweat. She looked at the clock. It was 4:30 am. She slid out of bed, showered and dressed for the funeral. She sat in her chaise lounge, staring out the window until the sun safely filled her room with the comfort of light.

The people filed in to pay their last respects to Theodore Johnson. They slowly walked past his coffin. Some touched the side of the coffin; others touched his skinny little hand; and others leaned in and kissed him.

His mother fainted. His grandmother screamed. And Raleigh looked stoically on. Christian stood there the longest, saying in quiet remorseful stares what McKenzie imagined was holding her spirit down in weights. But he knew, just as she, that words didn't cross over into the other world. Like a ball bouncing off of a wall, Christian's apologies, no matter how heartfelt, didn't get through. There would be no absolution. Not for him; and certainly not for her.

The choir sang some stupid A & B selections. McKenzie spent the entire two songs trying to figure out why Baptist churches still sang those gut-wrenching negro spirituals. And why they called the two most morbid songs ever A & B selections? They always said "A & B Selections."

The preacher got up and preached. About what, she couldn't tell you. She saw his mouth move, she saw the sweat gushing down the sides of his head, like little sprinklers were lodged right at his hair line, and every time he opened his mouth the sprinkler system would turn on, releasing streams of water down his face. But she couldn't repeat a single word he said.

The church officiant read proclamations that would *hereto and forever be placed lovingly in annals of the church records.* What the fuck did that mean? Is there a special file cabinet that holds these proclamations? What does the drawer label read "Loving Annals"?

Then it was her turn. The pastor introduced Theodore's "Faithful" wife, who stood by his side, morning and night. He went on and on about how this man *truly indeed, found himself a good helpmate when he found this wife.* McKenzie wanted to say, "Shut the fuck up already!" But she didn't. She waited patiently at the podium while Pastor Reverend Elder Doctor *So in So* stole another ten minutes of podium time to pontificate and expostulate on nothingness.

When he finally chewed the taste out of it he turned to McKenzie.

She had never sung for TJ. Well, there was their wedding day. But she'd never sung opera. And he'd asked her on several occasions but she'd refused. Every time she'd sung opera she'd wanted to vomit.

Her nausea caused by the fact that the Major got so much pleasure from hearing her sing. He'd make her sing, song after song, after song. One time, he made her sing while he was on top of her, another time while he took her from behind. He said it was a natural mood enhancer and caused his ejaculation to feel that much better.

Once she left that house, she vowed never to sing opera again. But she had nothing left to give her husband. And this was all he had ever asked from her *"Sing for me baby."* And so, hoping this might temper the gods, she would once again, honor his request. The piano began to play and before the congregation knew what hit them this powerful falsetto voice filled the church.

McKenzie sang Stevie Wonder's words from her core.

All is fair in love
Love's a crazy game
Two people vow to stay
In love as one they say

Tears streamed down her face, but her words were clear and strong as she thought about they resonated inside her. She thought about the vows she made to TJ. And how they changed with time. She had never seen this moment in her future. All she knew was that he had offered an opportunity to leave behind her past for what she thought was a picture perfect future with a man who loved her. And now, standing over his coffin, she had no idea what lay ahead.

But all is fair in love
I had to go away
A writer takes his pen
To write the words again
That all in love is fair

Stevie said that *All of fate's a chance that's either* good or bad. McKenzie had pondered on this one sentence long and hard. Had she chosen this fate when she said yes to TJ? To once again be alone, raising a child. Or, was that her fate? Did she choose or was it life's evil plan? All in in war is so cold. . . falling in love with a man she couldn't have, then losing the man she promised to love.

McKenzie looked into the crowd and locked onto Christian's bloodshot eyes. *She thought about their situation. "You either win or lose, When all is put away the loosing side I'll play"* She knew she was the loser in this situation. She wasn't with the man she loved, and wondered if she was being punished for being unfaithful to TJ? She didn't know. It was all too much: too much to process; too much to figure out.

McKenzie closed powerfully—conceding to her to tormented world.

A writer takes his pen
To write the words again
That all in love is fair

♋   ♋   ♋

417

CHAPTER FIFTEEN
The Truth

"Ma . . . Ma?" Ahmad said peeking his head through McKenzie's door. "Ma, you up?'

"No." she replied.

Ahmad walked in the room. He stood watching McKenzie. She looked like shit. He walked over and climbed in the bed with his mom. They lay face-to-face. McKenzie flinched looking into Ahmad's face. He looked so much like the Major. She smiled.

"I love you son." she rubbed his head.

"I love you too mom." Ahmad shifted nervously. "Mom, I've been thinking."

"Oh lord."

"Mom! I'm serious."

"OK, what is it Ahmad?" She grabbed a pillow and propped herself up.

"I'm . . . I've decided not to go back to school."

"The hell you ain't!"

"Mom, you need me here. Who's going to take care of Madison?" he said, his eyes welling up full of tears. "Who's going to take care of you?"

"I am, that's who." McKenzie sat up. "Look son." she said, grabbing his hand. "I've been depressed these past couple of days, but . . . I'm fine now. And you have to go back to school mister."

"No, Ma, I don't. I have to take care of you." Ahmad said, crying. McKenzie's heart warmed. She rubbed his back slowly.

"No you don't. That's not your job baby."

"I promised Christian I would . . . I'm the man of the house." he said in a feeble voice. McKenzie smiled down at her son who was tall enough and brave enough to be a man. But whose heart and demeanor screamed little boy.

"And you have son. You've gotten me through—not just this ordeal, but through life. You know that don't you?" she said grabbing his face and staring him in his eyes. He shook his head. "Yes, Ahmad, you have. You have been my rock . . . my light . . . my joy."

"What I need is for you to go back to school and do well. Seriously. TJ is gone. That's my reality now. I've got to move on. I've got to put my life back into some kind of order. And that's my problem, not yours. OK?"

Ahmad nodded. He looked helpless. McKenzie could tell he felt bad for her. She knew he just wanted her to be happy. And she also knew she looked miserable, despite what she said, causing her son to worry.

McKenzie reached out to her son. He moved into her arms.

"I'll tell Christian you kept your promise."

"For real?"

"For real." She said kissing the top of his head. "You have gotten me through lately, taking care of Madison, and keeping me on top of things. You have definitely taken charge of this house young man."

Ahmad smiled like a nine year old instead of an eighteen year old. But McKenzie loved it. It made her heart smile. It gave her hope for her bleak future.

♋   ♋   ♋

McKenzie watched Madison play on the floor in the den. She busied herself with her wooden blocks, trying to match up the shapes so she could hear the thump in the bottom of the canister.

When Madison was successful she had her own personal celebration. She said "Yaay!" and clapped her hands. She had the same amount of enthusiasm every time she heard the thump. McKenzie smiled and got up to go into the kitchen to fill Madison's juice cup. She washed the cup with soapy hot water, rinsed it, and rinsed it, and rinsed it again.

She turned to the refrigerator and pulled out the apple juice. She started to pour the juice into the cup when she heard Ahmad scream.

"Madison! Madison!" McKenzie's heart fell into her stomach hearing the panic in Ahmad's voice. She dropped the juice cup and ran into the den.

"What?" McKenzie froze in place.

Ahmad was holding Madison's limp body in his arms, shaking her. Fear gripped his face. McKenzie dashed down to his side, grabbing Madison out of his arms.

"What happened? What's wrong?" she screamed frantically. Madison's eyes were closed and she was burning up.

"I don't know! She was just lying in the middle of the floor when I walked in." He explained. "I checked her airways, felt her pulse—she didn't respond."

McKenzie did her own sweep of Madison's mouth. She laid her flat on her back and listened for breath. It was shallow.

"Ahmad, let's go!" she said, scooping Madison up and running for the door.

"Shouldn't we call 911?"

"Get the fucking keys, Ahmad, and open the fucking car door. I don't have time to wait for a fucking ambulance!" McKenzie snapped.

Ahmad grabbed her keys and ran in front of her, opening the front door and the car door. Ahmad jumped in the back seat with Madison and McKenzie slid in the driver's seat. She bolted out of the driveway and headed toward the emergency.

"Touch her forehead, Ahmad, how does it feel?" McKenzie instructed calmly. Ahmad touched her forehead. "She's burning up mom. And her heart is racing." His eyebrows were furrowed, his mouth twisted. He kept sliding his index finger under Madison's nose to make sure she was breathing.

"Maddie bum bum." he cooed in his baby sister's ear. "Wake up, baby girl. It's me Ah-ma. Wake up so we can play patty cake." he said, hoping it would make her open her eyes.

"Whoa!" Ahmad screamed.

The car swerved to miss a silver Toyota Celica in front of them. McKenzie was watching Ahmad in the rear view mirror, hoping Madison would open her eyes and almost rear-ended the Toyota.

"We're almost there, Madison. Hold on momma!" McKenzie said whipping the burgundy Volvo TJ bought her two weeks after he found out she was pregnant, into the emergency parking area.

She screeched into the ambulance-parking stall, jumped out, grabbed Madison and ran inside the double doors.

"Help me! Somebody please help me!" Two nurses ran to assist.

"What's wrong with her?" the first nurse, a tall Asian woman with long black hair cascading down her back, asked.

"She's despondent. She was playing . . . And her brother found her unconscious on the floor. She is burning up and is barely breathing."

"Did she swallow anything? A toy, a button? Could something be lodged in her air way?" The other nurse, an older Black woman with huge breasts, asked calmly. They took her in the triage room, checked her airways, her pulse, and bagged her.

"She was playing with blocks. Her brother swept her air passages, and I followed up and checked for obstructions too." The nurse jotted down notes in Madison's chart.

"Why didn't you call 911?" the nurse admonished. "It's always best that they receive ambulatory care—they're professionals and can catch things you're not trained to catch.

McKenzie watched as the lights started to blink and a loud beeping sound filled the room.

"She's flat lining! Code blue, stat!" the Asian nurse screamed. Another nurse rushed over a crash cart.

"What's going on?" Ahmad shouted, moving closer.

But the Black nurse shoved McKenzie and Ahmad out to the waiting area. McKenzie was speechless. She covered her mouth even though she stopped breathing the moment those beeping sounds filled the room.

"I need to be in there with my baby!" McKenzie pleaded with the nurse.

"No, you need to get out the way and let those people do what they do best." McKenzie crumbled. She broke down into tears. The nurse extended her arms and McKenzie fell into them. The nurse rubbed McKenzie's back while she lay comfortably on the nurse's huge breasts, crying.

Almost forty-five minutes later, the Asian nurse came out to the waiting room. "Mrs. Johnson?"

"Yes, is Madison OK?" McKenzie said, hands clenched, fear choking the voice out of her throat. All she could think was that she would die if her baby died. She knew it . . . she'd die.

"Yes, yes. She's fine. She stopped breathing momentarily but our team revived her right away."

"Why did she stop breathing?"

"She had a febrile seizure. She had a fever of 103.7, which caused her to seize, lose consciousness, and stop breathing. I wish you had called 911; they would've taken her to a pediatric hospital. We're not equipped for Peds here." she said agitated.

"Look B--," McKenzie caught herself. "I'ma tell you like I told her" McKenzie said looking at the other nurse "I saw my child unconscious. I didn't stop to think about calling 911. I reacted. My reaction was to bring her to a hospital. Now if you're ill equipped to treat my daughter, you just let me know--"

"She just would have received better care Mrs. Johnson. We've stabilized her, but I've arranged a transport for her to Little Company of Mary Hospital in Long Beach. They have a special pediatric ward." She hesitated. "Our preliminary tests can't seem to determine the cause of her illness."

"She needs a blood transfusion." Dr. Reed, the Attending Doctor, said.

Madison's condition had worsened at the Little Company of Mary hospital. They had stabilized her and ran a battery of tests but within a couple of hours Madison had taken a turn for the worst.

"A blood transfusion?" McKenzie said. The words shook her to the core. "What for, what's wrong?"

"Her condition has escalated Mrs. Johnson," the doctor said.

"What condition? You ain't told me shit!" McKenzie screamed in his face, frustrated. "You don't know what the fuck is wrong with my daughter, do you, Peter?" she asked, reading his badge.

The doctor remained calm. "I believe she has some sort of viral infection."

"You *believe* she has a viral infection, huh? And what makes you believe that, Peter?"

He cleared his throat. "The symptoms. The high fever came out of nowhere. She has diarrhea, rapid heartbeat, shortness of breath, and she's getting progressively weaker. Her labs haven't detected any bacteria in her system. I'm thinking it has to be viral."

McKenzie listened intently. "You're thinking? How can you know for sure? Are there tests you can run for viral infections? Are their medications you can give her?" McKenzie said rubbing her arms absent-mindedly.

"Well, according to her charts the Emergency room staff already administered Madison twenty cc's of Penicillin. They probably suspected the same thing, too. But when her symptoms didn't change, they thought we'd do a better job of diagnosing her—what with our specializing in pediatrics."

"Little good your specializing in pediatrics is doing for my daughter right now, Peter." she said less sarcastically and more as an observation.

"We're not done yet Mrs. Johnson." Dr. Reed said. "Are there any other relatives you can call to come test to see if their blood type matches Madison's? She has a rare blood type, 0 negative?"

McKenzie froze. She immediately thought of Christian. He was her father. But things were so complicated now. She had called

TJ's family who were on their way, but none of them would be a match unless God decided to show her grace . . .

"I'm here and her brother is here. Test us."

"How old is her brother?" Dr. Reed said. To him, Ahmad didn't look a day over fourteen.

"He's eighteen."

McKenzie and Ahmad followed Dr. Reed to the lab to get tested. The corridor was bright and long. McKenzie prayed the entire time. *Lord. Please let one of us be a match for Madison. Please don't punish my baby because of my sins.*

♋   ♋   ♋

"Neither you nor your son is a match Mrs. Johnson. I'm sorry. What about her father, or any other family member—another sibling maybe?" Dr. Reed said, distressed. Madison's condition was worsening and he was frustrated that they hadn't identified the cause. The blood transfusions were critical to her survival.

"I'm her mother. I carried her for nine months. What do you mean I don't match?" McKenzie fretted. *Shit.* "Her father . . . her father. . ."

"Passed two weeks ago." Ahmad finished her sentence. Silence filled the room. Dr. Reed felt horrible for McKenzie.

"Well" Dr. Reed said, scratching his head. "Because this is such a rare blood type, there's a limited amount of 0 negative blood the hospital allows for each patient."

"What kind of shit is that?" McKenzie screamed. Dr. Reed held his hands up in protest.

"It's hospital policy. And it's to be fair to other patients in need. The nurse has been on the phone calling local blood banks.

Unfortunately, with all of the natural disasters this year, blood banks are even more desperate than we are. So we need to find a match. Is there anyone you can call?"

McKenzie wrapped her arms tightly around her shoulders.

"I'll call . . . friends . . . family members . . ." she whispered.

⊚   ⊚   ⊚

"McKenzie!" Raleigh said, rushing up to her in the waiting room. "How's my niece?" Mrs. Johnson walked in behind Raleigh, looking distraught.

"Lord Jesus, you don't need this right now." Mrs. Johnson said, embracing McKenzie.

McKenzie tried to muster a smile. "I'm OK."

Raleigh looked at McKenzie. She looked worn and tattered. He'd watched her on vigil by TJ's side the entire 9 months. And they all knew this was too much. She was a strong woman, but everyone had their breaking points.

"What do we need to do sis?" Raleigh said.

McKenzie smiled. "Go down to the basement and get tested to see if you're a match. She needs a blood transfusion."

"Blessed savior!" Mrs. Johnson screamed. "The child ain't two yet. A blood transfusion. Are you sure McKenzie? Did you get a second opinion?"

"No I'm *not* sure. It's what the doctor told me, and *no* I haven't gotten a second opinion because my baby's life is hanging in the balance right now. So, if you want to help – go get your blood tested. But if not, then I'm going to ask you to either leave, or push pause on the second-guessing over there. Right now, we're going to trust the people who actually went to medical school, OK?" Mrs. Johnson went silent.

"I'm sure momma was just trying to help Mac." Raleigh said.

426

"Well, check this. That shit ain't helping. *Go get your blood tested.* That's all I need right now, OK?" McKenzie turned her back on TJ's family.

"Sure." Raleigh said. "We'll go right now."

Raleigh quietly ushered his mother out the waiting room. McKenzie heard Mrs. Johnson talking as she walked down the hall.

"Raleigh, you know I didn't mean nothing by that, right? Dr. Oz always says, get a second opinion. I was just trying to help."

"I know ma, but you have to remember McKenzie just lost TJ. She's got to be frantic right now. Just . . . just stay clear of her for awhile, ok?"

"Well OK." Mrs. Johnson said. "I'm not sure if I can give blood with my diabetes son."

"The lab tech will let us know."

But McKenzie knew in her gut already, none of them would have the DNA to save her baby's life.

McKenzie paced the waiting room. She ran her fingers through her curls. Madison needed another transfusion. So far, no one had been a match. *Who should she call? Her mother who she hadn't exchanged seven words within two years? Christian, who had no idea Madison was his biological daughter?* McKenzie couldn't breathe. She sat in a chair and buried her head in her hands. She cried—no she sobbed, the gut-wrenching kind of sob that made your body jerk on the exhale.

McKenzie's cell rang.

"Hello?"

"McKenzie. It's Denny. What's going on, sweetie?"

"Oh my God Denny!" McKenzie sobbed into the phone. "God is punishing me!"

Denny held the phone as McKenzie continued to cry. She felt horrible for her best friend.

"No honey. God is not punishing you. Life is happening. That's all. We get over one hurdle just to catch enough breath to jump over another."

"Shit. My husband has been dead 2 weeks. Two weeks, Denny! You think that's enough time to catch my breath? How about *No*, my lungs are collapsing under all this fucking bull shit."

"I know honey. What can I do? I have Jermaine looking for flights."

"Denny, no. You were just here baby. Let's just wait. The doctor seems to believe it's just a viral infection." McKenzie reached in her purse for tissue. She blew her nose.

"Whatever. My friend needs me. And, what if I'm a match?"

"What's your blood type?"

"AB--"

"You're not a match. And God *is* punishing me."

"Punishing you for what McKenzie!"

"For having sex with my husband's best friend and getting pregnant!" McKenzie screamed then quickly scanned the room to see if anyone had heard her confession. Luckily no one was around. There was silence on the phone. "I told you" McKenzie whispered. "I'm awful."

"Oh shut up bitch. My ass is in shock over here. My silence is not saying you're awful. It's saying '*What the fuck*?'" They laughed.

"Maddie is? "

"Christian's daughter. We conceived her in St. Lucia." McKenzie said feeling lighter after sharing her secret.

"And you guys decided to keep it from TJ because he was sick?"

"'*I*' decided. Christian doesn't know Maddie is his."

"What?" Denny screamed into the phone.

"Mac!" The deep voice came from the door.

McKenzie turned to see Christian and Ahmad staring at her from the door well. She quickly hung up the phone and wiped the tears from her face. Her heart stopped beating and the air in the room turned into hot gas that burned her lungs as she held her breath waiting for the shoe to drop. She searched Christian's face to see if he had heard her confession. Christian extended his arms to her. Relieved, McKenzie exhaled and slowly moved into them. He held her tight.

"Oh Christian." she moaned. He rubbed her back. "Madison . . . Madison might die." she said into his chest.

"No baby, she's not going to die."

"The hospital said they could only give her 5 units of blood in 24 hours and she has a rare blood type--"

"I know. . . I know. I just left the lab Mac. I'm a match. She's going to be fine."

McKenzie pulled back to look at him; her eyes were full of relief. She hugged him tight. She wanted to tell him right then and there that he had just saved his daughter's life. But she didn't.

♋   ♋   ♋

"We've discovered the problem." Dr. Reed said rubbing his tired eyes.

He hadn't left the hospital since Madison arrived. The head nurse told McKenzie he was on his way home from a thirty six-hour shift when he received the call about Madison.

McKenzie felt like shit for talking so rudely to him. She thanked the nurse for telling her, found Dr. Reed and apologized for her behavior. Dr. Reed hugged McKenzie and assured her that folks had said worse things to him than what she'd said; and understood that she was talking from fear and anger about her daughter.

McKenzie, Christian, and Ahmad immediately stood up and crowded around the doctor.

"What is it?" McKenzie said. She was in knots about her sick baby.

"It's a disease called Autoimmune Hemolytic Anemia." He motioned for them to go back to their chairs. They all took a seat. Dr. Reed sat across from them and explained Madison's condition.

"Autoimmune hemolytic anemia is a condition in which your body's immune system mistakenly attacks its own red blood cells, causing them to disintegrate, or 'hemolyse.'"

"Is it a genetic or hereditary disease Dr. Reed?" Christian asked. "I mean, how did she get it?"

"There are many causes of hemolysis, the breaking up of red blood cells. Some are congenital, like sickle cell disease. Some are due to other diseases, and some are caused by drugs, but they all lead to anemia. The autoimmune hemolytic anemias, of which there are many types, occur when antibodies attack red blood cells."

McKenzie gasped. "Isn't that Leukemia?"

"Leukemia can certainly cause hemolysis, but thankfully, in Madison's case, she has not tested positive for Leukemia."

"Well, what caused it then?" Ahmad shouted.

Everyone looked his way. He was clearly agitated. Christian wrapped his arm around his shoulder and pulled him in to him. Ahmad didn't pull away.

"Well, son," Dr. Reed said addressing Ahmad specifically "in most cases, abnormal immune function leads the body to attack normal red blood cells. Causes of the underlying abnormal immune function include drugs like Alpha-methyldopa and L-dopa" He said turning to face McKenzie and Christian.

"None of which she'd been administered. Then there are infections. And if you recall, I was certain she had a viral infection. But she tested negative for mononucleosis and mycoplasma pneumonia—the two likely viral infections to lead to hemolysis." He scratched his head and rubbed his beard. "And of course there are the cancers, leukemia, lymphoma, non-Hodgkin's but also, occasionally, Hodgkin's, collagen-vascular autoimmune diseases like lupus—but again, she tested negative for all of these."

"So, what is it?" McKenzie said.

"In some cases of autoimmune hemolysis, medications may attach to red cells, leading to targeting for destruction by the immune system. In Madison's case, it was penicillin. The medical team suspected she had a viral infection and administered her cephalosporin, a derivative of penicillin, which caused the hemolysis."

"That's some crazy shit." McKenzie said, exasperated. "How did you know?"

"I didn't. All I knew was that she had the symptoms. And no matter what we did, we couldn't cure them. Then when she needed so many blood transfusions I used deductive reasoning to eliminate the cause." he sighed and stood up. They all stood up.

"Thank you Dr. Reed. I'm sorry again for my mouth--" she started to say. But he held his hand up in resignation.

"Madison is fine. That's all that matters. Anything before or after that is inconsequential, right?" he said with a beautiful bright smile that let you know he meant it.

"Right." she said, grateful for the doctor's forgiving spirit and tenacity. He had saved her daughter's life. What a humbling feeling.

He hugged McKenzie, shook Christian and Ahmad's hands and finally ended his shift--64 hours later.

"Madison's going to be fine fellas." McKenzie said, elated.

"Thanks to Christian." Ahmad beamed. "You saved my sister's life." The thought suddenly overtook him. He quickly turned away. Christian walked up behind him and grabbed his shoulders.

"Hey young blood." Christian turned Ahmad to face him. "Thanks to you. You made the call. You saved your sister's life." He pulled him into his chest and rubbed his back while Ahmad released built up tensions from the past 24 hours. "It's OK." He whispered in the top of his head. "It's OK."

McKenzie stood watching. Her heart was warm and heavy at the same time. She was so grateful to Christian. *She* hadn't made the call that saved their daughter's life—her son had. And now, he was comforting Ahmad the way he had comforted her so many times before. Her heart was warm and heavy.

Madison was in the hospital for seven days. Then they brought her home. McKenzie allowed Ahmad to stay home three days after Madison came home and then made him return to Howard.

He called four times a day the first week back until he felt sure his Maddie bum bum was fine.

McKenzie was relieved that Madison was fine, but was a wreck about when she would tell Christian the truth about Madison's paternity. She was almost a year old. For nearly one year McKenzie kept Christian's daughter a secret from him. She sighed. Her head remained in perpetual pain.

McKenzie walked outside to get the mail. On the way back to the house, she thumbed through the letters. A plain grey envelope addressed from Williams, Harris & Smith LLP caught her eye. That was TJ's attorney. James Harris had been his attorney for years. He had drafted their prenuptial agreement, their living trust, and Madison's trust fund.

Ripping open the letter, McKenzie began reading the contents of the letter:

Your presence is requested, October 7th at 2:30 pm in the office of Williams, Harris, & Smith LLP for the official reading of the Johnson living trust.

McKenzie froze in place. *The reading of TJ's trust.* With Madison's hospital scare, she hadn't really had time to mourn TJ. She walked into the house and sat on her couch. This was just too much to deal with. McKenzie felt overwhelmed.

"Hello Mrs. Johnson." James said shaking her hand. "Thank you for coming." He said showing her to the conference room. "How is the family?"

432

"Please, McKenzie. And everyone is doing fine, thank you." McKenzie walked into the conference room and took a seat.

"That's wonderful." He said leafing through his notepad. "We're just waiting for a Mr. Christian Malveaux and we'll get started."

She turned to face the attorney. "Christian's coming?"

"Yes, he should be here any minute." He replied, smiling casually as he left the room.

McKenzie sat quietly contemplating the idea of Christian's presence. Of course it made sense: he was TJ's best friend and Madison's godfather. She just wasn't feeling too great being in his presence knowing she hadn't told him about Madison.

"Ah, here we go." James said, leading Christian into the conference room. "Mrs. Johnson, Mr. Malveaux has arrived. We can get started now."

Christian walked over to McKenzie who stood up. They hugged and then took their seats.

"Thank you both for coming today." James said shuffling through papers. "The purpose of today's meeting is to settle the matter of the distribution of assets from the living trust of Mr. Theodore Johnson." McKenzie looked on. And Christian looked unimpressed.

"Yes, well . . . let's get on with it." McKenzie said.

"Of course." James said smiling easily. "Teddy and I had been friends for years" he said casually. "We went to high school together. After graduating from law school, I ran into him at a conference and we stayed close every since. As a matter of fact, he was one of my first clients with the firm." he said fondly. "His premature death at such a young age was both a tragic loss and a shock to everyone. My sincerest condolences." He directed his statement to them both.

"Thank you." McKenzie said. Christian nodded.

"The trust is pretty simple. All of his assets are bequeathed to you Mrs. Johnson." James handed her a sheet of paper detailing his assets. McKenzie reviewed the paper. Nothing seemed out of the ordinary.

"Can you tell me why I'm here?" Christian said.

"Absolutely." James reached in his mahogany desk and pulled out a letter. "For the reading." He grabbed a pair of glasses and opened the letter. "There, now, are we ready?" He looked at both McKenzie and Christian. They nodded. It was just the three of them in the huge conference room.

"A-hem." He said clearing his throat.

Dear McKenzie,
I believe I love you more than life itself. You have shown me the true meaning of the word love. You are loving, kind, forgiving and warm.

I will be eternally grateful for all that you've given to me. A man couldn't ask for a better wife. I am so sorry for all the pain I caused you. I know you never forgave me. But you stayed with me to the very end. And even in the very end, I felt more loved and honored than I have in my entire life.

I don't know if you will ever understand just how much your dedication to me means. I know the personal sacrifices you made were great, and I just want you to know that I do appreciate them, and you. And now that I am gone I want you to be happy.

Go be with the man you truly love. Christian. You stood by me and loved me even though your heart belonged to him. I know I was wrong to keep you with me, I should have let you go be with him McKenzie, but I just loved you so.

And when I found out I was dying, I thought it wasn't so bad—it would only be for a little while . . . I hope you can forgive me. For everything fucked up I did to you. For keeping you here with me when I knew everything . . .
My last dying wish is for you to finally be happy. And to have the love you so selflessly gave me. You are a magnificent woman!
I love you, heart, body and soul,
- TJ

McKenzie sat frozen in her seat, eyes opened wide, biting her bottom lip. She was too embarrassed to look at the attorney . . . too embarrassed to look at Christian. The huge conference room suddenly felt small. She tried to think of something to say, but James simply pulled out another letter and moved on.

> *"C",*
>
> *You have been my best friend since college. My deepest and scariest secrets will go to the grave with you. It is because of our bond as brothers and my love for you that I give you my blessing to be with McKenzie.*
>
> *I know you love her, and I know she loves you. It took me a while to figure it out, but when I did it made complete sense. I only wish you had told me sooner, although it probably wouldn't have stopped me from falling in love with her. But at least only one person would have been devastated instead of five.*
>
> *But that's water under the bridge, eh "C"? Right now you get to love McKenzie like she deserves to be loved. You get to be the father to your daughter that you deserve to be.*

"A daughter? What the fuck?" Christian shouted.

Confused, he turned to look at McKenzie who looked completely mortified. She dropped her head into her hands and began to cry. Christian was enraged—elated, sad, but mostly confused. *Madison was his daughter? But when, how? TJ knew? McKenzie didn't tell him?* He was a ball of mixed emotions. The attorney resumed reading when Christian sat back in his chair.

> *I will always love her even though she doesn't share a drop of my blood. I can't believe how loving and selfless you are, to let me have her as my child for the time that I had her.*
>
> *You have always looked out for me, and this was the biggest gift ever. A daughter. I found out during the*

radiotherapy that I was sterile. After that, I put two and two together and realized that was why McKenzie was so depressed that whole month after the trip.

She loved you, was carrying your child, and was stuck with me, her sick husband that she probably hated, but pitied enough to stay with.

But she never made me feel unloved. Actually, it was quite the opposite—and why-- even after I found out everything, I couldn't walk away. She made me feel alive! She made me feel special, loved, and I knew her heart was with you. But she managed to make me feel whole Christian. And I couldn't walk away.

I'm sitting here thinking how awesome McKenzie's love must be . . . if faking it made me feel so good, how awesome it must feel to get the real stuff?

I feel really blessed to have had you as a brother Christian. I'm not sure I could have made the personal sacrifices you made for me to be happy. I can't say I could have Bruh. But on the Shield, I love You—and I hope one day you can forgive me for not being the man I should've been to McKenzie, and the brother I should've been to you.

I hope my blessing somehow levels the score? Forever your Friend, Eternally Your Brother - TJ

Christian sat motionless trying to absorb everything he just heard. He turned to face James who tried to maintain a blank face, but failed miserably. Anyone could look at his face and tell he was thinking what Christian was feeling, *that this was some fucked up shit to have read to you.*

"McKenzie." Christian said slowly between clenched teeth. "Madison is *my* daughter?"

McKenzie's head was spinning. First, from the shock of hearing that TJ knew all of this all along. And second, from the shock and fear of having Christian find out about Madison this way. It was all so horrible and not at all how she planned on telling him.

"Yes, Christian—but I can explain."

Christian stood up, turning the chair over from the force of his motion.

"No, you can't explain. There's nothing you can say to me that will make this make sense to me." He grabbed his jacket and headed for the door.

"Christian, wait. There is a reasonable, logical explanation!"

Christian paused at the door. The look on his face made the attorney turn away in embarrassment for McKenzie. It made her turn to mush inside.

"Fuck you McKenzie."

CHAPTER SIXTEEN
Closure

"Christian, what's up man? I can't reach my mom." Ahmad said over the phone. Christian instinctively answered on the first ring, but now he wished he had let it go to voice mail.

"I don't know what to tell you young blood. Keep trying her," he said dryly. Christian left the attorney's office in a daze. He had been driving around the city for hours, trying to make sense of this situation.

He couldn't believe that McKenzie could betray him this way—his own daughter! He had a daughter who he'd been treating like a goddaughter, who he'd held and kissed—and loved, for over a year—and she was his own flesh and blood. How could a person do something that heartless? At that moment, he felt like he didn't know McKenzie at all. In a million years, he never thought she could be capable of doing something that low down and dirty.

"What's up "C"?" Ahmad said. "What's wrong?"

Christian half smiled. It was amazing that Ahmad could tell something was wrong. Although, they had become pretty tight over the past year, he didn't know what it was about this kid, but he just loved him. He really did love Ahmad.

They practically talked every day when he first went to college. Ahmad called him about everything--from registration, picking classes, his roommate, some girl he was feeling—to being conflicted over that because of Crystal. They had put in some hours. And he was truly a cool kid.

Ahmad was the one who had called him when Madison was sick. If it hadn't been for Ahmad, his daughter might have died. The anger welled up inside him again. McKenzie knew he was Madison's father when she was in the hospital—she should have called him herself. She should have told him the truth!

"Aw, naw man. This is some shit that has nothing to do with you." Christian said into the phone.

"Then why can't you tell me what's up?" Christian paused. He knew he shouldn't be talking to Ahmad about this.

"Because it's about your mother. And despite anything that happens between me and your mother, that's your mother. I ain't trying to damage your relationship--" Christian started to explain, but Ahmad cut him off.

"Dude. I thought we established our boundaries way back when? I thought *we* were friends? Has that changed?" Ahmad said sounding wounded.

"Of course we're friends, Ahmad, but this is different."

"How?"

"Because . . . your mom did something . . . I don't know if I'll ever be able to forgive her for . . ." Christian said the words that had had his heart so heavy. He loved McKenzie, but how could he work around this ugly sense of betrayal he felt?

The question that consumed him was *how long was she going to let TJ believe he was Madison's father?* If he hadn't gotten sick, would she have allowed his best friend to raise his child? The thought enraged him. Who did she think she was?

"Christian. I love my mom. But I know my moms has done some fucked up shit—case and point, marrying your best friend. That was some fucked up shit. BUT! I know you two love each other, and eventually ya'll gone work that twisted shit out."

"Naw, Ahmad. I don't think so young blood. This shit is . . . it's too much." Christian said rubbing his temple. Christian looked out into the evening sky. The day was winding down and the sun was settling into its peaceful slumber. The sky was splashed with a mixture of magenta and burnt orange hues.

"Just tell me. Whatever it is, it's not going to make me stop loving my mother and it's not going to make me stop loving you." Ahmad said with trepidation. He'd wanted to tell Christian a long time ago that he loved him. But he didn't know how. And he didn't want to make him feel weird.

Christian had been the closest thing to a father Ahmad ever had. And it was the best feeling he ever felt. He loved his mom with all his heart but to be able to call up Christian and talk to him about his feelings as a man—Man! That was some shit! And Christian always made him feel special. Even when he did fucked up shit.

Ahmad got drunk his first semester at Howard. He was so sick he missed class for two days. When he told Christian, he went off.

"Dog, you gotta know your limits. You are at college to learn. That's your priority. So, if you're going to party—party. But not at the expense of your education. Education first, everything else follows." And that'd been Ahmad's credo ever since.

"Ahmad . . ." Christian paused, touched by Ahmad's confession. "I love you too son. " He paused. "And it's because of my love for you—and your mother, that I don't want to cause any confusion between you two."

"All right. I'm on my way home."

"What? On your way home? What are you talking about boy?" Christian said irritated.

"Well, I can't get in contact with my mom and you're not talking. So, I guess I need to come home and find out what the hell is going on?" Christian could hear doors slamming open and shut. Ahmad was packing!

"Whoa, whoa! Slow your roll!" Christian said trying to think this through. "OK. I'll tell you. I'll tell you," he said marveling at this kid. The noise in the background stopped.

"OK, shoot!" Ahmad sat on the corner of his twin bed and listened.

"We had the reading of TJ's will today. And I found out . . . that Madison is my biological daughter."

"What the fuck?" Ahmad shouted into the telephone. "What? How? I mean – whoa!" Ahmad and Christian sat silent for a few minutes. "Wow."

"Yeah, right?" Christian frowned and rubbed his temple.

"Wait, hold up. You said, you found out. So that means . . . my mom didn't tell you. She knew? That's why you don't know if you can forgive her . . . for not telling you Madison was your daughter?" Ahmad talked through his understanding. They sat silent another couple of minutes.

"Christian. I don't know why my mom didn't tell you. I want to say there has to be a good reason why. But I just can't imagine what that could be, not to tell a man he has a daughter." He paused.

441

Christian smiled despite himself, listening to Ahmad speak. He'd always thought Ahmad was mature beyond his years.

"But check this . . . "

"I'm checking . . . what's up?" Christian said, tickled that Ahmad sounded as if he was about to kick some knowledge.

"Madison is your daughter." Ahmad said calmly. The air between them seemed to fill the telephone with an unspoken joy. "My Maddie bum bum is *your* daughter! Is that, like, the best thing ever? I mean—no disrespect, TJ was a cool dude and all. But Madison Johnson is really Madison Malveaux! That means I get to love her like a million times more—if that's even possible." Ahmad was rambling and Christian was grinning from ear to ear.

He listened to Ahmad go on and on about being happy that Madison had his bloodline, like it was something special. It made Christian smile. He knew how much Ahmad loved his mom, and now, hearing how much he loved him—and how that love would be showered on the little girl that shared both their genealogy—was just the most amazing thing to hear.

It was just what he needed to hear to help him put things into their proper perspective.

♋   ♋   ♋

McKenzie was home with Madison when she received the call. She had been back and forth to the bathroom with diarrhea—probably stress from the way things went down at the attorney's office.

It was almost 8:00 p.m. and Christian called to ask if he could come over. She said yes and the telephone went dead. McKenzie paced the room. Her anxiety level was to the roof, and no matter how many times she went over in her head the reasons why she didn't tell Christian that Madison was his daughter they all seemed to sound so weak and stupid.

Shit! She thought to herself *You fucked up now girl.* And she knew she had. The look on Christian's face when he turned to her and said "Fuck You" was almost more than she could bear.

It definitely meant more to her knowing that TJ knew she had been unfaithful to him--that she had slept with his best friend, and that Madison was not his daughter. She rationalized that it was because TJ wasn't here, and anyways, he had forgiven her for her deception with Madison and actually seen it as a selfless gift of love. And, he had given them his blessings.

Madison was playing on the floor when the doorbell rang. McKenzie's throat tightened. She stood in place for several seconds until the second ring of the bell jarred her into motion. She nervously walked over to the door and opened it. Christian stepped inside the foyer.

"Hello McKenzie."

McKenzie's heart dropped. Christian never called her by her full name—with the exception of when he told her "Fuck you, McKenzie." She knew he felt hurt, angry, and betrayed. These are all the things she told herself he would feel if he ever found out Madison was his daughter before she told him. But for some reason, all the explanations she had prepared to justify her decision just didn't hold up at this moment.

"Hi Christian" she said, closing the door behind him. Madison heard his voice, dropped her toys and took off running toward him.

"Chriss-tan!" She shouted with delight.

Christian stooped down and stretched out his arms to her. She ran and jumped up into his arms, wrapping her arms around his neck. He hugged her tight, kissed her face, and closely examined her features. *My daughter* he thought. And for the first time it dawned on him *My and McKenzie's daughter*.

Christian carried Madison back to her toys in the middle of the living room floor. He watched her expertly place wooden blocks into the correctly shaped holes. Each time she did, she turned to him for praise and he obediently clapped. She ran back into his arms and poked her lips out for a kiss.

"Smackums!" she demanded. Christian laughed from deep inside.

"Where did she learn that one?" He said, finally turning to speak to McKenzie.

"Her big brother" McKenzie said smiling. "He showers her with kisses and hugs. I think he's ruined her."

"Nothing wrong with a little affection."

McKenzie didn't reply. She was happy that he was talking to her without anger in his voice. She just smiled and hugged herself. He rubbed Madison's back. She turned to look at him and flashed the biggest brightest smile. In that moment she reminded him of McKenzie—happy.

"Why didn't you tell me Mac?" Christian whispered.

"I was wrong for not telling you. There is no excuse . . . I'm sorry."

"Ok . . . thank you. But I still want to know why you didn't tell me." Christian turned to face her. McKenzie looked pained. She ran her fingers through her curls, tugged at her t-shirt, and rubbed her hands together.

"Well, when we came back from St. Lucia . . . I was going to leave TJ." She looked at him sadly. "I really was. But when we got back, he tried so hard to make up for the shit he did on the island. He told me he was serious about his vows . . . and that he loved me."

"I loved you Mac. Besides not leaving Jada sooner, what have I done to hurt you?"

McKenzie looked Christian in the eyes. He seemed so sincere. She knew he loved her—at least back then. And he was the only one who had been by her side even knowing all she'd been through.

"Nothing Christian." she said, embarrassed. She walked into another room to wipe away the tears that were welling up in her eyes.

"You didn't deserve this... TJ didn't deserve this." She turned to face Christian. "I've fucked up everything Christian. I'm so sorry." The tears streamed down her cheek. She quickly wiped her face. Christian instinctively moved toward her. He pulled her into his chest and rubbed her back.

"Shhh. It's OK. It's all right. Shh." He kissed her curls.

"I wish you were right." McKenzie said sobbing. "But the truth is . . . I don't know how it can ever be all right." She pulled away and walked over to the couch to sit. Christian followed and sat next to her.

"I was so angry at TJ for what happened in St. Lucia. But the more I thought about it, the more I realized it was my fault."

"How was any of that your fault Mac? He should have protected you, not violated you!" Christian screamed.

"And I should have fought. I should have protested—not gone along with it. You said so yourself. I caused it to happen." McKenzie said.

"That's bullshit McKenzie and you know it!" Christian said.

"It's the truth . . . and so when I got back to the States, I started thinking. I'm going to leave this man for doing what I basically allowed him to do? Maybe if I had said something, done something sooner—it would have never happened?" McKenzie looked forlorn and lost, like she was still searching for answers. "I thought, maybe I could fix the problem. And I thought, maybe I owed that much to him?"

Christian sat and listened to McKenzie's thought process. It all sounded so warped. *Did she really believe the shit she was telling him?* He watched her face and knew she was serious.

"And so, that's why you stayed with him?"

"Yes. I thought I had to at least try. If, after trying, it didn't work, I was going to leave. But I was so fucking depressed. All I could do was sit in my room and cry. I tried to be happy. I tried to engage with him—but I was so fucking miserable." Christian remembered TJ talking to him about McKenzie's depression.

"That went on for about a month. Then I didn't get my period." She ran her hands through her curls. "At first, I didn't trip because I was under so much stress and knew I was depressed, I thought it was just throwing me off a couple of days. But then, my nipples became tender and I was feeling sick all the time. And it dawned on me that that's exactly how I felt with Ahmad." She was absentmindedly rubbing her stomach as she spoke. Christian watched her.

"I went and got a home pregnancy test and it came back positive. I took two more that week—same results." She turned to face Christian. "I knew it was yours. I hadn't had sex with TJ since before we left for St. Lucia." She rubbed her hand across her jeans. Then she looked at him with the most sincere look.

"I was so happy. The happiest I'd been in my entire life." She smiled a genuinely happy smile that made Christian involuntarily smile. "I was carrying *your* child. *Our* child. For the first two weeks I was on cloud nine. Just the thought made me giddy inside."

"I went to the doctor and had a blood test to make sure. Of course it was positive. And that was that. I was going to leave TJ. But before I could tell him, we got the news that he had prostate cancer. And then I just couldn't tell him. I couldn't leave him." McKenzie said, everything sounding like it happened in warped speed – one thing after another.

"OK, fine, I understand not wanting to tell TJ. But why didn't you tell me?"

"Christian . . . can you honestly tell me that if I'd told you I was carrying your child, you would have kept it a secret?"

"Why should I have kept it a secret?"

"Because your best friend had just been given a death sentence. Stage 4 Prostate Cancer. Do you think he needed to deal with death, betrayal, and disrespect?"

Christian sat quietly for a moment. "No. That would have been too hurtful." he whispered.

"I thought so too. There was a small possibility with the radiotherapy that he could have survived. If I had told him I was pregnant with your child and wanted to leave him, he would have given up hope. He wouldn't have fought as hard as he did. You know he only did that for me and Madison." Christian dropped his head and gently massaged his temples. He hadn't thought about any of this situation this way. He looked up at McKenzie.

"You certainly had a lot to deal with all alone, didn't you?"

He felt sorry for her. He tried to imagine all the stress she endured carrying around that lie, being strong for TJ, and staying by his side, when, all the time, she wanted to be with him. Christian reached out and grabbed McKenzie's hand.

"I'm sorry you had to keep such a huge secret. What a massive burden to bear. I'm sorry you went through all of that alone."

"It's OK. I just didn't want things to end badly. I wanted him to have peace in his last days. Can you understand that?" she said, pleading with her eyes. "I know it wasn't necessarily the right thing to do but I honestly believe it was the best thing to do."

"It would have been awful for TJ to die hating us. That's no way to leave this earth. Feeling betrayed by the two people you love and trust the most?" She shook her head and chuckled. "And it turns out, he knew all along."

"Not really."

"Hello? That's how you found out, remember? TJ's letter?"

"He didn't know that you got pregnant in St. Lucia. He didn't know that you were depressed that month because you were struggling with the decision to leave him before you even knew you were pregnant. C'mon, Mac, he thanked us for being selfless! He thanked me for 'loaning' him Madison. He fucking gave us his blessing to be together—no, darling, he didn't know shit."

McKenzie sat and thought about Christian's points. And she had to agree. TJ couldn't have known the real truth. But he knew enough to piece together that she and Christian were in love. He knew enough to believe they had put him over their relationship. And, as twisted as it all turned out—TJ gave them his blessing to have a happy life together.

But sitting on the couch, telling Christian her story, she didn't know if her good intentions were enough to erase all the ill feelings he harbored against her.

"He knew I loved you. How he knew that, I'll never know."

"He found your diary."

"What? He read my diary? How do you know that?" McKenzie replied pissed off at the thought TJ had violated her personal space like that.

"The attorney said TJ had read your diary where you went into great detail about how much you loved me." Christian stared straight ahead.

McKenzie sat dumbfounded. She tried to recall all the things she had written in her diary but couldn't. She just shook her head.

"I hope . . . I hope you can forgive me some day, Christian. I had every intention of telling you Madison was your daughter. But I wanted to do it right. I wanted to wait a little while after TJ passed. But then she got sick in the hospital, and I was just too – I didn't think that was a good time. And then, things just spun out of control."

Christian just nodded in understanding. He was not happy about how everything went down. He looked over at Madison and thought about all the months he had missed in her life. But then he thought about all the years he would have with her and it put things in their proper perspective.

Madison jumped up and ran to McKenzie. "Potty mom. Potty."

"Ooh! Good girl!" She turned to Christian. "Quick learner. She obviously got that from my side of the family." Christian chuckled as she winked and led Madison off to her potty.

He lay back on the sofa and rubbed his temples. He couldn't believe all the things McKenzie had endured in her life. She was, by far, the strongest woman he knew. She was the bravest person. The telephone rang.

"Christian, can you get that?" McKenzie shouted from the bathroom.

"Yeah!" Christian replied walking over to the telephone. "Hello?" he said into the receiver.

"Yes, hello . . . may I speak to Theodore Johnson please?" a high-pitched voice said across the line.

"Who's calling please?" Christian said, perturbed.

"Yes, this is Brenda Reisen. Is he available please?"

"No ma'am. Theodore passed about two weeks ago." Christian said in a strained voice.

"Oh my!" She stammered. It sounded like she dropped the phone for a minute. "Hello?"

"Yes, hello. I'm still here."

"Did you say Mr. Johnson is deceased?"

"Yes ma'am, I did. How can I help you?"

"Well . . . actually, I'm looking for his wife. McKenzie. It's just, he called us the last time, and so I thought I would contact him."

"Who are you ma'am?" Christian asked annoyed at her long drawn out explanation that wasn't telling him anything.

"Oh my, I'm Brenda Reisen. McKenzie's mother." She replied, flustered. The news of TJ's death obviously caught her off guard. "You mean to say, McKenzie's a widow?"

"I suppose that's true, yes." Having full knowledge of her relationship with her mother, Christian was annoyed with her questions. "Ms. Reisen, again, how can I help you?"

"Oh. McKenzie's dad had a major heart attack and is in the hospital. The surgeons are telling me they don't believe he's going to make it . . ." Christian could hear her weeping on the other side of the phone. "So I thought I would call McKenzie and let her know."

Christian was enraged! The nerve of the mother, to call as if McKenzie would want to say anything to that controlling, abusive, child molester!

"What hospital is he in? I'll give her the message." Was all he could say civilly in reply. He jotted down the information on a nearby bill and assured her he'd give her the information along with her telephone number.

As soon as he placed the receiver on the base, McKenzie walked in holding Madison's hand.

"Guess who stayed dry and pottied in her pot like a big girl?" McKenzie said grinning from ear to ear.

"Madison!" Madison said proudly, pulling away from McKenzie to clap her hands. Christian fell out into complete laughter and joined in the celebration by clapping as well.

"Madison, what a big girl you are!" Christian said, stretching his hands out to her. As always, she ran into them, laughing all the while. He picked her up and spun her around. She laughed and shrieked and held her hands out as they spun around.

"I can see she's going to love roller coasters when she gets older. Look at her!" Christian said laughing. "She's going to get on the fastest rides and hold her hands up the entire time!" They all laughed together.

"Who was on the phone?" McKenzie said sitting down on the couch.

"Uh . . . your mom. It was your mom calling."

"My who?" she said sitting straight up.

Christian placed Madison down to continue playing and sat next to McKenzie.

"It was your mother calling. Apparently the Major has had a massive heart attack and she thought you'd want to know."

"Why in the fuck would she think that? I wish the mutha fucka had died!"

"Well, I took down all the information—and your mom's telephone number. It's over there on one of your bills."

"For what? I'm not going to see his ass. And I won't need to call her for shit. How did she get my number anyway?" McKenzie said looking distressed.

"I don't know. But she did ask for TJ when she called."

"That's right! He did call them when we were getting married. She probably kept the number from then." She said. McKenzie bit her bottom lip and ran her fingers unconsciously through her curls. She looked up at Christian who was watching her closely. He knew she was struggling inside. There was so much evidence of pain outside and he didn't know what to do to help.

"Why would she call me, Christian? Why would she think I'd want to see his rotten ass?" McKenzie said tears caught in her throat.

Christian sighed. "Because she knows, like you know, that you need closure. And the only way that's going to happen is if you go see him."

McKenzie had the same look when they were out on the quad and the Major had her pinned up on the wall. It was complete terror.

They sat in the parking lot for nearly forty-five minutes before McKenzie would go inside.

"Just let his ass die. Then all my pain and hurt can die with his ugly ass."

Christian sat patiently, holding her, rubbing her back as she cried and protested.

"We can leave right now, Mac. I'm not going to force you to confront him." He kissed her head. "But I know you can do this. I think you should do this. And I promise, I'll be right by your side. He won't be able to hurt you baby—I won't let him."

His words filled her heart and lifted a heavy burden off her soul. But the innate fear and shear panic she felt just thinking about being in the same room with the Major caused her to shudder. Christian rubbed her arms.

"Are you cold?"

"I'm afraid."

"Then let's go get Madison and go home. Obviously this is too much for you emotionally. Let his punk ass die. He's going to hell anyway."

McKenzie smiled. She knew Christian was trying to make her feel better. She also knew that she needed to go confront this man once and for all so that he wouldn't forever have a hold on her.

She opened her door. "You'll be right by my side, right?" McKenzie said sounding like a scared child instead of a grown woman.

Christian took her hand. "Every second."

At the room, McKenzie paused, took a deep breath, then slowly pushed the door open. Her mother turned to face them. She smiled brightly.

"McKenzie! I knew you'd come!" She stood and started fussing over the Major. "He can speak, but it's labored. The doctor's say he's had a massive heart attack and he's undergone lots of trauma and internal damage." She was rambling as she straightened out the sheets over and over. "But they don't know the Major. He's survived wars. He's a survivor."

"Sh-ut . . . up . . . Bren-duh . . ." the Major said. Mrs. Reisen immediately stopped talking. Embarrassed, she sat quietly in the seat next to his bed.

451

"I see you haven't changed a bit. Still treating your wife like shit." McKenzie said.

"Don't . . . curse—" the Major said. But McKenzie cut him off.

"Shit! Fuck! Got dammit! Mutha fucka! Bitch! Whore! Punk ass! Bitch ass! Dick! Pussy! And cunt!" McKenzie spewed. Christian, Mrs. Reisen, and the Major all turned to look at her in shock. "Don't tell me what the fuck to say or how the fuck to say it! You are not my father! As a matter of fact, you don't mean a piece of shit to me!" the anger glared in her eyes as she spoke.

"Filth! . . . Wasn't . . . never . . . gone . . . be . . . shit . . . anyway--"

Christian moved forward but McKenzie tightened her grip on his hand.

"Well now" McKenzie said with an eerie calmness, "Is that what you told yourself to make you feel better? Because if there ever was any hope that I would have been something, you certainly killed all hope of that happening. Didn't you, Mister Minister Molester?" She stared him in his eyes. The mother turned her attention to a small pillow she was stitching and never looked up.

"I . . . was . . . grooming . . . you . . . to . . ."

"You were *molesting me*!" McKenzie said. "I was eleven for god's sake! You don't groom an eleven year old by shoving your dick inside her virgin vagina! You don't groom someone by copulating, and sodomizing, and putting the fear of god in her for *rejecting* the vile and disgusting shit you were doing to her!" McKenzie screamed.

The nurse on duty ran to the door and listened in. She gasped at the accusations that were being thrown around.

"You . . . weren't . . . going . . . to . . . be . . . shit . . ." Then he reared up and said "That's . . . my . . . son!" He said wickedly.

Christian was so full of rage that he charged the bed.

"Look, you sick piece of shit. You don't get to determine who the fuck is going to be something in life. Despite all the vile and disgusting things you've done to this woman, she has turned out to be the most loving, dedicated, and devoted woman I've ever known. She's smart, and compassionate, and she loves with a force you obviously have never known."

"You think you broke her spirit, mutha fucka? You're wrong." Christian said, leaning into the Major's face. "You didn't break shit. She's stronger and mightier than ever!" Their eyes locked on each other.

"And that boy is not your son. He is *my* son. And he'll learn how to love and cherish women, because that's what *I* will teach him! He has all the best qualities of McKenzie and nothing of your vile, sick ass!" The Major focused on Christian's face. His eyes registered recognition. He struggled to laugh, but it came out as a gurgle.

"This . . . ain't . . . no . . . knight . . . and . . . shining . . . armor. He . . . will . . . leave . . . you . . . e-ventually. Cause . . ."

"Cause I ain't shit! I know, I know." McKenzie said as she walked closer to the bed. The change in tone caused Mrs. Reisen to look up from her pillow stitching. McKenzie smoothed out the pillow next to the Major's head. She leaned in close to his ear and whispered:

"Here's what I figured out, Chester the molester. I figured out that you figured out early on that I am actually quite remarkable." The Major started to talk but McKenzie grabbed his lips and clamped them shut with her fingers.

"Uh uh, Bitch, I'm talking," she said politely. "What was I saying? Oh yes. You figured out that I was going to be a phenomenal woman, with a thinking brain, and a vocal mouth—that I'd have opinions of my own, and goals in life that didn't have shit to do with you. And you just couldn't handle that, could you, Mister Minister Molester?" McKenzie said very confidently. She pinched his lips tightly as he tried to speak. He couldn't move his limbs, he was helpless, and McKenzie enjoyed every minute of it.

"Oh, you don't like that, do you?" She taunted him. "Doesn't feel so good being helpless, does it, Major in the military, strong and mighty man?" She sneered. Tears started to fill up in his eyes; his breath started to become irregular.

"No tears!" She commanded, like he used to say to her. "This is for your own good!"

Christian felt sick to the stomach. He wanted to grab McKenzie and just take her away from there.

"There's your bitch, right there!" McKenzie said looking over at her mother. "Hers is the only spirit you've broken, the only pride you've taken, the only mind you've managed to brainwash!"

Her mother looked at McKenzie in shock. McKenzie stood and released the Major's lips. He took long, deep gaping breaths.

"And you allowed him to torment your only child. To rape her. To get her pregnant. To steal her dignity and self worth. *You Did That*." she said directly to her mother, who started to protest. But McKenzie raised her hand to silence her.

"There's nothing you can say to me. Nothing. Keep the words for your journey to hell." She turned to face the Major. "Both of you will have to account for your sins and there is no way in the fucking world Jesus Christ will forgive you for those atrocities."

The nurse listened through the crack in the door, gasping with her hand over her mouth at what McKenzie had said. She turned and ran toward the nurse's station.

McKenzie reached her hand out to Christian who immediately grabbed it. But before they could leave the room, the Major replied.

"You . . . ain't . . . shit! . . . never . . . gone . . . be--" But before he could finish the sentence, they heard a muffled sound. McKenzie and Christian turned to see what had happened.

Brenda Reisen had her palm-sized pillow placed firmly over the Major's nose and mouth. His limp, lifeless limbs couldn't come to his defense. She stood there, motionless, tears streaming down her face as she smothered the last breaths of life from her husband.

McKenzie was shocked. Christian stood motionless. Christian ushered McKenzie out the door but not before she heard her mother say:

"McKenzie is a phenomenal woman, with a thinking brain, and a vocal mouth. She has opinions of her own, and goals in life that don't have shit to do with you . . ."

CHAPTER SEVENTEEN
A Soft Place to Fall

They were quiet on the drive home.

"How do you feel Mac?" Christian asked.

He was worried. So many terrible things were said today. That wasn't quite how he had expected it to go. He wondered if she'd gotten any closure at all.

The Major didn't admit or own up to anything. He had hoped he would ask for forgiveness and give McKenzie some reassurance that his actions were because of his sickness and not her innate ineptitude—but instead, he insisted on telling her she wasn't shit.

"Oh, Christian, I don't know." McKenzie almost whispered. "Intellectually, I think I've always known he was wrong." She stared out the passenger window as she spoke. "But I can't lie and say there hasn't been a part of me that believes because of all of that, I don't deserve better."

"That's not true. You deserve the best and not just because you survived that horrible past. But because you, and you alone, are worthy of the best—never ever doing another fucking thing in your life. Just because you're you," he said in the most sincere voice she'd ever heard.

McKenzie smiled. She turned to look at him and knew without a doubt that this man loved her unconditionally. For him to be able to say something so beautiful to her knowing all that she'd been through.

"Intellectually I agree. But . . . emotionally, I'm never quite so sure. I still question Melvin and TJ—and why they felt so comfortable--"

"It wasn't because you deserved it!" Christian shouted. He gripped the steering wheel. "It was because they had issues of their own and they took them out on you. It was pure bad luck McKenzie."

She smiled at his attempt to persuade her. She loved him for trying so hard to make her feel whole. But the Major had stripped her of that security. On the outside, she did a very good job of looking secure and acting confident, but inside . . . deep inside, she battled constantly with feelings of inadequacy and insecurity that no man could talk away.

"I'm not ready to go home yet, you?" Christian said.

"No, not really. Where you wanna go?"

"Just sit back. I got a spot."

McKenzie smiled as they turned into the parking lot of Zuma beach. She fondly remembered their first time here together. She turned to face Christian.

"You getting sentimental on me?"

"It's become a favorite place of mine," he said, thinking about all the times he'd driven to Zuma during their relationship.

"It's a beautiful place."

"It always reminds me of you." McKenzie blushed.

They strolled along the shore talking about McKenzie's feelings about the Major, the possibility of her mother going to jail, what their relationship might be if she didn't, what Christian said about Ahmad in the hospital. They talked about Madison . . . Christian confessed that he was so happy about Madison being their daughter and shared with her his conversation with Ahmad and how he'd been able to move past the anger.

They walked and talked for hours until their souls felt cleansed. On the way back to his car, Christian turned to face McKenzie.

"Are you going to let me love you, Mac?"

McKenzie blinked several times before responding.

"What does that mean, Christian?" .She turned away.

"You know what I mean Mac. Stop playing me." He turned her to face him. He looked her straight in the eyes. "I know the worst there is to know about you. And I love your dirty draws, girl." He cooed in his most sexy voice. They laughed.

McKenzie felt warm inside. She marveled at Christian's ability to openly express his most vulnerable feelings to her like that. She smiled.

"And I love you, too. Honestly, I do."

"Do I hear a 'but' in there somewhere?" He said, wrapping his arms snuggly around her waist.

"No. You don't hear any buts in there. I'm just not sure I'm the woman for you."

Christian frowned. He tried to be patient with McKenzie and understand that she was struggling with her past. But he felt he had demonstrated his loyalty to her. And felt like she should know she could trust him.

He looked her in the eyes for a brief moment, then slowly and gently kissed her. He pulled her face into his and passionately swirled his tongue inside her mouth. She returned the passion, sliding her arms around his neck and pulling him into her.

The sun was setting behind them. Dark purples, settled at the horizon, followed by deep dark blues. Fuchsia and magenta hues cascaded around the burnt orange disk that was slowly and steadily finding its way below the ocean's surface.

They were in a small alcove near a bluff. Christian slowly began to undress her. McKenzie did not protest. Her body was impatient with his slow and intentional motions. She moved her hands to help him but he pushed her hands away intent on moving slowly.

He wanted to take his time. In his mind, his heart, and his soul, he knew she was worth the time it would take to make her believe, to make her understand how deeply he felt for her. And Christian would show her. Right now it was with his touch.

Tomorrow, it would be with her mom. Next week it would be with Ahmad. In his mind, he had a lifetime of opportunities to show her she was worth it.

McKenzie finally gave up and allowed Christian to take control of the moment. He tenderly kissed her neck and shoulder as he slid her blouse down and off her shoulder. She moaned gently.

He moved around to her clavicle bone, gently kissing it and causing shooting waves of stimuli to her nipples.

"Oh Christian." she whispered.

He slid his hand underneath her flowing skirt and in between her legs. His fingers were greeted with an onslaught of slippery wet juices. Christian's dick instantly jumped to attention.

"Damn baby, you are wet," he whispered in her mouth as he kissed her.

"Uh huh. I'm ready for you," she said in a silky sexy voice.

Christian smiled, intent on taking his time. He kissed her and slowly moved her down to the cool sand. She lay back and spread her legs open. Christian smiled understanding her desire. He pulled down his shorts and slid in between her legs.

Like air fills the lungs, and as naturally as night turns into day, their bodies melded. He slid inside her, sending a wave of electrical currents through her body. She wrapped her legs around his waist and instantly began to shake.

"Whoa! Momma. Wait for me."

"Oh don't worry. There are plenty more where that one came from baby," she moaned in response. Christian laughed and began his slow and steady motion. McKenzie closed her eyes oblivious to the sand in her hair or clothes. She only felt, saw, and smelled Christian. She heard his deep breaths in her ear. She felt his dick, long and hard inside her. She pulled up to meet him, pulling him deeper inside her.

"Oh shit, yes!"

They moved in time with each other. Each thrust more urgent than the last. They kissed each other fervently as if this would be the last time their tongues would touch. With a hunger she'd never felt before, she engulfed him. With a passion he'd never felt before, he enveloped her.

Their bodies collided like the ocean waves behind them, rising and falling to the heat and passion of their love. Once they reached their climax together, they lay there entangled in each other's limbs, staring up at the blackness of the night.

"Are you going to let me love you Mac?" Christian asked again.

"Yes, baby. I am going to let you love me." she said thinking back to that verse in the Teena Marie song, *I hope this heart of mine will do what you want it to . . .*

They pulled out of the parking lot in complete silence, each digesting their current situation and what it meant to them. McKenzie was worried. She knew she loved Christian, she just didn't know if she could give him the type of love she felt he deserved.

He had been by her side today, supporting her, fighting for her dignity—believing in her. Even in St. Lucia he had been so comforting and supportive. She knew he truly believed in her.

The problem was, she just didn't know how to love. She could give her body—she was used to that. Staying in her relationship with TJ was only painful because she really wanted to be with Christian. But what did it really mean to let someone love you? What did it really mean to give your heart to someone? The thought terrified her. More importantly, she didn't want to let Christian down.

Christian was in heaven. He knew he had a long way to go with McKenzie. She had had so many people hurt her. He knew it would take some time to build up the trust they would need to have a solid relationship. But he was excited that McKenzie wanted to make that type of commitment.

He reached under his seat and pulled out his CD holder. He flipped through a couple of pages until he found the CD he was looking for. Silence still permeated the STS. Christian slid the CD into the changer. The music played and he bellowed out the smoothest alto rendition of the song.

Girl it's been a long, long time comin', yes it has
But I, I know that it's been worth the wait
It feels like springtime in winter
It feels like Christmas in June
It feels like heaven has opened up its gates for me and you

McKenzie blushed uncontrollably. Christian changed pitches to accompany Babyface's melodic soprano voice in a way that made you believe the song was written for two people to sing. It was a perfect harmony.

Every time I close my eyes
I thank the lord that I've got you
And you've got me too
And every time I think of it
I pinch myself cuz I don't believe it's true
That someone like you loves me too

McKenzie's stomach dropped when Christian said he thought she was truly somethin', and every bit of a dream come true. Knowing all that he knew about her, her past with the Major, and then with TJ she just couldn't understand how he could feel this way about her. She felt, if anything, he should be running for the hills— trying to get as far away from her as possible. But here he was telling her that with her it never rains and the sun always shines when he's near her. She couldn't remember a time in her life sense her grandmother that anyone ever told her that she was a blessing.

McKenzie blushed, finding it hard not to turn away from the sincere look of Christian's stare. She was filled with so many emotions at that moment listening to Christian express the way he felt for her through the amazing words of this song.

To think of all the nights I've cried myself to sleep
You really oughta know how much you mean to me
It's only right, it's only right (In my life)
that you be in my life right here with me

At the song's end, Christian turned to face McKenzie. "That's how I feel about you Mac. Is that OK?"

"Christian . . . I don't know what to say. I don't know what I'm supposed to say to that . . . It was beautiful . . . I'm overwhelmed . . . I . . . I don't know what you want me to say?"

Christian took the corner on PCH easily, rounding it with ease and concentration. Once around the bend he said:

"Do you know what I mean by 'Let me love you?'"

"I think. But I'm not sure."

"Can I tell you?" He looked her way to find her looking stressed and worried.

"Sure."

"Before my mom passed we used to do Sunday lunches together. She'd pick a restaurant and I'd treat." McKenzie laughed. Christian looked over her way and chuckled. "Yes, she was special. But I didn't mind. I just loved seeing her happy. And my mom was happy when she was eating!" He smiled thinking about his mom.

"And she had a very nice figure too." McKenzie listened as Christian told his story. "Anyway, we talked about everything from investments, to politics, from sex, to genocide. She was well versed on many subjects. And I loved it." He merged onto the 405 Freeway South.

"One of the things my mother always told me was in order for a relationship to work, both partners had to want it to work." He turned to look at her. "Sounds simple, doesn't it?" McKenzie nodded her head. "But think about it for a minute . . . think about your relationship with TJ. Did you want it to work? I mean, really? Or were you just going through the motions?" McKenzie thought for a moment.

"I think I was just going through the motions."

"So was I with Jada. I said I was honoring my vows, but was I really? I mean I wasn't really. I wasn't honoring or cherishing her.

I couldn't, I didn't love her." He looked over at McKenzie who was listening intently.

"I didn't hit her, or curse at her, I paid all the bills, bought her whatever she wanted in terms of materialistic things, and in public, was the perfect gentleman—but the truth was I wasn't letting her love me." He stared straight ahead. "She wanted to comfort me and be a part of my life at school and at work, but I didn't let her in." He sighed rubbing his head.

"And I couldn't let her in anymore because she had violated my trust so much . . . so many times, that I had built up this protective wall and refused to let her in. I didn't let her love me. And the sad reality was, I didn't love her back." McKenzie nodded as if to say she understood what he was saying.

"And so, anyway, back to my mom. One day she told me that a good man needs a good woman. A good woman will be strong, supportive, loving, and give of herself. But a Good Man for that kind of woman--a strong woman--is a man who will provide her with a Soft Place to Fall." He paused to let McKenzie think about that for a moment.

"What did she mean by that?" McKenzie finally asked.

"She said, 'A strong woman is going to always excel, exceed, and achieve. But she's human. She's going to eventually get tired, become overwhelmed, burnt out—and even though she will eventually pick herself back up (cause that's what strong women do), what she needs most from her man, is simply to be a soft place to fall. Because when you're at the top, there's nowhere to go but down.

And maybe it won't be through any fault of her own. A strong woman usually has a plan. But she'll trip, maybe by a trap set by others, or the stars just didn't align correctly. Whatever the case, that strong woman is going to fall." They sat silently for a few minutes, letting Christian's definition simmer in the air.

"When I ask you if you will let me love you, McKenzie, I'm asking you if you will let me be that that soft place for you to fall?" He turned to look at her.

McKenzie's eyes welled up with tears. Of all the beautiful things Christian had said to her, this was by far the most beautiful.

"You are the strongest, fiercest, most resilient woman I know. You don't *need* me. But if you want me . . . if you let me in,

and allow me to love you . . . to be that soft place for you to fall—
that place where you can be vulnerable and feel safe, then I know
we'll be all right."

They drove about a mile before Christian got up enough
courage to ask her again. "So. What do you think? Now that you
understand my question, and what I'm asking you to do, have you
changed your mind?"

McKenzie sat quietly for a moment. "Christian, I don't know
what I did to deserve you" she said in between tears. "But I swear I
feel like you make up for all the horrible shit I've gone through in
my life." She wiped her tears on the back of her sandy sleeve.
"Shit!" They laughed at the sandy streak of tears smeared down her
face.

"Now, I know you're not perfect—by any stretch of the
imagination, Mr. Malveaux."

"No?" Christian replied, his eyebrows arching in feigned
disbelief.

"Uh—no" McKenzie said, laughing. "But I honestly believe
you are perfect for me." She reached over and grabbed his hand. She
gently kissed his palm.

"Now, I feel like that Babyface song." Christian looked over
at McKenzie and smiled. She pinched herself.

*"And every time I think of it, I pinch myself cuz I don't
believe it's true. That someone like you . . . loves me too."*

     ♋   ♋   ♋